William & Lucy

A TALE OF SUSPICION AND LOVE

Inspired by the William Wordsworth poem
She Dwelt Among the Untrodden Ways

A NOVEL

by

MICHAEL BROWN

D0465977

This novel is a work of historical fiction/romance. While some names, characters, and incidents are based upon real characters and events, this story is the product of the author's imagination.

Fiction/Historical/Romance – Registered WGA
William & Lucy / by Michael Brown
Tarn Publishing
Printed in the United States

Library of Congress Cataloging in Publication
Library of Congress Control Number:
PCN 2011922022
PCC PR 830.M73
ISBN-13:978-1456361433
ISBN-10: 1456361430

Available in print through all Bookstores, Amazon.com, Kindle, and on-line booksellers.

Smashwords Edition License Notes

For Holly

❧ INTRODUCTION ❧

*D*uring the Summer of 1798, twenty-eight-year-old William Wordsworth and his sister, Dorothy, two years his junior, were living in Alfoxden House, a short walk from the Bristol Channel, an arm of the Celtic Sea in the English West Country. King George III was on the English throne and his country was involved in a protracted war with France.

The end of the 18th century marked the dawn of the Romantic Era in poetry. William Wordsworth and Samuel Taylor Coleridge led the way with their book, *Lyrical Ballads*. One of the poems included in the tome was, *She Dwelt Among the Untrodden Ways,* written by Wordsworth. It was one of five *Lucy* poems he wrote, three of which are attributed to the inspiration of a young woman who may have lived in rural Somerset. Lucy has been the subject of debate in literary circles ever since the poems were first published. Wordsworth never revealed her true identity.

Who was Lucy? Where did she come from? Did she ever exist? No one will ever know.

This is William and Lucy's story…

❧ CHAPTER ONE ❧

illiam strode purposefully along the wheel-rutted country lane that curled through the forested Quantock Hills of Somerset, determined to out-distance the dark thunderheads of a threatening storm that blew toward him from the distant horizon. He squinted as rays of sunlight suddenly broke through the low ceiling of grey clouds roiling above him, the beams prompting him to pull the wide brim of his brown felt hat lower on his forehead. Feeling a cold breeze sweep down from the hills, he snuggled his lean form into the folds of his cape, grateful for its warmth and the protection it afforded. Soft alternations of light and shade followed each other on every side of William as his thoughts drifted to the morning and early afternoon hours spent at Samuel Coleridge's home in nearby Nether Stowey, where the day's intermittent rainstorms had kept him indoors longer than anticipated. Normally, he would have been thrilled for the

excuse to extend his writing session with Samuel, but today his mind had been frustratingly unproductive. Each and every line he composed had been a struggle. It hadn't helped at all that Samuel's newborn son, Hartley, had been colicky and had cried most of the day in spite of his mother's vain attempts to nurse him to sleep. William felt a tinge of guilt as he remembered how he had paced to and fro like a caged animal in his friends' small living room, likely contributing to the baby's irritation.

Thankfully, the rains had let up and a wave of relief had flowed through him, leaving him feeling that he had just been saved from drowning at sea. Taking advantage of the break in the weather, he had hastily bid good-day to Samuel and Sara and set out for Alfoxden House.

But now, only minutes later, the sun's promising rays were being choked off by the dark mass of thunderclouds sweeping inland from the Bristol Channel. In all probability, William thought, he would be caught in another thunderstorm, this time without the protection of a roof. Several yards ahead, rounding a bend in the road, a farmer driving a horse and cartload of hay appeared, rushing in an attempt to avoid the impending downpour. William stepped to the side of the track and tipped his hat to the farmer, who nodded in return. Watching the man disappear, William wondered what kind of life the farmer had. It was probably a different existence, he ventured, with success or failure dependent upon the whims of Mother Nature. Certainly the farmer's life couldn't be more troubled than his own. Just the thought of the dubious state of his affairs prompted the muscles in his chest to constrict and, he imagined, for a moment, that the tentacles of a sea monster had encircled his ribcage and were squeezing the living breath from him. He coughed hard and broke the spell. *Why was his life filled with so much turmoil? Why couldn't he simply concentrate on his poetry? And, why couldn't he sell the verses that he had written?* The answers seemed as randomly elusive as the vagaries that gave one man success and another failure.

Stepping around a puddle, he dug hands into his pockets, seeking warmth. The fingers of his right hand touched a few shillings and rubbed them together, a keen reminder that he had no savings to fall back upon, and he was in dire financial straits. Money that periodically arrived from poems he had had published was barely enough to cover food and minor expenses. Subsequently, he was in danger of losing the leasehold on his home. To top that off, he thought miserably, he had no woman in his life other than his sister for companionship. His last real relationship had been over seven years ago in France and *that*, he remembered all too vividly, had ended in disaster.

William kicked a ridge of mud out of his path. It splattered into hundreds of globules, a fine metaphor for the life he had led; a shattered personal, artistic and financial debacle. His future seemed equally bleak. He felt a pang of hunger and thought of his sister, Dorothy, who in all likelihood was in the kitchen at Alfoxden House, preparing their supper. Dorothy had always been his favorite sibling, the only girl among five children, and the only one, he felt, who understood him. After the death of his parents and a separation of several years from his sister—imposed by their orphaned status—he had located Dorothy, who had been working as a maidservant for one of his penurious uncles. She had been extremely unhappy and had pleaded with her brother to save her from the dull, hard and friendless life. Responding to her plight, almost two years ago now, William had rented a buggy and driven to his uncle's home late at night, and had helped Dorothy escape. She had been living with him ever since, which, of course, had added to his expenses. A sense of shame prompted William to consider Dorothy's value; she was a loving sister, a trustworthy friend and an intelligent companion. Yes, he nodded to himself, she gave much more to him than he deserved, both with her keen sense of observation and with an editing talent that had become a blessing.

Preoccupied, William took a moment to realize he was walking into a puddle. He stepped aside and trudged around it, his spirit in turmoil. He sighed as he tried to figure a way out of his economic morass. If only he had been born with the talent or desire to become an attorney like his father, John Wordsworth, a property manager for the hugely wealthy Sir John Lowther, Earl of Lonsdale; or a clergyman like one of his uncles; or a tradesman or even a farmer; then he would have been able to find employment and pay off his annoying creditors. But it wasn't to be; he knew he had only one vocation, one talent, and that was to write poetry. This was a curse, of course; he was sure of it. The Gods must be repaying him for a past offense he had committed. No sane man would intentionally pick a profession that almost certainly assured him a life of poverty.

William shook his head wearily. Reaching into the worn leather satchel he wore slung over his shoulder, he withdrew a thin journal and a stubby pencil. He opened the book to study his writing: Perhaps, he ventured hopefully, he had been too pessimistic and his composition might be a tad less onerous than he had previously thought. When his eyes focused on the lines, he read words that were exactly as he had remembered—purely useless, as rambling and nonsensical as King George himself. Misery seeped further into his soul.

William was tempted to throw the offending pages into the stream that ran alongside the road. He stared myopically at the small tributary. The cold waters cascaded and swirled over and around rocks and boulders, forming small pools that mirrored the leaden sky. The waters had lost their glitter as certainly as his soul had lost its creativity.

Unexpectedly, the sun once again broke through its grey mantel and, the wind changed, holding the thunderheads at bay. Random patches of blue began to appear, stretching across the sky. Raindrops, clinging to greenery, glistened in the sunlight. With the promise of fair weather, at least for the moment, William felt the soothing balm of nature flood his being. After a time he inhaled deeply, and cheered himself by communing with the bubbling song of the stream, the low whistle of the wind and the sweet chirping of birds.

Attuned to the impressions surrounding him, the nucleus of an idea began to ferment. His brow rose speculatively. *Had the God of whimsy run off to harass another poor soul? Perhaps.* He slowed his pace as the inner voice that had eluded him all day eagerly approached like a long-lost friend. He lifted his pencil and began to scribble on the page. Occasionally, as he walked and wrote, his eyes darted to the side of the road so that he could avoid milestone markers that lay hidden in the grass. More than once he had almost sprained an ankle tripping over these impediments, which had been laid out almost a hundred years ago when coach companies had first begun to spring up all over England.

He finished writing the end of a line and stopped to study his composition. He read aloud,

> "My stockings there I often knit,
> My kerchief there I hem:
> And there within the glade I sit,
> And sing a song for them.
>
> And often after sunset, sir,
> In embers of distant light,
> I carry my little porringer..."

William's hopes fell like the blade of a guillotine. "No!" he exclaimed. "The Muses avoid me still!"

His stomach growled again.

"Quiet! I don't need your opinion."

His stomach rumbled in response.

"Enough. Not another comment."

He felt his intestines twist defiantly.

"Bah," he uttered with exasperation.

Fortunately, a familiar structure presented itself a short distance ahead. The King's Head Inn was a rambling two-story building, vaguely Norman in design with white stucco walls and crisscrossed half-timbers. Curling wisps of smoke rose from a stone chimney, which protruded from the high-pitched roof of grey slate that covered the Inn and the attached barn. William caught a whiff of homemade meat pies. He inhaled the savory aromas, yearning for a taste of the hearty fare the proprietor made daily and set out on the kitchen's covered window sill to lure travelers off the road.

He knew he should walk past the Inn to save the few shillings in his pocket, but his rapacious hunger devoured that argument. *Besides*, he reasoned, *a half-pint of ale and a small bite of pie would be just the thing to give my spirits a lift!* He snapped his journal shut, walking now at a quickened pace.

❧ CHAPTER TWO ❧

he port of Bristol was teeming with ships; sloops, schooners, brigantines and barges of all sizes and shapes. Two grand gunboats from His Majesty's fleet, bristling with eighty cannon apiece, were at anchor near the entrance to the harbor, on guard to protect England from attack by the French. Several merchant ships, flying flags from all over the world, were moored at buoys, while others were tied to busy docks, loading and unloading textiles, sugar, glass and tobacco. In city center, a metropolis of 65,000 inhabitants, the cobblestone streets echoed with the clatter of carriages and drays while the sidewalks swarmed with shoppers, clerks, runners and carters, all scurrying about their business.

Geoffrey Walsh, a large man sporting a wide-brimmed black hat and suit, strode through the crowd like a battering ram, ignoring the stench of horse dung and unwashed bodies. His sharp scythe of a nose and angular Slavic features were odd for an Englishman and caused a certain amount of alarm as he walked amongst his fellow men; he found this gratifying. At the moment his dark eyes were smoldering with annoyance at having been summoned to the Home Office by a distant in-law, the Lord Chief Justice John Peel. His hand brushed aside the flap of his coat to rest momentarily upon the lethal looking flintlock pistol that lay strapped to his chest. It was his talisman ... a weapon he had confiscated after killing, with his bare hands, the thief who had been its original owner. Walsh turned up the steps to an imposing, three-story limestone building identified by words chiseled into the portico: H.M. HOME OFFICE.

An hour later he was standing in the office of the Lord Chief Justice John Peel, himself, a small wiry man in his late sixties, who paced to and fro in front of a bay window overlooking the harbor. Walsh had a difficult time listening to the old man, or anyone for that matter, who dared to lecture him on constabulary protocol. John Peel was, at the moment, droning on about Walsh's career, "...and furthermore, Geoffrey, it's been ten years since I sponsored your appointment and you are still only a first-grade constable."

Walsh imagined wrapping his fingers around the man's scrawny neck and throttling him to within an inch of his life. Instead, he answered with a tinge of bitterness, "Lord Chief Justice, my superiors have no appreciation for a man who obeys the letter of the law."

"Or, one who disobeys explicit orders," the old man countered in a condemning tone, then added, "Geoffrey, what makes you so self-righteous and intractable?

Walsh felt his bile rise. "My superiors are politicians with few morals. I refuse to manipulate the law to accommodate their needs. If that is self-righteous and intractable, then so be it."

Peel stared at him with what appeared to be sadness. "Your moral stance is laudable, but you are not a knight in shining armor. You are expected to obey orders. Not always an easy choice I agree, but for the sake of my poor niece..."

"My wife and children have all they need," Walsh interrupted.

Peel's eyes hardened. "Don't be impertinent, sir! It does nothing to help your situation."

The Chief Justice turned to the window and gazed out over the harbor. "Now then, in spite of your uneven performance, I am going to offer you an opportunity to improve your situation." He walked to his desk and picked up a small black notebook. "It may be your last."

Walsh bowed and replied disingenuously, "I am your humble servant."

"His Majesty's Government has received information that a French spy has taken up residence in Somerset. He will be summoned to appear in Bristol Court within a month's time. You are to investigate this individual and supply proof of his treachery." He held the black book up, offering it to Walsh. "All the information you'll need is in here."

Walsh took the notebook in hand. The old man continued, "The spy hails from Cumbria and was educated at Cambridge, so he should stick out like a sore thumb among those cider-swilling yokels."

The Chief Justice's eyes bored into him. "I warn you, these seditious bastards are devious. If you fail to substantiate incriminating evidence against the man but believe he is guilty, then I expect you to be … how shall I put this … inventive? Do I make myself clear?"

Walsh bit back a quick response, knowing that Peel was testing him; was he willing to perjure himself for the sake of convicting a suspected spy? Walsh remained non-committal. *Later, when he had all the facts in hand he would decide how to handle the situation and, if the man was guilty, he was as good as dead.* He nodded to Peel, acknowledging that he had certainly made his point.

The Chief Justice grunted and continued, "When the spy is hung from the gallows, your status and your future are assured. If not, then… ."

"His name?"

Peel nodded to the notebook. Geoffrey's eyes dropped to the black cover in his hand. When he opened it his eyes widened with surprise.

illiam stepped into the King's Head Inn, stopping by the door to allow his eyes to adjust to the darkness. He knew from painful experience that anyone over five and a half feet tall had to duck when crossing into the room, lest he crack his skull on the low, heavy ceiling beams. Half of the room's interior was furnished with scarred wooden tables and chairs placed randomly before a large stone fireplace where the glow of a peat fire offered a semicircle of warmth. The remainder of the first floor was taken up by a row of stools which stood before a long bar made of hand-hewn planks. Upon this, two oil lamps flickered, illuminating Simon, the innkeeper, who busied himself pulling pints of ale from one of three casks stacked against the back wall.

William remembered Simon, the balding thin-as-a-rail grandfather, as a convivial sort, who always had an opinion on politics, women and the ever-changing weather.

In the corner beyond the bar, a narrow staircase led up to the second floor, where a road-weary traveler could rent one of several rooms for five shillings a night. Couched beneath the stairs was a narrow door that opened to the kitchen, where meat pies were roasting in cast-iron ovens.

William swallowed quickly, the tantalizing smells making him salivate. He grinned as he anticipated eating, but before stepping forward into the room, he became alerted to the sound of angry voices. Peering into the shadows at the back of the bar, he recognized the hulking Sutton brothers, Ben and Walt, seated next to each other. Simon set two pints on the planks in front of the siblings, who were engaged in a heated discussion, their words slurred by drink.

The Suttons, William recalled, were local pig farmers with a reputation for being troublemakers. Their faces and odor reminded him of the hogs they tended. Whenever possible, William had made a point of avoiding any encounter with the unsavory duo, who had also taken a dislike to him. He backed up, reaching for the door, when Simon's voice beckoned, "William, come in, lad. I'll pour ya a pint."

William acquiesced, unable to retreat gracefully. He nodded a greeting to the innkeeper and moved into the room, doffing his hat.

"Thank you, Simon," William said. "A half-pint will do." He ducked to miss the low beams as he stepped over to the fireplace. "I'll warm myself by the hearth."

"You'll have a full pint and I won't be takin' a farthin' for it neither," Simon said. "And I not be takin' *no* fer an answer."

William knew better than to argue with the kind man. He nodded, offering his thanks, well aware that Simon's gesture emanated from the Innkeeper's knowledge of his precarious financial position: It was an embarrassing subject, and one he certainly didn't wish to argue about with the Suttons present. He recalled now that the Suttons had been making disparaging remarks about him, and spreading rumors regarding his, and others', loyalty to the Crown. It was the type of malicious gossip that always stirred up trouble. He had considered confronting the Suttons, and prevailing upon them to put a stop to their dangerous lies, but now he cautioned himself against an encounter. Trying to have a rational discussion when they were sober was dicey enough, but talking to them in their inebriated state would be foolhardy. He would ignore the brothers, if he could.

Ben took a drink from his mug, catching sight of William. He brought the mug down hard on the bar top and glared; ale dripped from his unshaven mouth. He spoke a little too loudly, "I don't know that I want to be drinkin' in the same pub with a French-lovin' sod." He turned to his sibling. "What about yerself, Walt?"

Walt glanced in William's direction with bloodshot eyes. "I'd just as soon drink piss."

William felt his heart begin to pound. Holding the brothers' gaze, he realized he was feeling just irritated enough to get himself into trouble if he didn't mind his words.

Simon spoke up as he pulled a pint from the ale cask, "Ya two shut yer faces or yer ta walk on outta 'ere."

"Bugger off," Ben said.

Simon put aside the pint and reached for his trusty persuader; a stout Irish shillelagh.

"Let it lie, Simon," William said.

Simon hesitated, lowering the heavy club. William took a step toward the Suttons. "You and I have a talk coming, you can be assured of that, but it's not going to be today. Neither one of you would remember a word I said."

"As if anythin' ya said was gonna be worth a load o' shit," Walt said. "Yer a French spy, ain't ya? Admit it!"

William turned his back on the Suttons. He stepped to the fireplace, hoping the two would lose interest if he didn't respond to their insult. He knew that if an altercation were in the offing, he might as well write his obituary now for all the chance he'd have against the two brutes. He raised his hands toward the peat fire, oblivious to the warmth radiating up to his palms, his pleasure eclipsed by the rueful thought that he had picked the wrong day to stop in for a pint.

Ben spat on the floor and glared querulously at Simon. "Givin' pints to an enemy of the Crown is dangerous deeds, Simon."

"I warned ya ta shut yer face," Simon said, still gripping his club.

Walt scoffed blaringly. "Wordsworth keeps a French whore. I seen 'em walkin' together holdin' hands."

William felt heat rise up his neck and burn his ears, but the heat didn't come from the fireplace. Struggling to rein in his temper, but unwilling to let another insult slide by, he turned to his assailants and said with forced calmness, "I sincerely hope you are not referring to my dear sister."

Ben snorted. "She's no sister. We all know thet, Wordsworth. An' another thing, Somerset's no place fer sympathizers of the Revolution. Ya understand me?"

Cold sweat trickled down William's spine, yet his temper began to override his trepidation. He heard himself saying, "I find it difficult to understand men who spread lies about their neighbors and deride the honor of a beautiful lady. Your misinformed ramblings are as repulsive as your lack of manners."

Ben choked on his ale, spitting it onto the floor. He slammed his mug to the countertop and sputtered, "Ya fuckin' traitor!"

William knew he had blown a bed of coals into a roaring fire and was now certain to be roasted alive. Running for the door seemed tempting, but he stood his ground; he clenched and unclenched his fists behind his back. *Damned if he'd cower and slink away.* His eyes focused on Ben as the big man moved aggressively forward, followed by his brother.

"No trouble, Ben!" the Innkeeper warned. "Ya'll never git another pint in 'ere again."

"Yer swill ain't worth drinkin'," Ben snarled as he and Walt crowded William.

Inexplicably, William felt himself grin. He knew that these men were bullies and would first try to simply intimidate him with their sheer size. He straightened his spine and stood up to his full height. *Intimidation works two ways,* he thought,

13

then noted with discomfort that his head was several inches below the brothers' noses. Their foul body odor almost made him gag; or was it the fear of dying that had brought bile to his throat? Gathering what courage he could summon, he said, "Ben, I want an apology from you and your brother for the salacious lies you've been spreading about me, and the use of your basest vocabulary in reference to my good sister."

Ben blinked, taking a moment to decipher the King's English, then said, "Rot in hell, Wordsworth! I've a feelin' ya won't be speakin' so fancy with yer teeth knocked out, now will ya?"

Backing up to give himself fighting room, William felt his legs tremble and hoped they wouldn't give out beneath him. As Ben and Walt crowded in from two sides, William guessed that each brother outweighed him by at least a hundred pounds. *He recalled getting into only two fights in his early school years and on both occasions coming out the loser.*

Being a civilized person, he had learned to avoid or negotiate his way out of most altercations. But it was obvious he would be wasting his breath with these cretins. Besides, now that he was committed, he was mildly looking forward to hitting the Suttons, striking out against everything they represented. He humored himself with the thought that tonight's altercation could be Fate, taking a hand in his feeble career: As a living poet he'd barely been able to scratch out a living; perhaps if he died a brave death, he would gain posthumous recognition, and his sister would have security from the sale of his works. But, he then reasoned, there *was* a real downside to letting these brutes kill him, as he would be quite dead.

William felt the back of his legs bump against the hearth's railing and knew he should feel panic; instead, he felt something akin to excitement. He smiled inwardly, thinking it a curious anomaly that nature pumped courage into one's system shortly before it asked for the ultimate sacrifice.

Ben barked, "Grab 'is arms, Walt!"

As Walt charged him, William swung a fist at his head. The man ducked and grabbed both of his arms, twisting his limbs up behind his back. William grimaced as bone and sinew were stretched to the breaking point. He found himself held in place like a trussed animal, one that was about to be slaughtered. He stared helplessly into Ben's leering face.

"Kiss yer bloody teeth goodbye, ya French lovin' swine."

The big man's fist hurtled forward—William spun at the same instant. Ben's knuckles missed him by a centimeter and slammed into Walt's nose. William heard the sound of bone breaking and felt Walt's grip fall away.

Ben and Walt squealed like wounded hogs and hopped to and fro. Ben stopped jumping about to stare incredulously at his hand, which appeared to be broken. Walt, eyes tearing, reached for his bloody, flattened nose. "Damn it, Ben, ya broke me nose! Ya bloody idiot!"

Ben, face contorted in pain, muttered, "Me hand, me hand is ruined."

William sucked in a breath and grabbed an iron poker from the fireplace, just in case the brothers had any fight left in them.

Simon rushed over, wielding his shillelagh. "Enough! I warned ya there's ta be no fightin' in me pub, ya hear me?"

Ben wheeled about to face William and snarled, "I'm gonna kill ya with me one good 'and!"

"Mr. Sutton," William said, "I suggest you rethink that idea." To emphasize his point, he slapped the iron rod onto the palm of his hand.

William watched Ben's gaze fall to the iron bar.

Simon said, "Ben, git out of 'ere and take yer brother with ya. Ya both need a doctor."

"Back off, Simon," Ben responded, his animosity diminishing.

"Me nose is killin' me," Walt said, holding his bloody snout.

William stared into Ben's eyes and held his gaze, ready to strike out if he or his brother attacked. After a long moment, Ben exhaled heavily and said, "Wordsworth, ya'll be seein' us again. I can promise ya that." He turned for the door, gesturing to his brother. "Walt."

William watched the Suttons hobble out of the inn and then replaced the poker by the hearth. He heard Simon chuckle. "They had that comin' fer years an' the funny thing is they did it ta themselves." Simon turned away, adding, "Come over ta the bar, lad. Yer pint's waitin' fer ya, an' a slice of meat pie to go with it. 'Aven't had such an entertainin' afternoon in years."

William felt his spirits lighten. "Neither have I, Simon. Neither have I."

ucy Sims stared impatiently at the two Hawkins children. They were eyeing their grammar books with bored, indifferent looks as they sat across from her on a flat outcrop of slate, midway up a long grassy hillside. She was doing her best to affect a stern, uncompromising look—not an easy task when one is born with lips that curl up at the ends as if on the verge of breaking into a smile. Her dark blue eyes, full of fun and bedevilment, seemed to be at odds with her forced attitude as she peered down her graceful nose at the children. She was waiting for a response to an English grammar question asked moments before and directed at twelve-year-old Emily and her younger brother, Henry.

Earlier this morning she had seen to it that the children had dressed warmly, with the addition of rain capes and hats. Their clothes and the shoes they wore were far more expensive than her own simple brown wool skirt and the white, buttoned shirtfront, worn beneath an old navy blue rain cloak.

Lucy repeated an earlier question. "Emily, Henry, once more, can either of you conjugate the verb 'to take'?"

The children kept their eyes downcast, avoiding her as they fidgeted with their books. Lucy sighed. She knew neither child was much of a student but normally gave both credit for trying. Today, however, they were being insufferably obstinate. *Well, if they were going to make this into a game of wills, she could outwait them.* Lucy was in no particular hurry: She was enjoying the warm feel of the stone beneath her. The slate, quick to dry after a rain, absorbed warmth even under a cool, almost sunless sky like today's. She knew this place was treasured by the children, offering a welcome respite from lessons held within the stuffy, cool interior of their parents' rambling manor house. The home was perched on the hilltop directly above them. With its heavy thatched roof, it appeared to be the large disheveled nest of some graceless bird.

Suddenly Lucy observed a rainbow that had appeared in the sky. Its multicolored stripes rose from nearby hills to arc across a bank of clouds before falling back to earth, where it illuminated a small meadow splashed with yellow primroses. Lucy caught her breath … marveling … wishing she could hold onto the colorful image long enough to capture it on canvas. She glanced longingly toward the foldable painter's easel and the two wicker baskets lying beside it. The larger basket contained her precious painting supplies and a half-finished landscape on a small canvas. The second basket held sandwiches and accouterments for today's outing.

She glanced over her shoulder and noticed dark clouds rising from the horizon. She frowned: *Would the rains never stop?* She said, "Children, there's a storm coming. We haven't much time before it's upon us. Emily, for the third time, please conjugate the verb 'to take'."

Emily said, "Why do we have to learn verbs? I hate verbs."

Henry added, "Nobody even uses verbs very much."

Lucy reminded herself to be patient, and explained for what she imagined to be the millionth time, "Emily, Henry, I'm teaching you verbs so you'll be able to speak proper English."

"Proper is … so uppity." Emily stuck her nose in the air and gave a good imitation of the stiffest of upper lips. "My dearest Henry, would you be so veddy kind, as to pass me

English book over so that I can study them simply wonderful verbs?"

Lucy bit her tongue and succeeded in hiding her smile. "Emily, you know better. The correct verbiage is: pass *my* book, not *me*, and; that I *may* study, not *can*. And next time, say; study *those* simply wonderful verbs, not *them*."

Emily shrugged. "Everyone knows what I was saying."

"But *how you say it* is far more important."

"We speak proper enough," Emily said. "Just like Mama and Papa."

Henry nodded. "They speak purty good and they lived on a farm without no governess ta teach 'em."

"That's beside the point," Lucy said. "They're gentry now, and so are you."

Lucy cast her gaze toward the large ungainly house on the hilltop, while searching her memory for words that wouldn't demean the elder Hawkins' less-than-sophisticated usage of the English language.

Henry took advantage of his governess' concentration on the manor to stare surreptitiously at her, as he often did when he thought she wouldn't notice. His bright, mischievous eyes, set in a chubby, freckled face, roamed as freely as a ten-year-old imagination would allow.

Lucy, returning her attention to the children, said, "The Squire and Lady Hawkins have asked me to tutor you in the King's English. Emily, they wish you to speak like a lady and you, Henry, like a gentleman."

"Miss Lucy," Henry said, "how come you know how to talk so proper? Were you once a lady?"

Emily responded, "Henry, she only be seventeen. She had no time to be a lady." Lucy smiled and her heart went out to her wards. They were so bright, so full of fun and lighthearted rebellion. *Had she been the same as a child? Perhaps.* And perhaps that was why she felt so close to them. She said, "To answer your question, Henry, I am not a lady in the proper sense of the word as you might consider someone with peerage to be, or one who was born into royalty. But, my mother was a well-educated schoolmistress who taught me how to speak properly, like a lady. She had high hopes for me. My being a governess is only a temporary condition."

A frown creased Henry's forehead. "Are you going to leave us?"

"Why do you ask? Would you miss me?"

He blushed. "Emily would."

"But you wouldn't?" she probed, in a teasing manner.

Henry shrugged and turned away.

Lucy refrained from giving him a hug; his obvious affection for her made up for all his mischievous ways. She thought if she were to have children, she would wish for character traits that matched those of her two wards. But, she knew in her heart these were distant musings; there would be little opportunity for marriage or a family for her as she intended to pursue her all-consuming interest in painting: The seed of this passion had blossomed when, as a child standing at her father's knee, she had watched him paint landscapes with meticulous care. The beautiful images had been captivating, and had imbued her with a love that would grow into an obsession—to dedicate her life to painting. And, day by day, she was working toward her goal and the freedom to attain it.

Lucy glanced to the darkening horizon. She would have just enough time to pursue her one indulgence before they would need to make a mad dash up the hill to the manor house. "Children, that's all the instruction for today. Tomorrow we'll review today's verbs and then conjugate four new ones." She took their books and placed them into the smaller basket.

Henry leaped to his feet as though he had just been released from purgatory and retrieved a small ball from the pocket of his rain cape. "Let's play catch, Miss Lucy. I'll be the runner."

Emily tugged at her brother's trousers. "No, Henry! It's my turn to be runner."

"It's not so!"

"Hold on, both of you. Lazy students don't deserve rewards. I'm not playing catch with either of you today. And if you want me to play catch tomorrow, you'd better apply yourselves to your studies."

"We will. We promise," Emily said. "But *only* if you play catch with us now."

Lucy affected another version of her stern look, one of the many she had practiced in her bedroom mirror for just these occasions. Hopefully, it informed the children the subject was closed. "Emily, take your brother and away with you. It's my time now." She turned to the three long thin pieces of wood lying beside her, picked them up and began to assemble the artist's easel.

"Why do you always have to paint?" Emily asked plaintively.

"I've told you a hundred times," she said, refusing to discuss the matter further. "Now go on. It will be raining within the hour and I don't want to listen to the two of you complaining about having no time to play outdoors. Off with you. Go."

Henry tossed his ball in the air and caught it. "Come on, Emily. She's no fun."

"Miss Lucy, we may not study verbs at all tomorrow," Emily said rebelliously, then turned and dashed off. "Throw it high, Henry. I'll catch the most balls. Throw it! Throw it high!"

Lucy smiled as she watched Henry follow his sister. He threw the ball high into the air, cheering gleefully when his sister ran after it and, trying to catch it, dropped the ball. Emily retrieved it, threw it even higher into the air and they were off, running across the hillside.

*inally,* Lucy thought with a sigh of relief, *a few precious moments to herself.* She took a long screw from one of the baskets and threaded it through holes at the ends of the easel poles. Then, securing the screw in place with a wing nut, she spread the skinny legs out to form a triangle. Next, she raised a short section of wood dangling from one of the poles and fastened it midway up one of the struts, creating a small crossbar to support a canvas.

She nodded with approval at the easel that rose a foot higher than the top of her head and then knelt beside the baskets, opening the larger one and carefully withdrawing a partially-painted, twelve-by-fourteen-inch landscape. She examined the canvas with a touch of pride and placed the painting on the easel's crossbar. Turning back to the basket, she extracted three long thin paintbrushes and a small oval palette bearing residue of colored oils. She selected the longest and most delicate of the brushes: Its finely tapered tip was made from the finest Russian sable, as extravagance even for professional painters. It had been a gift from her beloved father,

Thomas Sims. She held it up with reverence, caressing it between her fingertips. She imagined a jeweler would have the same feeling when holding a priceless gem.

Staring at the brush, Lucy suffered a pang of grief as she recalled her parents' deaths. Her whole world had fallen apart two years ago when Thomas and Josie had passed away in their late thirties, succumbing to tuberculosis. Lucy, an only child, had been sent to live with relatives, with whom she had little in common, and who had been raising far too many children of their own to really care about her: It had been the unhappiest time of her life. Without the means to support herself, and too proud to be dependent upon relatives with financial problems of their own, she had sought employment. She searched newspapers and small periodicals and scoured all advertisements for a governess position.

Within a few months, she had found a position at Hawkins Manor, tending to the owners' two children, Emily and Henry. At first, being a governess had been an answer to her prayers and would have continued to be so were it not for the presence of the master of the household: Squire George Hawkins was another matter entirely.

Lucy shuddered, recalling the man's most recent and inappropriate remarks regarding the growing swell of her bosom, and also the way his looks undressed her.

The paintbrush trembled in her hand as she recalled nightmares of Squire Hawkins, pursuing her as she ran to remote corners of the manor, where he would rip her clothes away and force his flabby body upon her. Lucy inhaled deeply to calm herself, but she couldn't shake the image. She knew her fears were well-founded, as the manor house was rife with stories of the Squire taking liberties with the help. So far she had been able to fend off his annoying advances, but soon, she suspected, he would become bolder. She was coming to realize her time at Hawkins House was running out. She sighed heavily: She had been delaying her departure for the sake of the children, and also because her savings were meager, but it couldn't go on much longer. She lifted her paintbrush and began to paint—and soon the frightening images began to fade away.

❧ CHAPTER SIX ❧

illiam trudged along the muddy road to Alfoxden House, reviewing his confrontation with Ben and Walt Sutton. He grinned, pulling his cape closer about him to seal out the penetrating chill. He was grateful that the brothers had maimed one another, and that he had been able to avoid bodily harm. But, he acknowledged, losing his grin, it would probably have been better if the brutes had not been injured. He knew there would be unpleasant repercussions. *Damn it! The last thing he needed was more trouble.*

William shook his head in frustration. Hoping to take his mind off the altercation, he withdrew the journal from his satchel, opened it and scanned the few verses he had written. He could plainly see the words did not adequately describe the awe he felt for the world around him. After awhile, as he walked on, the memory of the Suttons faded, the cooing of a nearby dove bringing his concentration back to the natural beauty of the sky and the woods, the mosses and the flowers, a study that always soothed him and made him feel at home. As often happened when he least expected it, new ideas began to form into words, as if some divine force had set to work cultivating his creativity. He retrieved his stub of a pencil and a penknife and began to shape a new point to replace the tip that had broken earlier. His thoughts, shaping themselves into verse, were interrupted by the pounding of hooves coming up fast behind him.

He turned and raised an eyebrow when he saw three horsemen in brilliant red cavalry uniforms approaching at a canter. A white-haired man, wearing a lieutenant's uniform and riding a handsome steed, was followed by two younger men dressed as privates.

William stepped quickly to the side of the road to allow them passage, but the Lieutenant raised his hand and the riders checked their mounts to a slow trot. William felt a trickle of fear. *Had Ben and Walt Sutton run into the soldiers and fabricated charges against him? Was he about to be arrested?* The horsemen swerved off the track to halt abruptly before him, splattering his trousers with mud.

William peered at his soiled pants with irritation. *Look at this! My best trousers covered in muck! Insufferable!*

The white-haired lieutenant leaned down in his saddle. "Mr. William Wordsworth?"

Believing it prudent to hide his annoyance, he replied as calmly as he could manage, "Indeed, Lieutenant, but how did you find me?"

"We stopped off at the King's Head Inn. The proprietor told us you'd been there and we'd find you on the road."

He relaxed a bit; apparently there was no connection between the cavalrymen and the Suttons.

The lieutenant opened a leather satchel and withdrew an official-looking envelope. "Mr. William Wordsworth, as an officer of the Crown, I have been instructed to serve you with this summons. You are to appear before the Home Secretary, the Duke of Portland, in Bristol Court on September twenty-first of this year, 1798."

William's mind began to race. *What in hell was this all about? The Duke of Portland summoning him to court?* He grimaced as he took the envelope from the lieutenant.

"Failure to appear will result in your arrest and incarceration."

"There must be some mistake. What is the charge against me?" he asked, voicing his consternation.

"The charges are outlined in the subpoena. Good day to you, Sir." The lieutenant and his guards wheeled their mounts and trotted off.

William tore the envelope open and scanned the contents of the single page writ, his heart pounding. He exclaimed, "Those Royal bastards!"

His hands shook as he replaced the letter into its envelope and jammed it and the journal into his satchel. He stepped back onto the road, the fragments of the budding poem forgotten.

On the horizon, thunderheads were blowing in from the sea, scattering a flock of white clouds before them, like sheep being pursued by a pack of grey wolves. William tightened his cloak. Anxiety overcame him. *How, in God's name, was he going to fight the charges against him?*

ucy, with one eye on the advancing clouds, was still painting at her easel when she noticed Emily and Henry running up the hill toward her. The children came to a halt a few feet from the baskets and stood there, breathing quite a bit harder than was necessary as they waited for her to acknowledge them.

No, no you don't, little ones. This is my time.

When she pointedly ignored their presence, the children began shuffling their feet to draw her attention.

She withheld a smile, and continued to paint as if they weren't there.

Emily, obviously not brave enough to interrupt her governess' few precious moments at the easel, nudged Henry and motioned for him to step forward. Henry shook his head but then noisily cleared his throat. Emily must have thought that a good approach, for she began to cough loudly.

Lucy tried not to laugh out loud at their antics; she continued to ignore them as she applied a dab of green oil to a stand of trees on the canvas.

Frowning with impatience, Emily finally blurted out, "Miss Lucy, your painting's gonna take a long time an' Henry and me need you to play catch with us before the rains come."

"Yeah," Henry said. "It's no fun, just the two of us."

Lucy glanced nonchalantly to the horizon. The storm clouds were rolling forward, dropping sheets of rain in the distance. *About another twenty minutes to paint before the first raindrops fell, but with the children hovering beside her, it was hopeless!* She sighed, lowered her palette and brush and began to disassemble the easel.

Henry beamed. "Miss Lucy, you're gonna play with us now?"

"I believe we've already had this conversation."

Emily said, "But we need you to play with us."

Lucy ignored Emily, knowing better than to launch a debate with her two precocious wards.

Henry stamped his foot on the ground in annoyance. After a moment, his eyes fell to the palette and paintbrush lying on top of one of the baskets. A mischievous grin appeared on his face. He surreptitiously reached toward it.

Lucy saw Henry's intent and gently tapped his hand. "Away with you!"

The boy ducked and, moving nimbly to elude his governess' reach, snatched up the paintbrush and palette. He quickly backed further away, giggling triumphantly and waving his trophies in the air. "Emily, catch!" Henry threw the paintbrush to his sister, who caught it with a conspirator's answering giggle.

Oh, the little brats! "Give those to me at once," Lucy said. It had taken her two predawn hours this morning to grind the pigments and mix them with the oils for the palette and if they were wasted it would cost her a week's savings to purchase new colors.

The siblings laughed in unison. "Catch us!" They ran down the hill, waving their misbegotten trophies.

"Oh, you awful little monsters." Lucy said as she gathered her skirts to her knees and gave chase.

CHAPTER EIGHT

William had left the road several yards behind the spot where he stood now, searching for the stream that had suddenly and perversely, he thought, veered into a grove of trees. If he didn't rinse the splattered mud from his favorite pair of trousers, they would be permanently stained. He kicked his way through a patch of brambles, dour still from the sting of the Home Office summons, his rift with the Suttons, the paralyzed state of his writing and his precarious financial affairs. He stepped upon a lump of undergrowth, and an explosion of feathers burst into the air as a covey of flapping, screeching quail took flight. Raising his arms protectively, he lost his footing and pitched forward down the path. As a tree branch materialized before him, he reached up and grabbed onto it, arresting what certainly would have been an ungainly tumble. While catching his breath, he focused on the sight before him: Hundreds of flowering water lilies floated in a small pond beneath tall Elm trees, forming an idyllic setting at the edge of a small meadow. William had come upon Dove Springs. He had been told of its existence but had yet to investigate its location. He noticed its waters bubbled up from the earth in several places, flowed into the pond, and then over its bank into the stream that had been the object of his search. The latter, he knew, curled through the Quantock Hills where, a short distance to the northwest, it joined the River Parrett. Two miles later, the river flowed into Bridgwater Bay and the Bristol Channel.

Remembering his muddied trousers, William withdrew a handkerchief from his satchel and knelt on the bank of the pond, laying his bag down beside him. He dipped the white cloth into the water, wrung the fabric slightly and began to wash the mud away.

He heard the sound of children giggling and turned to locate its source. As he did, a blurred flash of clothing hurtled toward him and suddenly a body slammed into his chest, knocking the wind from his lungs. He rolled on the grass, a boy tumbling next to him. He gasped for breath and was struggling to his knees when another figure, this time a young girl, catapulted into his backside, casting him headfirst toward the boy, all of them becoming a tangle of arms and legs.

The ground rotated around William, eventually righting itself. He rolled over and gingerly loosened himself from the knot he had formed with the two screaming bodies. He pushed himself up to a sitting position, feeling dazed. His attention was then drawn to the figure of a young woman, moving forward with an easy elegance of limbs and body, who hurried into the glen, apparently in pursuit of the children. She was tall, slim of waist with attractive curves in the right places. Her pleasing face was lined with worry as she rushed over to the thin girl, who lay on the ground gasping for air beside a red-faced, but seemingly unharmed, boy.

"Emily, are you hurt?" the young woman asked, taking the girl into her arms with a look of concern on her beautiful face.

The girl regained her breath. "I be fine, Miss Lucy," she said, sitting up, looking a bit shaken but otherwise unharmed.

The boy, whose round, yet stocky build made him less prone to injury, leaped to his feet with a display of bravado. His face dropped when he saw the attention his sister was receiving.

"Me leg," the boy said, suddenly grabbing the limb. "I think I twisted it purty bad."

The young woman helped the girl to her feet, then reached over for the boy. "Henry, my brave little man. I thought nothing could ever hurt you."

The boy seemed momentarily taken aback, then stood up as straight as one of the King's Guard and flexed his stout little body. "It's nothing. I be fine."

William's eyes had never left the face of the lovely young woman. He mused: *If the display of a little distress worked for the lad, might it work for him?* He groaned.

The young woman turned to him, appearing anxious. She took a tentative step forward then hesitated. "Sir, are you hurt?"

"I believe I may be slightly injured," William said, pleased by her look of concern. To better emphasize the point he held his ribs with crossed arms, and leaned slightly forward, grimacing.

"I'm so sorry. The children were running. I'm afraid they didn't see you." As she spoke, he noticed she had moved another step closer to him. "An unfortunate accident," she added.

So, this is an interesting turn of events, he thought, and rose unsteadily to his feet. Noticing the young woman's eyes for the first time, he caught his breath: They were large and tender and quietly thoughtful; their color—a kaleidoscope of indigo, cobalt and cerulean, all sparkling like precious gemstones—yet soft and ever changing, exhibiting glimpses of intelligence and innocence in their innermost depths. Their astonishing beauty and warmth, so seldom seen in real life, captivated him. Shockingly, he began to feel aroused.

A moment passed ... or had it been two or three? He would never know how long he stood there staring, unable to move. Finally, he brushed an imaginary blade of grass from the front of his trousers and was grateful to find that his physical stirrings didn't show.

The young woman suddenly gasped for breath. William noticed her cheeks were flushed. *Could she have experienced a similar phenomenon? Or was her blush the result of exertion from running after the children?* William was, for the moment, speechless.

The children's voices interrupted his musings.

"He was in our way," the boy said. "It's his fault!"

"Yes," the girl chimed in. "We didn't even see him."

William ignored the children as his eyes surreptitiously took in the young woman's slim, lovely figure and came to rest upon a fair and oval face with exquisite features. He noticed she was fumbling with her long black curls, unsuccessfully trying to push them back under a straw hat. Finding his voice, he responded, "I suppose they are right about that. I guess I shouldn't have let my mind wander in a field in which a couple of young pups might be running."

"We're not pups," Henry said. "We're children."

"Your manners, please," the young woman replied to the children. Then she turned back to him, lowering those incredible eyes. "Sir, I must apologize for their…"

"No, Miss Lucy," Henry interjected, assuming the stance of a protective bulldog. "Don't apologize. This be Hawkins property. Sir, you be trespassing."

Lucy corrected him, "This *is* Hawkins property. Sir, you *are* trespassing," and then quickly added, "Sir, I didn't mean that for you."

"Yes!" the girl named Emily said. "You shouldn't even be here."

"Just a moment," William said. "I merely stepped off the public road for some water when you two barreled into me."

"The stream and pond be on our property. You're to leave at once!" Henry puffed up his little barrel chest.

William withheld a smile, staring at the two impetuous monsters. Knowing better than to argue with children, he reluctantly turned away from the young woman to pick up his satchel and hat.

Henry suddenly burst out laughing, pointing to the rear of William's trousers. Emily also began to laugh. The young woman's eyebrow's rose with alarm.

Wondering at the object of their amusement, William turned around and glanced at his backside. His eyes widened at a display of green, brown and gray oil paint smeared on the seat of his trousers. He blanched. "Oh, no... ."

Instead of showing sympathy, the young woman the children called Miss Lucy began to look around in an apparent state of distress. "My palette," she exclaimed. "Where is it?" She ignored him completely and began to search through the grass. Emily's and Henry's smiles faded as they, too, joined in the hunt.

"There it be," Henry exclaimed, "in them rocks!"

William watched as the young woman gently pulled the fragile piece of wood from between two rocks and examined its surface with trembling fingers.

William peeked over her shoulder for a closer appraisal. He noted that the palette had suffered nary a crack, while his best pair of trousers was certainly ruined. With an air of disgust for the attention paid to such a trivial matter, he bent to pick up his satchel by the bank of the pond, and noticed its contents had spilled out. Scooping his possessions into the bag, his heart froze. *My journal! Where is my journal?* He glanced around anxiously. "I have a small book missing," he called out. "Please, everyone, take a moment to help me find it. It's a very important book."

The young woman continued to ignore him as she asked the children, "Have you seen my paintbrush?"

Emily and Henry silently winced. They hurriedly spread out to hunt among the small meadow's grass and rocks.

William called to them. "I say, would you please help me locate my lost journal? It's a thin, flat book ... very, very important."

"That be it?" Emily pointed to the middle of the pond.

William flushed with alarm. He could see his journal floating, partially submerged, among the lily pads; it would soon sink and be lost.

Feeling panic radiate throughout his body, he rapidly stripped off his waistcoat and shoes, threw them aside, and splashed out into the knee-high water. His feet immediately began to slip on the moss covered rocks beneath him. He held his breath, cautioning himself to advance more slowly but it didn't help. His legs were splaying out, and in spite of his efforts to pull them back together, continued to spread. A feeling of dread rushed over him. Wind-milling his arms out in broad circles, he fought to correct his balance, but lost it and fell backward. The water splashed over his head, entering his nose and mouth. He coughed and spat as he rolled over and crawled toward his journal, which was floating only a few feet away. Jagged rocks scraped his knees and elbows. Ignoring the pain, driven to save his poems, he lunged for the tome. His fingers grasped and encircled it. Hope surged as he pulled it to him and with pleading eyes riffled through the pages, praying that the writing—almost all of which was in ink—had not blurred nor run. His heart sank as he saw that the pages, other than the few he had penciled in today, were quite indecipherable.

"This is a disaster!" he muttered, sick at heart. "Complete and absolute disaster."

William turned to the perpetrators, expecting sympathy, but they were busy with their own search.

"It has to be here," Lucy said, parting a tuft of grass. "I must not lose it. It was my father's gift to me before he died."

Emily glanced to her with sympathetic eyes. "Don't worry. We'll find it."

"It surely don't got wings." Henry said. "It be nearby."

A look of hopelessness marred Lucy's lovely features. "Unless it went into the pond ... and it surely *doesn't have* wings."

William dragged himself out of the water, grasping his journal. The muscles in his body ached from the cuts and bruises, and a dank cold had seeped into his bones. Dripping from head to toe, he brandished his soggy pages over his head. "Look at my journal. Look what you little fiends have done."

The fiends gave him the briefest of glances and returned their attention to the grass.

"I said, look at my pages," he repeated, raising his voice. "You've destroyed weeks and weeks of work. Hundreds of hours of... ." His voice tapered off. He could see the children were indifferent to his distress. *The spoiled brats!* Suppressing an urge to pummel them, William walked over to the remainder of his belongings. He gathered everything into his arms and marched off on bare feet, heading for the road, murmuring words that Lucy and the children were better off not hearing.

William stepped onto the rutted track, and immediately jumped back up onto the grass to avoid squishing barefoot through mud. "I don't care if it is their blasted property," he groused, as a flash of lightening split the sky.

ucy and the children had spread out across the small glen and were turning over stones, examining rocky crevices and parting calf-high grass, in their search for the missing paintbrush. Lucy's heart felt like a ball of lead in her chest ... she was on the verge of sobbing. Fighting back the tears, she noticed that Emily and Henry were uncommonly silent, perhaps feeling guilt that their prank had caused her such angst. *Good ... they should feel shame.* She lowered her eyes to the thick clumps of grass, and hunted along the edge of the pool, praying the paintbrush hadn't flown into the water and been washed away by the current.

While searching, Lucy was surprised to find she could still feel a yearning deep inside her that she had experienced when her eyes had looked into those of the stranger, and that kept prodding her thoughts back to him.

His sudden appearance and her physical reaction to him had startled her beyond anything she had ever known in her seventeen years of life. Shocked, she couldn't decide if she had been experiencing pain or pleasure … or a combination of both.

Embarrassed by these private thoughts that even now caused her to blush, she made an effort to push the astonishing encounter aside, but the effort was made in vain. *How could the mere appearance of a man, a complete stranger, affect her in such a way? Who was he and where did he live? Would she ever see him again?* Her forehead furrowed. *In all probability he was married and had at least six children … not that the stranger or his marital situation mattered a bit to her.*

A fat raindrop fell on her cheek, interrupting her musings. She looked up to see that the dark storm clouds had almost filled the sky. Within minutes she and the children would be caught in a deluge.

She called to Emily and Henry, "Children, it's about to rain. We must go. Hurry, we'll just make it in time."

CHAPTER TEN

Claps of thunder exploded across the courtyard like a barrage of cannon fire as Lucy led the squealing children up the steps to the manor's front door. They burst inside just in time to escape the rain that began to slap heavily upon the cobblestones.

Emily and Henry yelled with exhilaration in the foyer, jumping up and down as they looked out at the falling rain.

"I knew we could beat the storm," yelled Emily. "Yahoo!"

"Just in time," said Henry. "Yippee!"

"Quiet, children. Enough," she said, holding her easel in one hand while she kicked the door shut and gathered a basket from Emily.

Henry, holding onto her other basket, looked to his sister and asked, "Emily, where's my ball?"

"I don't have it."

"You egghead," he shouted. "You must of left it in the glen."

"Don't call me an egghead," Emily responded, her voice rising, "you little ass!"

"Emily!" Lucy reprimanded, "Young ladies never use that word."

"He called me an egghead!"

"You are an egghead," Henry reiterated loudly. "An' you ain't no young lady, neither."

"Quiet children! Your prattle is enough to wake the dead in Saint Mary's cemetery." Lucy said, precariously balancing her easel and a basket as she started into the great room. "A minute more and we would have been soaked to the skin. Henry, bring that basket along."

They crossed the fan-shaped marbled entrance and swept into a large room furnished with heavy, ornate tables, chairs and sofas. Paintings of Lady Hawkins' ancestors were placed about the wood-paneled walls. The faces on the portraits reminded Lucy more of turnips and cabbages than human beings. There were also a few landscapes that, to her eye, were the efforts of secondary artists. The tall windows in the room were framed with faded, once-rich brocades that needed replacing. Even the tapestries, depicting hunting scenes, looked forlorn as they drooped from wrought iron poles beneath the heavily beamed ceiling.

"Miss Lucy," Emily said, hurrying to keep up with her. "We're so sorry about your father's paintbrush. We'll help you look for it again tomorrow."

"Yes, we be sure to find it then," Henry said. "Unless that trespasser stole it."

Lucy stopped beside a section of wall where she pushed on a beveled mahogany panel which swung open to reveal a small, dark storage room. Henry dropped his basket at her feet.

"Thank you," Lucy said, sidestepping through the opening to place her painting paraphernalia inside. "I want you two upstairs now to wash and dress for supper. It's your parents' anniversary. You should look your best."

"We're not dirty," Henry protested.

"I've seen cleaner mud pies. Now, off with you. I'm not in any mood to argue."

Henry opened his mouth to protest, but, before he could utter a word, his sister grabbed his arm. "We've been enough trouble for one day, Henry. Come along."

Lucy glanced after the children as the manor's three maids, Beth, Molly and Mary, entered from the kitchen area; they wore their best black dresses with white aprons and matching linen caps. Each carried an assortment of china and silverware to the twelve-place Jacobean dining table.

They were quibbling amongst themselves as usual. Beth, the tallest of the trio, had once been a comely young woman, but now, in her late thirties, was showing the effects of overdrinking. Molly, a buxom girl in her early twenties, who enjoyed flaunting her cleavage by wearing low-cut necklines, was almost pretty. Her features were just slightly off, Lucy thought, as if sculpted by an apprentice artisan instead of a master. Mary, a short, spry sixty-five-year-old, placed her stack of china on the table and bustled out while the other women set the table.

Lucy leaned back into the closet and was placing her last basket on a shelf when a red aura suddenly materialized in the darkness, burning a hole in her vision. She staggered back against the doorframe, feeling dizzy. *Oh, no! Please, not now!* She closed her eyes to squeeze out the light, but the intense glow penetrated her senses. She forced her eyes to open a crack, peered at the two servants, then cautiously inched backwards into the darkness of the storage room. *Dear God, don't let them see me like this. Please...* Then another wave of dizziness swept over her.

The floor tilted and started to spin. Lucy grabbed onto the wall to keep from falling and began to hyperventilate. Desperate to hide, she struggled to edge further back into the closet.

She gasped as muscles began to spasm in her arms, back, and legs. She heard a suppressed scream and then realized it was her own voice, echoing silently in her brain. She gripped the shelves, but couldn't hold on. She crumbled to the floor and began to shake. *Dear God, help me. Let it pass. Please, let it pass. Don't let them see me like this.*

Lucy held back a scream as a second, more powerful tremor coursed through her torso, forcing her to arch and twist in a vain attempt to avoid the stabbing pains. A suppressed moan escaped clenched teeth. Her eyes, beyond control now, rolled up in their sockets. Swirls of inky blackness descended as if someone had thrown a cloak over her. The last things she remembered were the sounds of heavy footsteps, the creak of the door swung wide and the feel of strong arms lifting her from the floor.

❧ CHAPTER ELEVEN ❦

ucy was only half-awake when she felt someone fumbling with the buttons on the front of her blouse. She opened her eyes and tried to focus. Squire George Hawkins was bent over her as she lay in her bed, alone with him in the servants' attic room. He breathed heavily; the fumes from his fetid breath sickened her. His face was porcine; reminding her of the pigs he had raised before his wife's rich uncle had died, leaving them the manor. Coming fully awake, she looked down and blanched … *she was more than halfway unbuttoned!* Her heart jumped as his intent became clear.

"No, Sir, please," she said, pushing his hands away and pulling the covers up to her neck. *What did he think he was doing? And why was he alone with her in her bedroom? Where was everyone else? Ah, the party …*

"Just tryin' ta help ya, Lucy dear," he said, ogling her heaving bosom. "Yer bodice looks so tight, I thought it might help if I was ta give ya some room ta breathe."

Lucy pressed the covers to her chin. Trying to keep the shock from her voice, she said, "I can breathe just fine, Sir." A look of displeasure crossed his features.

Flashes of lightning pulsed through the dormer windows, illuminating the small room. When Lucy saw the bedroom door was closed, she trembled. Eerie shadows played over the Squire's face, transforming his features into a gargoyle-like mask. The beast smiled at her. *If he went a step further, she would scream.* A boom of thunder shook the windowpanes as the storm began in earnest. *Would anyone hear her cries for help above the pounding of the rain on the roof and cobblestones?*

The door to the bedroom opened and,

Mary, one of the servants, looked in. She gave the Squire a look of disapproval.

The Squire turned on her with irritation. "Away with you, woman."

The maid glared at him for a condemning moment, then bowed her head and slowly stepped away, leaving the door open.

Lucy noticed the Squire's rummy eyes blink rapidly, as if he were reconsidering his lustful intentions; he reminded her of the barn cat that had sneaked into the kitchen last week and been caught a moment before being able to devour a piece of mutton stolen from the counter. Lightening flashed, followed by the rumble of thunder. The Squire let out an unhappy sigh and forced a wan smile, showing ochred teeth; the appearance of the maid had ruined his plans. He sat down beside Lucy on the edge of the small bed.

"Don't fret, Lass. 'Tis nothing but a little rain," he said in a not-unkindly voice. "Close yer eyes and sleep. I'll be watching over ya 'til the good doctor arrives. You've nothing ta fear now. I'm with ya."

Lucy tried to get up and run, but she couldn't seem to move. The Squire reached over and stroked her hands as they clutched the covers. Lucy managed to withdraw them and hunched back into her pillow, as far as the fabric would allow. *How could she trust him to keep his word?* Lucy's eyes fluttered as a wave of exhaustion swept over her. She fought to keep her eyelids open. *She couldn't allow herself to fall asleep ... she mustn't.* Visions of the Squire taking liberties with the servants flooded what was left of her awareness: On more than one occasion, she had seen him in an uncompromising position with Beth, when he thought no one had been looking.

Now she remembered a dream she'd had while unconscious from her seizure: Large hands had fondled her as she was carried her to her quarters. She was mindful, now, that it most likely hadn't been a dream.

Beth appeared at the door, breathing hard, as if she had just run upstairs. She gave the Squire a withering look and stepped into the room. "There's no need for ya to be here, yer Lordship. I'll be seein' after Miss Lucy."

The Squire hesitated, pursed his lips, and rose slowly to his feet, throwing the maid a piercing look. "See that ya do, Beth.

The Squire brushed past her, leaving the two women alone.

Lucy smiled weakly. "Thank you, Beth. Thank you so much."

"Think nothin' of it, dearie. His Lordship is randy as a billy goat. I wouldn't want him doin' ya no harm and I wouldn't want him ta get ta like ya neither, if ya know what I mean."

She understood what Beth was implying. The last thing on earth Lucy wished for was to replace Beth as the Squire's paramour.

light rain beat gently upon the windowpane beside Dorothy as she sat at her brother William's writing desk in the tastefully-decorated parlor of Alfoxden House. She looked up from the letter she had been reading and gazed out through mottled glass. Squinting, she was just able to discern the muddy road that ran in front of the property: A frown creased her pleasant features when she saw that it was deserted. Where was William? It was unlike him to be late for supper, and she was hoping he had found refuge from the earlier downpour on his way home from Samuel's cottage. The aroma of a chicken supper filled the downstairs rooms. She was pleased she had chosen to make a hearty stew … it would hold for hours if need be. She absently pulled at a lock of brown hair that had fallen from her white linen cap and twisted it, preoccupied with her concern for William; how easily the combination of wet and cold could cause illness! Since there was nothing on earth she could do to alter the weather, she returned her attention to the letter. It had arrived earlier in the day addressed to Mr. William

Wordsworth from the new owner of their leased residence, Alfoxden House. A few hours ago, she had opened her brother's mail, as was her custom, and now she edged the page closer to the flame of the candlestick that burned on the table beside her. Reviewing the letter for the umpteenth time, she focused on its message:

SOMERSET COUNTY SOLICITOR'S OFFICE
Termination of lease. Lessee is hereby ordered to quit the premises within sixty days.

The letter went on to explain that Alfoxden House had been sold and the new owner, a Mrs. Albyn, was no longer prepared to honor the one-year lease given to William three months previously.

The news had at first alarmed her. But now, the more she thought about it, the more she was convinced the order must be illegal. After all, she and William had a valid lease that had been properly witnessed by a solicitor. She lowered the page and tapped it pensively on the tabletop. Hiring an attorney to handle the matter would be a luxury they couldn't afford, but they had to respond and let this Mrs. Albyn know they had no intention of vacating the premises.

Dorothy was at a loss to understand why they were being asked to leave. They had certainly been good tenants and had always been able to come up with the rent on time. It didn't make any sense.

She mumbled an oath, raised her eyes to the heavens for forgiveness and scanned the document again. Its content offered no motive for the landlord's sudden action. Perhaps Mrs. Albyn realized how far below market the former owner had set their rent and the letter was a ploy to increase it. She had to admit twenty-three pounds a year was a miraculously low amount to pay for leasing the sumptuous estate. Or maybe this Mrs. Albyn intended to move in herself!

The sound of a man sneezing drew her attention to the window.

Well, and it's about time, she thought, smiling when she recognized William, sloshing resolutely up the front path. Her smile faded when she saw his state of dishevelment; he looked like a puppy that had been lost for days in the moors.

She slipped the letter back into its envelope and placed it in the pocket of her apron. It would be best to discuss the subject of their lease after a good meal.

She stood as William entered with wind and rain at his heels. He leaned back against the door, ousting the inhospitable elements as he pressed it shut. Shivering severely, he began to peel off his satchel and soggy hat.

Dorothy hurried over to him and helped remove his cloak. Touching his shirt, she said with some alarm, "William, you're wet all the way through. You'll catch your death."

"It would be a fitting end to a most wretched day," he said, and sneezed.

"God bless you. I'm so sorry you've had a bad day."

"It was wretched ... abjectly dismal. I wasted Samuel's time and my own: I couldn't write a dashed word that made any sense. And then I stopped by the King's Head Inn and was accosted by those pig farmers, the Suttons. They are two of the most feral sots on the planet and I'm afraid I told them so."

Dorothy stepped back, upset. "Oh no, you didn't really, did you?"

"I certainly did," he said, before sneezing again.

"Bless you. What happened?" she asked, hanging his cloak on the coat-stand by the door.

"We had a slight altercation ... nothing for you to worry your head about."

"Those men are brutes," she said. She gave him a questioning look. "They let you walk away after you insulted them?"

"I'll spare you the details," he said, avoiding the physical aspects of his encounter that he knew would upset his sister. He turned his attention to the task of pulling off his boots. "But on the road home, I was stopped by three of the Crown's horsemen. They served me a summons issued by the Home Office."

"A summons? For what?"

"And that's not the half of it. Moments after they rode off, I was almost drowned in a pond by some little brats. I'm bruised, cut, drenched and... ." He reached into his satchel and fished out his sodden journal, opening it. "Look! Look at my work ... ruined ... unreadable. A month's worth, completely lost."

"Oh, no," she exclaimed sympathizing with his tale of woe. "I am so sorry for you."

While he was retrieving a wet handkerchief from his pocket to blow his nose, he knocked over his satchel.

Dorothy raised an eyebrow as she noticed what appeared to be a long, thin pen roll out onto the floor at her feet. Stooping to recover the object she said, "What are you doing with a paintbrush?"

William blew his nose and stared at the slim foot-long piece of wood with its fine animal-haired tip. He said, "It must belong to that girl."

"What girl?"

"Oh, she was ... ahh ... ahh ... ahhchoo!" He raised a hand for patience, overcome by an outburst of sneezing.

"Never mind," Dorothy said, deciding she could find out more about all of this later. "I'll just leave it here." She placed the delicate brush on a small Chippendale side table. "William, I want you upstairs, out of those wet clothes and into your bed. Now!"

He glanced at the paintbrush and frowned. "After all the misery that thing reminds me of, I should burn it."

"William, that's quite unlike you."

He responded by blowing his nose again. "You haven't seen the final indignity." He turned, displaying a grotesque stain on the seat of his trousers.

"Oh, my goodness! You poor thing! Are you ill?"

"No! No! It's paint ... it's just paint. I sat on that fool girl's palette."

His sister tried to stifle her amusement, but a small squeak escaped.

William kicked his satchel. It hit the china cabinet, rattling the dishes inside.

She stared at him, surprised by his uncharacteristic outburst.

"Sorry, Dorothy," he defended. "These are my best—and very nearly my only—trousers and they're ruined! This has been one of the most hopeless days of ... ahh ... ahh ... ." He pinched his nose and staved off another sneeze. "...of my entire life!"

Seeing that his health wasn't improving, she instructed, "William, we have much to talk about, but not now. I want you upstairs." She gave him a gentle push toward the stairway. "Go on ... to bed with you. I'll bring up a bowl of chicken stew for supper. It will do you good."

Although William had pulled off his boots, she noticed that he still tracked footprints across the slate floor as he made his way to the central staircase. Part way up, he stopped and turned. "Thank you for your ... ahh ... ahhh ... ahhchoo!"

"Bless you."

William offered a wan smile, but his eyes were troubled. He climbed to his room.

ucy inhaled apprehensively as Doctor Deegan, a portly bespectacled man in his sixties, lifted a clear glass jar of greenish-black leeches from his physician's bag and set it on the table beside her bed. She beat down a wave of nausea as she watched the undulating worms, three to four inches in length, slither around each other.

Doctor Deegan threw her a comforting smile, then said, "You recall our little friends here don't you, Lucy, dear?"

She replied with trembling lips. "Yes, Doctor."

"They helped you once before. Remember?"

Lucy answered with a nod although she wasn't in the least convinced the leeches had had a healing effect when he'd first used them on her months earlier. She had an urge to leap out of bed and bolt from the room, but the moment passed as she reasoned there was no alternative. A prisoner to the doctor's good intentions, she whispered a prayer placing her fate in his hands.

Emily and Henry stood close to her, staring mutely at the slimy creatures. Several of the household servants had crowded into the doorway behind them. The fact that some were crossing themselves or fingering rosary beads wasn't at all comforting!

"There's a darkness in that Miss Lucy; that's for sure," she heard one of the maids whisper.

"Aye, 'tis the Devil's doing," Molly concurred. "I told ya before, she be possessed."

In Lucy's weakened state, she found it difficult to dismiss these superstitious opinions. *Could the servants be right? Was she possessed by the Devil? Is that why she had terrible dizzy spells? She could not recall any transgression or untoward act in her life that might have angered God enough that He would inflict such a terrible punishment upon her.*

Doctor Deegan placed a cooling hand upon her forehead. "Easy, lass. Pay no attention to that ignorant lot." He leaned away and took a pair of metal pincers from his bag and, dipping it into the glass jar, trapped one of the bloodsuckers between its prongs.

The Doctor lifted the slippery parasite from its container and turned to her. "You'll have to hold perfectly still now. I don't want to drop this little fellow."

"They be the Devil's helpers," the cook said loud enough for all to hear.

Molly grunted her agreement.

The Doctor turned to face them, the leech still curling, snake-like, in his forceps. "Quiet! You should be ashamed of yourselves. I've told you all before, this young lady has the falling sickness. Her blood is bad. The Devil has nothing to do with it. Now, all of you, out! Get out!"

The servants murmured apologies, but none of them moved; they were obviously hoping to witness the bloodletting.

The Doctor took a step toward them, brandishing the leech in front of him. Miraculously, it did not fall. "Am I going to have to bleed the lot of you?"

Alarmed, the servants backed reluctantly out of the doorway.

Emily and Henry exchanged anxious glances. "May we stay, Doctor Deegan?" Emily asked. "We know there's no devil in Miss Lucy."

"Yes," Henry said. "We know that for sure."

Lucy lifted her head from the pillow. "Let them stay, Doctor ... please."

Deegan eyed the children with a severe look but then his countenance softened. "You may stay if you're quiet. Shut the door."

Henry closed the door and rejoined his sister at Lucy's side.

"Careful," the doctor said. "Don't be crowding me."

Lucy whimpered quietly, trying to be brave as her eyes followed the doctor's hand, lowering the writhing leech to her right temple. She winced, gripping the side of the bed with white-knuckles as the hungry mouth locked itself onto her flesh. She felt an immediate but short-lived prickling sensation. This ordeal caused tears to well in her eyes, but she remained steadfastly silent.

Emily, living every moment of this experience through her governess, empathized. "Oh, Miss Lucy. It must hurt terribly."

Lucy forced a shadow of a smile, her eyes never leaving the doctor as he dipped his instrument into the jar a second time.

"We'll need two of these," he said. "One for each side to draw the bad blood out twice as fast."

"'Taint no bad blood in her," Henry said.

A faint involuntary giggle escaped her. "Thank you, Henry. Doctor Deegan knows what he's doing."

"What does it feel like, Miss Lucy?" Emily asked, staring in wide-eyed fascination.

"I can hardly feel anything now. A slight pulling sensation is all."

Doctor Deegan explained, "That's because leeches have a painkiller in their saliva."

"Saliva?" Henry asked. "What be saliva?"

"Henry," Lucy said, raising an admonishing finger, "It's: What *is* saliva?"

Henry rolled his eyes, and asked again, "What is saliva?"

"Spit," Deegan replied as he placed the second leech, a four-incher, against Lucy's other temple.

She flinched despite her best effort not to.

"I'm sorry," Deegan said. "It will soon be over."

She nodded bravely. A lone teardrop trailed down her cheek. Emily reached over and wiped it away. "Miss Lucy, Henry and I are going to give you more time to paint. We can play by ourselves most of the time."

"Oh, looky!" Henry said. "The worms are getting fat."

"That means they're doing exactly what they're supposed to do," Doctor Deegan said. "Now, be quiet, young man and let the leeches do their work."

Emily, seeing the tears in her governess's eyes, bent over and kissed her cheek. "It's all right to cry, Miss Lucy. I cry when I get hurt."

"Me, too," Henry said, then added as an afterthought, "But girls cry a lot more."

A smile flitted across Lucy's face as tears brimmed over and streamed down her cheeks.

❧ CHAPTER FOURTEEN ❧

illiam's eyes were watering from what he feared might be the onslaught of a cold. He dabbed his eyelids with his handkerchief and blew his nose. *At least,* he consoled himself, *he was warm and comfortable.* He sat in bed, propped up against pillows, wearing his flannel nightshirt and balancing a new journal on his knees. He picked a quill pen from the side table and stared at the blank pages, struggling to recall his lost verses and notes and commit them to paper. But every few minutes he had to put the pen down and blow his nose into the handkerchief. "This is not worth it," he muttered. He jammed the quill into its inkwell. "Maybe tomorrow... ."

His attention was drawn to the doorway as his sister appeared carrying a serving tray with a pot of tea, cups and two bowls of steaming stew. "Knock, knock," Dorothy said, unable to free a hand to strike the doorframe as was her custom before entering his bedroom.

"Come in ... come in," he said, tossing his journal aside. "I hope my black mood won't distress you."

"It's nothing I haven't suffered before." Smiling warmly, she set the tray on his bedside table.

William inhaled the stew's aroma. "Ah, food ... perhaps it will help to soothe the internal tempest. Now that I think about it, I believe I'm famished."

"A sense of smell and an appetite are good signs. Your sniffles should be gone by morning."

His eyes went to a slim journal she had tucked under an arm. "What is the book you have there?"

"Oh. Just a bit of my copying," she said nonchalantly and handed him the journal.

Intrigued, William began to leaf through the pages. A look of astonishment spread across his features. He couldn't believe his eyes: His poems, in various stages of development, except for today's entries, of course, were neatly written on the pages in Dorothy's small, precise hand. "Astounding!" He looked up. "Dorothy, you are a Godsend!" He threw the covers aside, sprang from the bed and embraced her, kissing her on the forehead. "Bless you. Bless you! *Bless you!* You are the finest sister a brother ever had." Still incredulous, William gave her a questioning look. "But you have never copied my unfinished verse before. What inspired you to do so this time?"

Dorothy smiled slowly, obviously savoring the moment. William recalled she had made it a habit to copy his final drafts when she had come to live with him, almost two years ago, shortly after her twenty-fourth birthday. She had first begun copying his writings with the poem 'Salisbury Plain.' Later, after he had read the comments she had penned beneath the poems, he informed Dorothy that he found them perceptive. He had sought her advice on unfinished works as well but, before now, she had never copied poems in their undeveloped state.

"I knew they weren't ready to copy yet, but... ." She shrugged, still smiling. "I can only do so much needlepoint when I cannot sleep at night, so I'm trying to use my time constructively." She nodded to the journal. "You'll see I've also added my rather opinionated comments to the bottom of each page."

He squeezed her hand. "I love your notes; they're invaluable to me." With the lone exception of Samuel Coleridge, Dorothy had become William's most valued critic.

He knew that looking over his work satisfied Dorothy's creative impulse while at the same time giving her a way to reimburse him for his support. Although Dorothy spent many pleasurable hours writing verses of her own, she seldom showed her efforts to anyone. Her only literary ambition was to see her brother's poems in print.

"William! You're shivering. Back into bed with you. You can read my notes when you're warm under the covers."

Still grinning, and feeling that some good had come of the day at last, he crawled back into bed, clutching his sister's work. "Coleridge and I have been rewriting these poems for weeks. When I tell him what you've done, he'll walk all the way to Bristol to buy you a new dress."

"If I know Samuel, and I believe I do, he'll celebrate by walking into the nearest pub and draining a few pints."

William retrieved his bowl from the bedside table. "Don't forget, it was in a pub that he negotiated the rent for the roof over our heads. If it hadn't been for him, we'd still be in that little cottage in Dorset."

He noticed a flicker of worry cross his sister's face and added, "If you're concerned about Samuel's drinking, don't be. He has some self-control." When she rolled her eyes he added, "Well, most of the time. Besides, I know you enjoy his company, and drink never dulls his quick wit."

Sensing a protracted discussion of his friend coming on, she said, "It's not Samuel's sassy humor I'm worried about. It's your health. Now eat your stew before it gets cold."

"Dorothy, you're beginning to sound just like our mother, bless her soul," he replied, lifting his spoon.

They settled into a comfortable silence as they ate. Presently, curiosity got the better of her. "I am more than anxious to hear the details of this confrontation with the Sutton brothers."

Sure, you are, he thought. He avoided a direct answer by swallowing a mouthful of stew. He said, "This is delicious."

She gave him an impatient look. "William... ."

He had no intention of relating the insults Ben and Walt had hurled at his sister, but finally, wanting to mollify her, he summarized, "It was nothing to speak of, really. We had a slight disagreement. They accused me of being a Francophile. They kept at me, insulting things I hold dear, and eventually I divulged my opinion of their views. Then we parted."

Dorothy clanged her spoon purposefully into her bowl, folded her arms and stared at him.

"Yes … well," he said hesitantly. "There might have been a little more to it than that. Ben took a swipe at me, but I bent over in time; his fist hit Walt's nose. I believe he broke it and his own hand. Divine justice." He grinned. "The whole episode was rather amusing, actually."

"It's not the least bit amusing," she said, her face darkening. "You were fortunate you weren't seriously injured; if you see the Suttons again, you must avoid them. Run if you have to."

"Dorothy, I'm neither a fighter nor a runner."

"You'll run if you don't want the life beaten out of you."

He laughed, which brought on a coughing spell. Finally, he rasped, "All right. To make you happy, I'll carry Father's walking staff. Remember Old Hickory? It's rapped a few heads in its day.

Some of Dorothy's color returned to her cheeks. She retrieved her spoon. "Now, tell me about this summons you mentioned."

He took a moment to savor another bite of food. Then, again trying not to alarm her, but knowing she wouldn't be satisfied until she had heard an explanation, he said, "A stupid annoyance. I must appear at Bristol Court next month. Apparently, some of our meddlesome neighbors wrote the Home Office claiming I'm a French sympathizer and possibly a spy. Can you believe it? They think that because I don't actively condemn the French Revolution, I must therefore favor it and foster seditious ideas against our own Monarchy. It's utter nonsense."

As he spoke, Dorothy's face became more somber. "William, this cannot be taken lightly."

He knew her concern stemmed from his often outspoken admiration of Parisian culture. And yes, he *had* been interested in the French Revolution. He had read both Edmund Burke's *Reflection on the Revolution in France* and Tom Paine's response to it in *The Rights of Man*. These tomes had strengthened William's belief that men in all nations had the right to be represented in their own governments. If this opinion upset the locals, who considered any rational discourse on man's freedom of speech an act of treason, William really didn't give a damn. But he didn't tell his sister that. Instead, he said, "All right ... I can deal with it."

"What will you do?"

"I'll go to court and explain myself. I don't believe our less-than-perfect king has started hanging men for voicing honest differences of opinion; at least not yet."

"No, but the court could hang you if they somehow proved you've made subversive statements while we're at war with France."

"No one can prove that because it isn't true."

"Nevertheless, rumors alone have taken many an honest man to the gallows," she said. "You must be careful what you say."

William emitted a sigh. "All right, the next time someone asks my opinion, my response will be; 'Sorry, but the King's got my tongue.'"

"I'm just making a point, and that is, you're far too candid for your own good."

"You worry too much. If they hang me for anything, it will be because they don't understand my poetry. That's what's behind this summons; they want me in court to explain why I consider man and nature to have any import."

Dorothy smiled, but became serious again as she reached into her pocket. "I suppose it's best to discuss all the unpleasantness at once and get it out of the way." She withdrew the solicitor's letter and placed it on William's tray. "More distressing news, I'm afraid."

William blew his nose yet again into his handkerchief and then picked up the correspondence. Glancing at the lawyer's return address, he raised an eyebrow and withdrew the letter from its envelope. After scanning it quickly, he read it more slowly. "There must be some mistake! We have a year's lease. I'll have a conversation with Mr. Bartholomew tomorrow and set things right ... he represents Mrs. Albyn now."

"It could just be a tactic to raise our rent. If so, that too could be a problem."

William nodded, knowing how short of funds they were. "We'll have a few more pounds soon enough."

"Are you keeping something from me?" she asked hopefully. "Is Raisley's bequest finally coming through?"

"Unfortunately, no," he replied. "Even after two years, the will remains stuck in probate with no resolution in sight."

He reflected upon his deceased friend, Raisley Calvert, who had believed William to be talented and had wished to sponsor his poetic endeavors. Sickly and dying at the early age of twenty-one, Raisley had bequeathed William an amount of nine hundred pounds. It was a handsome sum, enough for him and Dorothy to live without having to pursue common work. But the funds had been tied up in court by relatives with claims of their own, which could halve the amount. Whatever the final outcome, there seemed to be little chance of a settlement in the near future.

William glanced at his gold watch fob and chain, lying on the side table. There was no watch attached. "I feel one of my poems will sell shortly," he said, with more enthusiasm than he felt. "But in the meantime we need money to live and pay the rent ... that is, if I'm successful in straightening out the lease situation." He lifted the gold chain from the table. "No sense in hanging onto this without a timepiece to go with it."

"No, William!" Dorothy said. "I will not let you sell it. It's all you have left of Father. I would never have allowed you to sell the watch in the first place had I known what you were up to."

"Material objects are luxuries we neither need nor can afford. Besides, we will always carry our memories of Mother and Father in our hearts."

William thought back to the burial of his parents. He could still see the spray of yellow nosegays his father had placed upon his mother's coffin. But, rather than remembering the scent of the flowers, he recalled the stench of rotting garbage as he and other mourners had walked behind the hearse, through the slimy cobblestone streets of Penrith to the parish church cemetery. The smell had lingered, even as his mother's casket had been lowered into its final resting place. He had just celebrated his eighth birthday.

Five years later, his father had died and because of extenuating circumstances, had left the Wordsworth siblings, Richard, Christopher, William, John and Dorothy, with no income and few precious mementos. The Wordsworths had been a well-to-do family, living in a large country home with servants and carriages. But following the parents' deaths, the children's inheritance had been placed under the control of a wealthy landowner for whom their father had worked: This Lord, for years, had done everything in his power to keep control of the funds. The children, with no mother or father and no money, had suffered the indignity of becoming orphans: Relatives had divided the siblings and sent them to live with two stern and stingy uncles; Dorothy, who had always been William's favorite, had been miserable under the strict supervision of her Uncle William, who had treated her as one of the household servants; William had been sent to live with his Uncle Richard and had also been unhappy under the rigid rule of a man who had begrudgingly paid for his education and, in return, had expected him to become a parson, an idea William had abhorred. Despite his uncle's wishes, William had rebelled and pursued his poetic impulses.

"The fob and chain are not luxuries; they are keepsakes." The sound of his sister's voice, quivering with emotion, startled him out of his reverie. She added, "I absolutely forbid you to sell them."

William grimaced at Dorothy's uncustomary display of passion.

She continued. "If we must sell something, I have Mother's silver service. We can certainly do without it. I've yet to use it entertaining our friends, who are much more at home with pewter."

"Out of the question! It's your only heirloom from Mother and I know that you treasure it."

They locked eyes and glared. He was the first to see the futility of their argument and said, "We're a fine pair: Poor as street urchins bickering over a few precious crumbs. For the time being, we'll hold onto our cherished items and fight off the evil landlord. And now, with my journal intact, I'll send a few poems off to my publisher. He's sure to send me an advance."

After a moment Dorothy nodded, seemingly appeased. "Now, tell me about this mysterious paintbrush that fell from your bag. You said it belonged to a girl? Obviously she is an artist?"

He leaned back into his pillows and allowed his memory to drift back to the grassy glen where he had first met the young woman. *Had her elegance of form, her lovely face with those remarkable blue eyes—eyes that had moved him with surprising passion—had she truly been as real and exquisite as he now remembered?*

"William?"

He blinked and Dorothy came back into focus. "Yes," he said, "you wanted to know about the young woman?"

Dorothy nodded.

"So do I," he replied, suddenly feeling an unaccountable sense of loss. "But I don't know a thing about her. Not even her name."

ucy rolled over in her bed and opened her eyes to the rays of moonlight filtering into the room from the small attic windows. She realized it must still be the middle of the night. She could just make out the shadowy forms of Molly and Mary, who were sound asleep, breathing rhythmically beneath their bedcovers. A moment later, memory of the day's events paraded before her. *The tall slim stranger—who was he?*

Lucy searched her memory to recall his features; a fine-looking man … dark hair, a high forehead, whose nose was, perhaps, a trifle too long. His eyes—she might never forget his eyes—were light amber and had observed her with such an awareness! His mouth had been wide, with well-curved lips above a cleft in his chin. *What would it feel like to touch that dimple?* She smiled at her impetuosity. He wasn't what one would call handsome, but he was certainly attractive. She laid a hand on her chest; the mere thought of him had caused her heart to flutter.

Lucy pulled the covers up over her head, endeavoring to close off further musings, but her mind rebelled. She sighed—*all these wakeful hours because of an accidental encounter with a stranger. It was so silly, wasting time over a man whom, in all probability, she would never see again.* She squeezed her eyes shut, once more attempting to block him from her consciousness.

The cocoon-like feeling beneath the covers was comforting and, as her heartbeat returned to normal, she was finally able to focus elsewhere; her missing paintbrush drifted to mind. She recalled the saddest moment in her life, standing beside her father's deathbed the evening he had given it to her, along with his final blessing. And now, the paintbrush, too, she would probably never see again. Lucy's hand brushed against the small plasters affixed to her temples where the leeches had drained her affected blood. She recalled the servants' unkind comments. *Could tainted blood be a sign that Satin had possessed her? Was it possible the Devil could reside within any human being?* She sat upright and opened her eyes, chiding herself for contemplating such superstitious nonsense. Lucy's gaze traveled to the wall where three of her canvases hung in the shadows. They suddenly appeared morose and melancholy. She frowned.

Heavy footsteps clomped up the stairway, distracting her musings. Lucy settled back under the covers and listened. The boots scraped to a stop in front of Beth's bedroom, which was separated from the servants' room by a thin wall. There was a soft knock; followed by an urgent whisper from Squire Hawkin's. Beth's door opened and closed quietly.

Moments later, Lucy heard muffled conversation and laughter filtering through the thin partition, as they had many nights in the past. She covered her ears, but still couldn't block out the titter and occasional cries. The idea that the Squire and Beth were having intercourse was disturbing, but not as disturbing as the fact that they sounded like animals. *Wasn't the act of making love supposed to be something beautiful?*

In the next bed, Molly rolled over and whispered. "They be at it again, eh?"

Lucy lay still, pretending to be asleep.

"I know yer not sleepin', little Miss Purity. Tell me somethin'. What does his Lordship see in that old cow? I'm twice the woman she'll ever be. I'm tellin' ya, he don't know what he's missin'. I'd spoil him, I would."

She remained as quiet as a mouse.

"I know yer awake. Yer a sneaky little one. Ya look through key holes, too, don't ya?"

Lucy marveled that her roommate had just admitted to spying. *Was there no end to Molly's loathsome ways?* Lucy kept still, hoping the girl would take a hint.

"I do," Molly continued. "Ya wouldn't believe what me own two eyes have seen. Could fill a book, I could."

Obviously, Molly was not going to be put off. Lucy closed her eyes and whispered, "Go to sleep."

"Ah ha. I knew it," Molly gloated. "An' how am I ta go ta sleep with them two bellowin' like swine?"

"It will be over soon."

"That it will." Molly giggled. "An' one of these nights it's going to be yer turn."

Lucy's eyes bolted open.

"Ya should've seen the look on his Lordship's face when he found ya on the closet floor with yer skirts up over your knees. If we hadn't been there, ya can bet he would've done more than just carry ya up ta your bed. 'Course we all know why he did it! So he could feel yer bubbies and nice little bottom."

Lucy released a breath of mortification. "You're making this up."

"Ask Beth. She saw him pawin' you. Jealous as I've ever seen her."

"*I want nothing to do with him,*" Lucy said emphatically.

"Listen to old Beth in there. Havin' a good time she is, an' she gets a shilling fer her favors. Ya could use a few shillins, couldn't ya?"

Lucy could not stand to hear anymore. She rolled toward the wall and pulled the blankets over her head.

Molly chuckled. "Sweet dreams, little Miss Purity."

Lucy stared into the darkness, unsettled. She found it impossible to accept that some people took pleasure in taunting and upsetting others. In her limited experience, she had found bullying to be rooted in insecurity; *Molly must be intimidated by anyone more educated, or perhaps because the Squire showed more interest ... Oh, the Squire!* She fervently hoped he had not touched her body, although he certainly had been undoing the buttons on her blouse! Why was life so complicated?

Hearing the Squire moan again, Lucy pressed her hands to her ears in an attempt to block out the annoying sounds. There was truth to Molly's prediction, Lucy acknowledged: It was just a matter of time until the Squire began to pursue her in earnest. The image of the Squire pushing his fleshy, tainted mass onto her infused her with fury. *If he dared lay a hand on her, she would claw his eyes out!* To further complicate matters, the Squire's attraction to her was sure to cause friction between herself and Beth, who would certainly protect her adulterous relationship as tightly as a miser hoards gold. Then there was Molly, who would add fuel to the fire out of pure, jealous spite.

The situation was depressing. She steeled her resolve; *she would rather die first than suffer any kind of abuse!* Soon she fell into a troubled sleep.

illiam strode along the country lane wielding Old Hickory. Once he had gotten over the pretentiousness of carrying the forty-inch ornately-carved piece of wood, he had to admit it provided him with a certain degree of security. Let the Suttons attempt to harass him again and he would be prepared to give them a thrashing.

As he walked, his gaze rose above the Quantock Hills, to the horizon, where the wind blew a flotilla of white, puffy clouds across a sea of blue. He smiled, happy the rains were gone, happy to have recovered his lost verse, and happy that he had awakened this morning without a trace of the cold that had put him to bed the previous evening. Breathing in the rejuvenating sea-scented air that blew in from Bristol Bay, he made a vow not to let anything ruin his day, especially not thoughts of the ominous summons from the Home Office nor his plan to confront his landowner's agent, Mr. John Bartholomew, later this afternoon.

His enjoyment of the twitter of birds and the cascading waters from the stream beside him was interrupted by a horse's whinny, and the Exeter-to-Bristol mail coach with its team of four as it rumbled up behind him. He stepped off the narrow track and, as the coach drew nearer, recognized the driver: Davey was a country youth with rosy cheeks and a ready smile whom he had met at the King's Head Inn.

He lifted his walking stick in a salute to Davey who, in turn, tipped his hat and said, "Good day, Mr. Wordsworth."

Inside the cab, the Crown's agent, Geoffrey Walsh, leaned forward to glance out the window.

William caught a glimpse of the man peering out of the coach. He had ebony eyes, set oddly atop high, wide cheekbones, and a sharp scythe of a nose, perched above a mouth which bowed downward as if in continual judgment of his fellow man. *Ominous-looking fellow*, mused William, as the coach lumbered by. He thought nothing more of the passenger's stern countenance as he stepped into the wake of the vehicle and continued on his journey.

A half mile up the road, a familiar hill came into view. His heart quickened as he realized he was not far from the site of yesterday's encounter with the remarkably captivating young woman. Within minutes, he had tucked Old Hickory under his arm and was moving along at a full-blown trot, when he suddenly realized it would be inappropriate to appear too anxious to make her acquaintance again, if indeed she would be nearby. He forced himself to a more presentable gait, using his walking stick to pace his steps.

CHAPTER SEVENTEEN

*E*arlier in the morning, in an effort to forget the disquieting events of the previous day—her seizure and the Squire's libidinous advances— Lucy had gone alone to the glen, the same one she had already searched for her father's lost paintbrush. Today's search had also been in vain. After completing the children's studies on the hillside hours later, she had set them free to play, but Emily and Henry had surprised her by giving up their games to return to the glen and hunt for the brush. Not wishing to spend more time on what she now considered a futile endeavor, she had taken the opportunity to paint.

Standing before her easel, with a short stubby brush in hand, Lucy studied her subject; the abandoned granary at the bottom of the hill that stood within a stone's throw of the glen. She frowned. *The brush strokes were too heavy, not nearly as fine as those rendered by her father's paintbrush.* She blew out a breath of frustration, knowing if she continued to paint, it would mean settling for mediocrity.

A light breeze blew a curl free from under Lucy's hat; it landed on her nose. She brushed the errant tendril away, but when it rebelliously returned, she impatiently tucked it up under the brim, and pulled the hat down with more vigor than was necessary. *Why was she so upset? Perhaps it was the Squire's lewd behavior that rankled her, forcing her to come to grips with her dangerous, untenable living situation.* Then, there was the stranger; ever since their chaotic meeting, her emotions had run amok, as if they belonged to someone else entirely. Or, she reasoned, perhaps her unsettled state was caused by the aftermath of her seizure and the loss of her most dear possession—dear in both senses of the word; she wouldn't be able to afford to replace her father's paintbrush with a new one of similar quality.

"I hope I'm not interrupting," said a deep voice behind her.

She jumped and turned. *The stranger! Where had he come from?*

"Sorry. I didn't mean to startle you."

Lucy's hands fluttered up to touch the small plasters affixed to her temples. *She must look so ridiculous!* She felt her cheeks flush. *Why was she blushing like an adolescent?* Aware she had been staring at him, she lowered her eyes. "Sir, I didn't hear you approach."

"Forgive me," he said. "My big feet usually announce my arrival. My sister says I walk like a Clydesdale."

Lucy hadn't noticed the soft, melodious tone of his voice before. "I ... I was so involved in painting, I didn't hear you."

"I understand. I'm the same way when I'm writing."

"Oh, your journal!" she said, suddenly recalling his loss. "It must have been ruined. I am so sorry."

"Fortunately my sister had made a copy of my work, although I didn't know it at the time. Please accept an apology for my rude behavior." He leaned an ornately carved walking stick against his thigh, and reached a long and graceful hand into his satchel. "Somehow, this found its way into my bag." He withdrew her paintbrush!

Lucy's heart skipped a beat. Losing all sense of propriety she rushed to him and took her father's gift carefully from his hands. "Oh, thank you. Thank you!"

She felt his eyes upon her. Lifting her gaze to his, she was startled to feel a thrill once again shoot through her. She could neither resist nor explain the phenomenon. *Who is this man?* She wanted to know more, but her tongue wouldn't move. Her gaze fell to the brush in her hands.

She heard herself saying, "Sir, this paintbrush means much to me." Her deep blue irises darted up as she suddenly remembered another of the previous day's mishaps. "Your trousers! I am so sorry. They were ruined, I'm sure."

"It matters not. I didn't care for them anyway."

"Oh, but the unkind way we laughed at your misfortune." She smiled at the memory.

"It's nothing, really," he said with a shrug. "I laugh, myself, whenever I think about it. I must have been quite a sight."

His eyes focused on her. Yes, they were amber and so warm ... so sensitive!

Lucy was suddenly aware he was speaking, " ... sometimes, I believe, accidents are not always what they appear to be."

She caught her breath. *He was suggesting that their meeting was somehow an act of fate.* She noticed that he was smiling at her, a little too broadly, but charmingly, she had to admit.

"My name is William Wordsworth. I live not far from here, at Alfoxden House. If you don't mind my asking ... ."

It took her a moment to realize he had paused so that she might offer her introduction. "I am governess to Squire Hawkins' children," she said with a nod to the manor house on the hill. "I am Lucy Sims."

"Beautiful."

Lucy's pulse jumped. *Was he referring to her ... or to her name?*

"Emily, it's the trespasser!" Henry shouted. He and his sister, having left the glen, were climbing the hill.

Lucy noticed William turn toward the children disparagingly. He swung his satchel over his shoulder and lifted the walking stick. "I'd best be off before I'm trampled again. Are you here often, Miss Sims?"

Momentarily taken aback by William's obviously forward question, she wondered: *How she could answer without seeming too anxious?* While struggling to find a decorous reply, she realized he was a moment away from walking out of her life. She overcame her reticence. "I might be here a small part of every day."

"Are you ever free of feral companions?"

She found herself nodding. "Only when the family's at church."

"Then I shall see you Sunday morning. Good day, Miss Lucy Sims."

Before she could respond, he had already turned, and was walking briskly down the opposite side of the hill. She watched after him with a feeling of dismay. *How could she meet with a perfect stranger? She had never done anything like this before in her life. Well, perhaps it wasn't so scandalous; after all they had met once before, even if it had been under rather unconventional and trying circumstances.* A smile slowly appeared. *What if fate did have something to do with their meeting?* She recalled his name: William Wordsworth … a solid sounding name … very respectable. But she didn't know who he was, or what he did. She mulled this over. *Would she really see him on Sunday?*

Emily and Henry bounded up to her side, out of breath. "Was that man bothering you, Miss Lu … ?" Emily's voice trailed off as she observed Lucy's unusual countenance.

Henry glared after the retreating stranger. "If that basher comes back, I'll set the hounds on him!"

"No, no. He wasn't bothering me at all. Look what he brought me." She held up her paintbrush. "It had fallen into his satchel."

Emily beamed. "Oh, Miss Lucy. That's simply amazing!"

Henry sulked. "We looked a long time for your paintbrush and he had it all along. That pig turd!"

"Henry!! You know better than to use that kind of language," she scolded. At another time, her admonition would have been stronger, but at this moment she didn't feel like censuring anyone. She reached into one of her baskets and withdrew a ball. "Anyone for a game of catch?"

Emily and Henry cheered. "I want to be first," Henry said. He sprinted away, holding his hands up to catch the ball.

"No, no. Throw it to *me* first." Emily dashed in the opposite direction.

Lucy laughed and threw the ball to Henry, who deftly caught it and giggled. "Catch me, Emily! Come on ... you have to catch me."

Emily yelled exuberantly and gave chase. Lucy, running after them, realized they had forgotten all about the stranger, but she knew it would be a long time before she thought of anything else.

avey braked the mail coach to a stop beneath the King's Head Inn porte-cochere; the wooden canopy provided passengers precious little protection from inclement weather. Two redheaded boys, ten and twelve years of age and wearing ragged clothing, darted out of the attached barn with water and feedbags for the horses. The coach door opened and the Crown's agent, Geoffrey Walsh, looking like an undertaker in his dark clothing, stepped to the ground with travel bag in hand. As the driver tied his team to a rail, he cast a curious glance at the passenger; the odd-looking chap reminded him of a large predatory bird. Davey's attentive eye appraised the man's worn suit and inexpensive shoes. *If he were a thief,* he thought, *he certainly hadn't been a very successful one.*

Davey, observing company instructions to be polite to customers, said, "Mr. Walsh, you'll find good food and lodgings inside."

Walsh's bkack eyes cast a discerning look on the building. "That would be a welcome surprise."

The driver spat on the ground, then gestured to the boys. "You lads take good care of me horses and there's a halfpenny for each of you."

"Yes, Sir, Mr. Davey," the older boy said.

The two men stepped up onto the porch and entered the inn.

They stopped inside the front door to allow their eyes to adjust to the darkness. "Watch your head," the driver warned, indicating the low ceiling with its heavy, unyielding timbers.

"I've been in better looking barns," growled Walsh.

The driver's eyes narrowed. "'Tis me favorite pub, been here over a hundred years." Having enough of company rules, he added, "If you don't like it, Sir, you could go elsewhere."

Walsh glared at the insolent whelp. "Maybe it will grow on me." He ducked to avoid the beams as the driver led the way to a plank bar, where a balding old man was wiping the countertop.

At their approach, the innkeeper glanced up. "Hello, Davey. Ya be wantin' a pint?"

"That I do, Simon. Got you a boarder here from Bristol."

Simon eyed the man dressed in black. "Ya be Walsh?"

"Mr. Geoffrey Walsh," the man said pointedly. "Reservations have been made in that name."

"That they 'ave, Mr. Geoffrey Walsh," the old hosteller responded, immediately disliking the man. "Up the stairs, first door on yer left." He passed the driver a pint of ale and asked the new boarder, "Ya be wantin' somethin' to drink?"

"Gin. A double."

"Mr. Geoffrey Walsh," the innkeeper said, reaching for a bottle, "if you don't mind me askin', what brings you to this part of Somerset?"

Walsh scowled. He didn't like questions, especially ones from a snooping barkeep. He finally replied, "I'm a writer. I've left the city for some peace and quiet so that I may concentrate on my composition."

"Well, you've got plenty of writers to keep you company 'round here," Davey said. "Don't he, Simon?"

"We 'ave our share … poets mostly."

"Oh?" Walsh glanced to Simon with an air of curiosity. "I'm always interested in my fellow writers. Anyone I might know of?"

illiam sat on the edge of the brown leather sofa in lawyer Bartholomew's oak-paneled waiting room, fidgeting with his stick, tapping it on the Oriental carpet. For the better part of the day he had been avoiding thoughts associated with the Alfoxden House lease, but now it was time to settle the matter. He had a valid agreement on the house, but with a new landowner there could be unforeseen changes. As he waited for his meeting, his thoughts drifted to his recent new acquaintance, Miss Lucy Sims. Since leaving the hilltop this morning, he had spent an inordinate amount time reflecting upon their two encounters. Their first meeting in the glen had left him interested, and, he had to admit, a bit disheveled. The second encounter had left him spellbound—if that's indeed what it was. *How had she reached so deeply into his very soul?* She was attuned to expressions of nature, as he was, and, certainly, this could explain the attraction. But, he hadn't known she was a painter when they had first met. *What was this quality Lucy Sims possessed that attracted him like a bee to pollen?* She surely wasn't the most beautiful female he had ever encountered. No!

But she did have an inner quality that shone in her eyes ... that seemed to parallel his very being! He lifted Old Hickory and tapped his head. *Was he unsound ... or infatuated?* Perhaps a combination of both, he allowed. His fingers curled around the walking stick as he re-experienced the fleeting touch of her hand as he had returned the paintbrush. *Had she noticed his fingers had been trembling?*

He wondered if she might be at her easel now, painting on the hilltop. Her technique and interpretation had disclosed a rare ability and exceptional sensitivity. Yet, there had been something missing. The landscape she crafted had been darker than the scene being painted: Joyless shadows and somber hues had made their way onto the canvas. Certainly, it must be a purposeful technique ... *or, were there difficulties in her life? Well, of course, there were difficulties in everyone's life.* As a poet, he was all too aware how one's work could be affected by disturbing circumstances. If that were the case, what could possibly be haunting Lucy Sims?

The sound of the solicitor's door opening interrupted his reverie.

Mr. Bartholomew, a well-dressed middle-aged man of medium height, beckoned the ponderer into his office. "Please ... come in, Mr. Wordsworth." William lifted his satchel and walking stick and followed Mr. Bartholomew.

Inside the office, the solicitor gestured to a chair in front of a sizable antique desk. Taking his seat behind it, Mr. Bartholomew said, "I assume you received my letter regarding Mrs. Albyn's decision to terminate your lease?"

William sat in the chair facing him. "Yes. I was hoping to persuade you and your client to honor the lease as originally agreed upon."

Bartholomew's shrewd eyes bore into him. "I am an honorable man, but at the time the twelve-month lease was executed on your behalf by your friend Samuel Coleridge, I was under the impression I was helping a needy poet, not a political rabble rouser."

William felt his face redden. *How dare this misinformed prig insinuate he was an agitator? It was quite obvious Bartholomew had heard rumors regarding his loyalty to the Crown, perpetuated by his own neighbors!*

"Therefore," the solicitor continued, "the lease agreement was made under false pretenses and I consider it null and void. However, Mr. Wordsworth, all is not lost. If I can convince you to curtail your political activities and simply concentrate on your writing, I believe I may be able to persuade Mrs. Albyn on your behalf. Then, I believe, we will be able to draw up a more suitable lease agreement."

William gripped Old Hickory and leaned forward in his chair. "First, allow me to correct your false impression of me. I am not, as you put it, a rabble-rouser. And, I do not appreciate being asked to censor myself, to modify my character and beliefs for the sake of appeasing my illiterate and rumor-mongering neighbors; living at Alfoxden is not worth that!"

"Wordsworth, all my client and I are asking you to do is keep your political opinions and theories to yourself. Having a radical as a tenant reflects poorly upon me, and Mrs. Albyn, of course, and would not be in our best interests."

"If I were to agree, I imagine a more suitable lease would mean you wish to renegotiate the rent?"

"You're a perceptive young man," the solicitor said. "Fifty pounds a year is a fair price for that estate."

William was tempted to slam his stick down upon Bartholomew's desktop but checked his impulse and stood up. He replied as calmly as he could manage, "It is a fair price, but one I cannot afford. Mr. Bartholomew, I don't appreciate threats, nor do I care for the likes of you and Mrs. Albyn. People of your ilk will never censor the way I think, nor the words I say and write. Inform your employer that my sister and I will be out of Alfoxden House within sixty days."

CHAPTER TWENTY

s Dorothy stepped from the kitchen carrying two bowls of steaming porridge, she said, "William, I am so proud of you." Setting their breakfast down on the parlor table, she added, "I knew exactly what those scoundrels were up to the minute I read that eviction notice. Asking fifty pounds a month for our rent … impossible, and they knew it." She pulled out a chair and sat down. "I have to tell you, I am very relieved."

"Relieved?' he asked, raising a small pitcher and pouring milk into his bowl. "I thought surely you would be saddened by having to leave Alfoxden."

"No, not at all. This is a beautiful home but it is much too big for the two of us. Without servants, I can barely keep up with the household chores. I've dusted and mopped far too many hours away, with little time for myself. I'm thrilled to be moving! I slept more soundly last night than I have in weeks."

"I'm sorry, Dorothy, I hadn't realized how much of your time has been misspent."

She waved away his apology. "Men seldom realize the effort it takes to maintain a large home. It's not in your realm of responsibility, so why would you notice? A smaller house will suit us very well. Perhaps a place closer to Nether Stowey and Samuel; that way, when the weather is inclement, you won't have to spend half a day getting drenched."

"That's a splendid idea! I'll talk to Samuel."

They were both silent for a moment while they ate. After a time, Dorothy asked, "Tell me, how is your writing coming along?"

"Slowly, but today, I feel, may be different … productive even." As Dorothy focused her gaze upon him, he smiled, but refrained from divulging the real source of his inspiration. "I've been concentrating too much on politics and finances. Today, I will walk to the lakes and do nothing but put pen to paper … and think optimistically about our future."

She nodded approvingly. "Good, William."

He gazed out the window at the garden, but his eyes were focused inward. He didn't believe he should mention that a dream of an arresting young woman had awakened him during the night, bringing a new sense of excitement into his life. Overnight, winter had become spring. As for his plans to visit Lucy next Sunday—the less his sister knew about that, the better. Yes, it was best to ensure that Lucy remained his special secret.

 eoffrey Walsh had risen early, departing the King's Head Inn after having obtained directions to the Wordsworth residence from a local tradesman. He had walked for less than an hour when he came upon the granite stone that bore the inscription:

ALFOXDEN HOUSE.

He stopped mid-stride, gaping past the marker at a three-story stone mansion. It was a hundred yards off the road, facing a lush expanse of grass where a flock of sheep grazed, and edged on three sides with thick woods. Confusion percolated through him. *There must be some mistake!* The setting was opulent, fit for a merchant or a lesser nobleman—certainly not a lowly poet. But before he could focus on the befuddling observation, he saw a man leaving the residence. From the description given at the Inn, he knew he was looking at William Wordsworth. Walsh quickly hid in a copse of trees. He removed his hat to avoid detection and waited.

Within minutes the poet walked by, passing within twenty paces of his position without glancing in his direction. Walsh remembered seeing him from the coach window, when they had passed on the road. Walsh released a quiet grunt of disgust. To look at Wordsworth, walking stick in hand, a pleasant look upon his patrician face, one would think the man hadn't a care in the world. The detective's bile rose. He hated anyone who affected an air of privilege; anyone who thought himself to be above the poor soul who had to labor and sweat for his meager existence. He spat on the ground; he hated spies even more ... the scurrilous men and women who would sell out Mother England for a few pieces of silver. Walsh glared after William, making himself a promise. *Wordsworth, you damnable traitor, I'm going to see to it that your high life-style ends abruptly ... at the end of a hangman's noose. It won't take me long to discover the source of your funds and the identity of your French contacts.* Walsh rubbed the grip on his flintlock pistol, anticipating their arrests. It would be the highlight of his career if he were to prove Wordsworth a spy, and, in the process, uncover his co-conspirators. Walsh grinned as he enjoyed an image of the poet and his cell of seditious French supporters hanging by their necks. He replaced his hat and pulled its brim low over his forehead. After waiting for what he considered an appropriate amount of time, he left the trees and began tracking his suspect.

amuel Coleridge, an average-sized man in his mid-twenties, with the beginnings of a pot belly, was perched at a table in the living room of his modest Nether Stowey home. The nib of his pen dashed erratically across the pages of his journal. The goose-feather quill swept within inches of a prominent nose and full Bacchanalian mouth, one that was normally inclined to wry mirth, but that was, at the moment, twitching with frustration. His pen hesitated as dark, fiery eyes examined and judged each and every word on the page. "Confound it!" he exclaimed, in a soft Northern burr. "Not clever at all!" He scratched out every line in a feathery flurry. Sucking in a ragged breath, he turned the page and began rewriting, pausing moments later to evaluate new verse through a prism of intense self-criticism. He scowled at his efforts and began to read the unfinished text:

> *"I hurried with him to our orchard-plot,*
> *And he beheld the moon, and, hushed at once,*
> *Suspends his sobs, and laughs most silently,*
> *While his fair eyes, … that swam with … ,*
> *Did glitter in the yellow moon-beam! Well!—*
> *It is a father's tale: But … if that Heaven*
> *Should give me … life, his childhood shall grow up*
> *Familiar with … ."*

"…with," he repeated. Dropping the pen, he clenched his unruly black hair with both hands, pulling it back from a high forehead. It had been several days since he had had his tincture of laudanum. "A scourge on my dull mind and the entire English language." He grabbed the pen up and jammed it into an inkpot as black as his mood. "Curse the urge to create and curse me for being a slave to the insidious urge!" He glared at the empty chair facing him. "Where in bloody hell are you, William?"

His wife, Sara, a comely young woman, came through the front door carrying a watering can and their three-month-old baby, Hartley, on one hip. She set the can on the floor and wiped her hand on an apron that protected her earthen brown dress. "Everything needed water," he heard her say in her customary pessimistic monotone. "The rain never touches the plants under the eaves. They were half dead."

"I sympathize with them. I'd pour the entire Bristol Channel on me if it would revive my wilted wit."

"I might be the first to douse you if I thought it would help."

"Bah!" he said under his breath.

She crossed to the adjoining kitchen, placed the baby in a wooden rocking crib, and snatched a long poker off its hook. Opening the stove's iron door, she stirred and sparked a pan of wood cinders beneath a teakettle. "I saw William coming up the road."

"William? Why the devil didn't you say so?" Samuel rose from his chair and opened the door. "And not a moment too soon. If I hadn't been about to give up the English language for Chinese!"

Samuel stepped out onto the stoop and waved at William, who strode up the muddy path, swinging his staff in cadence with his carefree jaunt. "Good day to you, Samuel," he shouted.

Samuel pouted. "What is that stick? How can you be so cheerful?"

The grin broadened as William brandished his walking aid exuberantly. "Old Hickory belonged to my father. It's to ward off scoundrels who might try to do me harm. Gaze about you." He gestured to the blue sky. "The rain has hastened away. It's a sublime day. I've spent the morning avoiding reality and I might very well be on the blissful path to insanity."

Samuel snorted. "You've come to the right place to complete your journey. I'm having a beastly day: I've lost the use of my native tongue; nothing rhymes; and my meters and syllables are at war with one another." He looked over his shoulder to be sure Sara wasn't listening, and in a lowered voice, added, "The woman is rattling my nerves and the baby sleeps all day and cries all night. I tell you, William, marriage must have been designed for saints, not for common men. It's especially injurious to the poetic soul."

"Say what you will, but marriage has saved you from your overindulgent ways."

"Tosh! My indulgences are my own."

CHAPTER TWENTY-THREE

*J*ust past the small village of Nether Stowey, Wordsworth had turned off the road, approaching a stone cottage via a short path. Geoffrey Walsh had halted a cautious two hundred paces behind him. He had watched with interest as another man opened the door. The two had chatted briefly, and had then entered the cottage. Walsh's hand fell to the butt of his pistol, caressing it. Excitement coursed through him as though he were a huntsman who had just located a den of foxes. His eyes narrowed pensively. *Was Wordsworth having a rendezvous with a French agent and, if so, what might they be planning? He would find out.* He was about to retrace his steps the short distance back to Nether Stowey, to make inquiries regarding the tenant of the cottage, when a farmer appeared, leading a pony bearing several bags of vegetables.

"Excuse me, Sir," Walsh said, approaching the farmer. "I believe I'm lost. I'm looking for Eliza Pimlott. Would that be her cottage, by chance?" He pointed to the small stone house.

The farmer came to a stop and stared at him with a local's distrust of strangers. "Where're ya from?"

Walsh bit back his annoyance and answered with a tinge of impatience, "I'm up from Bristol. I was hoping to locate my cousin, Eliza."

"We got no Pimlott's livin' 'round here. I don't recall we ever 'ad any neither."

He cursed himself for not picking a more common name and added quickly. "How silly of me. Pimlott was my cousin's maiden name. She's married now, but I'm having the demon of a time recalling her husband's surname. But I do remember her saying she lived just outside of Nether Stowey in a stone cottage much like that one."

The man shook his head. "There's no Eliza hereabouts neither." The farmer turned away, tugging on the pony's halter, adding, "That be the Samuel Coleridge cottage."

Walsh felt a rush of excitement. Samuel Taylor Coleridge? That was a familiar name … . The poet was known to the Home Office as a political dissident and trouble-maker: He was the publisher of *The Watchman*, a subversive newspaper from which he derived a small income.

As the farmer continued on down the road, Geoffrey scanned the surrounding area to be sure he was not being observed; not a soul was in sight. He stepped quickly into a stand of elms that grew to within a few feet of the cottage and stealthily made his way to one side of it. Crouching beneath a partially opened window, he removed his notebook and a freshly-sharpened pencil from his waistcoat. He rose up carefully to the sill and peeked inside. A woman, evidently Mrs. Coleridge, stood beside a baby's crib, filling a caddy with tealeaves, while a man, who must be Samuel, sat at a desk. Wordsworth stood nearby, watching their baby, and asking, "How is young Hartley today?"

"Asleep, thank God. Now don't you be waking him," Sara said. "Between the babe and himself over there I don't have a moment's peace."

Coleridge's eyes held those of Wordsworth for an instant. "It would be best not to get the woman started. Now, about your need to self-protect, to what scoundrels were you referring?"

William felt his sunny mood begin to slip away. "I had a run-in with the Sutton brothers yesterday at the King's Head Inn. It's not worth going into... ."

"The hell it isn't," Samuel said. "The Sutton Brothers! It's a damned miracle you're here! Tell me exactly what happened."

"Hmmm. Same response as Dorothy. It's not really worth repeating."

Samuel folded his arms and waited.

"Oh, all right ... all right. Ben and Walt called me an 'Enemy of the Crown' and referred to Dorothy as a 'French woman of ill-repute.'"

"An outrage! And your response was?"

"I ignored them for a while but, eventually, countered with some truths regarding their intelligence. And, as you would expect, they took offence and became aggressive. Within seconds, Walt seized me and pinned my arms behind my back. Ben threw a punch but it missed me and hit Walt's nose, breaking it and Ben's hand."

"Bravo! Well done, my friend!" Samuel exclaimed, and roared with laughter. Catching his breath, he added, "I would give five pounds to have been there. What a sensational, rousing sight it must have been! The Suttons are bullies but they'll think twice before assaulting a man with a stout cane."

William grinned wryly, his morning's resolve to forget his troubles simply gone. He sat in his usual chair, a high-backed rocker near the desk. "Well, Samuel, to be honest, the brutes are the least of my difficulties. I have other challenges ... ."

"You're not alone in that regard," Coleridge said. "I have new challenges, old challenges and challenges that haven't happened yet." He looked at his friend as though expecting a laugh. When none was forthcoming, he added, "If it's money you need, I've a few pounds you can borrow."

Sara, having just finished filling the water kettle, dropped it nosily onto the stovetop—a comment on her husband's largesse. William noted the fiery looks she and Samuel exchanged, and added, "Thank you, but it's a bit more serious than that. I received an eviction notice. I'm moving out of Alfoxden House."

"Ballocks!" Coleridge roared. "You can't be evicted. There must be nine months left on that lease."

Outside, Walsh sneered, gratified to hear the poet was having financial difficulty. He checked his position and then crouched lower, cocking an ear to catch Wordsworth's next words.

"Bartholemew's terms made it impossible for me to continue living there," William said. "We'll be out by the end of next month."

"The weasel can't do that. You have an agreement for a year's lease at twenty-three pounds a year! I'll see to it this coxcomb keeps his word. We'll fight it, by God!"

"No, I don't care to fight," William responded, feeling at peace with his decision. "Dorothy and I are ready to leave Alfoxden, and hope to find a smaller place nearer to you here in Nether Stowey. We need a change; the house is too big … and the neighbors are gossiping behind my back, accusing me of treasonous actions against the Crown."

"Busybodies! They've nothing better to do with their worthless lives. I'm afraid neighbors here are spreading rumors about me, too. It's time I rounded up a few of them and cracked their addled heads. Let me heft that stick of yours. Pass it over."

William handed Samuel the length of hickory. "The damage has already been done: A letter was posted to the Home Office, accusing me of seditious activities. I'm to stand before Bristol Court for a hearing next month. If I fail to make an appearance, I'll be arrested."

Coleridge leaped to his feet and slammed the walking stick onto his desk with such vigor that Walsh, kneeling outside beneath the window, seized the grip of his flintlock, ready to pull it if need be.

"Good Lord, you too?" Samuel bellowed. "Poor John Thelwall is actually *facing the gallows* for his work with Hardy and Tooke in the London Corresponding Society. Preposterous! Is a man not free to voice his thoughts without the threat of incarceration? Have English politics been completely subverted by degenerate aristocrats who don't understand God-given freedoms? The rights of a commoner are in dire jeopardy, I say. We cannot stand by and allow England to sink into the abyss of the dark ages. We must fight back," he declared, swinging the hickory stick in imitation of a battle axe.

Outside, Walsh smiled with grim satisfaction. This was turning out to be better than he had hoped. He wrote down, "politics subverted by degenerate aristocrats," and underlined the phrase.

Wordsworth put a hand on his friend's shoulder, forcing him back into his seat and taking possession of his father's wooden heirloom. "Samuel, these accusations are against me, not you. Let me fight them in my own way. I'll appear in court and explain my political positions in clear, unthreatening terms. They'll see that my opinions are no danger to England."

"Ha! They may hang you on the same gibbet as Thelwall."

"Words are my tools," he countered. "Have a little more confidence in me."

Samuel sighed. "You're too infernally honest for your own good; you'll convict yourself. You can't fight politicians with candid rhetoric! You have to wheedle and scheme ... sink to their Machiavellian level... ." A gleam entered Coleridge's eyes. "And who's better at that than I? We'll defend every seditious word you may ever have uttered."

William shook his head at his friend's loyalty, but raised a hand in protest. "Samuel... ."

"Correction. We'll defend every honest thought you've ever voiced. Freedom of expression is at the very core of intellectual inspiration. Our poetry could never exist without it! In truth, an attack against you is an attack against artists everywhere. I'll gather supporters for you: Oxford dons, esteemed scholars, renowned writers. We'll cause a sensation that will make those politicians at Bristol Court shrink to nothing under their powdered wigs."

Walsh licked the point of his pencil and put a period after *gathering supporters to fight the Crown*. He was pleased with himself as he transcribed every mutinous word the two renegades uttered. *If this were any indication of how easy it would be to gather incriminating evidence against Wordsworth, the man would surely hang before Christmas.*

Suddenly, he heard voices from the road: Three farmers were approaching, arguing noisily among themselves. Walsh comprehended it would not be in his best interest to be seen lurking near the cottage. He returned the notebook and pencil to his waistcoat and slipped quietly into the woods.

taring at William from across the table, Samuel asked, "Well, what do you think? Just say the word and we'll proceed at full gallop." Infused with self-satisfaction, he waited for an answer.

William looked at his friend blankly, realizing his mind had been elsewhere. Only part of a phrase presented itself: *"Proceed at full gallop?" What was he talking about?* "Let me mull it over," William said with hesitation, trying to cover his lapse of attention. With only a touch of self–admonition did he realize he had been day dreaming. *How could he have been thinking of Lucy at such a critical time?*

"Don't take too long," Samuel said. "It's your neck in the noose."

The kettle on the stove began to whistle. "Water's boiling. Tea anyone?" Sara interrupted from the kitchen.

"Thank you. I could use a cup," murmured William, as he turned to gaze out the window: He was not yet willing to part with his reverie.

"A shepherd's pie is in the oven for later, not that Himself over there deserves my good cooking."

Samuel snipped, "I may not be deserving, but I do need it to sustain a physical presence."

"You sustain that body much more and you're going to need a new pair of britches."

Samuel sullenly pushed his journal across the desk to William. "Enough gibberish, enough of politics. It's time for some collaboration; we've important work to accomplish, starting with these pages. I've squandered the entire morning on six contrary lines. Read this and tell me..." He hesitated, looking up, and noticed his writing partner was apparently enchanted with the garden. Samuel rapped his fingers on the pages, eventually slapping the whole flat of his hand on the book. William spun around, disoriented.

"William! Our verse."

"I'm sorry," he stammered. "My mind seems not my own today."

"William, I understand your anxieties, but now you and I must concentrate on our work. You know, you and Dorothy are welcome to move here with us." He paused and leaned close to William to whisper with a nod in Sara's direction, "Although that one, with her sour temperament, might cause you to flee within a fortnight."

"Thank you, but I'm sure it won't be necessary." William's attention drifted back to the window.

Samuel boomed, "What can possibly be more fascinating out there than the pages I've put before you?"

William turned. "I've met a young woman."

Samuel's face fell. "You don't have enough troubles?"

"She's not any trouble."

"They're all trouble. As your friend, I should tell you: Women can be a poet's inspiration ... or his curse. You must be careful and very selective." Samuel paused, and when no response was forthcoming he said, "All right. Who is she? Where did you meet? From a reputable family, I hope? If there's one thing you'll need now more than ever, it's a substantial dowry."

William arched his back, stretching his muscles. He was in no mood to be lectured to or questioned, but, maintaining his civility, he said, "Samuel, you're putting the cart in front of the horse.   At the moment all I'm considering is a little companionship. Where did we meet? A short walk from here. Her family is of no concern."

Samuel sat back in his chair. "In other words she's as poor as a scullery maid ... is she a scullery maid?" Samuel waved the thought aside, and added, "We both know you can't possibly allow yourself to be serious about her." He pushed the journal closer to William. "Now, I truly need your help! Read this, please: I've got the concept of this stanza, but the words elude... ."   William had again turned to gaze outside. "Confound it! Stop staring out the bloody window."

William faced him.   "Have you ever looked into a woman's eyes and sensed everything in your world falling away except for her?"

Samuel's mouth fell open.

"Not only that, but your heart would be racing. You wouldn't be able to breathe. Yet you couldn't take your eyes from hers?"

"No.   Never," Samuel said.   Then, focusing on William's lovelorn expression, he exclaimed, "Good Lord... ."

"What am I to do?"

"I'll tell you what to do," he offered, with a conviction only experience could bring.   "Avoid this woman like an outbreak of the Black Death! It would be madness to become involved with someone who is beneath you. And you, of all people, can't afford another Annette."

He exhaled, mentally kicking himself for asking Samuel his opinion. The mention of Annette brought back memories of his impetuous love affair with the woman he had met seven years before. It had been a noteworthy mistake; one that had left him with responsibilities that continued to worry him to this day.

But his feelings for Lucy—so far, anyway—were startlingly different from those of his first love. Lucy inspired a depth of emotion within him that he had never experienced before, had never known existed! He couldn't shake her image from his mind for more than a few hours at a time.

"William, have you heard a blasted word I've said?"

His eyes focused on Samuel. Rather than try to explain his obsession with Lucy—which he didn't understand himself—and the differences between the two women—which would result in a long drawn out discussion—he said, "I realize I cannot afford another mistake."

"Good for you. Now forget this girl and find yourself a wealthy woman of good breeding." He glanced furtively at Sara, then lowered his voice. "If you have need of a few kisses, well … enjoy yourself, but then say a quick *au revior* and never see the woman again! Men of our station would be much better off if they didn't get involved with the lower classes. "

William knew he could never take advantage of Lucy and then abandon her. He said cautiously, "You may be right."

"William, there is no room here for *may*. I am right! You cannot waffle in these matters. Now, I want to hear it from you. Am I right or am I not?"

He gazed into Samuel's eyes long and hard. Everything his friend said made sense. Yet he sighed so deeply it made his chest ache. He had far too many troubles to even consider a new relationship. "You are right, Samuel. You are definitely right."

"Good fellow. Now read my beleaguered verse."

William glanced down at Samuel's poem. Although his mind accepted the logic of Samuel's argument, his heart rebelled.

alsh was careful not to step on anything that might snap beneath his feet as he crept closer to the candlelit windows of Alfoxden House. He had followed Wordsworth home from Coleridge's cottage an hour earlier. Although the two poets had talked until dusk, he had been unable to resume his position beneath the window; traffic on the road had made eavesdropping too risky. Settling himself beside a chestnut no more than twenty feet from Wordsworth's residence, he wrapped his arms about himself as an icy wind whistled through the woods, chilling him to the bone. All the suffering would be worthwhile if he could catch Wordsworth meeting with a French agent. His teeth chattered as he peered into the parlor window.

A woman entered the room with a steaming teacup and crossed to Wordsworth, who sat at a desk. *Perhaps she was the sister, or possibly his mistress. With the poet's morality, she could be both.* After placing the cup beside him, she kissed Wordsworth's forehead and left him, *perhaps going to their bedroom to await his illicit favors.*

Walsh knew all about England's creative clique and its deviant behavior. At University, he had spent a wasted year with a group of painters and writers. He could thank Providence he had not gone down their path of self-indulgence, and moral depravity. Walsh shook his head as he recalled how close he had come to becoming a writer and, yes, a poet, as his mother had wanted; after all, she had christened him with the first name of Geoffrey after Geoffrey Chaucer. But it wasn't to be; his father had died and he'd been pulled out of school to support his family. He was a better man for it, finding the Church, a good woman to marry and a respectable civil occupation that allowed him to serve and protect the King against potential enemies.

The idea of writing had faded over the years, but on occasion Geoffrey still read Chaucer and a few of the classical poets. He had no respect for the modern ones—spoiled individuals the likes of Wordsworth and Coleridge, who wrote contemporary rubbish about nature and common man. He could look about his surroundings and see all of this for himself, and it held no interest for him.

As he studied Wordsworth's well-appointed home, he felt a deep-seated animus grow in his belly. Life wasn't fair. Yes, the poet was being evicted, but he would in all probability move on to a similar residence, perhaps one even grander than this. A bitter taste twisted his tongue.

How could Wordsworth afford to live like an aristocrat while he, himself, labored hard to make ends meet? Where did the poet's money come from? Certainly it wasn't from hard work. Most likely, it was sent to him via couriers from France in payment for his seditious activities. Walsh made a mental note to investigate the traitor's finances and banking records. He would also find a way to break into Alfoxden House while the Wordsworths were out walking; there must be a mountain of evidence inside.

Anticipating the spy's arrest soothed Walsh's spirit; the long, miserable hours spent in the damp chilling wind were a small price to pay for bringing the Godless William Wordsworth to justice.

illiam's eyes were glassy; the stark page of his open journal awaited as the flickering glow of a candle illuminated the quill in his hand, the feather twirling idly. He sighed, lowered the pen and stared through the windowpane into the shadowy, moonlit night. A sudden flicker of movement in the trees caught his attention. He leaned forward. Was that a man's silhouette there by the sycamore? He rose apprehensively, moving to the door, and, opening it, scanned the woods more thoroughly. The silhouette however, had disappeared. The trees and shadows were still. The lonely hoot of an owl drifted to him through the chill air ... nothing more. Returning to his desk, he assumed the shadow had been one of his neighbors, taking a shortcut through the property.

After a moment, his thoughts drifted back to Lucy. He pictured her shy, lovely smile, the charm of her dove-like voice, and the sunshine that glowed within the depths of her clear and truthful eyes—eyes that his friend, Coleridge, never wanted him to gaze into again. Damn it! Why should circumstances dictate with whom he could or could not associate? Was he expected to give up the most extraordinary young woman he had ever encountered? He knew the wretched answer to his own question.

The image of Lucy's canvas continued to haunt him. As with some lines of poetry, her brush strokes spoke volumes about the artist. A critical component was missing. Alas, he would never be able to help her discover that element! They would never set out on exploratory walks through the verdant Quantock Hills to have conversations, to investigate and explore. Oh, how he longed to share experiences with her—to show her, from his perspective, how he interpreted the world about him and translated ideas and images into verse. He wished to share with her his vision of reality, of life and beauty, and the inspiration and passion he found therein.... He knew— if only circumstances permitted—he could help Lucy find that creative component that was eluding her; that spark of life that was missing on her canvas. And, as an artist, he also knew that she would understand the very emotions that had inspired him to devote his life to the poetic description of Man and Nature!

Dash it all to hell! He was sorely tempted to ignore Samuel's advice; his friend had a tendency to give his opinions when they were neither needed nor welcome. Did Coleridge think he wanted to marry her? Absolutely not; he barely knew the girl! No, all he longed for was intelligent conversation and companionship with a female other than his sister. But, confound it, what was it about the human condition that caused one to perversely undermine one's rational thought and better interest?

William sighed and glanced back to his journal. He read the single word he had penned on the page: *Lucy...*

CHAPTER TWENTY-SEVEN

*L*ucy tossed and turned in her bed. Glimpsing the moon through the dormer windows, she judged it to be near midnight, yet she felt wide awake. After staring at the ceiling for several moments, she was overcome with a compelling desire to paint—a new experience at this hour. It was too cold to leave her bed and sneak downstairs to gather her materials, so she rolled over and attempted to sleep; but sleep would not come. Eventually, she rose, grabbed a shawl from the peg on the wall and, very careful not to wake Mary and Molly, stole out of the room.

Lucy tiptoed into the kitchen two flights below her bedroom, and lit a candle using embers from the belly of the stove. With its light guiding her path, she made her way up the chilly front stairs to the great room and padded quietly across the cold parquet floor to the storage closet. She held her breath when she opened the panel door, praying it wouldn't squeak loudly and awaken anyone; she was relieved when the door swung open, obeying her wishes. Stepping into the small area, Lucy set her candlestick on a shelf and began to gather the apothecary compounds from her painting basket. She moved quietly and with haste, hoping to quell the shivers that were making her teeth chatter. Using a seashell as a mixing bowl, she combined small amounts of ocher, cinnabar and madder with linseed oil and ground them together. Several minutes later, she had produced a spoonful of red pigment.

By the time Lucy returned to her room, her bare feet were practically numb. She set the candlestick on her bedside table along with the paintbrush and seashell, with its small peak of oil. Then, moving as quietly as a shadow, she removed one of her landscapes from the wall and climbed back into bed, quickly pulling the covers up over her chest. Relishing the warmth, Lucy propped the canvas up against her knees. She nodded with satisfaction when she saw that the candle and moonlight afforded enough light to paint. She dipped the tip of her brush into the red mound and began to add delicate dabs of oil to the scene. After several strokes, she leaned back on her pillow and studied the results with a discerning eye. There was a notable transformation; by adding a small cluster of red roses, she had dramatically changed a corner of the painting, lending it an undeniable vitality. As she studied the small metamorphosis, a smile spread slowly across her lips. She brought the wooden end of the paintbrush to her lips and clicked it thoughtfully against her teeth. Her canvas was coming to life in such a pleasing manner. Elated, she massed additional roses onto the canvas.

William Wordsworth's name drifted into her consciousness. Idly, as she painted, her thoughts romped freely in her agile imagination. She envisioned them living together in a small cottage ... but, no! Even a social relationship between the two of them would be an impossible circumstance; he was a country gentleman and she a mere governess. Why then, she pondered, was her subconscious haunting her with a rendering of his seductive smile? Following this vision, William's amber eyes appeared, stirring her very depths, and a warm blush crept up her neck and cheeks. She spiraled her torso around to see if anyone might be watching, but Mary and Molly were asleep—not that they possibly could have seen anything in the dim light. Relaxing, her thoughts drifted back to her most recent conversation with William. What was it he had said when he had returned the paintbrush? She tried to recall his words, but, for the life of her, could not. She only knew that she had been so thrilled that she had almost thrown caution to the wind, and embraced him out of relief and gratitude. Now, she thought mischievously, she wished she had. She applied the last of the pigment to her canvas, then crept from her bed and re-hung the painting carefully.

Lifting her candlestick, she brought the flame to the landscape and couldn't help but notice how drab the neighboring canvases were by comparison. *Well, Mr. William Wordsworth, I may have more to thank you for than just the return of my father's paintbrush!* She wondered if he would appear this coming Sunday; or if he would realize how unsuitable their attraction was, and change his mind? *Well,* she thought, placing the candlestick on the side-table, *she wasn't going to worry about it. If he did or didn't appear, it wouldn't make the slightest bit of difference to her.* She blew out the flame and dove into bed. Snuggling beneath the warm covers, she smiled at her little white lie.

n Sunday morning Lucy stood on the hillside, painting at her easel, only vaguely aware of the blue sky above her with its towering white clouds on the horizon. A cool sea-scented breeze blew in from the coast, swirling the knee-high grass at her feet. She lifted her paintbrush and held it poised, unmoving in front of her landscape. Her focus wandered to the road below, as it had every few minutes for the last two hours. *Where was he?* The Hawkins family had returned from church a quarter of an hour earlier. The children had changed from their Sunday clothes and had descended upon her, expecting her undivided attention. Still clinging to the hope that William would arrive, she had sent them back to the manor to clean their rooms and read a chapter in their English book, promising playtime after those tasks had been completed.

Lucy turned once again to stare at the empty road. *Perhaps he had been detained by some unforeseen business.* Her brow furrowed. *He could have twisted an ankle and been unable to walk, or he might have contracted a sudden illness.*

Rising early this morning, she had felt the thrill of anticipation, but now she was becoming agitated. She breathed deeply, trying to calm herself.

❧ ❧ ❧

*W*illiam strode along the road toward Hawkins' Hill with the weight of Old Hickory becoming increasingly greater in his hand. He had fully intended to call upon Lucy earlier in the morning, but had procrastinated, delaying his departure from Alfoxden House while he struggled with the dilemma that held him in its embrace, as tightly as a huntsman's steel trap. Samuel's advice regarding his relationship with a penniless young woman had been sound, especially when he thought of his responsibilities and lack of steady income.

It would be selfish and unfair to pursue Lucy for purely self-serving reasons, when a young woman really should have a man who could afford to give her things she required—a roof over her head and ... financial security. Yet, despite this common sense that argued against any relationship, the thought of abandoning Lucy disturbed his equanimity. Why was forbidden fruit the most tempting? He stared ahead without seeing his surroundings, walking more by instinct than by sight, as he struggled to find a solution.

ucy suddenly realized she hadn't been paying attention to her painting and she now focused on the canvas; she had begun to paint a bank of clouds a deep forest green, having dipped the brush in the wrong color. She blew out a breath and chastised herself for pining away over an imagined friendship. The mere idea of her having a relationship with William Wordsworth was as insane as the thought of her marrying into royalty. Cleaning her brush, she dipped its tip into a mound of grey oil. But before she could lift it to the canvas, a flicker of movement caught her attention.

She glanced to the road. A man was striding up the track, measuring his pace with a walking stick. *William!* Her heart bounded in her chest; *he hadn't forgotten her.* Not wanting him to think her brazenly awaiting his arrival, she braced herself, the anxiety now becoming anticipation once again; turning back to the canvas, she pretended to paint. She continued to observe his progress from the corner of her eye, however. As he strode closer, she noticed, with a slight feeling of unease, that there was a very rigid manner to his gait. Moments later, she perceived that William hadn't glanced in her direction, not as much as a quick glimpse; even from this distance she could see that he seemed preoccupied and troubled.

Lucy turned toward him as he approached the base of the hill but he did not display any sign of recognition. *Certainly he must see her. Why wasn't he acknowledging her? Was he purposefully ignoring her?* She started to call out, but stopped herself, not wanting to embarrass them both. Slowly, she forced herself to turn away—to stare at the canvas that blurred before her.

After several minutes, she steadied herself, and blinked away her tears. She turned again to look at the road, but he was gone ... *without even having said a word!* For a long moment her gaze lingered; she hoped he was playing some sort of prankish game. When it became apparent that William wouldn't return, she felt a pain deep within her. She brought her hand to her chest and pressed down, hoping to soothe the ache, as she tried to understand his behavior. *Had she done something to offend him?* She couldn't imagine what that might have been. *Had he simply decided he wasn't interested in her or, as she had feared, had he realized her social status to be undesirable?* The latter, she knew, was entirely possible; there were many young women from well-to-do families in the vicinity, who were far more appropriate than she, for a man like William. Besides, to an obviously educated man, she must seem dull and unsophisticated. Her vision blurred again and she found a handkerchief in her basket to net the droplets as they traversed her lovely cheeks. Her breath was ragged as she inhaled, on the verge of a good cry, but she steeled herself: *I will not cry ... I will not.*

She chastised herself for all the foolish dreams his appearance had conjured up. Now, for her own peace of mind, she would have to push William Wordsworth completely out of her life. Willing herself to concentrate on the blurred canvas before her, she lifted the tip of her paintbrush.

Several moments passed before she became aware she

had added globs of grey to the green clouds; they were hideous. Her temper flared; she had allowed a perfect stranger to interfere with her most passionate aspiration. Well, she would not allow this to happen again! Unbidden, however, her body suddenly evoked the warm sensation that she had felt before, and she shook her head to erase the memory. *Stop! Stop it—enough of Mr. William Wordsworth. Never, never think of that man again!* She set her jaw and focused on the landscape before her. She began to paint, slowly at first and then with more assurance.

"Miss Lucy! Miss Lucy!" Emily and Henry's exuberant voices came from the top of the hill.

Lucy wiped the tears from her cheeks as the children came bounding down to her. Emily reached her first. "Miss Lucy, you're never going to guess what's coming to Bridgwater Bay."

"No, I guess I won't," she said composing herself. "I suppose you're just going to have to tell me."

"The fair!" Henry shouted. "The fair's coming … with gypsies an' minstrel shows an' all kinds of stuff."

"Papa just told us," Emily added. "It's to be this coming Saturday at the seashore, right below St. Mary's Church."

Lucy was familiar with St. Mary's, a beautiful stone church facing Bridgwater Bay, a seawater inlet that flowed into the Bristol Channel. Beneath the church, a sleepy community of cozy cottages surrounded the small cove, less than an hour's walk from Hawkins' House. She had often taken the children there to enjoy the beach and scavenge for seashells in the small pools created by its mild tides.

Henry danced in front of her. "And Mama and Papa say you can go with us."

"You'll come, won't you? Please … please." Emily begged.

Lucy was taken aback; she had never been asked to join the family on any previous outing. It would be a special treat. She recalled having seen gypsy caravans traveling the country roads two to three times a year, and marveled at the wide array of goods they carried. And now they would be gathered at

Bridgwater Bay.

Suddenly her day had brightened. Even the wind had subsided. She didn't need Mr. William Wordsworth to make her happy: She had her painting and the children and, as an immediate diversion, she would be going to the fair.

"Miss Lucy! You'll come, won't you?" Emily asked again.

"Yes, I would love to accompany you."

illiam upended his pint of ale, swallowing the dregs. He lowered the mug and caught Simon's eye for another. Before entering the pub, he had hesitated at the door, suspecting he might encounter Ben and Walt Sutton inside, but had gripped Old Hickory tightly in his fist and pushed onward. Prepared for a confrontation, he had found himself mildly disappointed by the absence of the two brothers. That had been an hour ago and now, with the bullies long forgotten, the taste of the brew lay bitter on his tongue.

He reconsidered his decision to remove himself from Lucy Sims' life. It had seemed so right that he had marched past her without even glancing in her direction, although his conscience was now nagging him unmercifully. *Damn the irksome inner voice that came unexpectedly, cross-examining him.*

He noted abstractly that Simon had, with an air of disapproval, set another pint before him. Breathing in the aroma of hops, William once again ruminated over his lack of money, the root of most of his agony. It was a condition that hounded him more tenaciously than a pack of dogs in pursuit of a fox. How unlucky were he and his siblings that the oblivious hand of fate had taken the lives of their well-to-do parents at a young age? And how calamitous that their inheritance had been impounded by Lord Lonsdale, his father's former employer; he steadfastly had refused to release the funds, claiming irregularities in the elder Wordsworth's accounting procedures. William knew this to be entirely false, but the conflicting viewpoints could not be reconciled. The more William drank, the more he inwardly cursed Lord Lonsdale and the English aristocracy; they seemed to get away with almost any offence, outright thievery being one of the lesser crimes.

William's only hope for an infusion of funds in the immediate future was the legacy he had inherited through the death of his friend, Raisley Calvert—*if it ever would come through. With luck it would probably materialize in time to pay his funeral costs.*

He lifted his mug and muttered a melancholy toast to unjust times and to an unjust world—one that, so far, had denied him any chance of fulfillment.

Simon passed by, carrying a tray of drinks to a trio of farmers, who were engrossed in conversation near the fireplace. He then shuffled to a shadowy corner and set a tumbler of gin in front of a dark stranger. For a moment, the man caught William's attention. He looked vaguely familiar, but, unable to place him, William lost interest and dropped his gaze to stare moodily into his mug.

Feeling a man's presence, William looked up to see Simon, who had stopped by his table.

"What is it?" William asked with barely veiled annoyance.

"I never seen ya so thirsty afore, Wordsworth. Yer sister's fine, is she?"

William stared at the innkeeper through an ale-induced fog. After a moment, he nodded his head but declined to speak, hoping to discourage further conversation.

Simon lingered. "Yer not in any trouble, are ya?"

"Define trouble."

Simon shrugged. "Trouble comes from all sides … health, politics, money, people, 'specially the fair sex."

Despite his black mood, William smiled. But for health, the innkeeper had summed up the sources for all his miseries. He lifted his pint and drank it down in one continuous gulp, then slammed the mug down with a resounding thud, wiping the back of his hand across his mouth. "You're a wise man, Simon." He rose and tossed a few coins on the table. "Thank you for your hospitality. Good day to you."

"Good day, Wordsworth."

William turned and wove his way to the door, unaware that the man in the corner was staring after him with predatory eyes.

he whinny of horses, followed by the clatter of iron horseshoes on the courtyard cobblestones, sent a wave of panic through Lucy as she raced around the servants' bedroom, smoothing her hair and taking her shawl from its peg above her bed. The family coach had arrived at the front entrance, with the Squire's matched pair of gray geldings now prancing in place. Lucy was late. She quickly bent to fasten the buckles on her best shoes. She heard the front door open, and the Squire's voice filtered in through the high window. "Hold them steady, Percy."

"Aye, Sir. That I will."

The door slammed and sounds of small feet, that could only be the children's, dashed across the courtyard and stopped short. "Where's Miss Lucy?" Emily asked.

Lady Hawkins's harsh voice cut through the brisk morning air. "Go and fetch her. If she not be ready, ya all can walk to the fair."

"I'll go for her," Henry shouted as his footsteps raced back toward the house.

"I'm coming too," Emily said.

Lucy kneeled and reached beneath her mattress. Beth, Molly and Mary hovered by the doorway as she withdrew a bulky satchel, then rose, hurrying from the room with the others following. Mary, scurrying along beside her, dropped a few shillings into Lucy's pocket. "Now don't forget," Mary said, "a stout hairbrush with pure boar bristles. Nothin' else will last. Ya must bargain, mind ya, or those gypsies will rob ya blind. Three shillin's, not a penny more."

"I'll do the best I can."

"And don't ferget," Beth said. "Four yards of dark blue cotton with a fine bit of lace fer a collar."

Lucy bounded down the stairs two at a time, almost colliding with the children at the bottom of the landing.

"Miss Lucy, you have to hurry." Henry said. "We be walking unless you come right now!"

"Henry, it's *we'll* be walking... ," she said, correcting his grammar.

"All right," he said. "Hurry, they'll leave us!"

"I'm coming. I'm coming." She pushed the children ahead of her across the great room, with the servants following, close on their heels.

Molly grabbed Lucy's sleeve as they passed through the front door. "Please, could ya buy me a large bag like the one yer carryin'?" Molly pressed two shillings into her hand.

Lucy hesitated, staring at the girl who had, at times, been surly and mean to her. Before she could reply, the children grabbed her arms and yanked her toward the coach. Lucy, put her foot on the carriage step and turned to the servants. "I'll do the best I can for all of you."

"Stop dillydallying out there!" Lady Hawkins yelled from inside the coach. "In with ya."

Lucy scrambled into the cab with the children pushing in behind her.

The coachman snapped his whip and the carriage lurched off.

illiam, making use of his walking stick, led Dorothy along the narrow streets of Bridgwater, the small city that was a short walk from Alfoxden House. They passed the seven hundred year old St. Mary's Church with its one hundred and seventy-four foot spire. William admired the handsome architecture with its masonry design of the red-sandstone and limestone walls.

A short time later, William and Dorothy found themselves at the edge of a walkway that led down a gentle path to the beach at Bridgwater Bay. They counted over twenty gypsy and trade wagons of all shapes, colors and painted designs. The large drays were parked randomly across sandy fairgrounds that spread out below the siblings, all the way to the edge of the shoreline. William and Dorothy exchanged surprised looks at the size of the bustling crowd; there were people from all walks of life in attendance. The venders, an energetic group of individuals, had attached canvas booths to the sides of their vehicles and were boisterously hawking their wares.

"William, this is going to be sublime," Dorothy said, raising her voice above the din of hungry gulls, squawking noisily overhead. "I'm pleased you decided to join me.

Wishing he shared his sister's enthusiasm, William took Dorothy's hand in his and guided her down the path. "I hadn't realized it was my decision."

"You're far too much of a gentleman to let me come here alone. And I do need your help to carry a few things home."

"I am grateful to be your proverbial beast of burden."

"Cheer up. We're going to have a good time."

He wasn't so sure. He had been feeling despondent for almost a week now over his mounting financial troubles and his foreswearing of Lucy, and had at first refused to attend the fair. It had taken much cajoling on Dorothy's part to temper his moodiness and convince him to accompany her.

As they approached the booths, his sister's face brightened at the large display of colorful fabrics. He followed her to the first stall, which brimmed with imports from India and the Far East, and she began to browse in earnest. After a few moments, William's impatience with textiles got the better of him. "Dorothy, I'll walk on. Maybe I can find us something to eat."

"There's no hurry on my behalf. Take your time."

enry, walking beside Lucy and Emily at the ocean's edge, shouted, "Look at all the food!" He pointed to several open pit grills where meat, fowl, fish and vegetables sizzled over hot coals, while boisterous crowds of men, women and children strolled past. Seagulls dropped from the sky, gathering on the sand to scavenge food scraps. "My gosh, Miss Lucy," he added. "They could feed all of the King's cavalry."

"I believe they could at that, Henry," Lucy said, pleased to be with the children and away from Squire and Lady Hawkins, who had gone off to see and be seen. She breathed in the flavorful cooking scents drifting across the fairgrounds. "It all smells so wonderful."

Henry and Emily grabbed her hands, pulling her into the crowd.

"How many people do you think be here, Miss Lucy?" Emily asked.

"Emily, it's *are* here," Lucy corrected, as she gazed over the throng of vendors, farmers and townspeople. She did a quick calculation, idly fingering the blue ribbons that dangled from her straw hat. She said, "I would guess well over two-hundred."

"They got more things here than I ever saw before," Henry added.

"...than *I've* ever *seen* before," she corrected.

"Yes, Miss Lucy," Henry said. He stopped to glance at an open grate where links of meat were roasting. "Can I go over there and buy a sausage on a stick?"

"Oh, I want one, too," Emily said. "Papa gave us money."

"All right, but come right back. I'll be here at the dry goods booth."

Lucy watched as the children scampered to the sausage stand and then she directed her attention to a display of fabrics and notions. Riffling through the odds and ends, she found the blue cloth and fragile lace Beth had asked for. She purchased them at a fair price along with a new satchel for Molly. While keeping an eye on the children as they waited in a line of customers, she allowed the migrating mass of people to carry her down the midway.

Lucy continued shopping, searching for a merchant with hairbrushes. She passed bountiful displays of clothes, crockery, combs, pens, corn-plasters, wine, ale, imported coffee and teas, candles and lamp oils.

She stopped to stare at a group of musicians and jesters, entertaining atop a small wooden stage. Henry and Emily ran up, chewing their savory treats. "Look!" Henry said. "Minstrels."

"My goodness!" Emily said. "And, look, a puppy!" She pointed to a juggler who balanced a small dog on top of a pole eight feet over his head. The little dog danced in circles.

Lucy said, "I've never seen anything like it."

"Henry! Emily!" called two nicely dressed youngsters on the edge of the crowd, a boy and a girl. "Can you come and play?"

The children looked expectantly to their governess. "Please, Miss Lucy?" Emily asked. "Arthur and Elizabeth are good friends and we haven't seen them in ever so long."

Lucy nodded. "All right, but you must stay close by, where I can see you."

"We will. We promise."

She watched as Henry and his sister ran off to join their friends. They entered an area of the beach that had been set aside for children; a teeter-totter, three swings and a pit for throwing horse shoes were encircled by a low fence. When Lucy saw that the children were safely—and happily—caught up in their games, she strolled over to the next stall and was pleased to discover a selection of hairbrushes.

A wizened old gypsy, wearing a lively yellow and green headscarf, greeted her. "Best brushes in all of England, an' fer the best prices, too. Which one's to yer likin'?"

"That one," Lucy said, pointing to a stout tortoiseshell brush. *It would be perfect for Mary's long hair.* "But only if it's made of real boar bristles."

"That it is. Here, ya can feel it fer yerself." The old woman pressed the brush into her hand: It certainly felt like it was made with boar bristles; being stiff and strong. A tag read, "Five shillings."

Lucy knew better than to appear eager; in fact, she had come prepared. She opened her bag, allowing the vendor to observe the contents of her purse as she removed a couple of coins. "I fear I have only two shillings to spend."

"'Tis yer bad luck, me lady. I couldn't let thet one go fer less than three shillin's, an' at thet I wouldn't be makin' more than a half-penny for meself."

Lucy kept her face immobile but smiled inside. *Bargaining was fun.* She pretended to search her purse and feigned surprise when she found the third coin at the bottom of her bag. "Oh, look. I do have another shilling."

The old woman's eyes flickered. Nodding sagely, she took the coins and handed Lucy the brush. "If I had a daughter the likes of ya, I'd be livin' in a fine house and countin' me pound sterlin'."

Lucy allowed herself to smile, despite its crude implication. "Thank you." She placed the brush in her bag and turned, bumping into a man's chest. Her heart jumped; she knew this man!

*L*ucy's throat became dry. Her limbs began to shake. There were suddenly no sounds in the world, except for the deafening crescendo of her heartbeats. The feelings of longing and passion she had been trying to suppress, came rushing to the surface; she found herself quite out of control as she stared into the eyes of a man with whom she was barely acquainted, yet somehow knew intimately. She abruptly realized that his face was actually only inches from hers. The shock of it made her unsteady. Embarrassed, she took a large step back and regained her propriety. Now that the distance between them had increased somewhat, she was able to remember that the man who stood before her was the same individual who had very recently treated her rather badly. *He had rebuffed her most fanciful hopes. He was certainly not deserving of any more of her time.*

She observed his expression change from surprise to embarrassment. He was blushing. *And so he should be. He had hurt her.* The silence between them grew. *Say something,*

William Wordsworth. The very least you can do is to apologize for your awful behavior.

When he failed to speak, she became more anxious—she tried to turn and flee but her feet wouldn't obey.

"Miss Sims," he finally said, seeming to gather his composure, "it's good to see you again."

Good to see her again! What did he mean by that? Well, she certainly was not going to wait around to find out. Now, if only she could move. She took a tentative step backward and then, when she saw that she had control over her muscles once again, she curtsied and said, "Good day, Mr. Wordsworth."

"Wait, please," he said, reaching out his hand, almost touching her.

When she hesitated, he dropped his arm and added, "I, ah ... I would like to explain myself, if you would allow it."

"It's not necessary," she said, nervously dropping one of her packages.

He retrieved it and passed it to her. "Have you found everything you need?"

"Yes, thank you," she said with reserve. "A few odds and ends for the servants."

Another silence loomed. She still trembled. She wanted to run, but she had the children to oversee.

"Nothing for yourself?" William asked, his eyes probing hers.

"Oh, no, although I admit I have been tempted," she said, noting his parcels. "And you?" She almost bit back the words. *Why was she being civil to this man who was certainly no gentleman?*

"I'm not much of a shopper," he said in a convivial manner, seemingly reading her mind and wishing to offer a better impression of himself. "These are my sister's purchases. She insisted I accompany her, as her beast of burden." He looked about quickly. "I would introduce you, only she's wandered off, no doubt buying more essentials for me to carry home. She loves these fairs."

"Yes," Lucy said. *If she couldn't run, she decided she might as well stay and show him what civility looked like: He might learn something.* "I had no idea these events were so exciting. I've never seen so many wonderful things in all my life." *That does not include you, Mr. William Wordsworth.*

He seemed taken aback. "This can't be your first visit to a fair?"

"Oh, but it is … my very first."

When he smiled, she noticed his fine teeth—even and white. *But,* she reminded herself, *many predatory animals have even white teeth.*

"Then, you're lucky," he said. "This is one of the better ones." Again she found herself staring into those observant eyes! He continued, "Aside from traveling to Bristol, Exeter or London for something exotic, I'd say a person should be able to find almost anything he needed right here." He bowed his head slightly. "Maybe even a chance to explain bad manners."

Is he going to apologize? Had there been a good reason for his rudeness? Not likely! She should leave at once.

"May I walk with you?" he said.

In spite of her determination to flee, she was moved by the soft voice and pleading eyes. "You may," she heard herself reply.

They walked side by side for several steps.

He said, "Miss Lucy Sims, you must find me contemptible."

She looked down at her feet as they moved through the crowd. *Contemptible? No, for some reason, she couldn't find it within herself to feel this. If he had offered 'be angry with' she might have agreed, as she still had hurt feelings.* "I don't have contempt for anyone," she said, deciding it was best to depersonalize her response. She raised her head and gazed past the fairgoers to the bay, and tried to change the subject. "I should come here more often. It's lovely by the shore."

"Yes," he said. "I've often dreamed of having a cottage by the sea."

They strolled on, their fingertips almost touching. The noise of the crowds made conversation difficult. Lucy's eye caught the figure of a man who seemed to be paying them unwarranted attention. Turning to William, she said, "There's a gentleman dressed all in black, who seems to be following us. Is he a friend of yours?"

William glanced over his shoulder. The man turned and slipped away into the crowd. Frowning, William watched after the fellow. "No friend of mine," he said. "Probably a pickpocket. They're thick as fleas on a hound at these fairs. I'm afraid he'd be sadly disappointed with the contents of my pockets." He turned to her. "Would you mind if we stepped away from all this noise? I need to talk to you."

She desperately wanted to hear him explain himself, but allowed none of her eagerness to show as she gestured to Emily and Henry, playing on the teeter-totter nearby with their young friends. "I must keep an eye on the children."

He pointed to the shore with his walking stick. "Perhaps just to the tide line?"

Glancing toward the gently breaking waves, she nodded. "Very well."

"May I carry your bags?"

"Thank you but I can manage." Allowing William to assist with her packages seemed too forgiving a gesture for her to allow. She shook her head; *it was all too confusing to think about.*

They continued along the surf line, deftly avoiding waves that whorled at their feet as thousands of tiny bubbles broke, disappearing on the sand.

Lucy stole a glance at William's face; it was pensive. *Was he experiencing the same internal drama?* Her hand accidentally brushed against his—both jumped—then looked at each other, offering nervous smiles.

"Miss Sims, there's something about you ... I find ... quite bewildering."

Well, she was having an effect upon him after all. But was it in a positive or negative manner? "I don't understand," she replied. "Would you prefer to walk alone?"

"No. No. Not at all. What I'm attempting to say is that, in spite of our differences, perhaps the two of us, artist and poet, are in some way kindred spirits."

Kindred spirits? She felt the blood rush to her cheeks. Her eyes moved to his, willing him to say more.

"Yes,' he said. "I believe that's it. I want to know you better, Miss Lucy Sims."

Unable to hold his gaze, she looked down.

"I have an apology to make," he offered.

"It's not necessary."

"Oh, yes, it is. Since, as you've said, you choose not to have contempt for anyone, I venture to say you must still think I am the worst possible sort of person."

"I really haven't given it much thought." *A big fat white lie, she acknowledged, but allowable since he was so persistent.*

"I wish I could say the same."

He has been thinking of me! She lifted her gaze and studied his features. Those amber eyes were so sincere, yet so troubled, they made her heart ache.

A raucous group of children appeared from nowhere and splashed into the surf, spraying them with water. William and Lucy backed away, smiling at the intrusion as they brushed droplets from their clothes.

He pointed Old Hickory to a small driftwood bench that sat on a slight knoll, a scant twenty feet from where they stood. "It may be quieter if we were to sit over there."

She noticed the settee, her eyebrows rising as she observed how close they would be sitting to one another. Pulling her gaze away, she turned to Henry and Emily, who were in the play area, now romping around with their friends. She could see that the knoll offered a slightly higher elevation to keep watch over the children. "Yes, I believe you are right."

They strode over to the small bench and sat side by side. They were so close that she could feel the warmth of his leg as it rested mere centimeters from her thigh. Her heart pounded.

He said, "This is much better."

She couldn't disagree, as a feeling of excitement dashed through her.

He turned to her. "Now, allow me to explain my rudeness."

Finally, she thought. Then, as if his explanation meant nothing in the world to her, she said, "Please. It really isn't necessary."

"Do you know what you've done to my life?"

Her eyes widened. "What I've done to your life? I'm afraid I don't understand."

"Neither do I," he said. "You're a complete enigma."

"I'm an enigma?"

"It's all very complicated," he said. "I seem to be captivated by a feeling that has invaded my very soul. I've fought against it to no avail. Perhaps talking with you will help." He hesitated, as if struggling, than added, "I know I'm not making sense. Please, bear with me."

The pain in his eyes was so distressing; she found herself tempted to take his hand in hers but fought back the inapt impulse. But her fingers, traitorous digits to her sense of decorum, had a will of their own; they moved the short distance between them ... and had almost touched his hand, when she was startled by the Squire's voice. "Miss Lucy, where be the children?"

Oh, my dear God! She turned to see Squire and Lady Hawkins standing nearby, laden with purchases and staring at her with disapproval.

Rising quickly, she straightened her skirts. *They must think I'm the worst governess in the world, talking to a man instead of watching after the children.* The children! She looked about quickly and when she saw Emily and Henry playing with their friends nearby, she sighed thankfully. She waved toward the children. "They're right over there by the sand dunes."

She noticed the Squire's glare darken. "That's where ya should be. Gather them up. We be leaving."

Flustered, she turned to William. "I must go."

He seemed equally upset at the intrusion. "I haven't begun to say what I meant to! When will we meet again?"

Lucy turned and hurried away.

illiam stared after Lucy until she had disappeared into the crowd with the Squire and his family.

"There you are, William," Dorothy said as she approached, struggling with a surfeit of packages. "I've been looking everywhere for you! Help me, please. My arms are about to stretch to the ground."

He hurried to his sister's side, tucking Old Hickory beneath his elbow as he relieved her of most of the burden. "You must stop shopping," he intoned. "We are out of hands to carry more things, and even if we could, we certainly must be out of money."

"I've spent pennies, nothing more. Who was that young woman you were talking with?"

"Ah, an acquaintance."

"Her name wouldn't be Lucy, would it?"

He sighed with a touch of annoyance, which confirmed her suspicion. Dorothy said, "I thought she might be here today."

He didn't quite understand his sister at times. "And yet you still dragged me away from the cottage, knowing that I might run into her?"

"It was a chance worth taking. I had to get you out into the fresh air. A week of your moping about in the confines of Alfoxden House was all I could bear. Besides, I believed if you ran into your young lady you might wish to re-evaluate your feelings for her. First impressions are very often misleading." She gave him an appraising glance. "But from the look on your face I would say I should have left you at home. You're still smitten, aren't you?" She raised a hand, adding quickly, "Don't bother to deny it, it's plain as day. I will say this, though; you look almost like your old self again. She seems a tonic for you. Pity, however, it would appear she is as poor as we are." She shook her head sadly. "You should stop it now, William."

"I know, Dorothy," he said. "I know that all too well."

eoffrey Walsh ran the palm of his hand over the butt of his flintlock as he watched Wordsworth and his sister walk up the stone stairway from the beach, leaving the fairgrounds. He couldn't help but think he had wasted the day. His attempts to eavesdrop on the poet's conversation with the young woman had been a failure, as the surf and overloud children had drowned out all other sounds. Frustrated, he had left them and caught up to Dorothy Wordsworth, whom he had found huddled with a group of French gypsies beside a wagon of dry goods. Edging up to them, close enough to hear them speak, he had been thwarted this time by his inability to speak or understand French, a language he noted the sister spoke fluently. He spat and used the heel of his boot to grind the spittle into the sand. For all he knew, the gypsies could be the conduit to the French underground. The fair was a perfect cover for spies and seditionists to meet and conspire. He chastised himself for having allowed William to come into eye contact with him. That wouldn't happen again. He couldn't afford to make the traitor suspicious.

ucy, the ache of fatigue pulsing behind her eyes, chastised herself, *"I should not lose sleep over a man I hardly know."* She had told herself the same thing all last night as she had tossed and turned in bed. And now, as she stood before her easel on Hawkins' hillside, she tapped the tip of her paintbrush against the palette in frustration. The castigation repeated itself … disturbing her.

A light breeze ruffled the blue ribbons that held her hat in place, as she redirected the brush and attempted to concentrate on the tiny red roses in her landscape. She soon nodded with approval as the flecks grew in number, creating splashes of color among the darker trees and rocks. An image of William's pleasant smile drifted into her consciousness. She recalled their meeting at the fair, and reviewed their conversation. *What was it he had been on the verge of revealing when the Squire had interrupted them? How, she mused, would he have explained walking past her without so much as a nod or a hello?* Her brush froze in mid-stroke.

Perhaps he was engaged, or even married, and she shouldn't be talking to him at all! Peering at the empty road, she let out a sigh of disappointment. The answers to these musings would have to wait until … when?

She recalled, also, having overheard the household maids—Beth, Molly and Mary—jabbering on about the confusing deportment of the opposite sex, but she had never given male behavior much thought until now. *What did those misinformed women know about anything? None of them had an aspiration beyond pleasing Squire Hawkins.* Lucy shuddered at that image.

She remembered how excited the maids had been when she'd returned from the fair with their purchases. Molly had even given Lucy a kiss on the cheek when she had seen her new traveling bag.

Molly did have a few redeeming qualities, after all, but it was a shame she couldn't get along with the rest of the maids. The girl had sneered when Beth had asked her why she needed such a large bag and had snapped, "For me travels."

"You travel?" Beth had scoffed.

"Ya'd be daft if ya be thinkin' I'm stayin' here all me life. I got plans ta see the world."

"Right," Mary had jeered. "An' I got plans ta be the next queen of England."

Lucy's reverie was interrupted by a mellow voice, "I see you've added flowers. Quite lovely."

Lucy spun around to see William standing behind her, leaning on his walking stick as he appraised her landscape. A moment passed before she could speak. "I'm … I'm afraid you've caught me daydreaming."

"It must have been a most interesting dream."

"No! No! Nothing out of the ordinary." *Another white lie, but entirely permissible.* Lucy unconsciously dipped the tip of her brush into one small peak of oil after the other. "I'm pleased you like the flowers. I felt something was missing." *What would Mr. Wordsworth say if he knew himself to be her inspiration? Maybe, one day she would be able to tell him.*

William threw a quick look around and seemed satisfied they had the hillside to themselves, with the exception of meadow starlings and the larger tarn hawks that flew overhead in wide circles, searching for rabbits and field mice.

He said, "I'm thankful to finally have this opportunity to pass a quiet moment with you. I didn't have a chance to explain myself at the fair."

Her eyes were drawn to a multicolored glob on the end of her paintbrush. *How had she managed to do that?* She tilted her head up to William. *What had he just said? Lucy, concentrate.* She didn't have any trouble focusing on his eyes, which reminded her of a translucent pigment she had once mixed on her palette and had used to precisely color a yellowish-brown sunrise. Thankfully, he didn't now seem to notice her slight lapse of attention, nor the effect he was having upon her; he was so intent on explaining himself! William continued, "It's important that you understand why I walked past you the other day. At the time, I believed I was doing us both a favor. I didn't want to hurt you."

Lucy's brow wrinkled. *A favor? But he did hurt her.* She suddenly felt a premonition. *He was about to explain why they should never see one another. The whys didn't really matter. Explaining the details of his decision certainly wouldn't make her feel any better.* She turned her head away, unwilling to listen to his reasoning, but a certain desperation in his tone made her pay attention.

"...and there are some things you should know about me. I've lived a rather unsettled life, almost like a vagabond at times. I have incurred a number of financial obligations, ones that have made it difficult to survive on the little money I earn from time to time. I'm afraid I can't predict a change any time soon. Unfortunately, my debts have made any thought of having a relationship impossible. I have people who are dependent upon the little money I make and everyone is pressing me to find a woman quite above my station in life."

Lucy caught her breath. *There it was, in plain English.* She had difficulty maintaining her composure even though her female intuition had given her fair warning. The remainder of his explanation was smothered as she scolded herself. *I am a naive fool! How could I have allowed myself to be entranced by a man who wasn't just rejecting me, but was also insinuating I was too far beneath him to be acceptable?* A deep anger permeated her core. Lucy fought back the nausea that worked its way up her throat and swallowed, hoping she wouldn't vomit. *She should have known better: The hard realities of class distinction were everywhere, and were as old as society itself.* In spite of her struggle to remain composed she felt her eyes brim with tears and lowered her head so he wouldn't notice.

"Forgive me for sounding so insensitive," he continued, "but at the time I walked by you that's exactly why I couldn't stop, even though my heart was in torment... ."

She realized he had stopped talking, but she couldn't look up.

"I'm afraid I am doing a terrible job of trying to explain why I am here with you now."

"No. You've done quite well," she said, making an effort to keep any tremor from her voice. "I understand completely. You're a gentleman. I'm a governess. No further explanation is required."

"No! Miss Sims, no. Please, listen to me." He moved closer to her, his face strained. "There's more, much more. I managed to walk away from you once because I listened to my friends, and believed I was doing what was right for both of us. I thought by continuing to see you, I would have given you false hope, hope that we could have had a relationship when obligation and reality dictate, demand, that I pursue another path. I didn't want to hurt you."

"Please, just go. There's no need for you to..."

"Miss Sims," he interrupted, "walking away from you almost destroyed me. I felt like a dead man for days. I could not think, nor sleep, nor write. And then, when we met at the fair, I tried to walk away from you again, but I couldn't. Doesn't that mean anything to you?"

Bewildered, she shook her head. *What was he saying? She too, had been powerless to step away from him.*

"Miss Sims, look at me. Please."

She raised her eyes and felt a single tear spill down her cheek.

He raised a hand and wiped the droplet away. His voice was gentle, "It's all become very clear to me. My actions have been untruthful to my heart and to you. What kind of a man would I be if I were to allow outdated social custom to overrule my very soul?"

"A wise one?"

He smiled, then said, "There are individuals who might agree with that assessment, but I know now more than ever, there's something extraordinary between us. Please hear me when I say that this something, this bond, is stronger by far than any argument against us could ever be." His eyes searched hers. "You must feel it. Tell me … you must."

"I feel … something," Lucy admitted with all the prudence she could muster.

"When I said I had financial obligations that precluded a relationship, that was my brain speaking. Now, dear, sweet Miss Sims, I appeal to you from my heart."

She blinked away her tears and questioned him boldly. "Who rules William Wordsworth? His heart or his brain?"

"Certainly, my heart. Though I am a man of words, words fail me at this moment. Please, allow me to see you."

A ray of hope lightened her mood, but she eyed him speculatively. "I suppose we could exchange ideas on art and poetry." To prevent the conversation from becoming any more intense, she talked on, saying the first thing that came to mind. "I've read poetry all my life. My mother was a schoolmistress. She loved poetry and used to read to me almost every night."

"You were fortunate."

"She's gone now." Lucy looked down at her hands. They were trembling. "My father, too. He was an artist. I've always nurtured the belief that I inherited some of his talent."

"There's no doubt of it."

As she raised her eyes, he continued, "Lucy Sims, there are so many things I have to say to you and I want to know much more about you."

"Perhaps, once you do, you'll be disappointed."

"That isn't possible." William took a step closer to her. She caught her breath.

The clatter of hoofs and the creak of a carriage broke the moment, drawing Lucy's attention to the road where she could see the Squire and Lady Hawkins peering out the rear window of the family coach as it lumbered up the hill. The children, leaning from the side windows, waved and yelled her name. "Miss Lucy!"

ucy lamented, "Oh, no … this always seems to happen to us. I'm so sorry! I must leave to watch after the children." She read the disappointment on his features.

"Then I'd best be off myself," he managed.

"Perhaps you had," she said, keeping an anxious eye on the coach. "Good day, Mr. Wordsworth."

"Please! When may I talk with you again?"

"Maybe … next Sunday?"

"That seems a year away..."

"Yes," she agreed, "but that is all we can do… . I really must be on my way."

"Good bye, then." He held her gaze momentarily.

The stillness on the hillside was interrupted by the baying of hounds. Lucy and William turned toward the manor house. A pack of dogs appeared at the open gates and charged down the hill toward them.

"Run!" Lucy said. "Henry has set the hounds on you."

William's grip tightened about Old Hickory. "What about you?"

"They know me. I'm safe. Run, please!"

He turned without another word and dashed down the hillside.

As the barking, howling canines bounded closer, with Henry, Emily, and the Squire appearing behind them at the manor gates, the Squire yelled some indistinguishable curses and all three of them ran down the hill after the hounds.

Lucy held her breath as she turned back to watch William's progress. He leaped over a hedgerow, almost falling, then plowed through a thicket of heather. A few yards later, he found the road and ran.

The hounds bayed shrilly, pounding the earth with their downhill stride, then ripped through the tall grass, sweeping past her. A few moments later, Henry and Emily pulled up, out of breath, at her side. The Squire, huffing and puffing, followed quite a few yards behind.

Lucy grabbed Henry by the collar. "Call them back, right away!"

Henry tore loose from her grip and folded his arms resolutely. "He still be on Hawkins property."

She raised her voice to a level the children seldom heard. "Call the hounds off. *Immediately!*"

Emily flinched. "You better do it, Henry."

Henry lifted a hunting whistle and began to blow it halfheartedly as the Squire lumbered up to a stop beside them.

On the road below, Lucy could see William running as fast as his legs would carry him. But then, obviously seeing that he couldn't outdistance the dogs if he stayed on the current path, he leaped off the track and headed downhill toward the ruins of the old granary.

Lucy turned to Henry and skewered him with a pointed stare. "Henry!"

This time he blew the whistle louder.

William must have heard the shrill toot as he glanced over his shoulder.

The pack of hounds responded to the command and abruptly gave up the chase save for one small bitch that left the road and continued after William at full speed.

The poet could see the mutt, snarling now, was beginning to close the short distance between them.

William was nearing the granary wall. Lucy prayed he would be able to scale it before he was bitten. Lucy turned and scowled at Henry.

He shrugged with feigned innocence. "Can't call her back. She be deaf as a rock."

Lucy's eyes darted back to William, who was scrambling over the stone enclosure as the little hound launched herself through the air—clamping her teeth onto the seat of his trousers.

"Oh, Lord, no!" Lucy responded, raising her hand to her mouth.

William swatted his stick at the monster, but before he could make contact the fabric gave way.

Lucy could almost hear the tearing sound as the mouthful of cloth parted, leaving a hole the size of a grapefruit.

William disappeared quickly over the barrier. The cur turned away, growling, and shook her trophy between her teeth, but her effort to show off backfired as the fabric came loose and flew up onto the wall, where it stuck, hanging from an uneven stone.

Henry smiled proudly. "That chap won't be coming back any too soon."

"Henry," the Squire said. "Gather them hounds right now! Ya set them on a feller again, and I'll hide ya. Ya hear me?"

Henry's smile diminished. "Yes, Papa."

"Emily," the Squire said. "Help yer brother get them up ta the kennels."

"Yes, Papa."

Henry blew his whistle. Then he and Emily scampered off to gather up the hounds and usher them back to the kennels.

William squatted behind the wall, waiting for the commotion to end. As his pulse slowed, he began to relax and take in the surroundings. Here, before him, sat an abandoned granary with most of its roof rotted away. The ruined millhouse faced a cobblestone courtyard, surrounded by crumbling stone walls, one of which had provided the barrier between him and further misfortune! He noted that a few trees had cheated the odds, and were flourishing within the enclosure. Along the base of tumbled walls, bursts of color were everywhere; foxglove, gardenia, and iris grew wild, standing out against the backdrop of mossy stone. He drank in the beauty and vowed to return when he was in a more favorable mood.

After a while, he rose and realized that, with the granary's close proximity to the manor house, Lucy must surely know this spot. His could almost feel her presence ... and he stood savoring this thought for some time. *Would he see her next Sunday? How could he wait that long?*

A gust of wind drew his attention to the embarrassing tear in his trousers. He needed to walk to Samuel's cottage for their daily writing session, but now, with his posterior open to view, he dared not take the road there, nor could he go back home. He was pondering this dilemma, when his attention was drawn to the top the wall—the swatch of fabric torn from his pants was there, fluttering in the wind! Reaching up, he snatched it and stuffed it down the rear of his waistband. The breeze again alerted him that the patch afforded little protection from inquisitive travelers, who were sure to gawk and laugh at his indignity. It would be best, he decided, to take the back road, and the shorter journey, to the Coleridge cottage.

ucy's attention returned to the granary where William had just disappeared over the wall. She fervently hoped his unfortunate experience with the little hound would not discourage him from coming back! As she scanned the ruins for any sign of William, she recalled their first encounter in the glen, a short distance away: The dramatic comedy that had unfolded there should have discouraged them both from ever wanting to see one another. But, the opposite was true; she, at least, strongly craved this man's presence. It deepened her senses and made her see the world differently. This psychological and emotional yearning was manifesting itself in a very physical way, frightening her with in its sheer strength! *Was this lust or love?* Reluctantly, pushing aside thoughts that were better left unexplored for the time being, she pulled her eyes from the granary and turned to her easel. She lifted the canvas, placed it inside the larger of her two baskets and began to fold the stand's long wooden legs.

"I'll help ya with that," the Squire said.

Suddenly becoming aware of her employer, who still stood nearby, she said, "I can manage, Sir."

He ignored her protest, lifted the containers and smiled broadly. "I'll follow ya, Lucy." He nodded toward the manor. "Up the hill with ya, now."

His familiar manner made her skin crawl. She knew it would be inappropriate, possibly even dangerous, for her to refuse his assistance. *Oh, that awful man! What would the servants think if they saw the Squire carrying her baskets? It would certainly fuel rumors.* But she had no choice in the matter. She uttered a plea under her breath, picked up her easel and began to stride up the hill as he trailed closely behind.

"That was the same lad as was at the fair, I believe," the Squire said. "Ya be seeing him now?"

"We've just met, Sir."

"Ya be too young to have a lad courtin' ya. Ya've got enough on yer hands with Emily and Henry. They be a full time occupation. Best ya not be seein' him again."

Her easel slipped from her hand, hitting the ground with a thud. Picking it up, Lucy noticed her hands were shaking. "I would never jeopardize my time with the children, Sir."

The Squire now walked by her side. "I know that. Ya be a fine lass. And I be pleased the children like ya. But yer to 'ave no more of these meetin's. I can't have ya runnin' off with some lad now and leavin' the children. Ya understand me?"

"Yes, Sir," she replied through clenched teeth.

The Squire smiled as he transferred one of the baskets to his other hand and reached over to touch a small pink blemish on her temple that remained from Doctor Deegan's bloodletting. Lucy ducked away.

"Don't be skittish, Lass. My touch won't hurt ya. Them ugly suckin' leeches left hardly a mark on ya. They be little miracles, though, don't ya think?"

"I believe so, Sir," Lucy replied, half-listening, wondering if she and William would ever have the opportunity to see each other again.

The Squire's eyes roved downward over her figure. "Ya remember I took ya in me arms to yer bed?"

Lucy's attention snapped back. She could not believe the inappropriateness of this lewd man, but said flatly, "No, Sir. But Beth told me."

"Yer nothing but skin and bones, lass. 'Course, yer filled out in all the right places." Lucy saw that his gaze lingered on her breasts. She stepped ahead of him, as he added, "I couldn't help but feel ya, carryin' ya as I was."

Lucy felt the heat rise to her face, recalling the incident, and suspecting once again that he might have touched her inappropriately. Her lips tightened; it would give her great satisfaction to spit in the man's piggish face. But she resisted the urge, for the moment.

"Ya'll be needing a room of yer own one of these days. I'm thinkin' I could arrange it. Would ya like that?"

She recoiled, repulsed by the salacious offer. Everyone knew Beth, the Squire's mistress, was the only servant with a room of her own.

The Squire grinned lopsidedly. "Ya hear me offer?"

"Sir," Lucy said, struggling to contain her temper, "there are no empty bedrooms in the servant's quarters."

"Ya let me worry about that."

She said tightly, "I like things as they are, Sir."

"I be thinkin' ya might change yer mind. A lass like yerself could use a few extra shillin's in her purse, eh?"

She wanted to flee.

The Squire—ever insensitive—seemed to be encouraged by her silence. "Ya think on it now. It's not very often a young lass gets offered an opportunity ta better herself."

Lucy was on the brink of lashing out at him when Molly stepped from the manor house several yards ahead of them, carrying a rug. The girl began to shake it vigorously. Molly glanced in their direction, her mouth dropping open as she noticed the Squire carrying Lucy's baskets. The girl's eyes flickered and then narrowed to jealous slits.

The color drained from Lucy's face, as a chill closed in on her: The relative peace and security she had known at Hawkins House was eroding at an alarming rate.

illiam inhaled the aroma of spiced jasmine as he sipped the warm tea, his eyes and ears attuned to Samuel, who sat on the other side of the desk, reading the newspaper. William squirmed in his seat, feeling conspicuous in a pair of his good friend's breeches, sewn from green and red striped silk and sporting gold ribbons at waist and knee. When he had first seen the pants, he had thought Samuel to be playing a joke, that the 'costume' must certainly have been purchased for some theatrical event. Samuel had taken umbrage, stating that the breeches were the latest fad in London and had been made for him by one of the city's finest tailors. William had–in the end–decided it would be better to wear the bizarre attire than to sit nude in front of Sara, as she stitched up the seat of his trousers, while holding a sleeping Hartley. Even as her needle flew, William noticed that Sara was eavesdropping, a customary habit of hers.

Samuel slid the newspaper toward his friend, pointing to a column. "Read this bit here … an article on our compatriot, John Thelwall."

William lifted the broadsheet and began to read. "…the political radical, John Thelwall, has been acquitted of all charges of high treason." He glanced to Samuel. "This is wonderful news."

"You see, if they couldn't hang John, they'll never be able to ensnare that skinny neck of yours."

William chortled with good humor, but as he read further, his cheerfulness subsided. "Samuel, listen to this rot: 'John Thelwall is a known extremist who often associated with the poet, William Wordsworth. He stayed for extended periods at Wordsworth's residences, first at Racedown in Dorset and, more recently, at Alfoxden House in Somerset. Wordsworth is a suspected revolutionary and antimonarchist, as well as being a French sympathizer and possibly even a spy. He is currently under investigation by the Home Office.'" William threw the paper aside with disgust. "These are outright lies! John came to visit but he never stayed the night. And my views are completely misrepresented! This vile publisher wants to hasten me to the gallows."

"No chance of that with me orating your defense in court," Samuel said. "Trust me: You have nothing to worry about. The scandalmonger who wrote that refuse is simply stirring up controversy, trying to sell newspapers."

"I've a mind to sue for libel. This sort of thing will ruin my name and damage me professionally."

"William, unless we get some new verse written soon, there'll be nothing to ruin or damage."

"The article says I'm being investigated." William squinted, delving into his memory. "There was a man at the fair. I've seen him somewhere before, but for the life of me I can't place him. Do you think the Home Office has assigned someone to follow me?"

Samuel looked up with interest. "I wouldn't put anything past them. What did he look like?"

142

"Fairly tall, lank, with odd, almost Slavic features. His eyes, as I recall, were dark. He was wearing a wide-brimmed hat and suit, both black. Somber looking fellow."

"Perhaps he was a cemetery salesman," Samuel said raising his voice for effect, "out to sell plots of earth to those about to die." He guffawed.

"Not funny."

"William, relax! He's probably just a bookkeeper or a solicitor up from Exeter."

"Possibly, but all the same I don't relish the idea of being followed nor having my politics investigated. I'm fed up with false accusations. With all the specious lies my neighbors are spreading, maybe it's time for me to get out of the country for awhile." His eyes took on a faraway cast. "You know, Dorothy and I loved Germany, even though we were there ever so briefly."

"Germany! A wonderful idea." Samuel's eyes sparked then focused on him. "But you two cannot leave without me. We have work to accomplish. If you decide to go, we'll accompany you. Besides, Sara needs a change."

"Speak for yourself," Sara said.

Samuel ignored her. "Think of the intellectual challenges. We'll learn to speak German, explore the cities, villages and countryside. Why, it will be a wonderful educational and writing adventure, we'll feast on German sausage, sauerbraten and Weiner schnitzel; and wash it all down with the finest beer in Europe!"

"And how will the two of you finance this bacchanalian escapade?" Sara asked.

Samuel, lines etching his youthful face, said, "'Tis not your worry."

Sara scoffed. "Hartley and I will be right here when you come crawling back home, tired, hungry and with not a penny left in your pockets."

Samuel pounded his desktop. "You and the baby will accompany us."

"No! Not in this lifetime!"

William had been silent, regretting his initial suggestion. He had witnessed the Coleridge's unpleasant disputes before; and so, to defuse the situation, he said, "I spoke too soon. It's not possible to leave just yet. I must prove my innocence before the court. Otherwise I will be hounded for the rest of my life. The trip will come later, after I have been acquitted."

"Here, here!" Samuel said, his disagreement with Sara overshadowed by the reminder of William's legal problems. "I heartily concur. If it's a choice between a good contest of words and a good trip, I'll take the words any day. We stay, we fight, we win. And then, by God, we'll travel to Germany and write poetry the world has never conceived–nor even dreamed– of."

Sara groaned and shook her head. "The dreamers of this world ... pity the woman married to a poet."

Samuel threw her a look that would have crushed a lesser woman. "Pity the poet married to a woman who pities the woman married to a poet."

Sara scowled. "Would that you could turn words into shillings as quickly as you turn them into banter."

"Ha!" he bellowed. "I thought that was quite clever, myself. Not that I would expect you to appreciate gifted repartee."

William stood and crossed to the sewing table, again hoping to divert their argument. "What's the verdict on my trousers?"

Sara put down her needle. "Salvageable, but you won't be wearing them to any fancy outings."

Samuel emitted a barking laugh. "William, this girl of yours is doing her best to diminish your wardrobe. You've seen her twice, and twice your trousers have been ruined. Do you think the fates are dispatching a message?"

William hadn't mentioned seeing Lucy at the fair and he thought it prudent to keep the encounter to himself. "Ha! Yes. I believe Providence is suggesting that I look far better half-clad than any other man in England."

Sara chuckled and held up the garment to inspect her needle work. "'Tis a shame to sew up your trousers and disappoint all the ladies."

William nodded with approval as he inspected her sewing. "Thank you, Sara. They almost look new again."

Samuel folded the newspaper and put it aside. "William, you and I should be focusing on our writing. At the rate we're dragging along, we'll both be in our nineties before either of us produces another manuscript."

Cognizant of this fact, William said, "That's changing as of today. I'm feeling inspired."

"Be careful, William," Sara said. "Your new source of inspiration is running you out of trousers."

ucy relaxed in the chair between Emily and Henry's beds, stretching back to ease her tired muscles. She closed Gulliver's Travels, which she had been reading, and set it on the night table, where a single candle burned. "That's enough of Jonathan Swift for tonight."

Emily pulled covers up to her chin. "One more chapter, please."

Henry yawned, barely able to keep his eyes open. "How do Gulliver get away from the Lill-i-put-ians, him being tied up and all?"

"You'll find out tomorrow," she said, standing. "We'll read the next chapter together."

Henry pouted. "I can't read them big words."

"*Those* big words," she corrected. "Nonsense, you're becoming a better reader every day."

"I can read almost all of the big words," Emily said.

Lucy smiled and gave each child a kiss on the forehead. "Sleep tight. I'll see you in the morning."

"Miss Lucy," Henry said. "I be sorry I set the hounds on that chap."

"Why, thank you, Henry. Offering an apology is very grown-up."

Henry beamed.

"Do you love him, Miss Lucy?" Emily asked.

The governess' eyes widened. "Emily! I've only just met the gentleman."

"Remember Romeo and Juliet? They fell in love at first sight."

Lucy raised an eyebrow: Emily's intuition never failed to surprise her. She suggested, "I've been reading you far too many love stories."

Emily giggled. "I can tell you like him."

"Oh?" she asked, with a curious tilt of her head. "And how's that?"

"Because you seem so happy."

She considered this for a moment. *Is it that obvious?*

Henry yawned again, then voiced his opinion, "She's happy because she got her papa's paintbrush back."

"Thank you, Henry," she said. "That did please me. Now it's time for both of you to sleep." She blew out the candle and exited the room, leaving the door ajar, and stopping just outside to be sure her little charges stayed in bed.

"She be in love," Emily whispered.

"Never! That chap's not fer her."

"I'm a woman. I know these things."

"You're only a girl. You don't know nothing."

"Wait and see."

"That chap better not be coming around here again. Next time I won't be calling the hounds back."

Lucy smiled as she turned and tip-toed away. Clearly, there were two men in love with her.

ucy hummed cheerfully to herself as she strode along the hallway, and was almost skipping by the time she bounded down the stairs and entered the kitchen. There, she found Molly ensconced in front of the sink, alternately scrubbing pots and pans, and picking at the remains of a chocolate cake on the counter. "Hello, Molly," she said, reaching into the cupboard for a teacup. "Long day?"

"Longer for some than others," she grumbled. "I seen ya with the Squire today. What did ya do ta get him ta tote yer baskets?"

Taken aback by the thinly-veiled accusation, Lucy spun around and dropped the teacup, her mood and the china shattering. She bent to pick up the shards. "Molly, why do you always think the worst of people?"

Molly grinned wickedly. "Ha! Don't try ta weasel out of it. I knew ya was after him all along."

Lucy felt anger, yet also pity, for the servant girl, who seemed to live in a world of jealousy. "Molly, when you want something from someone you can be very pleasant, but it never seems to last. You ought to think about who you are, what kind of a person you want to be and then change your ways. Otherwise, you're going to end up very unhappy."

"Blither off, ya trollop."

Lucy let her breath out. Molly wasn't worth getting upset over. She defended, "I feel truly sorry for you, but I'm not going to stand here and let you insult me."

"I know what I seen with me own eyes," Molly taunted, then thrust a large chunk of cake into her mouth.

"You didn't see anything because nothing happened."

"I surely did," she said, licking frosting from her fingers. "Ya was courtin' his Lordship."

Disgust shone in Lucy's eyes. "That's not true and you know it. The Squire is the last person on Earth in whom I would be interested."

The churlish girl laughed derisively. "Yer a smart one, ya are, Lucy Sims. Ya had me fooled fer a while with that act of yers, eyes rollin' up into yer head and twistin' about on the floor like a serpent. Oh, ya got the devil in ya alright, but it ain't from the fallin' sickness. Ya were fakin' it ta get the Squire to carry ya to yer bed so he could feel that little body of yers. And now ya got him chasing after ya like one of his hounds chasin' a bitch in heat."

Lucy's mouth fell open, dumbfounded by Molly's crude thoughts. She couldn't understand how anyone would actually wish to touch the Squire, let alone sleep with him. It had to be the promise of money—and what a low goal that was. "Molly, you're making this all up. Believe me, there's no reason for you to be jealous of me."

"Jealous?" Molly spat. "I ain't jealous of a skinny bird the likes of ya. Ha! I'm twice the woman ya are." She scooped up another piece of cake and bit into it with a satisfied smirk.

"No, not quite twice the woman I am. But at the rate you eat desserts, you soon will be."

Molly breathed in a bit of cake, and choked on it, coughing as Lucy turned and left the room. The governess hid her smile until she was well into the hallway.

quire Hawkins strode out the front door of the manor into the courtyard, where his wife waited in the family carriage, with its driver and team of four. The horses were prancing anxiously, their iron shoes clattering on the cobblestones. Lucy and the children, carrying baskets and easel, trailed behind.

"Papa," Emily said. "Will you bring us a surprise?"

Henry clapped his hands. "Yes, yes! A surprise."

"I might, if ya try extra hard to learn yer studies."

"We will. Won't we, Henry?"

"Yes, we'll learn everything real good."

The Squire's eyes shifted to Lucy. "I'll get ya a little somethin' too, Miss Lucy."

"Oh, no, Sir," she asserted, feeling uncomfortable. "Please, just the children."

The Squire ignored her. "I can buy ya somethin' if it pleases me." He stepped closer to her, lowering his voice. "It'll be somethin' special from me to ya."

Lucy recoiled—the man's breath was as foul as his implied intimacy.

"George!" Lady Hawkins yelled. "Quit dawdlin'. I'll be late for me fittin'."

"Comin', dear."

The Squire winked at Lucy, as if to imply they had a secret between them, then hurried into the coach, slamming the door.

The coachman snapped the end of his whip and the team leaped forward, pulling the slack out of the harnesses, and throwing the passengers back onto their seats. The carriage lurched away.

Lucy was relieved to see them go. Life without the Squire lurking about was suddenly more pleasant. She led the children out of the courtyard. They strolled toward the hillside for another morning class, Emily and Henry skipping along after their governess.

"What did Papa whisper to you?" Emily asked.

How like Emily to pick up on her father's aside to her. She answered quietly. "Something about the surprises."

"Oh, good," the girl said innocently, and added, "I'm so happy Papa's going to get you something, too."

Henry charged ahead, swinging an imaginary saber. "I hope Papa buys me toy soldiers."

"And I'd like a new fashion doll," Emily said.

Lucy whispered to herself, "I'd just like to be left alone."

orothy was suddenly aware she had been standing in front of the kitchen sink, drying the same plate for the last five minutes. She shook her head, perturbed that she had allowed herself to worry away most of the morning. She stacked the remainder of the breakfast china in the cupboard, poured a cup of tea, and carried it into the parlor. She settled down in her usual chair beneath the window, and gazed out onto the front garden, unaware that she fidgeted with the saucer as she waited for William to come downstairs. Finally, she lifted the cup and sipped, while considering the best way to approach him with her concerns. Perhaps she should speak to him while on a walk, using their old tradition of expressing uncertainties while strolling through the countryside. Nature's unique aura offered solace to the soul, her beauty diminishing one's troubles, and her truth offering solutions.

Dorothy heard the sound of feet descending the stairs. She sat upright and assumed a pleasant demeanor. When William reached the landing, he bowed and turned around, modeling his new britches. "How do they look?"

She thought him to be quite handsome in his new pair of dark green wool trousers. "Never mind how they look," she said. "How do they feel?"

"Very comfortable, indeed," he said, continuing down the stairs. "As if hand-sewn by the finest tailor in all of England ... and they were! Thank you, Dorothy." He crossed into the parlor and kissed her forehead. She caught his reflection in a wall mirror. "Look at yourself."

William glanced to the mirror and admired the cut of his trousers. "Rather stylish, eh?"

Dorothy smiled, pleased by the compliment. She didn't have much confidence in herself as a seamstress, but had to admit the garment looked surprisingly well-tailored. "You could be a nobleman in the court of King George, himself."

"I believe I could, at that," he acknowledged. "While there, I could offer advice to our misguided King: Abdicate the throne, abolish the monarchy, repeal the Crown's oppressive laws, end the power of the Church and the aristocracy, and initiate a Republican form of government. And that would just be my opening statement," he concluded with a twinkle in his eye.

Dorothy didn't mind if William was politically outspoken in front of her, but she did grasp the seriousness of being so in public. She pleaded, "Talk like that will surely place you in prison, if not on the gallows. Please don't speak about these matters to anyone but me!"

He shrugged. "Criticism is healthy. Besides, the King actually deserves it. George is quite addled and everyone knows it. He's an embarrassment to all Englishmen."

Dorothy placed her cup of tea unsteadily on its saucer. It was time for her to engage William in another, more personal subject. She rose and crossed to a coat rack where she lifted two capes from their pegs. "A little fresh air will do us both good. A walk to show off your new trousers?"

William seemed momentarily puzzled, and then a knowing look spread across his features. He reached for his cape. "Lead the way."

mily and Henry sat across from Miss Lucy on the outcropping of rock below the manor house. Emily noticed their governess seemed distracted as she read from Jonathan Swift's novel. "...and so after Gulliver swore a peace with the Lilliputian Emperor and agreed to the Articles for the Recovery of his Liberty, the King had him unchained." Miss Lucy paused and passed the book to Henry. "Your turn."

Henry stared mutely at the open page, his face contorted as he ran his finger along the lines of type, in an apparent struggle to decipher all the words.

Emily eyed her teacher as Miss Lucy's gaze drifted down the hill to the granary, as if she were waiting for something to happen. Emily saw that she stared at the spot on the wall where they had seen her gentleman last. *She must really be in love.* Emily swore to herself that she would tell no one, above all, not Henry. He was too young to understand these things. Besides, if he did find out, he might set the hounds on the poor man again.

Henry began to read. "Gulliver was given his lib-er-er-ty and a sa-sailing boat and, and . . ."

Emily interrupted. "Miss Lucy, if the tallest of the Lilliputians be not even six inches, how big be their babies?"

Lucy continued to gaze down the hill, a dreamy expression on her face. Emily smiled.

Henry also noticed his governess's preoccupation and grinned like an imp. He began to read faster, words Emily knew Reverend Swift had never written. "...and Gulliver scooped up ten of them little chaps, dipped them in a pot of gravy, added salt and pepper and then started to eat them, chewing up one little chap after the other, starting with their yummy toes and ending with their crunchy heads and squishy eyeballs... ."

Emily began to giggle. Henry joined her. One led the other on, until both were quaking with laughter.

Miss Lucy popped out of her reverie. "What is so funny? Henry, what were you reading?"

Henry was incapable of answering: He rolled over, chortling beyond control. Emily, too, couldn't catch her breath. Miss Lucy reddened with embarrassment, knowing she had been caught daydreaming.

illiam and Dorothy walked along the leafy path in silence for several minutes, passing beneath a stand of elms where sunlight filtering through branches brightened their way with dappled light. Ever since they had begun living in the same house, it had become their custom to take long walks in the countryside, day and night. They were often joined by Samuel Coleridge and an array of poet friends from all walks of life, who carried notebooks to record observations as concepts for future writings, on nature, politics and humanity. It was because of these nocturnal outings that neighbors had labeled them *suspicious individuals*.

Then, as now, the participants usually took turns conversing: one simply listened while the others expressed feelings or ideas. Today, however, just brother and sister were walking, and William could sense from Dorothy's demeanor that he was in for a serious conversation. He suspected why a troubled look had appeared on her features, but he wasn't in the mood to discuss his love life.

To ward off what he imagined would be an uncomfortable discussion, he enthused, "Dorothy, I awoke in the middle of the night with an idea as to how we might finance a return trip to Germany."

After several paces Dorothy turned to him. "Germany? Well, are you going to tell me, or keep me in suspense?"

He smiled. His tack had been successful, if only for a few moments. "I'll tell you in due time. I don't wish to build up your hopes until I've discussed the idea with Samuel. His cooperation is necessary."

"Samuel and Sara would be accompanying us?"

"I believe so."

"I would welcome that! But, Sara doesn't enjoy traveling, and this will be especially true now that they have Hartley."

"If we can find a way to fund the trip, I believe she'll come around. If she doesn't, I have a feeling Samuel will accompany us without the family. He's not one to miss out on an adventure. Besides, he enjoys your company. He's always had an eye for you, you know. Rather infatuated, I'd say."

"Oh, William, don't start," she said, blushing. "You know that's nonsense!"

"I'm simply stating my observations."

His sister was quiet for a moment as they entered a copse of trees that were abuzz with the chirping of sparrows and thrush. They spent several moments delighting in the sounds, and finally Dorothy spoke. "This young woman who paints, have you seen her again?"

He exhaled. *So much for deflection.* Yielding, he answered, "Yes."

"I would like it if you could describe her to me."

William eyed the leaves underfoot as they trod on the path. *Lucy was so many things to him; indeed, she seemed to **be** him, and, yet, she also seemed to complete what was absent in him; and this dichotomy manifested itself as a dual desire for her companionship and as an intense physical yearning. How* *to describe this?* He said the first word that came to mind, "Extraordinary." Then added, "She's extraordinary."

Dorothy waited for him to expound further, but they walked on in silence. "That is all you have to say?"

"Extraordinary isn't enough?"

"I was hoping for a little more. Perhaps a name or a description ... age, background ... things of that nature."

One look at his sister's probing eyes told William her interrogation would continue until her curiosity was satisfied. He said, "Her name is Lucy. She's ... ah, not ... easy to describe. I'll put some words on paper and show them to you."

"How old is she?"

"Hmm, I'm not sure. Nineteen, twenty ... maybe twenty-one."

"Surely, you must know something more about her. Where she was born? What type of background is she from? Was I correct when I assumed she works?"

William knew confirming his sister's suspicions would unsettle her, especially since he had admitted to seeing Lucy again. But the truth had always worked best between them. "Yes. She's a governess ... ."

Dorothy's cheeks flushed as they invariably did when she was frustrated. "William, I admire any young woman who can read and write, but a governess is hardly appropriate for someone of your standing. You need to marry into a respectable family."

"Yes, I know. With a wife who will bring a substantial dowry. You and Samuel," he muttered. "But doesn't it seem wrong that we can have a profound empathy for those not as fortunate as us, and yet we maintain this ... this ... hierarchy of class inequalities?"

Dorothy turned to look pensively at the small brook bubbling over its stony bed beside the path. Finally, she answered, "Yes, there are inequities in our lives, and I believe, as I know you do, that it is our desire to change our world in a peaceful manner, but change comes slowly, and, in the meantime, I don't wish to see you hurt anyone—or be hurt."

"There's nothing for you to worry about. It isn't even a friendship yet. With all of my uncertainties, who is to say if it will ever evolve into anything more than a few conversations?"

"One thing leads to another," Dorothy said, envisioning the future. "Especially if she is, as you say, extraordinary."

"She is that. The first time I looked at her I perceived my own soul reflected there. It stayed my breath, and I couldn't will myself away from her. That's never happened to me before."

Dorothy stopped on the pathway. She turned to him with the dour expression of a fortune teller, one who bore her customer bad tidings. "William, your reaction to this young woman doesn't change a thing about your present circumstances. You are in no position to support another family."

"Dorothy, the thought of another family is the furthest thing from my mind," he replied, piqued by his sister's lecturing tone. "You do know that, if I publish *The Prelude* this year, there'll be more than enough ..."

She interjected, "*The Prelude* isn't nearly ready for publication. And only God knows how long it's going to take you to complete it. You have to be honest with yourself."

He swallowed a sharp retort, turned and strode up the lane, Dorothy in his wake. A crow shot past overhead, squawking harshly, as if agreeing with his sister's unsolicited comments. Yes, there were obstacles, William admitted begrudgingly to himself. They were perhaps insurmountable ones, yet they seemed unjust—even irrelevant—when compared to the pull Lucy had on his very spirit. He would continue to see the governess. And, if the plan that had come to him in the middle of the night were to work out, then he and Samuel would soon have enough money in hand to ease their financial plight.

"You must talk to your young lady," Dorothy said as she caught up with him. "Explain your circumstances."

"Dorothy, I already have," he said. "I've explained my situation. She knows I'm a humble poet."

"Does she know about your time in France with Annette? Or where your shillings go every month? Does she know that the Home Office currently suspects you of being a French spy? That many of our neighbors believe the same thing? Is she aware that I am, without any choice, dependent upon you for my existence? And that we'll soon be without a place to live?" Dorothy stopped to catch her breath, seeming to realize she had over-stepped her sisterly counsel. Her face softened. She laid a hand upon his arm. "William, go to her ... talk to her ... explain. If she's half the person you believe her to be, she'll understand there can be no future for the two of you. I am so, so sorry."

William clenched his jaw and kept his peace. After they had walked for a few minutes in silence, he regained some humor. "Dorothy, one of your most endearing qualities is your reluctance to voice your opinion."

A tinge of color returned to Dorothy's face. She smiled. "And how would you survive without my meddling advice?"

William laughed in spite of his troubles. He knew his sister's opinions were well-intentioned, and common sense told him she was right; if Lucy knew everything about his circumstances, she would in all likelihood run from him as quickly as he had run from the hounds.

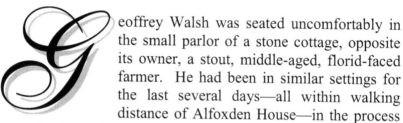eoffrey Walsh was seated uncomfortably in the small parlor of a stone cottage, opposite its owner, a stout, middle-aged, florid-faced farmer. He had been in similar settings for the last several days—all within walking distance of Alfoxden House—in the process of gathering evidence against Wordsworth. He scribbled an entry into his notebook.

A younger man and woman sat at the table, fanning smoke from their faces as their employer sucked on the end of a pipe. The farmer spoke, responding to Walsh's earlier question, "Wordsworth started a fight at the King's Head Inn with Ben and Walt Sutton. Broke Ben's hand and Walt's nose, and that ain't no easy thing ta do. The Suttons' be strong as bulls an' wicked as a pus-filled boil." The man laughed and added, "Ya can bet Wordsworth ain't seen the last of Ben and Walt; that's sure as the Devil himself."

The girl named Penny said, "Tommy 'ere an' I seen Wordsworth talkin' to some odd lookin' strangers."

Tommy nodded so vigorously that Walsh thought his thin neck might be in danger of breaking. "Yes sir. It were in the middle of the night, too."

Penny grasped Tommy's arm. "What God-fearing person would be fightin' in pubs an' traipsin' about in the dark?"

Walsh recalled Wordsworth's thin, aesthetic demeanor. He found it difficult to imagine the poet starting a brawl with two brutes and coming out the winner. Maybe he hadn't given the man enough credit. It brought to mind the old axiom: *Never underestimate the enemy.* Wordsworth might be a dangerous adversary. He wrote the names Ben and Walt Sutton in his notebook.

"That ain't the half of it," the farm owner said. "We all seen Wordsworth talkin' ta a foreign lookin' stranger down at Bridgwater Bay a fortnight ago."

Penny lowered her voice. "We sneaked up on 'em an' listened fer awhile."

Walsh's eyes narrowed. "What did you hear?"

"It was hard ta make out," Tommy said, "but it sounded like they was talkin' about a nosy spy."

"I heard it, too," the farmer said. "But they didn't call him nosy spy, they called him spy *Nosy*. A Frenchie, if ya ask me."

Walsh's lips curled with satisfaction. He wrote in his notebook; *a spy named Nosy.*

The farmer continued, "The Wordsworths are partial ta them frogs. I heard tell he lived in France fer a year or more. Ya can bet he was up to no good."

Tommy continued nodding, idiot-like. "They said things about King George that no loyal Englishman would say."

"What kind of things?"

"That he were mad as a March hare and belonged in an asylum."

Walsh hesitated to write down that piece of information, as it was a loosely held secret George III had been mentally unstable for years. "Anything else?"

"They never go ta church." Penny's mouth turned down with disapproval. "Not once since they been 'ere."

"An' that woman he be living with? She ain't no sister at all," Tommy said. "They hold hands in public."

"Ya can wager a gold Crown they do more than that," Penny said with a smirk. Then, to confirm her suspicions, she added, "An' she talks French."

Yes, he too, had heard the sister speaking French at the fair. He wrote the information he had gathered in his notebook, then asked, "Who do you believe she is?"

"Ya ever seen a picture of Josephine, General Bonaparte's wife?" asked Penny. "She's her spittin' image. She be a Frenchie alright, maybe even kin."

ucy and the children had been summoned to the library, where they awaited the Squire's arrival. Just minutes ago, Squire and Mrs. Hawkins had returned from their day of shopping in Nether Stowey. Now Lucy was dreading the thought that the Squire might have purchased something for her. *How dare he put her in this awkward position?* She rubbed her hands together, feeling her palms moist with perspiration. Emily and Henry bounced up and down beside her on the library's brown leather couch, trying to contain their excitement as they awaited their father's momentary entrance, along with his promised gifts. Lucy recalled the Squire's words when he left this morning; *"Something special from me to ya."*

She shuddered. *What could the Squire possibly be thinking, buying a present for her? What would the other servants say? What would Mrs. Hawkins and Mrs. Tennant*

think? It was an unpleasant situation, and one over which she had absolutely no control. Lucy imagined bolting from the room, running from the manor house and not stopping until she reached Bristol Bay. The view of the ocean had always calmed her, and she longed for it now.

The children fidgeted restlessly, staring at the door. Finally, they heard footsteps approaching, and sprang to their feet, squealing with delight. A moment later, Squire Hawkins strode into the room carrying three gaily wrapped presents. The children's eyes lit up as he placed the gifts on top of his large desk.

Emily rushed over and stared at the pretty boxes, her hands hovering above them in expectation. "Which one is mine?"

"Is the big one for me?" Henry asked, jostling his sister aside as he came up beside her.

The Squire grinned like a mischievous little boy. "What makes ya think any of them be for ya?"

Emily struck a coy pose, batting her eyelashes. "Papa! Please. Tell us."

Henry searched the packages, looking for a tag with his name on it. "Which one did ya get for me?"

The Squire peered down at them and then looked to Lucy with mock solemnity. "Miss Lucy, did they learn their studies well today?"

"Yes, Sir," she responded, keeping her gaze on the children.

The Squire glanced at the anticipatory expressions on his children's faces, and tantalized them by hesitating a few more seconds, then said, "The one in gold wrapping is fer ya, Emily. An' the blue one is yers, Henry."

The children yelped and tore at the wrappings like ravenous bear cubs savaging a hare. Henry opened his present first, removing several hand-painted toy soldiers. "Oh, goody! Soldiers," he said, displaying them for everyone's benefit. "Best I've ever seen. Look at them kilts and red coats."

"They be the 48th Royal Scots Fusiliers an' Twenty-first Foot," the Squire said. "Fought with distinction under the Earl of Marlborough at the Battle of Blenheim in 1704."

Emily lifted a little doll from its carton. "Oh, Papa. She's so beautiful." She rummaged in the box and found fashionable changes of clothes. "Look at these dresses!"

The Squire beamed. "Made in Italy. Cost a pretty penny, she did. Nothin' but the best fer the family." He picked up the last present, wrapped in gold paper and tied with a white lace ribbon. He looked at Lucy and held it out in front of her. "Told ya I'd bring ya somethin' special, Lucy."

"Oh, no, Sir," she said quickly, feeling her cheeks color as she stared at the expensively wrapped package. "I didn't want anything, Sir."

"Take it," he insisted.

Not wishing to make a scene, she reluctantly reached for the gift.

"Open it," Emily said.

Henry took his eyes off the brightly-painted lead soldiers for a moment. "Yes, open it, Miss Lucy."

She warily untied the bow and removed the ribbon and wrapping paper. Opening the carton's lid, she grimaced as she looked at its contents.

"Take it out," the Squire said. "It's not gonna bite ya."

Lucy tentatively lifted out a long, blue shirt-like garment.

"'Tis an artist's smock," the Squire said proudly. "I'm told ya wear it over yer dress to keep the paint splatters off."

In spite of her apprehensions, Lucy was intrigued. *A painter's smock! How appropriate ... for an inappropriate act.*

"Put it on," Henry said.

With help from Emily, Lucy slipped the smock over her dress and turned to a mirror to see her reflection. *It was actually something she needed. But how infuriating that he was the one to give it to her.*

"Ya look like a real artist now," Henry said.

"An' that she be." The Squire beamed like a gambler who had just placed money on a clever bet. "Lucy, me walls are covered with old paintin's of me wifes' relatives, I need a picture of meself fer the family. I want ya to paint me image to hang above the fireplace."

Lucy blushed, but not from embarrassment. This was an obvious ploy to gain her good graces and he was shamelessly manipulating her. She was being offered a rare opportunity to paint a member—albeit a poor example—of the upper class. Her painting, if she accepted the assignment, would hang in Hawkins Manor, where it could be seen by the Squire's guests. It would be an opportunity to perhaps gain some commissions. Lucy's eyes flitted to the gilt-framed ancestors on the walls. She raised a judicious eye as she studied the artistic style and workmanship of the paintings. The compositions, brushstrokes, and renderings of facial features were almost amateurish. She could certainly paint a better likeness of the Squire, even though portraits were not her chosen subject. Lucy was tempted to accept his offer, but knew that being in close proximity to the Squire for hours at a time would simply be foolish. "Sir," she said with slight disappointment in her voice, "I'm a landscape artist. I don't believe I'm the right person to do your likeness."

The Squire scoffed. "Yer an artist, aren't ya? Ya paint one thing, ya can paint another. And I want ya to paint me likeness. Yer ta start tonight."

Lucy was startled. "Tonight, Sir?"

The Squire nodded. "Yes. After ya put Emily an' Henry ta bed, yer ta come here and paint me image for an hour every night 'til it be finished."

Her breath caught in her throat. Being alone with the Squire at night when he would surely be drunk was an ordeal she didn't wish to contemplate. She had no experience in handling the advances of men, certainly none as crude as the Squire.

"I know 'tis extra work. I'll be givin' ya a new shillin' every night."

Lucy's stomach tightened. *Molly had been right. The old lecher was bent on seducing her or worse.* She avoided a response, removing the smock and folding it over her arm as she tried to think of a polite way to reject his offer.

"What be the matter?" the Squire asked. "I won't bite ya, ya know," he added with a disarming smile.

Her mind raced. *At the moment he looked far from dangerous. In fact, when the Squire was sober, as he was now, he almost appeared to be gentle—never a gentleman—but gentle. But when he became inebriated, he went out of control and she didn't know what he might do. Would he be foolish enough to try to molest her here in the library? If he did, she would make him live to regret it. She would scream and bite!*

Lucy gained confidence from the fact that fear of waking his wife and the entire household would protect her from his advances.

She needed time to think and pleaded, "Sir. I will attempt to paint your portrait but if you don't mind, would it be possible to start tomorrow night?"

His smile dropped. "What fer?"

Before she could respond, he added, "No, Miss Lucy, it would not be possible. We start tonight."

The Squire ended the conversation by turning his attention to Henry who was busily lining up toy soldiers on the floor.

Lucy tried to keep her aversion to the man from showing as she replaced the smock in its box and gathered up the wrappings from the floor.

She noticed that the Squire was standing on the last remaining piece of wrapping paper. *Had he stepped on it on purpose? She wouldn't put anything past him.*

"Excuse me, Sir," she said, indicating his shoe. The Squire didn't move. Instead, he stared at her for a disquieting moment. Finally, lifting his foot, he said, "Ya'll not be late now, ya hear?"

"Yes, Sir," she replied. Staying as far from him as she could manage, while still being able to reach the scrap, she grabbed it and moved away, as quickly as a mouse darts from a Tom cat. The Squire chuckled.

Lucy fumed. *He had done that on purpose!* She picked up her present and, taking the wrappings under her arm, left the room.

As she walked down the hallway, she was distraught; the thought of being alone with the Squire was frightening; and in spite of her willingness to scream and fight to protect herself, she could easily be overpowered and silenced while he forced himself upon her. *What could she do? She would have to think of some way to fend him off or else she could very well end up being disgraced.*

❧ CHAPTER FORTY-EIGHT ❦

oonlight walks were a custom William had enjoyed ever since establishing his residence in Somerset. More often than not, Dorothy would join him, and they would stroll the countryside lanes, conversing about nature and poetry, as well as the events of the world. Tonight, Dorothy had stayed home, which was fine with William, as he needed to be alone.

He thought back to his last conversation with Lucy, interrupted by the boisterous arrival of the Hawkins family and their unruly hounds, and realized his next opportunity to see her again would be almost a week away, on the following Sunday. Waiting that long was more than he could bear. And, because of that, he walked the road to Hawkins Hill, drawn by a desire to be close to her.

Now, having stood for some time at the base of the hill, gazing up at the ungainly manor house—where candlelight still glowed through the windows—he whispered, *"Miss Sims* ...

Lucy, I am standing here so near you ... yet you have never felt so far away. What are you doing at this moment?"

The shriek of a night bird pierced the stillness as it darted overhead. He watched it fly, across the road and down to the granary, where moonlight illuminated its broken walls. Remembering the courtyard and the roofless mill house with its lingering beauty, he moved toward it, compelled by an urge to write of these feelings.

William crawled over the crumbling stone wall and dropped into the courtyard. Seeing it for the first time in moonlight, the structure reminded him of a ruined church, but instead of statuary to grace its interior, there were trees, and, here and there, flowers among mossy stones. God would be pleased. He exhaled and began to walk, his breath forming a mist that trailed after him like a flight of translucent butterfly wings.

Passing an arch in which a door hung half-askew from broken hinges, he wondered how many years had gone by since men had labored in the mill, grinding wheat and barley. *How many of them were still alive today? Had anyone of them found a life of fulfillment? Perhaps fulfillment was an illusion for all mankind.*

Locating a flat area, he spread his cloak upon the cobblestones and sat, withdrawing his journal from the satchel he carried. With pencil poised, he looked about, wondering if Lucy might ever have wandered here to meditate on her own.

A dark shadow glided silently overhead. William recognized a large owl. He watched it bank away and then circle back, embarking on a low, feathery approach, as quiet as a newborn-baby's breath. It was no doubt hunting for rabbits or field mice, offering no warning before silently swooping down with deadly talons. William contemplated the contradictory elements of nature: its exhilarating beauty, and its depressing cruelty. He understood that man, too, was burdened with the conflicting dynamics of good and evil. Then his thoughts again turned to Lucy: *He hoped his obsession for her was not driving him to unethical lengths, nor his interest lending her false hope of a lasting relationship. Could there be a future for them together?*

William concluded that resolving any of this would require that he be completely honest with Lucy. When they met again, he would explain to her—in detail—all the reasons for which he would not be a good candidate for marriage. And then he would let her come to her own conclusion; one that would affect both of them for the remainder of their lives.

CHAPTER FORTY-NINE

*L*ucy reluctantly stood before her easel in the Hawkins library, sketching a preliminary drawing of the Squire, who sat in a heavy ornate chair in front of her. He wore the upper half of his best Gentleman's finery. A black silk coat, with gold embroidery on the lapels and cuffs, partially covered a red silk waistcoat. Beneath that, he wore a white shirt with a high frilly collar that seemed to truss his outsized porcine head as if it were being served on a platter. She had had to stifle a laugh when she had first entered the room and observed that, below the man's frippery, he wore his soiled day pants and scuffed boots. *If only he knew how foolish he looked.*

As the pencil flew in her hand she observed that he finished off a tumbler of wine and then poured another drink from a now more-than-half-empty decanter. She glanced to the grandfather clock standing against the wall behind him. It read nearly nine. Her hour with her employer was almost over and, thankfully, he had made no untoward advances. Maybe, she prayed, he was going to act like a gentleman.

"Lucy, ya do a fine image of me and ya'll get a handsome bonus."

"Thank you, Sir. I'm doing my best."

The clock chimed the nine o'clock hour.

The Squire drank off the remainder of his wine and lurched to his feet. "That be all fer tonight. Let me see what ya've done."

He was quite tipsy as he reeled around the easel and edged in close to her to peer at the drawing. He groused, "I be that portly?"

Lucy inhaled the Squire's wine-soured breath and took a step back. "No, Sir. It's the medium. The heavy pencils I use. Once I begin to paint, the oils will slim you down to size."

He nodded, accepting her subterfuge. "Ya think I be a good-looking chap?"

Lucy coughed, choking back a laugh: She bit her bottom lip, controlling the urge. *How could she get out of this without insulting the man?* She finally said, "It's not for me to say, Sir."

He stomped his foot. "Yes or no?"

Cornered, she answered as diplomatically as she could. "I'm sure Lady Hawkins thinks you are, Sir."

He burst out laughing. "Yer a smart one, Lucy Sims." He reached into his pocket and withdrew a coin. He seized her hand and pressed the silver piece into her palm, holding it there. "Here's the shillin' I promised."

His lingering touch sent waves of disgust through her.

"I want us ta be friends, Lucy. Good friends." Lucy felt him release her hand, but before she could get away, he placed both of his palms upon her shoulders and looked into her wide eyes. "Ya think that be possible?"

She played innocent. "I'm not your equal, Sir. People would talk."

He leaned in close, reeking, "Not if we kept it our little secret."

The repulsive oaf! Lucy pushed his arms aside and ducked out from under his grasp. In fewer than five seconds, she had gathered up her art paraphernalia. Not wishing to provoke a temperamental drunkard, she offered, "There are no secrets at Hawkins house. Beth would surely notice and I wouldn't want to hurt her."

The Squire's face flushed. "Don't ya worry about the servants blabbering, especially Beth. She be moving out soon, then ya can have her bedroom all ta yourself. I want ya ta think on it. Such an arrangement would be ta your benefit … ya can be sure of that."

"Yes, Sir." She turned and feeling his eyes boring into her as she strode to the door, escaped into the hallway.

Entering the great room, Lucy hurried across the polished hardwood floor to the closet under the main stairway, and flung the door open. She deposited her painting basket and easel inside, closed the panel and crossed toward the stairway to the kitchen. She had to get away from this house! After retrieving her cape, she threw open the back door, and taking the steps two at a time, hastened out into the night.

ith the full moon to light her path, Lucy ran breathlessly from the rear of the manor house. She swept past the front courtyard, bounded partway down the sloping terrain, and then ran unhesitatingly for the thicket of sycamore and larch, in case the Squire might be meaning to follow. After stopping to catch her breath, she hurried past the glen with its sparkling pond where she had first met William. *It had only been two weeks ago! How quickly one's life could change!*

Through the trees, Lucy spied the ruined walls of the granary. This would be a safer place to walk than the woods, where vagrants sometimes wandered.

Reaching the outer wall, she scaled a waist-high section of tumbled stones and entered the courtyard. The night was still as Lucy moved through the ruins, her eyes probing the shadows, alert for trespassers.

A few steps further on, a small gasp escaped her as she saw the figure of a man stretched out upon the ground. She retreated quickly behind a section of wall and tried to see more clearly. The man seemed to be asleep, curled up on his cape. Beside him, a journal lay open upon the ground, its white pages reflecting the moonlight. She was wondering what to do when she noticed a walking stick propped against a pile of stones beside him.

She stepped out from the wall and crept closer to the man—*could it be?* Drawn nearer now by a feeling of familiarity, she soon recognized William Wordsworth. Curious, she crept silently forward until she was standing beside him. He looked so peaceful, she dared not speak. Instead, her eyes moved to the journal, where a pencil lay upon an open page. She knelt at his side and silently read: 'An extraordinary maiden, unknown, save to me: A lovely violet by a moss-covered stone————' Here a pencil mark traversed the page, indicating the poet had fallen asleep.

Lucy smiled and turned her attention back to this remarkable man, so different from the unpleasant Squire. She reached out and allowed her fingers to lightly stroke his cheek. His eyes opened—and she drew back, catching her breath.

"Lucy ... ah, Miss Sims." He sat up, so close to her ... silence ... nothing existed between them but the vapor that appeared when the warmth of their breath met the chill of the night. She held his gaze and, in that moment, knew beyond a doubt that she was in love.

William finally spoke. "What fortune has brought you to me?" He raised a hand and gently brushed aside a lock of hair that had fallen across her cheek. Her skin tingled at his touch. His fingertips lingered, caressing her face, and Lucy closed her eyes, savoring the sweetness.

She answered, "I'm afraid it wasn't fortune that brought me here ... life in that house is so oppressive, so ... ." She paused and, deciding not to burden him with her problems, continued, "I was seeking solace. I often come here to think things through. And I found you here. What fortune brought *you* to this granary?"

William explained, "I came here to find inspiration. No, in all honesty, I came here to be near you, which could be the same thing ... I didn't know any other way ... ."

He came to the granary to be near her! *'An extraordinary maiden', he had written.* *Was she the inspiration?* *Surely, there must be more he had to say.* Her lovely, curved lips turned upward at the corners. "Tell me, Mr. Wordsworth, why would you come here to be near me?"

For a moment he didn't answer, then spoke, "This is an act of fate, Lucy—if I may call you that, I had the need to speak to you, and you have come to me. You see, I have to tell you some things about myself before you and I become closer, although I feel it is becoming too late for that: You see, I am not the person you believe me to be."

Lucy doubted this, but beckoned William to explain. "Please tell me anything you wish. And yes, call my Lucy." She seated herself next to him.

"All right. Well, how should I start? I am actually a very simple man and I lead a simple existence. I have, fortunately or unfortunately, dedicated my life to poetry: It's not an easy life. I am haunted by a unique perception of the world and a need to precisely explain it with my pen, ... but I don't believe my poems are like any of the ones your mother read to you."

"In what ways could they be so different?"

William sat back a bit, and took her hands in his— *sending a thrill through her.* He said, "It has to do with my writing style as well as my subject matter. My verse breaks most of the rules set down by other poets. I refuse to follow the accepted standards of their work, to mathematically formulate my words or to rhyme the end of every line with the one that preceded it. I can do that, of course." Lucy understood this departure from tradition—she did the same on her canvases! William continued, "Too, the words I choose to write are universal, easily understood even by those without a formal education. My poems are for the commonplace person ... not for academics and not for the church." William stopped, lifted her hands and lightly kissed them. *She felt a most delectable electric shock.* He paused. "I'm not tiring you?" She shook her head. He continued, "My words describe mostly simple, everyday subjects: farmers, peasants, merchants, and among those, the foolish, the ill, and the eccentrics of the world. I write about clouds and ponds, lichens and even yew-trees."

Lucy was intrigued by this and when he smiled whimsically at her, she realized, with a growing sense of familiarity, that his passions were not that far from her own. When he began to speak again, she hung on his every word. "Flora, fauna and the earth's elements, including all the colors of the rainbow and the darkest seas, are on the palette I draw from. As they are on yours, I believe." Lucy nodded, acknowledging the similarities and his awareness of them. He went on, "To my mind, I render my verse in a pleasing, lyrical manner. But, as you might well imagine, many critics look down their long noses at my poetry. To quote one of my latest reviewers: 'Mr. Wordsworth writes simple, rustic poems, some of them little more than doggerel.'"

Lucy smiled, completely at ease with this gentleman, who was able to affect her so deeply with a simple touch of his hand. She admired his passion for his work and his ability to poke fun at himself. She desperately wished to hear everything he had to say.

William returned her smile. "I'll give you an example, a small piece, of one of the so-called rustic poems I've been working on:

> "'No joyless forms shall regulate
> Our living calendar;
> We from today, my Friend, will date
> The opening of the year.
>
> Love, now a universal birth,
> From heart to heart is stealing;
> From earth to man, from man to earth:
> —It is the hour of feeling.'"

Lucy felt the emotion of his words. "It's beautiful," she said. "I would love to hear more."

"Asking a poet to recite his verse is like asking a cock to crow. You'd soon grow weary of me, and that's the last thing I wish to happen."

She laughed. "I haven't grown weary of you yet."

"That's because I've given you the impression I'm an independent soul who wanders about the countryside without a care in the world. Unfortunately, I have my share of woes. It's only fair that I warn you of some of them."

"You don't have to explain yourself to me."

"I'm afraid I do. You see, we are becoming entangled, you and I, and I must be sure you are aware of my past: And, the more you know of me, the less you may wish to see me again."

Lucy raised his hand and brushed her lips across the back of it, which made him smile. "There is always that possibility."

His smile faded and he confessed, "I've led an unusual life by most standards. My liaisons with women have not always turned out for the best." He must have seen her quizzical look, for he added quickly, "No, I am not married."

Lucy blushed. *He had read her thoughts.*

"Although, once I came very close to having a wife."

"You don't need to explain," Lucy offered, not sure she wished to hear more.

William's voice tightened, as if the memory gave him pain. "I'm afraid this is the part you must know. Seven years ago, while I was traveling through France, I met a woman, named Annette Vallon, in the city of Orleans. She was fluent in English and I, ever fascinated by language, was keen to improve my French ... she became my tutor. As the lessons progressed, we became friends and then ... lovers. I was twenty-one at the time; she was twenty-five. Our affair lasted several months..." He hesitated, then blew the remainder of the sentence out with one quick exhale, "...we have a daughter from that relationship."

Her surprise must surely have shown on her face. Silent for some time, she finally remarked, "But you said you weren't married."

"And I am not. I fully intended to do the honorable thing and marry Annette, but circumstances, and a subsequent war between our countries, made it impossible for me to live or find employment in France. You see, I had no money and no opportunities. Forced to return home, I hoped to find some kind of livelihood so that I could send for them. But, despite my efforts—and those of others—I was unable to find a position with a wage sufficient to support a family. Unfortunately, the ability to write poetry has always been my only talent. And so, when the war with France broke out, we were instantly cut off from one another. Months, and then years, went by. We corresponded, but we were unable to ever get back together again."

"And that's the last you saw of them?"

"No. There was a break in hostilities several years later, and the government allowed travel between our two countries. I booked passage to France, where she and I were reunited. Things had changed between us. We were old acquaintances who had come together with great hopes and expectations. But, the love we had had for one another no longer existed; perhaps it never had. All thoughts of marriage were dismissed by both of us. We parted as friends. We're still friends."

"How sad for your daughter. Where is she now?"

"Believe me, Anne Caroline is not unhappy. On the contrary, she has a wonderful zest for life and is surrounded by her mother's loving family in France. I keep in touch with her through correspondence and I help to pay for her upbringing and education." He stopped and let that sink in, and then rushed on, "And, so that you'll know everything about me, I also support my sister, Dorothy, who shares my home. That, too, is a problem. It's a home from which we are about to be evicted: My landlord disapproves of my outspoken political opinions."

Lucy's mind could hardly take it all in. She was relieved that William was not a married man, but his revelations were startling, to say the least! She managed, "It doesn't seem fair he should evict you for that."

She felt him squeeze her hand as he added, "It's worse than just this..." He looked Lucy in the eye, quite adorably. "...I've been summoned to the Home Office to defend myself against charges of radical activities against the Crown—charges drummed up by some who don't like me. If my defense is unsuccessful, it is possible I could be hung. I am innocent, of course."

They were both silent for a time, William seemingly afraid of the effect of his words, and Lucy contemplating them. Soon, she heard herself say, "I can't explain why, but I believe in you... ."

"Thank you for trusting me: You must know I am no anarchist. While I'm no admirer of the monarchy, I'm not a violent man, nor do I condone political insurrection. All I want is the freedom to express my ideas and the chance to make a living as a poet. But I'm failing at both. So, as you can see, I have very little to offer a woman as lovely as you."

His words, self-deprecating and painfully candid, had upset her, yet touched her deeply. She felt no change in her bond to him. "William, you have more good qualities than you are aware of. You're a gentleman, one who is thoughtful, intelligent, honest, and kind."

"I try to be a better man than I am," he said, "but I often fail ... quite often."

"We all fail at times. It's part of life. I admire you for knowing who you are and who you want to be. And I envy you your freedom. How wonderful it must be to travel and see so much of the world."

"Hardly any of that is true, I'm afraid. My freedom is curtailed by my meager purse. And I've seen far too little of the world."

Lucy had read much about travel to foreign cities, but her life, limited to the parish in which she had been born, had never provided her with the opportunity to meet anyone who had actually journeyed further than Bristol or Exeter. "William, tell me where you've traveled and what you've seen."

He appeared to be lost in thought for a moment, but then answered, "I've wandered about England a good bit ... and taken an extensive walking tour of North Wales. I was in France, of course, for two years, and in Germany a few months ago. I may be going there again. I've been to Switzerland and ... that is all. I'm hardly a world traveler."

"It's the universe to me. Is Paris as beautiful as people say?"

"Yes, it is. It's busy and filled with more people than you can imagine—all saying things you can't understand. But, I'd much rather be here now with you than dwell in any faraway places." They sat together in silence for a time, and then William said, "Now it's your turn. Tell me about Lucy Sims, if you wish to tell me."

"Oh, no," she replied, embarrassed by her provincial life. "There's nothing to say about Lucy Sims. I wish there were. But it's all trivial compared to your..."

"Tell me anyway," he persisted. "I want to know all about you."

Lucy acquiesced and slowly began, "I'm an only child. Both of my parents have passed away and I've lived my whole life within a few miles of Hawkins House."

"You've never traveled beyond this shire?"

"Not yet, but I hope to experience the world one day."

William gave her a long look, then asked, "Would a trip to Germany be of interest to you?"

"I would travel anywhere, but I could never afford any journey."

"Maybe that will change."

"No. Not for a long time, I'm afraid. But I do have an Aunt living in Bath who has offered me room and board. I'm going to accept her offer next year, when I turn eighteen. It's part of my life's master plan. You see, I'm not going to be a governess forever. I'm going to go out into the world and make my own way."

His brows drew together. "I know times are changing, Lucy, but there are very few women able to support themselves without the help of family or, dare I say it, a man."

"You're looking at one who is going to try," she said, her voice steely with determination. "I'm going to join the rarefied ranks of women who are not dependent upon anyone."

William chortled.

Was that skepticism in his tone? Yes, there was a touch of cynicism in those amber eyes. Lucy's eyes sparked fire. She argued, "I'll accomplish it by overcoming male prejudice, like that evidenced just now by your less-than-honorable laugh at my expense. I'm not expecting it to be easy. Nor am I naïve. I'm well aware it is a man's world and I'm prepared to sign my paintings 'George' or 'Thomas' or even 'Genghis Kahn' if I have to, until I've established a clientele. And then, after my skills are recognized, I'll reveal to the world that the newly-famous artist is a female—me."

William roared heartily and said, "Bravo! You are quite the most remarkable young woman I have ever met. And, please, while my laugh may have sounded a touch incredulous it was certainly not meant to be derisive. I really do wish you success."

"Really? Then you think I might have a chance?"

"Lucy Sims, I believe there's no force on earth that can stop you from becoming whatever you wish to be."

"Then I take back all the bad thoughts your laughter evoked in me."

"And I apologize for not having more faith in you. The more I am getting to know you, the more special you become."

❧❧❧ ❧❧❧ ❧❧❧

William and Lucy talked on through the evening without a thought to the passage of time. She reveled in the flowering relationship, one that was blossoming so extensively that she might be blending with the lovely blooms all about her. At a lull in the conversation, she looked up and noticed William's expression had become serious. His eyes were boring into hers … searching her very being.

As William leaned forward, Lucy closed her eyes and a moment later felt the warmth of his lips pressing gently upon hers. A quiver, then a tantalizing heat rushed delightfully through her. He kissed her again, ever so lightly, and then ... she responded, pressing back upon his full mouth, sharing a bouquet of emotions that transcended this earthly life, and yet was the very heart of it.

When they drew apart, she was breathless.

"You are so, so very rare," William said, his voice filled with awe at the discovery of this hidden treasure. "And you're not even aware of it, I think?"

In response Lucy kissed his lips slowly, lovingly ... then, without warning, her heart clutched painfully. A sense of alarm, of dread, and then of humiliation, raced through her as she recognized the telltale signs. A red aura materialized before her eyes, blocking William's image. She fell backwards, her body jerking. *Oh God, no! Please, not now.* Lucy wanted to run—to hide. But there was no time. Her breathing began to come in gasps. A powerful radiance burned scarlet holes in her sight, blinding her with its growing intensity.

William stilled and, watching closely, conveyed surprise and puzzlement. "Lucy, what is it?"

She raised her hands to wave off the fiery intensity that distorted her vision. Heartsick, she moaned. "William... ."

He clutched her hand, his face pinched with concern. "Tell me, what is happening? What is it? What is the matter?"

The muscles in her arms and legs quivered as the seizure took its terrifying hold. She was wretched as her illness bared itself. "Oh, William, I'm ... I'm so sorry." Another spasm set fire to nerve endings, making control of her limbs impossible.

"What is it? Lucy! Talk to me."

The tremors intensified. She struggled to speak. "I ... can ... not ... ." She gasped and began to writhe. " ... hoold me ... ho ... mee."

Momentarily bewildered, William quickly rallied and took Lucy into his arms, embracing her. Her spasms progressed into convulsions. She could not speak.

"I've got you, Lucy. I won't let go. I'll take care of you. Try not to talk. Try to stay calm until the spasms pass."

Lucy's eyes rolled up into her head; her body quivered and jerked. He held her closely for a long time, pressing her to his breast until the contortions began to ebb. Slowly, the fit began to recede and, after a long while, she regained some lucidity. As her vision began to clear, she stared at him with pain in her eyes. "Will ... ." she whispered.

He exhaled. "Don't try to speak. You gave me quite a scare."

She rested, then, until she had recovered a bit more. With a weak voice she said, "I have ... falling sickness. Thank you ... staying with me."

"I could never leave you."

"Some believe ... possessed by the devil."

William snorted. "Superstitious fools without an ounce of education. From what I've read, falling sickness isn't the proper name for your condition. Doctors in London have a medical term for it ... epilepsy, from the Greek word *epilambanein*, which means to seize upon or attack. Many famous people have suffered from it ... even Julius Caesar."

Lucy didn't speak, but he must have read the curiosity in her eyes. "You have a malady of the nerves. It comes and goes from time to time without warning. No one quite knows why."

Feeling drowsy from the effects of the seizure, she fought to stay awake. She said with effort, "How are you more learned than my doctor?"

He shrugged. "I read widely and, you remember, I love words."

Her eyelids drooped. *She was so tired.* "How long does one live with epilepsy?"

He held onto her, comforting her. "I believe you have a long life ahead of you, Lucy. I've read it's a malady one sometimes outgrows. Hopefully, in a year or two, it will be but a memory."

Lucy nodded, resting her head on his shoulder, and then slipped off to sleep.

❧ CHAPTER FIFTY ONE ❧

 s the first song of larks drifted into Lucy's consciousness, she opened her eyes. For a moment she was disoriented by a sky filled with dimming stars. Then she felt William's warm breath on her neck. He was curled next to her beneath the warmth of their cloaks, cradling her as gently as a quail's egg. Only then did she remember their chance meeting, her seizure and his kindness. She turned to study his face in the soft light. A moment later she realized something was amiss; *it was far too bright for moonlight!* She looked over her shoulder to the roofless walls of the granary where the first vermilion streaks of dawn were lighting the horizon.

"Oh, no," she cried, panic setting in.

William awoke with a start. "What is it?"

Lucy sat up, catching her breath. "It's morning! Everyone will be rising. I must leave at once."

William stood and placed Lucy's cape about her shoulders, helping her to her feet. "Come. I'll accompany you home."

They threaded their way through the shadowy courtyard and when they reached a low point in the wall, William assisted her over the tumbled stones.

"William, I have to run," she said.

"Can you? Are you all right?" When she nodded, he urged, "Well, go! I'm with you."

They dashed off, he keeping pace with her as they raced along the path where the first light of morning cast an orange glow upon the tops of the trees. They passed the pond where they'd first met, and then came to the road at the bottom of Hawkins Hill, where she halted, panting for breath. "William, I had better go on from here alone."

He nodded, taking her hand, holding on. "We must see each other again... ."

Her stomach quivered. "I don't know when... ."

"Tomorrow night?"

Her eyes darted toward the horizon, now a blushing radiance. "Yes."

"At the granary?"

She squeezed his hand. "I'll be late, at least an hour after I put the children to bed."

"I'll wait."

They kissed softly—there was little time—but there was urgency in it. Then she gathered her skirts up and sprinted away. As Lucy raced up the slope through the tall, dewy heather, two pheasants exploded out of the grass, squawking and flapping away. She cringed at their noisy clamor, praying she would reach the manor before the household staff rose to begin their morning chores.

Moments later, with her heart in her throat, Lucy eased open the kitchen door and peered in. It was dark and quiet. She stepped inside, knowing it would only be minutes before the cook or his assistant entered to kindle the fires. She breezed through the room and down the hallway.

Molly and Mary were asleep when she crept into the bedroom and tiptoed across the creaky floor. Lucy tossed her cape on the peg above the bed, untied her bodice and wiggled out of her dress. She was slipping on another when she heard a

189

pair of feet slap against the floor. She spun about to face a smirking Molly.

"Where've ya been?"

Taking a deep breath, Lucy thought quickly and replied, "I couldn't sleep. I went for a walk."

"That be some walk. Yer bed ain't been slept in all night."

Lucy picked up a hairbrush and ran it briskly through her hair. "It's no concern of yours."

"Ya been with the Squire, ain't that so?"

The question caught her off guard, and she laughed. "No, I haven't."

The girl smirked. "Yeh, sure. Feed that tale ta Beth after I tell her what I seen."

Lucy retorted, "You haven't seen a thing. And keep your wicked gossip to yourself."

Molly sneered. "Don't lose yer knickers. I'm just having fun wit ya. Me lips are sealed. It don't bother me none what ya two do under the blankets."

"I was not with the Squire!"

"Right ya are, dearie. Ya was up all night drinking tea."

Lucy clutched the hairbrush, fighting down an urge to throw it at the shrewish girl. On the other side of the room Mary snorted, rolled over and peeked from under her bedcovers. "If you two are jabbering about tea, I'll have a cuppa."

Lucy's anger dissolved as the older woman smiled at her.

"Good morning, Mary. Yes, I'm just leaving for the kitchen. I'll bring you a cup."

Molly flashed a buttery smile. "Me too, dearie?"

"Sorry, Molly. With two cups, I'm afraid I might trip and spill one over your head."

Molly made a face at her as Mary chortled. Lucy turned for the door and left the two maids getting out of their beds.

fter an uneventful breakfast and morning tutoring session, Lucy lounged on the grass with her eyes closed, listening to the birds' songs and the children's laughter coming from the sunny incline where they played. She had given them an hour's break from their lessons while she painted and then had put her brushes away early, hoping for a quick nap. But thoughts of William, her tenuous situation with the Squire and her uncertain future, pirouetted in her head like dancing ballerinas. Each image brought its own set of problems and worries that made a nap impossible, and yet she was exhausted. A sudden stillness prompted her to open an eye. She glimpsed the children who were sneaking up on her. Their mischievous looks told her they planned to wake her so she would play with them. Determined not to be bothered, she closed her eye and pretended to be asleep, hoping if she ignored them they would go away and allow her a few more minutes to herself.

Henry giggled. "Let's wake her up."

"You do it," Emily whispered, then noticed the canvas on their governess's easel. "Oh, look at her painting, all the flowers."

Henry glanced at it and shrugged. "So?"

"She's never painted flowers before. You know what this means?"

Lucy's eye opened a centimeter peering through her lashes. The children were now standing before the easel.

Henry shrugged. "Means naught to me."

"You don't know anything! It means Miss Lucy be in love."

"Don't be daft. Flowers don't mean love."

Lucy closed her eye. *How could Emily have possibly associated the changes in her painting with her love for William?* She smiled inwardly. Emily was indeed a perceptive child.

"It ain't just the flowers, stupid," Emily said. "It be the whole painting."

Henry grunted. "I'm gonna come right out and ask her, I am."

"Maybe we should let her be."

"Shh."

With her eyes tightly shut, Lucy waited to hear more, but for a long moment the only sound was the rustling of grass. *What was Henry up to?* She felt a gnat or a fly on her nose. She brushed it away, still pretending to be asleep. She heard Henry giggle. Another fly landed on her cheek, tickling her. Her eyes popped open. Henry knelt beside her, a furry thistle in his hand. Both children broke out laughing. Even she couldn't keep from smiling. She stood and teased, "Henry Hawkins, I'm going to get you for that."

Henry sprang to his feet, prepared to run. "First, can I ask you a question, Miss Lucy?"

"If you must, Henry, but it may be your last."

He hesitated, his cheeks flushing a bright crimson.

Emily elbowed him in the ribs. "Go on, Henry. Ask her."

Henry sucked air into his round little chest, gathering courage. "Be you in love, Miss Lucy?"

"Why would you ask such a personal thing?"

His face turned even redder, and his eyes dropped to stare at his shoes. "Ain't seen you paint so pretty a'fore now. Emily says it's because you be in love."

She turned to Emily, who nodded affirmatively.

"You little rascals. If I could persuade the two of you to pay as much attention to your studies as you do to my painting, you would both end up with scholarships to Hawkshead and maybe even Cambridge when you're grown."

Henry sneered. "Haw!"

Undaunted by her governess's evasions, Emily crossed her arms; her expression was one of determination. "Seriously, Miss Lucy, be you in love?"

"*Are* you in love?" she corrected. It was amazing to hear the children ask the very question she had pondered for days, but now knew to be true. Lucy didn't quite know what to say, so she picked up her paintbrush, dipped its tip into a daub of bright red oil and began painting. "What if I were to make this landscape even prettier? Would that tell you anything?"

Emily and Henry exchanged glances as Lucy applied a series of dazzling red roses to her landscape.

"You were right, Emily," Henry said. "She be doodle-headed."

Lucy's brush continued to sweep across the canvas, brightening the dark areas, adding warmth and color, as she celebrated the love she felt within.

❧ CHAPTER FIFTY–THREE ✦

*G*eoffrey Walsh stepped down from his rented buggy into the unkempt front yard of Ben and Walt Sutton's small, one-story stone farmhouse. He grimaced at the neglected shrubbery, weeds and vines that covered assorted rubbish. The brothers, he had heard, were bachelors who lived alone: It was no wonder; no female he knew would consider living in such squalor. He surmised that the inside of the house was as disorderly at its exterior.

Beyond the cottage's low sloping roofline, he could see a faded, two-story wooden barn. Walsh tied his horse to a post, and was making his way to the front steps, when he heard a bloodcurdling scream. The sound raised the hair on the back of his neck, stopping him in his tracks. His hand flew to his flintlock while his eyes darted about the property, searching for a woman in distress. Hearing sounds coming from the barn area, he scurried around to the side of the house and pulled his pistol from beneath his coat. He stopped near the end of the wall to check the flintlock's primer pan. Satisfied the weapon was ready to fire, Walsh edged closer to the corner. Another scream pierced the air. This time he recognized the pig's squeal and breathed out, releasing pent up anxiety.

When Walsh peered around the corner of the cottage, he eyed two burly men in their thirties, hopefully the Suttons. They were stripped to the waist, splattered with blood, and wielded sharp knives; they were in the process of slaughtering three full-grown pigs. The animals had been hung from ropes and hoisted above the ground by their front hooves.

One of the pigs had already had its throat slit, its carcass sliced open from neck to anus. It was being eviscerated by one of the brothers. The second Sutton, his right hand wrapped in a crude splint, cut at the pig's entrails with his good hand. He ripped the viscera out and threw the guts into two buckets; one for usable innards and the other for offal. The second pig, having just had its' throat slit, was in its death throes. The third animal, uncut as yet, squealed, staring at the butchers with rolling, terrified eyes.

Both Suttons were covered in gore up to their elbows, as if their hands and forearms had been dipped into a pail of scarlet paint.

Walsh grimaced, expressing his distaste for the bloody tableau as he holstered his pistol. He moved into the yard, purposefully kicking a pile of stones to announce his arrival.

The brothers spun around, knives in hand. One of them, with black and blue marks under his eyes and his nose quite flattened, demanded, "Who the 'ell are ya?"

Walsh's adrenalin surged at the man's confrontational tone, and he would have gladly shot him between his bruised eyes if it weren't for the fact that he was an agent of the Crown, sworn to uphold the law. He swallowed his irritation. "My name is Geoffrey Walsh. I'm a writer for the Bristol Daily News. I'm here to write an article on the poets in your area. I've been told you might be able to assist me with some background on Mr. William Wordsworth."

"Wordsworth!" the man with the bandaged hand exclaimed. "Thet French lovin' sack of dung! He's an enemy of England! Write thet in yer damn paper."

His brother spat on the ground. "He's a traitor and a spy. Next time we see 'im we'll do the Crown's work an' execute 'im." He slashed the air with his knife. "Gut 'im like one of our swine."

Walsh eyed the two men warily. Bullies, he could clearly see, and dangerous ones. Allowing them to kill Wordsworth would undermine his efforts; all of his labor would come to naught. There would be no adulation from the Home Office and no raise in his position or salary. He couldn't allow these two brutes to destroy his plans. Walsh hesitated to say anything for a moment as he mulled over his options. *He dare not inform the Suttons he was an agent of the Crown. If word reached Wordsworth that he was being investigated, the poet would surely flee the country before Walsh had gathered enough evidence to arrest him. But how to keep the two brothers at bay until he could discover Wordsworth's treasonous activities?* He finally said, "It would be a waste to see the two of you good English lads hung for the murder of a traitor like Wordsworth. If what you say is true, let me expose the spying bastard in the Bristol Daily News. Give me incriminating evidence of his guilt and I'll see to it he's prosecuted by the Crown and hung by the neck. As a reward, you'll both be invited to the hanging and the newspaper will compensate each of you with ten pounds sterling." He was pleased when he saw the Suttons' mouths fall open. They looked stunned. Ten pounds apiece would be a fortune to them. He added, "But, there's a condition. While I'm gathering evidence from other sources I'll need assurances from both of you that you will not accost Wordsworth in any way."

The brothers exchanged glances, obviously imagining what they could do with the money. Ben turned to him and said, "Fer ten guineas apiece we'll let the Crown hang the bloody traitor, ya can be sure o' thet."

Walt turned to the live pig wiggling at the end of its rope and with a sudden flash of blade sliced its neck open. Blood spurted like a fountain. Walt grinned and said, "Come around ta the 'ouse an' share a drink, Mr. Walsh. We'll give ya more'n enough information ta hang thet French-lovin' turn coat."

Walsh had to choke back a wicked laugh, pleased with the effect his false promises had had, and disgusted by the sight before him.

wo candelabra, each holding a half dozen burning candles, illuminated the library where Lucy stood before her easel, adding finishing touches to her pencil study of Squire Hawkins. Her eyes flew between the drawing and the Squire who lay, sprawled, in his oversized armchair, sipping wine from a glass. When he had first assumed this supine pose, she had had to squelch the impulse to giggle. The Squire obviously had been trying to look like an aristocrat, a bon vivant perhaps, but he, instead, resembled a beached whale.

Lucy lowered her pencil to study her drawing and, stifling a yawn, took an eraser to the Squire's jowl lines. She thinned his heavy features in an effort to make his likeness more presentable.

The Squire belched and said, "I see the children have been wearing ya out, eh, Lucy?"

"It's not them, Sir. I didn't sleep well last night."

Squire Hawkins struggled up from his chair. "Then enough of this posin'. Have a drink with me, an' off ya go ta yer bed."

"Thank you, Sir, but I don't drink spirits." Yawning again, she placed her pencils and sketching paper into a basket.

The Squire reached for the decanter on the table and poured wine into a second glass. "A wee splash will do ya good. Ya'll sleep like a suckled babe."

Lucy became wary as she watched him cross to stand next to her. He took her hand in his and pressed the tumbler into her fingers. He grinned and held it there with so much force that it frightened her. She pulled her hand free, but was left holding the sloshing glass of wine.

"Come," he said, "sit with me fer a bit an' have a taste." He waddled to the divan and plopped down, patting the cushion beside him. "Sit here. I need ta talk with ya."

Lucy searched her mind for an excuse to refuse him politely, but was at a loss. She hesitated, and observed that a red flush began to darken his features.

"Sit, I say!"

Still she hesitated. *Should she scream or flee?*

He struggled to rise, but the softness of the cushions kept his bulk trapped in the divan. After a moment's exertion, he fell back, panting. He said, almost pleading, "Please sit. I won't bite ya."

Lucy moved forward, hoping she could humor him for a few moments and then leave. She settled on a cushion, sitting as far from the Squire as she could manage.

He slanted toward her and clinked his tumbler against hers. "Now then, ta King George. Drink up. It'll do ya good."

She courteously raised her glass and took a small sip of the tawny fluid. Her tongue recoiled, and her lips curled in disgust.

The Squire laughed. "'Tis something ya'll get used to. Drink a wee bit more."

She shook her head. "It's not to my liking, Sir."

He grunted and edged closer to her. "Have ya thought over me offer of yer own room?"

Lucy attempted to sidle away, but the arm of the couch prodded into her back, limiting further retreat. "Begging your pardon, but I prefer to stay where I am."

The Squire's eyes suddenly blazed with fury. "That's not goin' ta be! Yer ta take Beth's bed. She be moving out at the end of the week."

"Certainly not on my account, Sir."

"Yes, on yer account. 'Tis over between Beth and me."

Lucy rose quickly to her feet. Chin held high, she said, "Sir, I will not be taking Beth's bed, and I have absolutely no intention of becoming your plaything."

The Squire, taken aback by her unexpected display of strength, sputtered, "Ya'll do as I say, or ya'll be seeking new employment. And ya'll be getting no references from me. I can promise ya that."

Lucy glared at him, shaken. *It would be almost impossible to find employment without references, but she wasn't going to allow him to intimidate her.* She squared her shoulders and looked directly into his dark little eyes. "As you wish, Sir. I'm sure Lady Hawkins and the children will understand when I explain my reasons for leaving." She saw color drain from his face. Without waiting for a response, she gathered up her easel and baskets and was at the door when she heard him squeal.

"Wait."

She turned the door handle.

"My dear," he cooed, finally managing to heave his bulk out of the divan. "'Tis a misunderstanding we be having. I'm not asking ya ta be me plaything; I just wanted ya ta have better quarters. Are ya troubled with that?"

Realizing she had been holding her breath, Lucy exhaled and said, "I'm quite happy in the servants' quarters with Mary and Molly, Sir."

He roared at her with the force of a blacksmith's bellows. "Then, damn it, stay where ya be! See if I try to do ya a good deed again." He turned his back on her, staring out the window.

"So, I am not dismissed?"

He turned around, shoulders slumping. "No, yer not."

Lucy stepped into the hallway and closed the door behind her, leaning back against it with a triumphant smile.

*T*he Squire's hands were shaking as he downed his wine and banged the tumbler on the tabletop. *Damn her!* He had not expected the timid governess to become so feisty. *How dare the uppity little tart threaten to tattle to his wife and children!* He poured another glass of wine and gulped half of it straight away, then slumped into his armchair. *He had certainly bungled this opportunity to screw the prettiest of the maids. How was it possible the bitch was turning down an opportunity to better herself? Was she after more than a few shillings and a room of her own? Well, Miss Lucy had better get used to the idea that she was no better than any of the other little quims he'd taken to bed.* The Squire grunted. *He had at least discovered a fiery passion beneath her sweet exterior and that certainly lent an air of excitement to the chase. Other opportunities were certain to present themselves. He would think of a clever way to maneuver her into his bed. Yes, it would be an interesting pursuit—one he was looking forward to. But that could wait until tomorrow when his mind wasn't so clouded.*

He drained his glass, let it drop to the floor and fell into a drunken slumber, dreaming of his future conquest.

CHAPTER FIFTY-FIVE

ucy entered her bedroom to find Mary and Molly slipping into their nightdresses by the light of a single candle. "And how's his Lordship's little lady tonight?" Molly asked. "I'm not his Lordship's little lady," she replied. "I never will be." Lucy unfastened her bodice, stepped out of her dress and reached for her nightgown.

"I know ya better than ya think," Molly said, in a taunting tone. "Ya see Beth with her own room and a purse full of shillin's and that's what ya be wanting."

"Leave her be, you ungrateful wench," Mary said, as she grabbed her new hairbrush and ran its bristles through her long hair. "Not many would be buying you a satchel. I'm telling you that."

Molly sneered. "Don't mean we be kissin' sisters. Why ya be sticking up fer her, ya old evesdropper?"

"Shut your mouth unless you've got something good to say," Mary said.

"Ya can kiss me bum."

The last thing Lucy felt like doing was arguing with Molly. She climbed into bed and pulled the covers over her head, hoping to drown out their bickering. Inside her cocoon, Lucy felt closed off from the world. She shut her eyes. *Now if they would just be quiet and let her go to sleep.*

Molly stepped over to her bed and pulled the covers back. "Ya can't fool me. I know what yer up to. Ya want the Squire all for yerself. Satan himself is workin' inside ya. Tell us the wicked things he makes ya do."

"Enough!" Mary said with disgust, and blew out the candle. "Molly, you're acting like a tramp. Go to bed."

Molly laughed and turned away. "The tramp already be in her bed."

Lucy felt warm tears slide down her cheeks. She pulled her covers up, rolled over on her pillow and stared into the darkness, dismayed by the cruelty of words and how they hurt, even when she was blameless.

blast of cold air swept into the pub as Geoffrey Walsh hastened in the front entrance. "Shut the damn door," Simon said, setting a tray of drinks down at a nearby table, occupied by two local merchants.

Walsh scowled at the innkeeper's offensive tone and took his time closing the door. He removed his hat and let his large, unfriendly eyes sweep the room. He saw Simon cast a furtive glance in his direction, and then sit down with tradesmen, becoming engaged in a hushed conversation.

Walsh's curiosity was piqued. He had an idea: Slapping his hat against his leg, he drew their attention as he crossed the room and ascended the stairs. At the top of the landing he walked heavily to his door, opened it, entered and slammed it closed. A moment later, he quietly reopened the door and tiptoed back to the top of the stairs, careful to avoid a few floorboards that had creaked on the way up. Hidden from sight, he listened to the men below, who—as he had hoped—no longer whispered.

"That chap's up ta no good if ya ask me," one of the men said.

"Name's Walsh," the innkeeper said. "Likes ta be called Mr. Geoffrey Walsh. Piss on him and his newspaper, too."

"He was nosing about today, askin' after the Wordsworths."

"What'd ya tell him?"

"I don't talk ta strangers about me neighbors, even if they be as odd as those Wordsworths."

"Good man," Simon said. "This scoundrel told me he was a writer, but I have a feeling he's more'n he says he is. Could be a government official, come ta raise our taxes."

❧ ❧ ❧

*G*eoffrey Walsh snorted as he crept back to his quarters to undress. The opinions of the fools in the bar were of no concern to him. Let them believe what they wished. His was a pursuit of morality, after all, and he worked hard to protect the public—even if some dupes didn't appreciate it.

All in all, it had been a frustrating day. He had spent it questioning Wordsworth's neighbors and acquaintances but, with the exception of the Sutton brothers, most of them had been close-mouthed, like those downstairs. The Suttons had revealed suspicions about the odd brother and sister who walked the woods late into the night for no apparent reason. This made no sense at all, unless they were on a mission to rendezvous secretly with enemies of the English government. The Wordsworths, they had confirmed, entertained all sorts of foreign-looking individuals. Some, they had suspected, were French spies. Unfortunately, neither brother had revealed concrete evidence that could be used to prosecute Wordsworth in a court of law.

Walsh slipped off his trousers, placed them over the back of a chair and recalled a question that had been hounding him for the better part of the day: *How had the Wordsworths managed to entertain visitors with no apparent means of income?* His eyes narrowed. *Perhaps the French government was subsidizing them. If so, they must have money. But then, why were they being evicted? Maybe their funds had been cut off, or delayed by the war. If those were the circumstances, the Wordsworths would be getting desperate. And desperate individuals made mistakes.*

Dressed only in his shorts and undershirt, Walsh lifted his coat from a chair, reached into a pocket and withdrew his flintlock and a letter. He checked the pistol's flash pan. Satisfied that it was primed, he placed it within easy reach, on the desk beside his bed. His obsidian eyes lingered on the deadly weapon: It was a source of power and authority. He had recently shot and killed two unarmed criminals with it—men who had murdered and raped—men who had deserved to die. *It could be that William Wordsworth deserved to die.*

But, where was the evidence to condemn the man? Shaking his head, he picked up the envelope with the official Home Office return address and withdrew a single sheet of paper. He stared at it for the umpteenth time since its arrival three days before. The letter demanded an overdue report on his investigation into the foe of the Crown.

Walsh sank heavily into the chair and leaned an elbow on the desk. He stared at the paper without seeing it as he considered the consequences of any report he might compose. *If he were to write the truth—that he had not yet obtained factual evidence to convict the poet—he would surely be recalled and judged incompetent by his enemies in the Home Office.*

Yes, he ruefully admitted, *he had plenty of detractors among his peers.* As a zealously God-fearing man, he had ruffled more than a few feathers by what some had considered his overly-obsessive approach to the law. And, to the sometimes bitter disdain of his colleagues, he saw no virtue in showing favoritism to men with influential friends and relatives: He judged all men equally, risking his life, if need be, to apprehend armed and dangerous criminals.

And, if any of these miscreants tried to escape, he would shoot to kill: It was the law.

Yes, he was a righteous man. And, with the arrest of Wordsworth, he would be beyond criticism.

He picked up a quill and a piece of paper. *If it were facts they were after, he would give them facts.* His pen began to scratch across the page. *If he embellished a few things for the moment, it wouldn't matter. He was certain that hard evidence would appear, as surely as Death itself. Soon enough, he'd have all the proof he needed to hang the traitor.*

His pen scribbled long into the night.

❧ C H A P T E R   F I F T Y – S E V E N ❦

illiam was planted at his desk in Alfoxden's parlor, surrounded by several journals: Two were heavily bookmarked; he yawned as he read from a third, accompanied by the gentle whistle of the night wind against the windowpane. He lowered his book and reached for the teacup beside him as the candle began to sputter. Opening the desk drawer, he withdrew a fresh candle and touched its wick to the dying flame. When it caught fire, he snuffed the old flame and replaced the stub with the new taper.

"A two-candle night, I see."

He looked up to see Dorothy descending the stairs in her robe and slippers. She held her own candlestick to light her way. "I guess inspiration knows neither day nor night."

He offered a tired smile. "Actually, I'm reading more than writing. And you … what are you doing up at this hour?"

She stepped to the hardwood floor and turned toward the adjoining kitchen. "I couldn't sleep. Perhaps some tea will help."

"Water's still hot."

Entering the kitchen, Dorothy filled a small silver spoon with tea leaves and soaked it in a cup of steaming water from the kettle. After placing it on a saucer and adding a spoonful of sugar, she padded back to William, stopping beside his desk. "Would I be intruding?"

He noticed a familiar expression on his sister's face, one he didn't welcome at the moment. But he gestured to the chair across from him. As she settled in, he realized he must be the cause of her insomnia. "There's no reason to lose sleep over me."

"You know me too well. Would you like to have a little chat?"

"No, not particularly." He saw her look of disappointment and added, "I believe I know what's on your mind. It has to do with a young woman. Am I correct?"

She nodded.

"I tried to end it," he said halfheartedly. "Well, I tried as best I could."

Dorothy set her cup and saucer on the table and waited for an explanation.

He sipped his tea, evaluating his response. *What could he tell his sister that would alleviate her worries?* When he realized it would be fruitless to even try, he said, "Dorothy, as I told you before, there's something about this young woman that's completely taken hold of me. My every waking moment and my dreams, too, are filled with images of her; the sound of her voice, the beauty of her smile, eyes that reach into my very soul... ." He sighed. "I know all your possible arguments against a relationship, and they are sound. I did see her since the last time you and I spoke of this and I did explain my circumstances to her, giving all the reasons why I am wrong for her, including my financial circumstances. But when we are together, I feel as though God were offering me a gift, one I cannot turn down. All I can think of is how *right* she is for me."

His sister shook her head with worry. "William, your work."

"*The Prelude* is on a temporary hiatus." His hand wandered to the journals beside him. "I've been reviewing a number of poems upon which Samuel and I have collaborated. Some of them are quite good, as you know. Good enough, I believe, to take us to Germany." She looked doubtful, and was about to question him when he added, "Don't ask. You'll find out in due time. Over the next few weeks, with Samuel's cooperation, I may have some very encouraging news for all of us." He picked up one of his journals. "But, for the moment, I'm consumed with a new poem. Would you care to hear what I've written?"

Dorothy nodded, her eyes finally showing a spark of hope as she lifted her cup. "I'm always eager to hear anything you've composed."

"It's a work in progress," William said, as he moved his journal closer to the candlelight.

> *"My hope is one, from cities far*
> *Nursed on a lonely hearth:*
> *Her lips are red as roses are,*
> *Her hair a woodbine wreath.*
>
> *She lives among the Untrodden ways*
> *Beside the Springs of Dove..."*

He raised his eyes and explained, "The Springs are a short walk from Hawkins House where she lives."

The spark in his sister's eyes died.

He lowered his gaze to his text and continued reading.

> *"A maid whom there are none to praise,*
> *And very few to love;*
> *A violet by a mossy stone,*
> *Half hidden from mine eye..."*

William looked up. "It's a beginning."

Dorothy rose, picked up the saucer, and set the teacup onto it with a shaky hand. "It's beautiful, as she must be." She stood still for a long moment, then sighed and picked up her candlestick. "Be cautious, William. Please." She kissed his forehead. "I'm so worried ... for both of you."

William watched Dorothy ascend the stairs, the tread of her footsteps sounding heavier than usual. The fact that she might lose sleep because of *his* troubles touched him deeply.

Dorothy was the one true constant in his life. He valued her as a sister, his best friend, his housekeeper and cook, and, most of all, he prized her editing skills: She was honest, intelligent—and an excellent writer, herself; he had often suggested she send her compositions to a publisher under a pseudonym, but Dorothy had politely declined; she wrote only for her own amusement and occasionally shared her writing with a small circle of friends. William wondered why she had never married. Her explanation was that she had never found a man to match her expectations.

He picked up his quill pen and twirled it between his fingers, thinking how lucky he was to have Dorothy for a sister. But, as images of Lucy crowded out his musings, he dipped the nib into its ink well and began to write.

rs. Tennant, the Hawkins housekeeper, hurried into the glass-enclosed greenhouse at the rear of the manor house. She stood by the door, wringing her hands, waiting for the Lady of the manor to acknowledge her presence.

Gertrude Hawkins was in the midst of instructing one of the gardeners, a wizened old Irishman, to move an assortment of potted flowers to the western end of the structure, where they would benefit from the afternoon sun. Her Ladyship had noticed Mrs. Tennant's entrance, but having been advised by one of her more genteel acquaintances to keep servants in their place by ignoring them for a suitable length of time, she picked up a small potted plant and pretended to inspect its condition. After a few minutes had passed, she acknowledged the woman. "Yes? What is it, Mrs. Tennant?"

"There's an urgent matter needing your attention, my Lady."

Lady Hawkins turned to her. "What urgent matter?"

"Some silver has disappeared. The Apostle Spoons."

Lady Hawkins dropped the pot, which shattered at her feet. "Me Apostle Spoons? Silver don't just walk off on its own, Mrs. Tennant!"

The servant nodded, her forehead creased with worry. "That's why I'm bringing it your attention, my Lady. I've gathered the maids in the parlor."

Lady Hawkins kicked the remnants of the plant out of her way, pushing past Mrs. Tennant as she hurried out of the greenhouse, the housekeeper following close on her heels.

The three maids stood nervously beside a ponderous Jacobean chest of drawers in the great room, as Lady Hawkins and Mrs. Tennant hurried in from the hallway. The top drawer was open.

"You can see for yourself, my Lady," Mrs. Tennant said, breathlessly, as they stopped before the bureau.

Lady Hawkins searched the inside of the drawer. It was filled with velvet-lined slots that held silver settings and serving pieces. A dozen spaces in the center of the drawer were conspicuously empty. "Damme, we've got filchers here!" she said, and turned to the housekeeper. "Ya've searched the kitchen cupboards, the sinks an' counters?"

"Yes, me Lady. I've had the entire upstairs scoured high and low, every nook and cranny."

Lady Hawkins flashed suspicious looks toward the maids. "Someone in this house stole me Apostle Spoons. They be copies of ones in Windsor Castle itself. They cost more than a year's wages for the lot of ya, and I want 'em back. Ya hear me?"

"If I be accused of stealin'," Molly said defiantly, "I be walkin' out of here!"

"If anyone nicked the silver," Beth said, "it were that shifty eyed cook or that no account helper of his."

"The silver were in the drawer yesterday," Mary said. "I saw it with me own eyes."

"Quiet, the lot of ya." Lady Hawkins spun on the housekeeper and screamed, "Find me silver, if ya have to turn this whole household upside down!"

"Yes, my Lady. I will personally search the servants' quarters again." Mrs. Tennant bustled off.

"No one leaves this house." Lady Hawkins said, glaring at the maids. "Yer all to wait right here with me."

❧❧ ❧❧ ❧❧

As soon as Lucy had opened the Hawkins' front door, Emily and Henry had scooted past her, whooping and laughing as they entered the great room. She followed close behind, carrying her painting materials. Suddenly, the children stopped in their tracks, and their exuberance was quashed as they saw their mother and the maids. The stern look on Lady Hawkins' face was unsettling as she hovered by the three uneasy servants, arms folded, foot tapping the floor. Lucy could feel the tension; it seemed to have drawn all the air out of the room. Something was definitely amiss.

"Miss Lucy," Lady Hawkins said, "ya'll join us over here while Mrs. Tennant searches the servants quarters."

"Searches for what, Mama?" Emily asked.

"Silver is missing. Me Apostle Spoons. We have a thief in the house."

Henry stepped in front of her and folded his arms. "It ain't Miss Lucy!"

"Certainly not," Emily concurred.

Lucy couldn't help but feel proud of how ardently her two wards defended her.

Lady Hawkins said, "No one be charged yet, but everyone stays in this room until Mrs. Tennant returns." She eyed the servants. "If the pieces are found among any of yer belongin's, I promise ya I'll call in the parish constable and press charges. I'll not have a thief under me roof."

Lucy realized she was still holding her art paraphernalia and handed it to the children, motioning them toward the storage closet. As Emily and Henry carried the materials away, she stepped over to join the servants. She could feel their apprehension; sometimes, innocence was a difficult thing to prove.

illiam pulled the broad brim of his hat down to shield his eyes from the sun as he strode along the road with a sense of determination, his mind churning with plans and ideas. For almost a week his thoughts had ricocheted back and forth between an imagined relationship with Lucy and an exploration of how to acquire funds. He adjusted the strap on his satchel that had been cutting a groove into his shoulder. It was heavier than normal due to the added weight of his old journals, which he had crowded into the bag for Coleridge to peruse. If Samuel agreed to the plan he had worked out, he was confident they would be able to finance a trip to Germany. But his biggest dilemma was Lucy: *Would he be able to persuade her to quit her position and accompany Dorothy, Samuel, and himself?*

The chuffing of horses interrupted his thoughts. He turned and saw a line of British cavalrymen cantering up the road behind him. He warily stepped off the track to allow them passage. He was soon relieved as he counted the riders; there were almost sixty of them—far more than the Home Office would send to arrest a private citizen. As they trotted by, he gazed at the proud faces of young men in bright red uniforms with shiny sabers glinting at their sides. His relief was tempered by sadness after they had passed. He knew that, in all probability, the soldiers were heading off to fight in the war with France. *How many would never come home?*

William sighed heavily, reminded that *he also* faced a risk of losing his life: Whether a man died under fire, or from being hung at the gallows, unjustly convicted of treason, both were terrible fates. His own appearance at Bristol Court was scheduled to take place in just two weeks!

After walking for another twenty minutes, William suddenly heard a man yelling. At first, he thought someone was being beaten or murdered, but the yells turned to screams and then laughter. Stopping to listen, he was able to narrow down the location of the outcries to a stand of trees, where the roadside stream disappeared into the sizable thicket.

He left the road to investigate, uncertain if he should be approaching what might turn out to be a sort of game ... or perhaps a maniac. Threading his way between the trees, he followed the stream toward the commotion.

William stopped short as he recognized a naked man frolicking in a swimming hole.

"Is that you, Samuel?"

"One and the same," Coleridge bellowed. "Come on in, William. The water is most refreshing."

"You're daft, man. It has to be near freezing."

"Aye. But it's warmer than my own hearth at the moment."

William chuckled. "Ah, Sara has come to her senses and thrown you out."

"I've left of my own accord," Samuel said somewhat defensively. "Her nagging ways were stifling my creative soul."

"Come out of there. You're making a spectacle of

yourself and, for once, I'm anxious to show you something."

Samuel splashed about like a happy adolescent. "I don't wish to go home just yet. Sara needs more time to suffer the pain of my absence."

William knew better than to try to reason with Samuel over the subject of his wife. He and Sara seemed to enjoy goading each other, taking great pleasure in their verbal spats. It had become a contest between two stubborn wills, oftentimes creating a tense atmosphere that made writing at Samuel's home an unpleasant and unproductive experience.

"We'll go to Alfoxden," William offered. "Dorothy would love to have you visit. For some strange reason she appreciates your caustic wit."

Samuel beamed. He stood up in the water, naked as a newborn, and stretched without a trace of modesty, as if fancying himself to be the Statue of David. "I believe she appreciates me for my winning charm and handsome physique. And, surely, what lady wouldn't?"

William laughed as Samuel splashed ashore, thinking his friend bore a closer resemblance to a pudgy orangutan.

enry and Emily had returned from placing Lucy's art material in the storage cabinet and were skipping around the great room, bored with waiting for Mrs. Tennant to reappear. "Children, you'll have to settle down," Lucy said. "Come sit beside me."

Lucy patted the brocade seats on either side of her. When at last the two joined her on the divan, she said, "Henry. Conjugate the verb 'to spin'."

Henry, his mind apparently elsewhere, was playing with the buckle on one of his shoes.

Emily leaned around her governess and said, "Miss Lucy's talking to you."

He snapped to attention with a look of confusion.

Lucy sighed. She couldn't blame the boy for being distracted. It was taking all of her concentration to block out the tension in the room, which was exacerbated by the *click-clicking* sound of her Ladyship's shoes, as she paced up and down the parquet floors. Lucy said, "I guess we'll do our verbs tomorrow."

The servants by the dining room table exchanged anxious glances as they halfheartedly busied themselves setting the table and polishing silver.

Her Ladyship strode past Lucy and the children, unexpectedly passing gas.

Emily's and Henry's eyebrows shot up. They giggled and made exaggerated gagging faces. Lucy, resisting her own urge to laugh, admonished them with the sternest look she could manage.

Mrs. Tennant entered the room, slightly out of breath and empty-handed.

Lady Hawkins stopped mid-click and frowned. "Ya've found nothin'?"

"Not a thing, my Lady. I've turned the servants' quarters upside down. If the spoons had been there, I would have found them."

Lady Hawkins' countenance darkened; she glowered at the staff. "One or maybe two of ya's a filcher. Unless me Apostle Spoons turn up by week's end, ya'll be dismissed ... the whole lot of ya. I won't be livin' with thieves under me own roof."

"Mama," Emily cried, "Miss Lucy is not a thief!"

Henry jumped off the couch, almost growling. "She surely ain't."

Lucy smiled at the children's loyalty and watched as Lady Hawkins shook a finger at her offspring and bellowed, "Shush! I don't need you two ruffians tellin' me what's what."

The children seemed to melt under their mother's anger. They were barely able to utter, "Yes, Mama."

Lady Hawkins turned and stared at Lucy with beady, judgmental eyes, as if assessing her possible guilt. She then turned to the servants. "If me silver turns out ta be accidentally misplaced, then ya'll get me apologies. If not, then each and every servant, includin' the governess, is out of me house. Now, if I were ya, I'd start lookin' high and low."

Lady Hawkins turned on her heel and *clickity-clicked* toward the hallway. Passing the divan, she said, "Miss Sims, the children need a bath. They smell."

Henry waited until his mother had disappeared before he said, "We smell? Mama gassed the whole room."

Lucy placed a finger to her lips. "Henry, shh."

Emily giggled. "It be true, Miss Lucy."

Their governess smiled in spite of herself, then sobered, as the threat of pending dismissals suddenly made the large room seem claustrophobic. If the silver Apostle Spoons were not located, she would certainly be discharged. It wouldn't overly disturb her if she had to leave Hawkins House, but she would dearly miss the children. Her love for them had grown with every day that had passed, and she would forever be concerned for their welfare and education in the care of two such churlish parents.

And, then there was William. *How could she possibly leave him?*

CHAPTER SIXTY-ONE

*S*imon said, "Mr. Geoffrey Walsh, mind if I sit a bit and rest me weary bones?"

Walsh cast a suspicious eye at the innkeeper, who had left the bar to stand beside him. "It's your table," said Walsh. *Why would this old man want to join him?*

"I'll take this seat … lets me keep an eye on the room." The proprietor pulled a chair from against the wall, lifting Walsh's coat which had been draped over it.

Walsh's arm lashed out. "Keep your hands off…" It was too late. A knowing look had already crossed the innkeeper's face as his fingers examined the bulky weight in one of the pockets. Walsh tore the garment from Simon's grasp and placed it on another chair.

The old man smirked, obviously having confirmed a

suspicion. "I didn't know it was customary for a writer ta carry a firearm."

Meddling old fool. Walsh's dark eyes narrowed. "It's for protection. I've been robbed more than once."

The innkeeper sat across from Walsh and stroked his chin thoughtfully. He said, "What's yer real line of work, Mr. Geoffrey Walsh?"

"It would be best if you didn't interfere in things that don't concern you."

"Maybe ya should follow yer own advice," Simon shot back. "Ya bein' the one who's been stickin' his nose inta other people's lives. What's yer interest in the Wordsworths?"

The insolent simpleton! He wanted to tell the old cod to get the hell away from him, but he had to be prudent. "My interest in the Wordsworths is solely academic; I am writing an article for the Bristol Daily News on contemporary English poets."

Simon seemed to be taken aback by this revelation. He remarked, "Oh, ya are, are ya?"

Walsh reached into his pocket and withdrew an expensively engraved piece of paper, which he tossed on the table. "My credentials. Maybe they will satisfy you, if you can read them, that is."

"I can read," the innkeeper said, but for the first time he appeared defensive. He picked up the paper.

Walsh watched carefully as the man scrutinized the document. The paper was a formally-addressed invitation to a Tory political function, but he doubted the innkeeper would know that.

"Well, I guess yer right," Simon said, lowering the paper. "How much longer are ya plannin' to stay?"

The government man retrieved the document, darkly amused that his gamble had paid off. But the innkeeper's question had irritated him, reminding him that the Home Office had allowed him ten days' expenses, and expected results for this outlay. The consequences would not be pleasant if he returned empty-handed. He felt perspiration trickle down his ribs. He said curtly, "A few days, at most."

Simon snorted. "I'll have yer bill ready."

Walsh watched the man walk off, his own mood becoming more bilious than usual. He needed bona fide proof of Wordsworth's guilt, and he needed it now. Time was running very short. He felt potential failure settling like a heavy yoke upon his shoulders. After a moment, he shook his head, ridding himself of the heavy mantel, vowing to pursue Wordsworth to the grave.

amuel lifted a knife from Wordworth's kitchen table and carved several wedges from a wheel of cheddar. "William, let me see if I understand you correctly," he said. "You're suggesting we compile some of our poems for a new book?"

"Yes, that's exactly what I'm proposing," William replied. He reached across the table for a piece of cheese. "Both of us have at least a dozen or more works we could contribute."

William watched as his friend mulled this over. Samuel glanced to Dorothy, who stood nearby at a counter, dicing carrots and onions beside the carcass of a plump pheasant, all to be added to a stewpot that was heating on the stove behind her. Samuel said, "Dorothy, my one true barometer of sanity, what thinkest thou?"

"Me thinkest," she replied playing upon his old English verbiage, "ye two shouldest carry on to savest us from the poor house."

"Aye." Samuel nodded and turned his full attention to William. "I must admit I'm rather taken by the idea ... saving you from the poor house, that is. You believe we could find a publisher willing to pay for this grand epic?"

"I already have ... you know Joseph Cottle? He's offered to give us a cash advance, more than enough to finance our tour of Germany."

"Then, by God, we'll do it!"

"This is a glorious surprise!" Dorothy exclaimed. "Oh, what a relief!"

William beamed, pleased that his plan had met with everyone's approval. "Our trip will be everything we need and want it to be ... a magnificent and creative adventure."

Samuel lifted his mug of ale. "A toast to the poetry-loving fools in this world. And, to the health and success of our new publisher, Joseph Cottle."

"Here, here," William chimed in, raising his drink. After a quaff, he said, "I have a suggestion for the title of our book. What do you think of ... *Lyrical Ballads*?"

Samuel wiped foam from his mouth, thought for a moment, then said, "Very apropos. I love it. But, there's one minor problem." He waited until they turned to him, then added, "I have nothing to contribute."

"Are you daft, Samuel?" William asked. "You've produced some of the finest poetry ever written! If you're too modest to select from you own works, then please allow Dorothy and me to make suggestions."

Samuel held up a hand. "Modesty, as you know, is not one of my weaknesses, but I am a perfectionist and there are very few of my poems that I consider publishable at this time."

Breaking off a chunk of bread, William quelled the urge to fling it at his friend. Fortunately, he knew most of Samuel's weaknesses, and one of them was flattery. He wasn't above taking advantage of that Achilles' heel to further their aims. "Samuel, I don't believe there's ever been a poem of such impressive proportions as 'The Rime of the Ancient Mariner'. It's splendid. I've heard you say you wouldn't change a single word of it. Certainly, that's one contribution you can make without reservation."

Samuel shot him a brooding scowl, perhaps sensing his manipulation, but he couldn't resist the compliment. Stifling a grin, he replied, "Well, yes, I suppose it may be rather complete. It is quite brilliant if I do say so myself. Did you enjoy reading it, Dorothy?"

"You know I loved every word of it, Samuel," she said, then brought the meat cleaver down on the cutting board ... THWACK ... splitting the pheasant in two. "I've told you that a dozen times."

She continued to chop the bird and then carried the pieces to the stove, dropping the lot into a sizzling frying pan to brown before adding them to the pot.

Samuel took another sip of brew, then allowed, "Yes, I suppose I could give you that one, William, but that's all. I have nothing else to contribute."

"Pshaw. You've several more. Let me select them for you."

Samuel raised his hand once more. "If you please, I believe I am my own best judge. Perhaps I could come up with one or two poems ... three at most, but only on one condition..." He waited again until he had their attention. "The book must be published anonymously."

William inhaled bread crumbs and began to cough. Dorothy reached for a ladle and dipped it into the small water pot on the counter; she grabbed a mug, filled it, and carried it to him. While William drank it down she asked Samuel, "Why, for heavens sake?"

"As you know, the critics hate me." He glanced at William. "And they hate you, too. We've criticized the old school of poets, the ones they kneel down to and praise like Gods. To them, this is tantamount to rubbing their noses in manure! Believe me, if they saw our names on a new volume, they would crucify us without so much as reading a single word. Unfortunately, critics, even bad ones, count in the world of literature. I don't wish to sacrifice what little reputation I still hang onto, for the sake of the enemy." He picked up a hunk of cheddar. He nibbled as he explained, "William, let's see what those reviewers have to write about our poems, without letting them know the works are by Wordsworth and Coleridge. It could be quite interesting! They might even read the book and, if they're honest, give us a sterling review. Wouldn't you love to see those literary misanthropes eat a little crow?"

William, who had cleared his throat, immediately grasped the cleverness of his colleague's strategy. "A splendid idea," he said. "I wholeheartedly agree, we publish anonymously. In addition to everything you've just mentioned, the Wordsworth name is currently an anathema in more than just literary circles."

"Don't worry about your name, William. It will soon be cleared. I'll see to it."

"Oh?" he asked curiously. "How do you plan to accomplish that?"

Samuel reached over to the cutting board and snagged two carrots. Dorothy, standing by the oven, swatted at him good naturedly with a spoon. He tossed one piece to William while he crunched on the other and said, "I'll accompany you to Bristol Court, where we'll outsmart the powdered wigs by proving that the accusations against you are based upon hearsay."

William admired Samuel's offer of assistance, but he wasn't sure his friend's bombastic presence in court would be such a good thing. "I appreciate your offer, Samuel, but, as Dorothy has reminded me, this is such a serious business. I believe I should hire a solicitor."

"Have you forgotten already? I intend to be your solicitor. If you place your life in someone else's hands, the odds are you will be hung for treason or, at the least, spend the next several years rotting in a hellhole like Newgate Prison. For purely selfish reasons, I will not let that happen. I need a writing partner and a companion for our soon-to-be-affordable trip to Germany."

William smiled at his friend's exuberance, pleased that Samuel would join them on their journey. But his smile faltered at the thought of allowing his friend to defend him in court.

Samuel must have seen his hesitation. He said, "Dorothy, tell this Doubting Thomas brother of yours to trust his brilliant advocate."

Dorothy, stripping thyme leaves into the stew, said, "William, you could do worse."

William digested his sister's comment. He knew Samuel to be all he claimed and more: Coleridge had been a child prodigy and had been considered a gifted intellectual among his peers at Jesus College in Cambridge, possessing a vast array of knowledge on virtually any subject. He was also an excellent public speaker, despite his tendency to exaggerate. His sister was right; he could do worse. He said, "All right. But if I hang, Dorothy, you have my permission to chop his inflated head off."

Samuel guffawed loudly, and they all fell silent for a while.

Dorothy, who had earlier borrowed William's journal from the kitchen table, now opened it on the counter with one hand while she stirred the stew with the other. She read his last entry to *Lines Written in Early Spring.* "You've made some progress on this one." She read aloud:

> *The budding twigs spread out their fan,*
> *To catch the breezy air;*
> *And I must think, do all I can,*
> *That there was pleasure there.*
>
> *If this belief from heaven be sent,*
> *If such be Nature's holy plan,*
> *Have I not reason to lament*
> *What man has made of man?"*

"The ending is adequate. But I've made little improvement on the whole piece." William ran his hand through his hair, pondering an abundance of inspiration yet a dearth of concentration that characterized his current writing attempts. "I haven't written much today."

Samuel quoted:

'Have I not reason to lament
What man has made of man?'

He continued, "That's all new. But your dilly-dallying comes as no surprise, since you've completely ignored my sage advice and seen that young lass again."

"I'm afraid she's stolen his senses," Dorothy said.

Samuel clucked his tongue. "He's been bitten, Dorothy. Only time will tell if it's by a love bug ... or a bed bug. Hopefully, it's the latter."

She put the journal down. "I pray those two bugs aren't one and the same."

"Stop it, you two!" William yelled. "You can't make fun of a friendship of which you are entirely ignorant."

"Listen to him, Samuel. As if the two of us can't identify the face of a lovesick loon when we see it."

"Quite right. We're rather doltish. Perceiving the obvious is way beyond our limited resources."

William groaned, but smiled as he entreated his friend, "Annoying as you are, you'll be staying for supper, I hope?"

Samuel inhaled the savory aroma coming from the stewpot and beamed. "An absolutely wonderful idea. Dorothy, my dearest, is your lovesick brother's invitation agreeable to the chef?"

"The chef heartily concurs," she answered with a twinkle in her eye. "But won't Sara be missing you?"

Samuel grinned devilishly. "I certainly hope so."

andlelight flickered upon the Squire as he once again lay sprawled in his armchair; Lucy drew at her easel a few feet in front of him. He lifted his ever-present glass of wine and pressed it to his lips, drinking as his bleary eyes took in her figure.

At the moment, Lucy's thoughts were with William, as she sketched the Squire's portrait with a graphite pencil. She was glad the preliminary drawing was almost finished and she could then begin painting with oil on canvas ... and quickly be done! Her pencil moved with care, but her mind was at the granary where she would soon meet her poet. The Squire suddenly belched, which directed her attention to his watery eyes and she now noticed they were focusing on her breasts. *The beast was trying to undress her with his eyes.* But, and here she gloated, she had thrown on the painter's smock he had given her, which covered her loosely, and gave him nothing to enjoy. Even so, she had a growing sense of unease.

"Lucy," he said, breaking the silence. "The missin' silver, any idea where it might've gone?"

"No, Sir," she said, not wishing to encourage conversation. "It was probably just misplaced."

He licked his plump liver colored lips. "Hopefully. I'd hate to see ya leave us. 'Course, ya bein' the governess an' all, maybe I can help ya."

She said, as neutrally as possible, "I appreciate that, Sir."

"And there be no strings attached."

"That's kind of you." She sighed inwardly, hoping the Squire had learned a lesson from his last attempt to seduce her. *On the contrary, though, he seemed coarsely flirtatious tonight.* She peeked at the grandfather clock. It was twenty minutes to nine, *twenty minutes before she could leave to meet William. Every minute seemed like a year!*

"Ya suppose if I saved yer position, ya might think more kindly of me?"

She replied cautiously. "If you saved *all* of our positions, I might think more kindly of you."

The Squire must have fancied a flicker of interest on her part, for now he looked encouraged. "That may be possible. I'm a regular fox when it comes ta locatin' lost items if I put me mind to it." He finished off his wine and poured another glassful. "Lucy, ya an' I might be friends after all."

She almost scoffed. *If he thought he could make idiotic promises to get closer to her, he was a bigger fool than she had imagined; but then, she reminded herself, fools could be dangerous.* She said, "It's difficult to be friends with one's employer, Sir."

"That depends on yer employer," he said with a hopeful leer. "I would be willin' ta look upon ya as an equal if ya were ta look on me as more than yer employer, say a close friend?"

"I don't believe her Ladyship and the children would appreciate us being friends, Sir," she said, feeling as if she were maneuvering her way around a pool of quicksand.

"I've thought that over," he said, slurring his words. "I don't care what ya say ta Gerty, but ya won't jabber nothin' to the children. I know ya, Lucy Sims. Yer too kind a person ta tattle. Their little hearts would surely break."

The pencil froze in her hand, her fingers tightening until her knuckles turned white. She struggled against the urge to scratch it across the course face in the portrait. *The old sot would take advantage of her vulnerability, her love for the children!*

"Now, me dear, if ya was ta come over here and treat me right, the Apostle Spoons will be found an' no one would be dismissed. I can promise ya that."

She took in a breath, holding it. *There was only one way the Squire could promise to find the stolen silver. He must have taken the spoons and hidden them to create the environment the servants now found themselves in, so that he could suddenly 'find' them and save everyone's jobs—if she would allow him to seduce her! Or, there was the prospect that he was lying. Perhaps he had no idea where the silver had gone and was simply using the promise of recovery as a way to take advantage of her. In either case, the man was completely disreputable, caring only for his lustful cravings. Why, for God's sake, wasn't he chasing after Molly, who would be happy to be his mistress?*

Lucy knew that if she wanted any peace in the future, she would have to put an end to the Squire's advances once and for all, no matter what the cost. Her position at Hawkins House was already precarious. If he fired her for what she was about to say, she decided she could accept it.

She lowered the pencil, setting her jaw with determination. "Sir, excuse me for saying so, but I won't be placed in a position where I have to barter myself with you just to live normally."

The Squire's face flushed crimson red. She almost faltered, but raised her head and looked him in the eye. "I will never be more to you than I am now."

His mouth dropped open, lips quivering. Silence hung in the air as ominously as in the moment between a close lightning strike and the impending roar of thunder. Finally, she said with a tone of modesty that belied her anger, "I beg your forgiveness, but I'm unable to concentrate this evening." She began to pack her art supplies.

The Squire stood quickly, almost knocking his chair over. "Ya stupid, ungrateful little wench. Get out of here! "

She recoiled at his outburst, but was relieved to be able to depart. "But now you'll not be mistaking how I feel." Unable to keep the triumph from her voice, she added, "Goodnight."

She gathered up her art materials and hurried out.

❧❧❧ ❧❧❧ ❧❧❧

*T*he Squire glared after her as the door closed. "Damn maidens all ta hell." He fell back into his chair, sloshing wine onto his clothes, then reached for the decanter with an unsteady hand and poured another glassful. "They don't know what their tails are made fer." He gulped down half the tumbler and his monologue dribbled off into incoherence. "Well, Miss Lucy, next time we be together it's me that's goin' ta be the schoolmaster. Ya'll learn real quick the lessons I be teachin' ya." Reveling in his fantasy, he chuckled. "Ya just wait. Once ya've had me cock in ya, ya'll be coming back ta me, beggin' fer more. And, I be just the man ta give it to ya."

ucy hurried down the hillside path from the manor house. The chill wind abraded her face, blowing her long hair and cape out behind her as she dashed across the road and then paralleled the pond that glistened with a thousand reflected stars. She reached the tumbled walls of the granary and climbed to its highest point, where she hesitated, her heart pounding, and peered into the dark courtyard.

There, at the far end of the enclosure, she could see a lone figure pacing the cobblestones: It was William. She caught her breath, leaped from the wall to the ground and ran to him. He must have heard her racing steps, for he turned in time to catch her as she flew into his arms. She grasped him tightly and buried her head in his shoulder, seeking strength and protection.

He gently pushed her back to arm's length, and stared at her. "Lucy, what is it?" What's wrong? There's sadness in your eyes."

She didn't know where to begin. But the reassuring warmth of his hand upon hers lent her courage. "My life is in complete disarray. It seems that I may have to leave Hawkins House."

Even in the moonlight, she saw the concern on his face. "Lucy, what is it?" he asked. "What's happened?"

She inhaled deeply and explained, "There's been a theft at the manor. Valuable silver pieces are missing, and her Ladyship, who is an inhumane and temperamental woman, has threatened to dismiss the entire staff unless the thief or the silver is found by week's end."

He shook his head in disbelief. "She couldn't possibly discharge all of the help. She'd be left with utter chaos."

"Oh, she's certainly capable of creating chaos."

"But where would you go? How would you survive?"

She answered with all the pluck she could muster, "I would go to Bath and live there with my Aunt. Perhaps it's time I did that anyway." She hesitated, then, "And there's a more pressing situation that makes my continued employment very difficult."

"What sort of situation?"

She shook her head, then said, "I shouldn't trouble you with this ... ."

"Lucy, you have to understand. Your problems are now mine also. Please ... I'm here to help ... if I can."

She looked at him for a long moment, debating whether or not to involve him in her difficulties. Before she had made up her mind, she heard herself say, "The Squire has been making untoward advances. I've been able to fend him off, but I fear there will be no end to it."

His face colored; the muscles in his jaw worked as his anger flared. "I will put a stop to that nonsense. I'll confront the Squire tomorrow."

"No. Please, don't," she said. She knew the inevitable outcome of any confrontation involving her and the Squire.

"You might put the fear of God into him, and that I would dearly love to witness, but I would surely be dismissed immediately thereafter. Or, in fact … I should leave. One way or the other, we may not have much more time together."

William drew her into a warm embrace and then, taking a step back, said, "Come, sit, and we'll discuss this further."

William spread his cloak on the ground to protect them from the damp earth. Lucy sat beside him, wishing she could share his optimism, but had little hope for their future. William moved closer to her and she noticed he was shivering. "You're cold," she said and undid her cape. He reached over, grabbed one side of the garment and helped wrap it about their shoulders.

William took her hands in his. "Lucy, I will not allow us to be parted. If indeed you are let go, you will come with me. I mentioned before a trip to Germany. I feel it may now be possible. The journey would be a wonderful experience for you and I would be flattered to have you accompany me, my sister and my friend."

She tightened her fingers around his. "Oh, William, I would so love to be your companion." She paused as she imagined the journey. "But I can't … it wouldn't be… ."

William inclined his head gravely toward her. "Forgive me. I didn't mean to imply that we would be involved … oh, no. I wouldn't do that to you. Not that I wouldn't want to," he added playfully. "It's just that I have a much more interesting offer."

She searched his eyes for meaning … a *more interesting offer. Could he possibly be suggesting… ?"*

Before Lucy could finish the thought, his arms had encircled her and he was squeezing her to his chest. With her ear pressed against his linen shirt she could hear the force of his heart. She inhaled his scent, a heady mixture of earth, wood smoke and pine. William placed his palms on either side of her face and tilted her head up so that he could look into her eyes. He whispered lovingly, "Lucy Sims, my feelings for you are more powerful than any love I've ever known or ever hoped to have."

Lucy looked deeply into his eyes … emitting a small cry as she saw adoration there; and her spirits soared. He released her and took her hands into his, raising her fingers to his lips. He kissed them gently. "I'm asking you to travel with me as my wife."

Lucy stared, then held back a sob. *This amazing man shared her feelings! He was her friend, her confidant, her protector … her very soul!* She steadied herself before she said, "My dear, sweet, William. If it's possible, I love you even more than you love me. But … I cannot marry. Not now."

His face fell. "Then when?"

"When I wouldn't be a burden to you. You have more than enough responsibilities without trying to support a wife and, in time, a family. And … we can't be struggling to put bread on the table and still have time to do the work we are born to do. Yes, we nourish each other's souls, and you inspire me to be a better painter, to sense this earth's beauty more deeply than before. I could never forgive myself if I … and above all *you*, had to give this up before we've even begun." William opened his mouth to object, but Lucy placed her fingers over his lips. She continued, "Our love can certainly exist and grow while we endeavor on our own paths. The sentiment we so dearly hold in our hearts is never going to change. Waiting a few months or even years to marry won't matter at all. To the contrary, it will lend us vision, and when we marry, it will be at a time that is right for both of us."

Lucy watched him closely as he struggled with the logic of her words. He seemed to come to a conclusion. "Lucy, for such a young woman, you have more wisdom than many of the scholars I've known. But, know this, and know it well; I am never going to let you get away from me. If you go to live in Bath, I will follow you."

"What of your trip to Germany?"

"Germany is but a whim. You, on the other hand, are very, very real; a day without you would be torture for me. I need to know that we can be together, to explore the hills and leas, to lie on the mossy banks of streams, to walk to the shore and be enveloped by the ocean mists ... I no longer wish to experience these things without you."

Lucy, seeing the images that his words described, fought back tears. "William, you are indeed an artist ... with words."

He smiled with her. "For too long, I've been a man alone, without a kindred spirit. Lucy Sims, I would follow you to the ends of this earth."

"Does that mean you would follow me if I were to move to Spain?" she asked coyly. "Or maybe Italy? Perhaps ... even China?"

William's eyes sparkled in the moonlight. "Spain and Italy surely, but China ... that's a long way to go for a mere bit of a lass."

Lucy laughed softly and held him close. "I won't travel that far, I promise."

As William leaned toward Lucy, she closed her eyes, raising her lips ... and, as his mouth touched hers so gently, and then more firmly, an exquisite sensation seized her ... and she was suddenly lost in the ascendence of a physical awakening.

Her body, without the least bit of shame, arched into William as his arms embraced her. The mounting rhythm of his heart played counterpoint to the rising rate of her pulse. His hands touched her body, evoking delightful sensations ... *it was so natural that he was caressing her.* Suddenly, he stopped, his hands lingering motionlessly on the halfway undone buttons. *Why did he stop?*

Breathless, she opened her eyes. He was looking at her with a query in his eyes—the air between them was heavy with implications...

"William ... I ... ," she said, "I ... we mustn't ... ."

He smiled. "A wise decision ... but we can kiss ... and touch ... ."

She pressed her body into the reassuring warmth of his embrace.

Between kisses, she moved her fingers tenderly through his hair and over his face, above his eyes, cheeks and mouth. She found the cleft in his chin that was rough with beard stubble. She inhaled his scent and trembled. Her physical being marveled at its new and erotic responses; ones that heightened as she became aware of his hardness between them. She whispered, "William, I love you so."

"Yes," he answered, lost in the same dance. "And I you."

When his mouth next touched hers he gently bit her lips. Her eyes widened as she relished the tease, and, staring at him as her passion grew, she smiled, and found herself leaning into him, responding in kind. Sensations raced through her that almost made her stop breathing. She was at a loss to understand the shameless longings that had taken control of her with a complete will of their own, overpowering all her steadfast rules of propriety; her heart now pounded with a wild and abandoned rhythm. When she felt his solid masculinity press up against her, she gasped, and then pressed back with equal ardor.

The tip of his tongue played lightly across her lips, their bodies quivered as one ... and she heard herself moan in a most unladylike fashion. *So this is what it's all about.* She whimpered with delight, and felt herself thrusting against William, her flesh ultrasensitive. As more tiny nerve endings fired, her tempo increased, as did his. Lucy was vaguely aware of a voice, pledging undying love, and then realized with a sense of bewilderment that the voice was hers.

Her breath became short and quick. She arched her hips upward, responding to the urgency they both felt.

A cry escaped her and then time stood still as deep pulsations rocked them both, and bonded them forever, in sweet shared pleasure.

CHAPTER SIXTY-FIVE

*L*ucy, resting in William's arms on the cobblestone floor of the granary, smiled up at the moon. *It was not clear who glowed more. Her mind, body and soul would never be the same again.*

"William, I don't ever want to lose this feeling. Surely, you're going to make a wanton woman of me."

"I find that very promising."

"Oh, look." She pointed to transparent sheets of vapor rising from the earth. She had often witnessed vapor coming off the fields, but tonight the mist that rose seemed ethereal ... heavenly...

"It's like the morning fog that lifts over the moors," he said. "It's as if our love were celebrating the best gifts of man and nature, making an offering to the moon."

"My loving poet," she said, and kissed his lips.

"I have my moments. Would you like to hear something I'm working on?"

Lucy nodded and nestled against him.

He spoke quietly, as to the heavens:

> *"And vital feelings of delight*
> *Shall rear her form to stately height,*
> *Her virgin bosom swell;*
> *Such thoughts to Lucy I will give*
> *While she and I together live*
> *Here in this happy dell."*

William kissed her tenderly on the lips. "There'll be more to come."

Lucy was pleased. "I'm in your poetry?"

"As surely as you reside in my heart."

A sudden breeze began to stir. Lucy felt William begin to shiver, and pulled away, turning for her cape that lay beside them.

"This happy dell of ours is freezing," she said picking up the cape.

"Yes, quickly, before we turn into blocks of ice."

She pulled the cloak over them. As they held and drew warmth from one another, she closed her eyes, overwhelmed with emotions of contentment and love. She had never been so deliriously happy. Lying face to face, she said, "My darling, darling William."

He pressed his lips once again to hers. As they drew apart, he said, "All my skill with words is inadequate to describe my longing for you."

"Our love will outlast this earth … it is God's reason for giving us birth."

"Ah, an artist *and* a poet." He smiled. "You intrigue me."

Lucy could not hold him close enough. She wished they could go on like this forever, but the position of the moon told her it was late. "I can't bear to say this, but I must be going."

"Not yet. Not just yet."

quire Hawkins's eyes were closed as he lay slumped in his library chair. On the table beside him a solitary candle was sputtering, casting shadows over his florid face. He lifted a goblet of wine to his lips. His eyelids opened a crack when he realized the glass was empty. Turning to the table, he focused on the wine decanter. It, too, had been depleted.

Groaning, the Squire rose unsteadily to his feet. He felt the room spin and leaned on his chair for support. About to stagger off to his bedroom, he noticed a flicker of movement outside the window. He stumbled over to the windowpane. Clouds were beginning to cover the moon, and he had to squint, but saw nothing.

Suddenly, as he was about to give up, he spied a shadowy figure moving across the dark grounds. As the figure drew closer, he recognized the children's governess. The Squire's eyes narrowed. *So, sweet young Miss Lucy had been stealing out at night to meet with that lad of hers, had she?*

"Sneaky little bitch," he muttered. *All this time she'd been pretending to be so pure and she wasn't innocent at all! Miss Lucy was a wicked little tramp.* He grinned in anticipation as a plan began to form in his murky brain. *Obviously, he had been using the wrong approach. Well, that would change. Women like Lucy Sims didn't understand gentlemen. What she craved was a strong, lustful man, one who would forcefully take advantage of her phony virtue. And, he was just the man for the job.* The Squire picked up the candlestick and lurched for the door.

ucy was humming to herself as she rounded the corner of the manor house. The gentle night wind had taken a turn, becoming stronger and carrying with it the smell of rain, but nothing could diminish her feelings of joy as her mind cosseted visions of William. She grinned impishly as she recalled the experiences of the last few hours. *Did she feel guilty?* She shook her head, her curls bouncing—*not at all. She should, but she didn't.* She knew she wouldn't be able to sleep for the remainder of the night.

She reached the back door and could see through the window that all the candles had been extinguished. Quietly lifting the latch, she slipped inside and stood with her back against the doorframe, allowing her eyes to adjust to the darkness. After a moment, she was able to discern the familiar shapes of the stove and the work tables. She moved cautiously forward, holding her breath, hoping she wouldn't bump into anything that would make noise and wake the household.

Lucy turned into the hallway and was startled by an arc of flame that swept toward her, stopping only inches in front of her face. Beyond the flickering candlestick, the Squire's distorted features appeared.

A cold shiver shot down her spine.

"Ah, 'tis my little molly-girl," he slurred, crowding her. "Out ruttin' in the fields with that lad of yers now, eh?"

His breath was acrid with soured wine. Lucy took a disgusted and wary step backward. "I couldn't sleep, Sir. I went for a walk."

The Squire pressed in upon her. "Yer no prim maiden, are ya? I'm thinkin' ya be like me hound bitches when they come inta heat."

A tremor of fear added an edge to her voice. "Please move, I wish to go to bed."

He ignored her. "Ya ought ta see them bitches dig an' chew ta get out'a them pens. They do anythin' ta get a male ta mount 'em."

"Please ... ," she said, trying to move around him. He blocked her path and pushed his bulk forward, backing her into the kitchen.

"No need ta hurry off," he said, setting the candlestick on a sideboard. Then he grabbed the edges of her cape, yanking her to him. Terrified, she swallowed a scream as he opened the cloak and stared bleary-eyed at her figure. "I been askin' meself, what be beneath this dress? What've ya been showin' off ta others an' hidin' from yer Lordship? A pretty little garden of delights, I'm thinkin'."

Her heart pounding, Lucy twisted and tried to pull away from his grip, but it was like iron.

"I'm tired," she said, angry now. "Please let go and allow me to pass."

"Not 'til I've had me eyeful, an' maybe more."

The Squire suddenly ripped her cape off. His arms encircled her and pulled her roughly to his copious belly.

"No! Stop. Stop it, damn you!" she asserted, her voice shaking with alarm and indignation.

Grabbing a handful of her hair, he twisted Lucy's face up to his and attempted to kiss her. She whipped her head from side to side, managing to avoid his fetid mouth.

"Ha," he panted, sweat on his face, "a little vixen now, are ya?"

She tried to struggle free, but to no avail.

Chortling at her plight, he lifted her up to his chest and carried her to a table. He held her with one hand while he brushed aside cooking utensils, sending them clanging across the floor.

Lucy felt her buttocks smacked down upon the edge of the tabletop; her toes dangled inches above the floor. Panic swept through her as he spread her legs and moved between her thighs. Horrified, she cried. "No! Stop! Stop it, damn you!"

When he pressed forward, she screamed! He clamped a hand over her mouth. "Ya'll do no screamin'," he said, the threat of additional violence appearing in his guttural voice. "Ya hear me? No screamin'!"

The Squire's hand dropped to paw at her chest, ripping at her bodice.

Lucy's mind was becoming molten-hot with fury. "Get your filthy hands off!" she yelled. "If you don't stop immediately, I'll feed you to your damned hounds!"

Snickering derisively, he tore at her clothing.

Lucy's rage erupted like liquefied lava, bursting through the earth's crust. She attacked the Squire with a furious assault of her fists, to his belly, arms, shoulders and face. She scratched his cheeks and jabbed her thumbs in his eyes. Squealing, he flailed back, slapping at her until a hard blow to the side of her head blackened her vision. Lucy fell back. Her hands were grabbed roughly, twisted and then pinned behind her back, immobilizing her.

The Squire grinned triumphantly, sweat running down his horribly flushed face, as he held her firmly with one fist and grasped the table with the other. "So this be the way ya like it?" he wheezed, saliva dripping from his mouth.

The blow had left Lucy faint and disoriented, and she found it hard to respond, although she managed weakly, "Stop it, damn you! Let go of me!"

"Ya know ya don't want me ta stop. Let's see these teats," he said, ripping away the remnants of her bodice.

"You monster!" Lucy yelled, as she rallied significantly and butted him in the face with her forehead. He groaned, momentarily stunned. She twisted in his arms and tried to bite his nose, but he effectively warded her off with his superior strength. She realized, with a growing sense of depression that she was as helpless as an injured fox, caught in the jaws of a hungry hound. She had one hope left: She would awaken the household. She screamed, louder this time than before.

The Squire's reaction was swift and vicious. He slapped her hard, once again momentarily blackening her vision. He yanked a dirty handkerchief from his pants pocket and jammed it into her mouth. "I warned ya!" He began to unlace his trousers. "Yer like one of me wild mares. All ya need is a good rider ta break ya."

Lucy recoiled as revolting substances on the Squire's handkerchief seeped onto her tongue; she heaved and gagged. She was unable to breathe.

The Squire, who noticed she was choking to death, pulled the filthy cloth from her mouth.

"Quiet! Ya be quiet now, or back it goes,' he threatened.

She gasped, sucking in air, choking on the bitter vomit that had risen in her throat as she desperately arched away from him. Inflamed by the rise of her hips, the Squire pulled his laces free and grinned, wolfishly eager to take advantage.

Suddenly, a shadowy figure in a white gown appeared behind the Squire. The wraithlike shape lifted a heavy frying pan from the stovetop and brought it down on his head with a resounding *thwack*. The Squire fell with a guttural exhale, dropping heavily on top of Lucy, his spittle drooling onto her breasts.

Lucy recognized Beth's livid face standing over the

unconscious Squire. The maid said, "May God forgive me, yer Lordship." With effort, Beth managed to push her employer's heavy body off of the governess so they lay side by side on the table, and then hurried over to a nearby pan of water that had been used to rinse last night's dishes. Lucy turned her head and was repulsed when she saw the Squire's piggish face, just inches from her own.

Beth rinsed a cloth and carried it back with shaking hands where she wiped the damp cloth over the governess's forehead. "Lucy, dear, ya'll be just fine now," Beth said. "Don't worry about a thing. The Squire won't be wakin' up fer a long while, I'm thinkin'."

Beth's words sounded muffled, as if the woman spoke from a distance, but her voice was calming. Lucy's eyes followed Beth as the older woman moved to the Squire and bent over him. Beth tossed her towel into the bowl and took ahold of her lover's jacket. "Now let me get this big lummox offa the table and lie him onta the floor."

Beth pulled on the Squire, her face turning crimson with the effort. Within moments she had him halfway off the table, but he slipped from her grasp. He fell hard, smacking his head loudly on the slate.

"Oh, dear," Beth said and kneeled down to take the unconscious Squire's head in her hands. "Oh, my, yer Lordship. I hope yer not hurt too bad, but ya deserve every lump ya get."

Beth glanced up at Lucy. "Don't think too poorly of him, Dearie. He's a fairly good man, he is, when he be sober; though when he be in his cups he's too randy fer his own good; and he can have a mean streak, that's fer sure."

Lucy took several breaths to steady herself and then sat up slowly. The chill air raised goose bumps on her flesh where her bodice had been torn open.

Attempting to re-button her clothes to cover herself, she saw it was hopeless; the fabric had been severely ripped. She said, "Beth, thank God… ." Realizing how close she had come to being ravaged, Lucy buried her face in her hands for a moment, struggling with the horror of it all, and then looked up. "How can I ever thank you?"

"'Tis nothin'. Bloody hell!" the maid muttered, as she laid the Squire's head on the floor and stood. "His Lordship deserved it an' more. He coulda come ta me bed for his needs instead of chasing ya ... ya sweet thing."

Lucy struggled against the urge to cry. It was obvious that the world in which she had been living, once so comfortable and secure, had rapidly vanished. She looked down at the prostrate form of the Squire and knew it would now be impossible for her to stay a moment longer at Hawkins House. The tears she had been withholding brimmed over and cascaded down her cheeks when she thought of the children. *What reason could she give them for leaving? She certainly couldn't explain the truth. And then there was William. How would she ever be able to see him again?* She shivered. Her plans for fleeing Hawkins Manor, once only contemplated, had suddenly become an urgent reality.

Lucy wiped her cheeks and straightened her shoulders. She became very quiet as she slipped into a sort of meditative state. She was a firm believer that one could derive strength from one's inner resources, and she now drew upon that resolve and courage. Lucy became serene, and suddenly knew exactly what to do. She turned to the maid. "Beth, I don't wish to go into my bedroom looking like this. Could you gather my wool dress and petticoat off the peg by my bed ... and my belongings? I'm leaving here tonight."

"What're ya saying, lass?" Beth asked. "Ya can't be leaving us."

Lucy's words, now spoken, helped to set her determination. "I'll be on the mail coach that leaves from the King's Head Inn in the morning."

"Ya can't just up and be gone, child. If it be the Squire that worries ya, he'll be too embarrassed ta talk about tonight." The maid winked. "And, as for his head, I'll swear from here to Christmas he took a fall in his cups and banged his noggin' on the floor."

Lucy slipped off the table, holding her tattered bodice together. On unsteady feet, she managed to retrieve her cloak from the floor and wrap it around herself. "It's not just tonight, Beth. It's living in this household. Most of the staff are wary of me. They believe I'm possessed by the Devil."

Beth sputtered with disgust. "Don't pay them simpletons no mind! I'll have a good talk with them."

"It wouldn't do any good, but thank you. Anyway, I need more time on my own ... time to study, to draw without interruptions... ." Beth's face lit up, as if she understood. Lucy continued, "My life and my future begin when I leave Hawkins Manor. The Squire, who may be a good person when he's sober, is not a good person when he's, as you so graciously say, 'in his cups', which makes him 'not a good person' in my eyes. He'll never stop drinking and if I remained here, he'd come after me again and again until he had his way with me. I would sooner die than suffer that indignity. I am leaving tonight."

Beth's face fell. "But, Dearie, if ya go inta the dead of night, her Ladyship'll think ya was the one that nicked her silver spoons."

Lucy considered that possibility, but she wouldn't let it deter her. "Her Ladyship can believe whatever she wishes. At least, with me leaving, you and the rest of the staff won't have to worry about being dismissed if the silver isn't found. I owe you that much for your quick thinking with the frying pan and for your friendship."

Beth, on the verge of tears, said, "Ya owe me naught. Don't be leavin' us, now."

"I have no choice in the matter."

"What about the young'uns?

Lucy cringed. "I'll miss them terribly," she said, knowing the children would be devastated by her departure, especially if she left without saying goodbye, but she couldn't tell them the truth! "If I may use your room, I'll write them a letter."

"Me room be yours," Beth said. "I'll gather yer things."

They hurried from the kitchen, leaving the Squire, who, in his drunken stupor, had begun to snore loudly.

Lucy followed Beth to her private bedroom and hesitated as the maid pushed the door open. There was a candle burning on a small desk. Beth said, "Quill, ink and paper be in the top drawer. Do ya have a carryall for yer things?"

"Yes, my travel bag. It's under my bed."

Beth nodded. "Hurry now. I'll meet you at the front entrance. Go, quick as ya can."

Lucy crossed to Beth's desk as the maid padded off. She sat down in the small chair, opened a drawer and withdrew pen and paper. She would write two letters, one to the children and one to William. Neither would be easy to compose under normal circumstances. Now, having to dash them off in minutes, it would be impossible to include everything she wished to say. She dipped the pen into an inkpot and began to quickly record her thoughts.

❧ C H A P T E R   S I X T Y – E I G H T ❦

*B*eth tiptoed down the hallway and opened the door to the servants' bedroom. Moonlight, mottled by thickening clouds, filtered in from the high dormer windows; she entered the room and padded like a cat around Molly and Mary to Lucy's bed. She lifted Lucy's dress and petticoat from its peg and then knelt on the floor beside her bed, fishing beneath the mattress for the travel bag. She found it and pulled it out, its wooden handles knocking loudly against the bed frame. She winced and froze. The servants stirred and rolled over, but continued to breathe steadily. Beth waited a moment to be sure the women still slept before she lifted the bag and filled it with Lucy's few belongings. She turned to leave, but a bolt of lightning lit the room, and her attention was drawn to the three landscapes hanging on the wall. She hastened over and removed the paintings from their hooks, placing them inside the satchel, as the sound of thunder rolled overhead.

Molly grunted sleepily and propped herself up on an elbow. "Miss High and Mighty is leavin' us, is she?"

Beth spun around to face Molly, as the girl added, "Good riddance to the Devil's keeper, I say."

"I wish ya was the one that was leavin', ya nasty bag o' suet," Beth said, and continued to stuff the canvases into the bag.

"Oh, do ya now? Ya must've seen the way the Squire's been lookin' at me lately."

Beth snorted. "The Squire has better taste than the likes of ya."

Molly laughed. "Ya sound a bit worried, old Beth."

"A pox on yer soul." Beth slipped out through the door, inching it closed behind her.

CHAPTER SIXTY-NINE

*L*ucy extinguished the candle in Beth's room and scurried out, holding her cloak closed as she crept silently along the hallway and down the darkened stairway into the great room. The light of a small flickering lantern drew her to Beth, who was waiting by the front door. Lucy motioned to the woman, indicating she had one quick stop to make. At the storage closet, she opened the paneled door and stepped inside.

The room was pitch black, but she didn't need a light to feel her way around the familiar confines. She quickly found her most precious painting materials and consolidated them into a single basket. Next, she gathered up her easel; its long poles presented a carrying dilemma, but she couldn't bear to leave it behind. She threaded the sticks beneath the handles of the basket, hoping she would be able to hold them in place. As she closed the door behind her, a flash of lightning illuminated the room, followed four heartbeats later by the clap of thunder; she carried her art materials across the length of the room. "Beth, I'm sorry to take so long."

The woman waved aside the apology and held up a petticoat and long dress. "Your woolen threads ... off with them rags."

"You're a Godsend." Lucy hugged Beth and slipped the cape off, allowing the torn dress and tattered undergarment to fall to her feet. Her bare skin shivered as she wriggled quickly into the shift and dress, grateful for the warmth of the wool.

Beth placed the cloak about Lucy's shoulders and lifted the small lantern and a pair of oversized boots from the floor. "Ya'll be needin' these, there's a storm coming. The boots are oiled and watertight. An' ya wouldn't be able ta see a thing without candlelight."

"I can't take those from you. You'll be needing them yourself."

"They be me gift to ya. An' don't ya be arguin' with me now. It'll do ya no good." She pressed the boots and the lantern into Lucy's hands. "This little storm lamp keeps its flame in the worst weather, so you won't be wanderin' off the road and getting' lost."

Lucy was overwhelmed by the woman's generosity. "I don't know how to thank you, Beth, you've been so ... ."

"Shh, I'm here to help ya. First now, pull them walkin' boots on over yer shoes." Lucy leaned against the wall and slipped her feet into the weatherproof footwear.

Beth picked up the torn dress and ripped off several long strips of material from the skirt. She deftly twisted and braided the pieces together, making a rope. She tied one end around the handle of Lucy's travel bag. "Now, hand me the basket," Beth said. When Lucy passed the container to her, Beth attached the other end of the rope around its handle and made it into a knot. After testing the strength of the two knots, the maid nodded with satisfaction. Then she lifted the center of the rope and looped it across Lucy's shoulders. Beth smiled proudly. "There ya be, like a pack horse."

Lucy felt some of her anxiety diminish. She did indeed feel like a pack animal with her bag, basket and easel dangling at her sides. "What can I ever do for you ... ?"

Beth grinned. "Ya can send me one of yer paintin's when ya get famous."

"Oh, I will. I promise you."

"A quick hug now, an' off with ya, even tho' I don't think ya should be goin' out. It's threatening to rain."

They embraced warmly and as they parted. Lucy kissed Beth's cheek. "I'll miss you." She reached into the pocket of her cape for the two letters she had written. "One of these is for the children and the other one is for my gentleman friend, Mr. Wordsworth."

"I'll see that they get them." Beth reached for the letters.

Lucy hesitated to release the few hurriedly composed lines; they were so inadequate. "I had so much to say, but … no time… ."

Beth nodded sympathetically and gently took the letters from her. "They'll understand."

"I pray they do."

Beth pocketed the envelopes and edged the front door open, revealing that rain had begun to beat down upon the cobblestones. "Now, off ya go, child, and may God be with ya."

Lucy lifted the hood of her cape and hurried out.

Lightning flashed again as she crossed the courtyard and she turned back for a final look at Hawkins House. The flicker of candlelight drew her attention to an upper windowpane. A woman's face was there; it was Molly. Lucy thought she spied a malicious grin spread across the girl's face before she pulled away, and the thunder rumbled overhead.

W illiam was oblivious to the rain that pelted the window beside his desk, as he concentrated on his newest verse. After a moment he lifted a quill and studied the words with a critical eye. He began to read the poem:

LUCY.
She dwells among the untrodden ways
Beside the springs of Dove,
A Maid whom there are none to praise
And very few to love:

He paused … no words could describe Lucy, really, but were these adequate? He went on…

A violet by a mossy stone,
Half hidden from the eye!
Fair as a star when only one
Is shining in the sky.

Yes, this verse was perfect, but there was more to write.

I told her this: her laughter light
Is ringing in my ears;

He examined his words again—ever the bane of the writer. He crossed out the last two lines and shaped new ones.

Eventually, he thrust the nib into its inkpot. He would improve the verse and start over.

But first, he felt a chill in the air. He stood and crossed to the fireplace, stirred the smoldering peat, and added another chunk to the hearth. When it glowed with rekindled warmth, he returned to his labor of love.

❧ ❧ ❧

*I*cy, stinging rain blurred Lucy's vision as she leaned into the gusting wind, struggling to keep her footing on the road that had quickly become an oozing ribbon of mud. She was thankful for Beth's lantern, which she clutched before her with numb fingers. Its dim light, casting eerie shadows, was all that saved her from losing her way.

Occasionally, Lucy passed the outline of a house or barn, but she wasn't familiar with these buildings. She had no idea how far she had come, nor how far she still had to travel before she would reach the warmth and safety of the King's Head Inn. *Would she arrive in time to depart on the mail coach? Would the coach even be traveling with the roads barely passable?*

Lucy pictured her mother's elderly sister, some sixty miles away in Bath. Half a year had passed since she had last corresponded with her aunt. *What if she found her aunt had moved away or, worse, had died?* Lucy's concerns were swept aside as a fierce blast of wind blew her hood back, causing her hair to fly into lashing tangles. Her cape flapped about her like the wings of a great albatross. Somehow, she managed to hold onto her few possessions until the gust subsided. When she pulled her hood up, rivulets of icy water streamed down the nape of her neck, taking her breath away. Lucy could feel the cold seeping into her bones and began to shiver severely; she thought the earth must surely be quaking beneath her feet. But she wouldn't allow the storm to break her! Sucking in a deep breath, she wiped her face with a renewed sense of determination. She pulled her cape tightly about her and strode forward against the punishing storm, toward the King's Head Inn and an uncertain future.

❧❧ ❧❧ ❧❧

he anemic purple glow of a stormy dawn barely illuminated the eastern horizon across from Hawkins House. Intermittent bolts of lightning pierced the grey sky in the west, great rolls of thunder following. Muted light seeped through the rain-mottled windows of the manor as the housekeeper bustled into the kitchen, followed by a huffing, pink-faced Lady Hawkins. They were still in their nightclothes. Her Ladyship almost tripped over the Squire, who lay prostrate on the floor, a stupid grin pasted on his face. The cook and his assistant, Percy, had been stepping gingerly around their master as they sifted flour to make bread and replenished the stove with squares of peat.

"This is where the staff found him, my Lady," Mrs. Tennant said.

"George, wake up!" Lady Hawkins nudged her husband with her toe. "Wake up, damn ya! Me earrin's have been stolen."

The Squire snorted and exhaled, flapping thick lips. Exasperated, Lady Hawkins nudged him harder, in the ribs. "George, I'm tellin' ya, I been robbed."

His Lordship's eyelids fluttered open. He winced and regarded his wife with confusion. "What ... what're ya sayin'?"

"Me ruby and diamond earrin's have been taken right out of our bedroom durin' the night." She frowned. "What're ya doin' sleepin' on the damn floor?"

The Squire's head throbbed. *What was he doing on the floor?* Squinting, he tried to remember the previous evening; he vaguely recalled his encounter with that tart, Lucy, lifting her up onto the kitchen table and tearing at her clothes. He grinned at the image, but then his mirth fell away as his memory of what had occurred next eluded him. He hoped there had been more to it than that, but his mind was a befuddled blank.

"George, I asked ya why were ya sleepin' on the bloody floor? An' why is yer face all scratched?"

The Squire scowled, as much from the shrill sound of his wife's voice as from the throbbing in his cheeks and the top of his skull. "I must've taken a fall," he said. Sitting up, he ran fingers along the side of his jaw and cringed. *The little bitch had scratched him.* Then he explored his hair, and his fingers found two bumps the size of eyeballs protruding from his scalp; touching them, he flinched ... they hurt like hell! *Had he really taken a fall? He would find Lucy and force her to tell him what had transpired. A little pain would be well worth it if he had bedded the wench.*

"Didn't you hear anythin' I said?" Lady Hawkins demanded. "Someone nicked me new earrin's."

He focused his bloodshot eyes on his wife. "Stolen, ya say?"

"Have ya gone deaf on me?" she said, raising her voice. "Yes, stolen, I say! I said it afore an' I'm sayin' it again. Now get yer bum off the damn floor an' find the thief afore they gets away."

Beth appeared in the doorway, fidgeting nervously with her apron. "Excuse me, me Lord and me Lady. Is something wrong?"

Mrs. Tennant strode toward the servant. "Yes. Something is dreadfully wrong. My Lady's ruby and diamond earrings have been stolen."

"There's a damn filcher in me house," Lady Hawkins yelled. "First me Apostle Spoons are taken and now me new earrin's. This is cussin' outrageous! Mrs. Tennant, send for the parish constable."

The housekeeper turned to the cook's assistant. "Percy, take a horse from the stable and summon Constable Hardy. Go now. Away with you!"

"Yes, ma'am." Percy grabbed a cape and scurried out the kitchen door.

"Someone lend me a hand," the Squire said.

Beth reached for him, grunting as she hauled him to his feet.

"George," his wife said. "I want the thief caught and prosecuted. Ya hear me?"

"I hear ya, Gerty. The constable will sort this out and ya'll get yer silver an' earrin's back."

She glared at her husband. "Damn ya, don't call me Gerty in front of the staff or ya'll be kissin' the floor again, I'm telling ya." She spun and faced the housekeeper. "Mrs. Tennant, no one is to leave the house. Ya understand?"

"Yes, my ... er ... Lady. I promise you we'll get to the bottom of this."

"An' fer the love of God, put on your clothes."

"Yes, my Lady," Mrs. Tennant replied, drawing her robe together.

Her Ladyship cast a reproachful look at the servants and then whirled out of the room like a dervish wind, with Mrs. Tennant following in her wake.

"Beth," the Squire said, edging over to the servant. "Look at the top of me head. See if the skin be broke. It hurts like the Devil."

Beth took his head in her hands and examined his skull. "The skin be fine, me Lord. Two little bumps is all. I think your noggin's in one piece."

The Squire elbowed her away with a dismissive grumble, racking his memory for his encounter with the governess: *They had had a little wrestling match, during which he had overpowered her and started to remove her dress. Then ... yes ... now he remembered; she had been helpless, he knew that.* His brow wrinkled with frustration. *But then what had happened? Why couldn't he remember any more? He certainly hoped he had taken advantage of her, but he would also like to remember it.* He touched his sore pate and was suddenly suspicious. *He had fallen on the top of his head? Not bloody likely.* Fingering his injury, he looked warily at Beth. "Beth, did ya come near the kitchen last night?"

"No, my Lord. I was in me bed, all by me lonesome."

The Squire grunted. "Go and fetch Miss Lucy."

"I'm afraid I can't do that, Sir. She's gone."

"Gone? Gone where? What're ya saying?"

"She's left Hawkins House, Sir. She said she won't be coming back."

"Won't be coming back?" His eyebrows rose. *Had the little trollop taken his wife's earrings as revenge for his indiscretions? It was entirely possible. She might have a dark side after all. Some of the servants had said she had the Devil in her. Yes, she could be much more devious than he had realized. Hadn't he caught her creeping back into the house after having sex with her lad in the fields?* The Squire touched the scratches along the side of his jaw as he mused. *Maybe the two of them were in this together. Her accomplice could have followed her into the kitchen and hit him over the head. Yes, then the two of them had made off with the valuables. She and her lover were partners in crime. So the servants had been right about Lucy Sims all along.*

"May I serve you a cup of tea, Sir?" Beth asked.

"No!" he thundered. "I don't want a damn cuppa tea. I want that thievin' little devil in jail."

CHAPTER SEVENTY - ONE

*G*eoffrey Walsh struggled to pull on his boots as he cursed the foul, rainy weather. He had slept poorly, having been kept awake first, by loud claps of thunder, and then, by a relentless downpour that had pounded on the roof. All of it had finally driven him from his bed early this morning. He was tempted to stay indoors and let the storm pass, but there seemed to be no letup in sight, and he had much to do. Now fully dressed, he stood and lifted his pistol from the nightstand. He checked the primer and then, confident it was charged, slipped it into his coat pocket. Rainstorm be damned, time was running out and today he had plans to visit Wordsworth's writing partner, Samuel Coleridge. This poet had an eccentric reputation; his critics had accused him of "being a misguided genius", had labeled him "fickle and childish with a passionate, troubled mind, given to extravagant—and often absurd—behavior." Coleridge was known for writing those modernistic poems that people would find boring and pedestrian. He was also rumored to use laudanum, along with other exotic drugs, a weakness Walsh thought he could exploit if the opportunity arose. His plan was to get Coleridge, a man who apparently loved the sound of his own voice, to inadvertently reveal the mystery of Wordsworth's income and his association with the French spy network in England.

Walsh's stomach was growling by the time he descended the stairs. He spotted Simon at the fireplace, throwing fuel onto the smoldering grate. It was not yet dawn.

"I'll have tea and a bowl of porridge," he said, taking a table near the hearth. "And I need to rent your horse and covered buggy for another day."

The innkeeper turned to him with a scowl. "Right-o, Mr. Geoffrey Walsh. I'll get yer vittles. The buggy'll cost ya ten shillin's."

"That's twice what I paid yesterday." he said, indignant at being overcharged. "It's outrageous!"

"Not in this pissin' rain. Odds are ya'll run off the road an' crack up me buggy."

He could see from the innkeeper's wry grin that the man would like nothing better than for him to have an accident, but he also realized there was some truth to the statement. A cautious man would have waited for the storm to pass, but he didn't have that luxury. He had to conclude his investigation and write his damning report. "Have the buggy brought around."

❦ ❦ ❦

Lucy slogged along the road under a low, dark sky, her ability to see diminished by the heaviness of the rain. A rhythm of sucking noises accompanied the sinking and rising of the thick soles of her oversized boots, in and out of the mud. Blisters burned the heels of her feet with every step. The fingers of her hands, blue with cold, ached, as she clutched onto the small lantern. Its' dim light began to flicker. Lucy panicked as she watched the candle inside sputter and smoke, water seeping past its protective seams. She prayed it wouldn't go out.

A noise suddenly impelled Lucy to raise her head. She gasped. A horse and buggy sped directly toward her! She caught a quick glimpse of the darkly-dressed and fierce-looking driver, as she leapt aside, to avoid being hit. She felt a hard blow to her hip as the buggy's wheel struck her and sent her sprawling to the side of the road. She rolled over in the soggy grass and came to a stop inches from a large boulder. Frightened and angry, Lucy peered after the buggy as it disappeared into the mist. *Had the driver even seen her? She doubted it or surely he would have stopped and offered her assistance. The idiot! He should look where he's going!* She slapped the earth with frustration and then cried out as a thousand needles pierced her partially-numbed fingers. Lucy cradled her aching hand inside her cloak for warmth and tentatively rubbed her torso and legs with her free hand, investigating her injuries: She located a sore area on her hip that would soon become an ugly bruise, but as far as she could tell, nothing was broken. The rain was beating down so powerfully, she thought she might dissolve into the very earth. Lucy pulled her soaking cape close about her and stood up on unsure feet, then became aware of a new darkness. *The lantern!* The cry of a wounded animal escaped her when she found the glass square lying in a puddle, its flame extinguished. *And, where were her baskets? They surely had flown off as she had fallen.*

Overhead, lightning ripped through the sky; Lucy threw her hands over her head in a futile gesture of self-protection. Thin jagged streaks of white fire cut through the night as thunder hammered across the heavens like the battle drums of an advancing army. Lucy covered her ears with her hands to stifle the reverberating roar.

Finally, she raised her hands upward in a sacrificial offering. *All right, here I am. I give up. If you must strike me, Lord, do it soon! Put me out of this misery!* Another fiery spear pierced the air. It forced her backwards as it momentarily illuminated a sign beneath the branches of a roadside tree. Lucy could barely believe her eyes. The sign read: King's Head Inn. She choked back a sob as her faith returned. *Oh God, I'm so sorry. Forgive me. Forgive me. I didn't really mean it. Thank you, God. Thank you.* She cupped a hand over her eyes and peered through the downpour. Yes, there … off the road, was the rambling two-story structure. Small lights dimly outlined the inn's windows.

Lucy searched on hands and knees for her possessions, and, finding them relatively unharmed, rehung them about her shoulders. She stood, lifted her cloak and skirts to her calves and plodded through the mire toward the front entrance of the inn.

✿ ✿ ✿

A gust of rain followed Lucy as she entered the roadhouse. She closed the door behind her as quickly as she could and leaned back against its timbers, savoring the warmth of the tavern. She muttered a prayer of gratitude as her eyes scanned the dark interior.

An older man, apparently the innkeeper, was the only person in the room. He seemed to be dozing in one of three armchairs facing a smoldering fireplace, the dim glow casting shadows over his craggy features. He stirred and smacked his lips. With eyes still closed, he grumbled, "If ya be here for the mail coach, it be runnin' late."

"Thank you," Lucy said, obviously relieved to hear that her transportation had not been aborted by the storm and that she had not missed it. "Yes, I am here for the coach."

Simon opened his eyes to scrutinize the bearer of such a pleasant voice. He sat up straight, his face registering concern; he saw a slim young lady shivering under a soaking cape. He rose and stoked the peat, stirring up flames. "Step over 'ere, Miss, and warm yerself. Ya look to be half frozen."

"Thank you." Lucy placed her dark lantern on the floor and slipped the rope from about her neck, setting down the basket, easel and travel bag. She removed her cloak and stretched her shoulders, wincing from the ache of bruised muscles.

"Bring that cape over here to dry by the fire."

"That's very kind of you." She crossed to the fireplace and spread the garment out by the side of the hearth, appreciating the warmth it afforded.

"Have a seat, Lass," the innkeeper said. "Where ya off to, all by yerself?"

Overcome by a wave of exhaustion, she gratefully sank into an armchair. She replied, "I'm traveling to Bath."

"A fairsome city, Bath. I were there once many years ago." He started for the kitchen. "Ya could use a cuppa tea an' a bit of porridge, I'm thinkin'."

"Oh, please!" she said, suddenly feeling her stomach cramp from hunger. "If it's not too much trouble."

"No trouble a'tall."

Lucy tried to run her fingers through her wet and tangled hair, but it was hopeless. She edged closer to the warmth of the fire and her eyes soon fixed upon thin wisps of smoke spiraling up the flu. Her thoughts wandered to Emily and Henry. *What would the children think of her when they discovered she had left them?* She hoped her letter would help soothe their hurt feelings. She prayed they would understand. She was going to miss them greatly and she would always worry about them in that terrible house.

And what of William ... their short time together ... the love she had for him had opened a new and breathtaking world ... and now she had to leave it behind. Would he ever follow her to Bath? She felt a pain deep inside her chest. *What would she ever do without him?*

CHAPTER SEVENTY – TWO

Beth, Molly and Mary sat at the kitchen table, eyeing each other uneasily as they ate breakfast in silence. Outside, the wind howled around the corners of the manor house like a wild beast, shrieking after its prey. The storm continued to rage. At the stove, the cook dropped chunks of onion into a steaming stockpot. His eyes, watery from cutting them, flitted to the windows where sheets of rain battered the panes. "Percy should be back by now," he said, in a worried tone.

"'Less he and the Constable got themselves washed inta the next county," Mary said.

"Our little thief be wishin' fer that, ya can be sure," Molly said with a snicker.

"Lucy is no thief," Beth defended.

Molly sneered. "Oh, do ya think not? What was she up ta last night when ya was packin' her things?"

"She was in me room, writing letters."

"Wouldn't take her but a minute ta run ta her Ladyship's bedroom an' nick them earrin's. Have ya thought of that?"

"Lucy wouldn't steal a farthing, ya can take me word on it," Beth said with conviction.

The children rushed in from in the hallway.

"Beth!" Emily said, her features tense with alarm. "Papa said Miss Lucy has left us. Is it true?"

"'Tis true," Beth said, withdrawing Lucy's letters from her pocket. "One of these be fer the two of ya, the other fer her lad."

"I'll take them," Emily said, snatching both envelopes from the woman's hand. She read the names neatly written in her governess's handwriting. "I'll see Mr. Wordsworth gets his letter," she said, tearing open the one addressed to her and Henry.

"What does it say?" Henry asked with an anxious frown.

"Shh, Henry! I'm trying to read." Emily stepped over to the windows for more light and privacy.

Henry followed her. "Emily, tell me!"

Emily began to read. "Miss Lucy says she is very sorry to be leaving us. She tells us to do our studies and promises to write to us later to explain why she didn't have time to say a proper goodbye." Emily's downcast features suddenly lightened. "She says we can visit her when she is settled in her new home. And she says to tell Mama and Papa she didn't steal the silver spoons."

Molly snorted. "Bloody liar! She nicked the silver an' her Ladyship's earrin's!"

"Shut your mouth, Molly," Beth said.

Molly concluded. "It be the Devil in her."

"Miss Lucy would never steal anything," Henry said. "And she's got no Devil in her."

Emily spoke up as she read the letter's last line. ". . . and she says she's going to miss us terribly, and that ... she loves us."

Henry turned away to hide the tears that welled in his eyes. A moment later he headed purposefully for the back door.

"Emily, come with me."

"Where to?"

Henry ignored his sister as he grabbed two cloaks from their pegs. He threw one to Emily. "Come on!"

"What are you doing?" she demanded.

Henry yanked open the door and ran out into the heavy downpour. After a sigh of frustration, Emily threw her cape on and chased after him.

Beth hurried to her feet and crossed to the gaping door.

"Emily! Henry!" Beth yelled, standing in the doorway with the rain pelting her face. "Get back in here right now!"

The children paid no attention to Beth as they splashed across the muddied yard toward the barn.

The servants crowded up to Beth at the door. "They'll be catchin' their death out there," Mary said.

"Those little urchins!" Beth said. "I'd best get me coat and go after 'em."

"I'll get the little buggers," Molly offered. "Me cloak's downstairs. Not to worry. I'll have 'em back in no time."

Beth looked after Molly, who rushed out to the stairway, surprised that the sullen servant girl would offer to do anything that wasn't required of her.

"There be Percy and Constable Hardy!" the cook yelled, peering out the doorway as he spotted two men riding up on horseback through a veil of rain.

The men dismounted in front of them. Hardy was a tall, severe-looking man in his fifties; he had a large nose, hazel eyes and a full, sandy beard. He wore a rain cape over a brown tweed suit and was oblivious to the downpour as he walked to the rear of his steed and lifted a hoof to inspect it. He spat on the ground and tore away a loose horseshoe. "Mud's playin' hell with these shoes. Percy, can you put a new one on for me?"

Percy wiped his wet face and nodded. "It'll take a while to get the fire in the shed goin', but I'll handle it fer ya."

"Good man," the Constable said. He handed his horse's reins to Percy and stepped into the kitchen.

❧❀❧ ❧❀❧ ❧❀❧

*H*enry and Emily ran through the barn, scattering a half dozen chickens that clucked angrily as they scurried out of the way. Horses snorted and pranced in several stalls that occupied the ground floor. Above stood an open gallery stacked high with pungent bales of hay. Emily followed Henry into the tack room at the far end of the structure and watched as he pulled a bridle down from its peg on the wall.

"Henry, what are you doing?" she demanded, almost stepping on a fat tabby cat that ran off with its tail as ruffled as its temper.

"I need Dobbin's saddle. Hurry!" He turned to lift a saddle blanket from a rail.

Emily reached for one of several saddles resting on a row of blocks. "Are you going to tell me what you're up to?" she asked impatiently, as she wrestled the saddle down.

Henry crossed to the first stall where a large brown gelding was prancing and whinnying. "We're going to bring Miss Lucy home," he replied as he rubbed the white star on the horse's forehead and unlatched the door.

"How are we ever going to find her in this storm?"

He stepped into the stall and crawled up onto a feed trough. "She be on the road to the King's Head Inn or maybe she be there by now. We'll find her." From his perch, he threw the blanket onto the gelding's broad back and then slipped the halter over its head. Holding onto the reins, he jumped down and led the horse out of the enclosure. "Bring the saddle."

Emily, not convinced this was a good idea, didn't move. Her eyes filled with tears as she contemplated life without Lucy.

"Come on, Emily! We've got to hurry. We can make Miss Lucy come home. I know it." He glanced at her imploringly. "She loves us."

Emily stifled a sob; then bolted forward and threw the saddle up onto Dobbin's back.

amuel seethed silently as he stared across his desk at a grim-faced Geoffrey Walsh, who was sucking the last of his tea from a cup. Walsh's horse and buggy could be seen through the rain-mottled front window, where they stood beneath a pine tree, semi-protected from the foul weather.

"Another cup of tea, Samuel?" Sara asked from the adjoining kitchen. She'd been eavesdropping as usual, he assumed, while she sat in a chair crocheting a baby's sweater. Hartley slept soundly in his crib nearby.

"Not until our guest has left us," Samuel said, having had his fill of the inquisition the man had been putting him through regarding William's background.

Walsh raised his empty cup, his eyes darting from his host to Sara. "I'll have a bit more."

"Not in this house, you won't," Samuel said. "Get yourself back to Bristol. You've outworn your welcome here."

"Being welcome is not my concern," Walsh answered with what Samuel considered contempt. "Tell me, what are you hiding about your friend Wordsworth? If you speak candidly I'll see to it that the Bristol Daily News, rewards you handsomely for any information that might be newsworthy."

"You're not a writer for any damned newspaper," Samuel declared, having had enough of the man's charade, a bad one at that.

Without bothering to deny the statement, Walsh tilted the teacup over his open mouth to catch the last drops on his tongue, and then lowered the container to the saucer with a resounding clank. "There have been rumors that Wordsworth is, how shall I put this, not as loyal to England as he should be. Your neighbors have had no problem discussing these allegations with me. Why should you?"

Samuel snorted. "Fools love to hear themselves prattle on. And a man who gives credence to fools is no less a fool himself."

Samuel was gratified that the man flinched as though he had been stung.

Walsh narrowed his eyes and said, "It would be wise for you not to antagonize me."

"Walsh, you're a liar, and as transparent as a jar of piss! You come into my house under the guise of a reporter and you have the cheek to challenge the reputation of William Wordsworth. How dare you! William is twice the man you'll ever be."

Walsh snarled, "There are those who say Wordsworth is a radical, dangerous man, one who is stirring up insurrection."

"Name one man of reputation who has had anything ill to say of William Wordsworth."

"One?" Welsh countered, raising his black notebook. "I have a dozen in here. Your friend is in very serious trouble."

"Who are you, Mr. Walsh?"

Walsh withdrew his credentials and displayed them proudly for Samuel to inspect. "I am an agent from the Home Office in Bristol, sent here by order of the Duke of Portland to investigate a suspected French spy, William Wordsworth. I will give a full report on his activities so that he can be prosecuted to the fullest extent of the law."

"William is no more a spy than I am!"

Welsh stared hard at him, as if pondering the likelihood of Samuel's loyalty to the Crown. "Who is Nozy?"

"Nozy?" Samuel said. "I've never known anyone by that name."

"Wordsworth was overheard talking to a spy by the name of Nozy," Walsh said, drilling deeper for an answer.

"Nozy? Oh, right you are," he said magnanimously as if suddenly remembering the man. He turned to his wife. "Sara, isn't Nozy coming over for tea this afternoon?"

"Yes, dear," she said, adroitly catching on to Samuel's private joke. "I believe Spy Nozy is joining us, along with the First Consul of France, General Napoleon Bonaparte."

Walsh blinked with irritation. "Allow me to remind you, this is a grievous matter! It's a criminal offense to harbor, aid and abet spies. The penalty is death by hanging." He paused, apparently to allow the weight of his words to sink in. "Once more now, Mr. Coleridge, for your sake and the sake of your family, I strongly urge you to answer honestly: Who is Nozy?"

Samuel rose to his feet knocking his chair over. "*You* are nosy. Get out of my home!"

Walsh stumbled from his seat and reached for his pistol as Samuel bore down upon him.

"How dare you come in here and threaten my friend and my family," Samuel bellowed. "Get out. Get out now before I throw you out."

Walsh backed up toward the door, his fingers clenched around the butt of his firearm, ready to draw it. "Mr. Coleridge, your defiance and lack of cooperation will be duly noted in my report to the Home Office. You, too, can expect a summons."

Samuel caught sight of Walsh's black notebook on the table. He swept it up and threw it at his visitor. "Move your arrogance out of my home or I'll take great pleasure in breaking both of your Goddamn legs, and maybe your head too!"

Walsh's face flushed a beet red; he appeared to be on the brink of losing control. Samuel's eyes fell to the investigator's hand, hidden inside his coat pocket. The outline of a pistol was evident. Walsh glared at him, breathing heavily and looking as though he hoped Samuel would be foolish enough to attack him.

Hartley, awakened by the loud voices, began to cry.

Sara put aside her knitting and lifted him from his crib, pleading, "Mr. Walsh, please leave our home."

Walsh's eyes darted to Sara, to Hartley, and then back to him. Samuel couldn't fathom what the interloper's next move might be but as a precaution, he tightly gripped his chair, prepared to swing it at Walsh's head if the man drew his pistol. The agent finally eased off and pulled an empty hand from his pocket. He stooped, picked up his notebook, then turned for the door. Walsh hesitated momentarily in the open doorway, staring out at the rain, then whirled around with a snarl on his face. "You sir, and your ilk, are a curse to England. I'll do everything in my power to see that you are all hung."

"And you," Samuel thundered as he walked to the door with chair in hand, "who certainly doesn't deserve the courtesy of being called 'Sir,' are a dangerous, overzealous simpleton! I shall do everything in my power to see that you are dismissed for gathering salacious gossip from other half-wits!"

Walsh, who had stepped out into the rain, spun around to retort. The door was slammed in his face.

Samuel fastened the door latch and yelled, "Damned, prying misanthrope."

"Samuel, you're scaring Hartley," she admonished, pulling her blouse aside to offer a breast to the squalling baby. Hartley stopped wailing as soon as his mouth found his mother's nipple. "You mustn't get so angry. It makes you sound like an irrational beast."

He flashed a wily smile as he returned to the table and set down the chair he was still holding. "That is one of my better acts, one I feign so as to intimidate and frighten. Fortunately, it works quite well with bullies who try to fabricate lies against good men in order to achieve their own ends."

"I thought you were going to strike him with the chair."

"Excellent!" he added gleefully. "Had I so intended, believe me, I would have thrashed him soundly. I do have my primitive moments."

"That you do," Sara replied, not smiling, all too happy to agree.

He sat at his desk and thought for a moment, drumming his fingers on his journal. "I'm afraid I haven't made it any easier for William. Walsh must be the sneaky bastard who's been following him. A bloody government man!"

"You'll have to get word to William," Sara said.

He peered through the window with a growing sense of apprehension, watching after Walsh's buggy as the Crown's man drove away through the rain and mud. "I'll go to Alfoxden as soon as this never-ending pissing stops."

ady Hawkins, who had changed from her nightclothes into a dress, sat with her husband and Constable Hardy at the kitchen table, which was laden with several teapots, steaming bowls of oatmeal, sliced baked ham, scones, orange marmalade and an assortment of cheeses. The household servants, Mrs. Tennant and the cook, hovered uneasily by the warmth of the stove. Hardy, halfway through his bowl of oats, spoke between mouthfuls. "... and do any of you know where Lucy Sims might have gone?"

The cook cleared his throat and said, "I'd wager she be goin' far from here ta sell them jewels an' silver, maybe ta London itself."

"Constable," Lady Hawkins said, "how will ya ever find her in this storm?"

"The inclement weather works for me, my Lady. If the mail coach is runnin' and if she be on it, I'll catch up to her by the end of the day. No coach moves as fast as a horse and rider on muddy roads."

"Thank God!"

"We'll want ta press charges," the Squire said, "so we'll know the little filcher goes ta prison where she belongs."

The door opened and Percy bustled in, his hat and cloak dripping. "Constable, yer all set," he said. "Sorry it took so long but that horse of yers be a bit bad tempered."

"I forgot to tell ya, he don't like his hooves hammered, 'specially when it's cold." Constable Hardy finished a last spoonful of cereal and then stood. Reaching for his cape and hat that rested on one of the chairs, he said, "Squire and my Lady, I thank ya for the nourishment. Ya'll soon be having yer property back and a fine prison term for Miss Sims."

The kitchen door flew open again and Beth, wearing her raingear and a look of alarm, hurried inside. "I can't find Molly or the children anywhere! An' Dobbin is gone."

"I thought I heard a rider go by the shed about a half hour ago," Percy said. "But I couldn't be sure; I was too busy buildin' a fire in me hearth to pay attention."

The Squire and Lady Hawkins rose quickly from the table. "I don't know a damn about Molly," the Squire said. "But I'll wager a pound sterling Emily and Henry have gone after Lucy."

"Squire, if I see them on the road—if I can see anyone on the road—I'll be sure they get back home," Constable Hardy said, slipping on his cape.

"Ya don't know my Emily and Henry," Lady Hawkins said. "They won't listen to ya."

"Percy," the Squire said, "bring me coach around! I'll be bringin' the young'uns home meself."

Percy ran for the back door, pulling his cloak about him as he dashed out.

The constable said, "Ya won't be making much time with your carriage, Squire. A saddle horse would suit you better."

"No, I want Emily an' Henry where I can control them. I've a strong team. They be used to the mud," the Squire said with determination. "Beth, gather me raingear."

Beth scurried from the room. Constable Hardy put on his hat and opened the door to the elements. He stood there a moment staring at the heavy rain. "'Tis a poor day to be chasing down a thief, but then, 'tis a poor day to be a thief," he said before he stepped out, closing the door behind him.

"George," Lady Hawkins said, "what is happenin' in this household?"

He answered, "It all be the fault of that Lucy Sims. But it will soon be over, I promise ya that!"

he children clung to Dobbin's back as the big horse cantered along the slippery road. Emily sat in front, gripping the horse's mane while Henry's arms circled her waist, holding onto the reins. With the wind and rain lashing their faces Emily leaned down, listening to the gelding's labored breathing. "Henry, this mud be too hard on Dobbin. Take to the grass."

Henry guided their mount onto the field paralleling the road. The animal's hooves gained traction in the turf and their progress improved.

"We can save time by crossing this pasture," she cried, pointing out a shortcut through a meadow, "if I remember right."

Henry reined Dobbin away from the road. Lightning flashed overhead, but the steady gelding ignored the spears of fire and the accompanying roll of thunder and, with a little urging, broke into a steady gallop. They swept over the countryside, passing through veil-like sheets of rain that saturated the earth. Emily blinked her eyes repeatedly, trying to clear her vision, then suddenly stiffened, eyes wide with terror: A tree limb had materialized in their path!

"Henry!" she screamed.

Before he could react, they were swept from Dobbin's back. They hit the ground and rolled head-over-heels across the rain-softened turf. Filthy and disheveled, Emily was the first to scramble to her feet, and she watched with distress as the horse galloped on without them.

"Dobbin!" she screamed. "Come back here. Come back!

"Dobbin, whoa!" Henry yelled, standing up beside her. "Whoa! Dobbin! Come back!"

She could see their yelling wasn't going to accomplish anything. Her brother started running after the gelding. "Come on, Emily. We've got to catch him."

Without much hope, she splashed across the meadow after him.

❦❦ ❦❦ ❦❦

*W*illiam and Dorothy were finishing a late breakfast of fried eggs and buttered toast with plum preserves as they sat at the table near their front window. The incessant rain pelted the windowpanes with the cadence of a military drum corps at a steady march. William read his journal, reviewing his latest efforts. Dorothy was paging through a week-old newspaper, when movement outside caught her attention. She looked through the window and her eyebrows shot up. "William, there's a horse in our yard!"

Lowering the journal, William squinted to see through the blurry panes. There was, indeed, a horse in their yard. It calmly flicked its tail and ears against the downpour as it grazed under a tree close by.

"Yes," he said, noticing the mount's empty saddle, "and it appears to have lost its rider." Laying aside his work, William rose from the table and crossed to the coat rack where he retrieved his hat and cloak from a peg and opened the front door. "I'd better have a look."

Dorothy followed him, grabbing her wrap. "I'm coming with you."

The two stepped outside into the gusting deluge. William was pleasantly surprised when the horse ignored their presence and continued feeding. Looking about for signs of a rider, he could see no one; the rain diminished visibility in every direction.

"Dorothy, stay where you are," he said in a monotone so as not to spook the horse. He slowly approached the gelding. "Hello, big fellow. Now where did you come from? And where is your rider?"

Out of the corner of his eye he saw Dorothy take a few steps back, watching anxiously.

The horse tossed a curious glance in William's direction and then lowered its muzzle to pull on the slippery grass. Gaining hope that it was a mellow animal, he walked quietly up to the gelding's side and patted its wet shoulder, noticing the skin was warm and steaming: It had been ridden hard recently. "Good boy," he said, taking hold of the reins that lay across the animal's neck. "Now, where might your master be? I'd say he took a fall. Let's hope he's not hurt." William glanced around, searching for clues that would help unravel the mystery. He noticed tracks in the grass where the horse's hooves had sunk into the soft earth, leaving distinct indentations.

Speaking up to be heard above the storm, he shouted, "Dorothy, there are hoof prints in the soil. If I take the horse and follow them, they might lead me to the rider. I think it's best if I leave immediately, as the rider may be hurt and the tracks may not last long."

"You may need a carriage if the rider is injured," she called back. "I'll try to borrow one from the Cottrells down the road and come after you."

William grabbed the horse's mane. It had been awhile since he had ridden and he hoped the animal was as tame as it seemed. "All right, I'll meet you somewhere along on the road and we'll return together. Be careful!" William placed a foot in the stirrup and vaulted up onto the gelding's back. The horse whinnied but didn't seem to mind. "Good boy," he said soothingly, patting the animal's neck. "You and I are going to get along just fine."

William touched heels to the mount's flanks and felt him respond, moving in the direction indicated by his pressure on the reins. He kept his eyes on the deep gouges cut in the grass and followed them at a slow canter.

Dorothy waited until they had disappeared before she ran for the Cottrell's home a few hundred yards distant.

❧ ❧ ❧

*M*inutes before, Geoffrey Walsh had been driving his rig through the rain-shrouded Quantock Hills, still smarting from his humiliating experience with Coleridge. Suddenly, Alfoxden House had loomed before him out of the fog-like surroundings. In the front yard, a saddled horse could be seen grazing. Thinking it odd no rider was in evidence, he moved to the side of the road, edging the buggy into a thicket where he could watch without being seen from the house. He had observed William and Dorothy as they had come out the front door. The poet had edged up to the mount, taken the reins, and then inspected the surrounding terrain and a few moments later, was in the saddle and riding off. Dorothy had then hurried desperately down the lane, almost passing the spot where Walsh was concealed.

This was the opportunity Walsh had been waiting for, the stroke of luck that would finally allow him access to Wordsworth's most private inner sanctum. The poet must certainly have papers and communications inside his home that would prove his guilt. Walsh's heart began to race as he climbed down from the trap. He secured his mare to a tree and hurried up the lane to Alfoxden.

Walsh reached the front entrance within moments and stepped up to the brass lion-head knocker. He rapped upon the imposing front door. He had heard from disgruntled neighbors that Wordsworth had dismissed all the servants, but he thought he should play it safe and be certain there was no one in residence. When no one answered, he knocked even louder, afraid the sound might have gone unheard over the rumbling of the thunder. He placed his ear against the oak door; he could hear no human movement. A thrill traveled up his spine. Walsh turned, made his way to a window and looked inside. The parlor was empty, as was the hallway beyond. Walking briskly around the house now, he peered through several more windows. No one was home. He looked about the property: what he could see of the landscape was uninhabited.

Walsh moved quickly now to the windows at the rear of the structure. As he had hoped, he found one that was unlatched. After another look around, he slid it open and climbed into Alfoxden House.

he team of four pulled the mail coach into the inn's courtyard, churning up great globs of mud before sliding to a stop beneath the porte-cochere. The innkeeper's sons scurried from the barn carrying feedbags, heavy with oats.

"Hello, Davey," the tallest boy called.

Water spilled from the driver's broad-brimmed hat as he leaped to the ground. "G'day, lads. Some weather, eh? I've a hungry team fer ya."

"We'll take care of 'em," the smaller lad said.

Davey secured the reins to a hitching post and reached back to fetch a canvas pouch from beneath his driver's seat. Turning to the passenger cabin he opened the door and said, "A short stop fer nourishment ma'am an' then we be on our way."

A hooded figure on the rear seat said, "I'm not hungry. Hurry it up."

❧❧❧ ❧❧❧ ❧❧❧

*L*ucy's eyes were fixed on the warming glow of the hearth when the front door burst open letting in a gust of wind that drove a spray of sparks up the chimney. She turned to see a young man enter. He doffed his hat and squeezed water from his long red hair. "Damn hat's got more holes in it than a sieve. Mornin', Simon. 'Tis a beautiful day if ever I saw one." He tossed the mail pouch to the innkeeper.

"Davey, yer as blind as a mud brick. How bad is it out there, really?"

"Like sailin' through a sea of molasses," said Davey with a laugh, peeling off his cape.

Simon reached into the mail pouch and withdrew a number of letters. He gaped at them with the same blank look the children displayed when they ran into new words. Lucy, who was watching the exchange, guessed that, like most people of his class, the innkeeper could not read.

She felt Davey's brown puppy-dog eyes look upon her as she lifted her mug. "Any of that tea left?" he asked. "I could use a cup and a hot bowl of porridge."

The Innkeeper waved a hand. "Take a seat, Davey. I'll fix ya up an' get the return mail. The lady there is yer passenger. Goin' to Bath, she is."

The coachman bowed to her with youthful gallantry. "Ah, me Lady. I'm Davey, the finest mail coach driver between here and London."

Lucy nodded, suppressing a smile with polite reserve.

He pulled out a chair and sat at one of the nearby tables. "'Tis me lucky day. Another lady passenger to accompany me in this foul weather."

The door swept open and a hooded figure stepped into the room, carrying a large travel bag. "It's freezin' out there," the passenger announced. "I be needin' a cuppa tea."

Lucy was stunned to recognize Molly. She carried the same satchel Lucy had purchased for her at the fair. Molly swept her hood off and grinned. "Well, well. Looky who's here, Lucy Sims herself. Ya look awful, ya do."

"Molly, what are you doing here?"

"Stopped the mail coach on the road. I'm gettin' meself out of the backwoods an' inta the city where I belong. An' yerself?"

"I've left my post."

"Well, so have I, Dearie. Left that damned house fer good. Them Hawkins are nothin' but pigs, accusin' innocent people of bein' thieves. I wouldn't stand fer it. I'm goin' ta London, I am." Molly turned impatiently to the coachman. "Driver, when are we leavin'? I'm in a hurry ta see the big city."

"London ain't going anyplace. And neither are we until I've had me breakfast." He gestured to the innkeeper and said, "Simon, a cup for the lady." He turned back to Molly. "There's an empty chair by the fire." He added under his breath, "It might warm your personality."

Molly heard his remark. Her features twisted into a scowl. "I'd like ta warm yer face with the back of me hand."

Davey's eyes crinkled with amusement. "Easy now, Duchess. 'Tis a long walk ta London."

Molly huffed and crossed to the fireplace, plopping down into the armchair beside Lucy. "Insolent bastard," Molly whispered. "I'll smack him good at the end of me ride. I can't wait ta be gone from this place. You, too, I'll wager, with the law after ya and all."

Lucy's heart skipped a beat. Even though she had anticipated being accused of theft, hearing that it was now a reality was frightening. She voiced her alarm. "I suppose I'm being blamed for the lost silver?"

"That ya are, Dearie. Sent for Constable Hardy, they did. He'll be coming for ya, ya can bet on that." Molly shot her a sly look. "Ya nicked them Apostle Spoons, didn't ya?"

"No. I didn't take any silver."

"Don't matter. They'll put ya in jail just 'cause yer a suspect. That's why I'm out of there. I didn't want them turnin' on me."

Lucy twisted away from the servant girl, clasped her hands together, and stared into the hearth; just like the peat, her life was going up in smoke. Lucy glanced nervously at the entrance. *How much time did she have before the constable would charge in to arrest her? If the mail coach left now she would have a chance to escape.* Her eyes darted to the coach driver as the innkeeper was setting a bowl of porridge before him. Davey looked over to her and saluted with his spoon; then, he began to eat at a distressingly slow pace. Her hopes sank.

fter searching the house quickly to ascertain that he had the premises to himself, Walsh returned to the parlor and settled down at Wordsworth's writing desk. He began rummaging through its contents. Within moments he came across a document that interested him ... the lease agreement for Alfoxden House. He was surprised to discover that the rent was less than he was paying on his own small cottage. *How could it be that Wordsworth had been paying the sum of only twenty-three pounds a year?* He made a note in his black book to look further into the matter. Sorting through the drawers he found another letter, one that confirmed the conversation he had overheard outside Coleridge's window regarding the traitor's eviction. It seemed real enough. Additional correspondence revealed that Wordsworth had been periodically sending a small amount of money to an Annette Vallon in France. *Interesting. Why would the poet be sending a few pounds to anyone in France? Unless, of course, the funds were a ruse. The letters*

could have carried coded messages to a spy cell that would then be forwarded to the French War Ministry. Clever.

In the back of the drawer he found bank records. He quickly read through the reports and realized that, if the statements were true, his suspect was basically a pauper. Wordsworth showed no income other than money that periodically came in from the sale of his poetry which was negligible and was barely enough to pay the household bills. Walsh drummed his fingers on the table, contemplating his findings. *Spies could be devious individuals. The bank statements could be a plant to deflect the eyes of the law.* Walsh smirked as he dwelled upon his growing suspicion. *Yes, acting the part of a penniless poet was, indeed, a clever ploy, but one he could see through. Wordsworth must have secret caches of money and very possibly a personal account in one of the fancy Paris banks.* Walsh grinned: He would see to it that the traitor never got his hands on those funds.

When he was done hunting through the drawers, finding nothing of additional interest, Walsh noticed Wordsworth's journals stacked neatly on the desk. Perhaps there was further evidence of the poet's treachery hidden between their covers.

CHAPTER SEVENTY-EIGHT

*E*mily and Henry tramped across the meadow under the unremitting rainfall, following Dobbin's trail of churned soil. Henry, several yards ahead, turned and yelled. "Hurry up, Emily!"

"Why? Dobbin's probably halfway to London by now."

"Come on. He's too lazy to go very far."

Hoof beats, sounding at first like an angry otter slapping its tail on a riverbank, grew closer. Henry shielded his eyes and barely discerned the shapes of a horse and rider in the distance.

"Emily," he yelled, "it's Dobbin! And the man who got his breeches chewed."

Emily jogged up to Henry's side, panting for breath. "It be William!" She started to jump up and down waving her arms. "Hello! Over here! Over here!"

A sudden gust of wind and rain forced them beneath the protective canopy of a large tree as William trotted forward and stopped before them.

"That be me horse you're riding," Henry said, jamming fists onto his hips. "You're to get off of him right now."

William suppressed a smile. "And a fine 'thank you' to you, too."

"Henry, be nice. We'll need to hurry."

Her brother grunted and stepped forward, grabbing the gelding's bridal. "I need me horse. We got to catch up to Miss Lucy."

William gave him a startled look. "What's that you're saying?"

"Miss Lucy has left our house," Emily offered. She withdrew an envelope from her pocket and handed it up to William. "She left this for you."

William tore the sheath open, withdrawing a single page. Scattered raindrops fell from the canopy of branches, smearing the ink as he read:

My dearest William,

The events I mentioned to you have transpired. By the time you read this letter I will be in Bath with my dear Aunt. I will write and give you my address as soon as I am settled. This parting is only temporary. I need you and dream of spending the rest of my life embraced by your love.

I am yours forever,
Lucy.

William quickly stuffed the letter under his cape. "How long ago did she leave?"

"Sometime during the night," she said worriedly . "We think she be at the King's Head Inn waiting for the morning mail coach."

William frowned. "Good God. We may have only minutes to stop her." He offered an arm. "Up behind me. Hurry!"

Emily and Henry hesitated, exchanging uncertain glances.

"Last chance."

Emily was the first to relent. She took William's hand and was pulled up behind him. William offered Henry his hand.

As Henry shied back, William said firmly, "There's no time to argue. Take my hand now or we're off without you."

Henry's face twisted rebelliously but he grabbed William's hand and was hauled up behind Emily.

"Hold tight!" William kicked Dobbin's flanks and the big gelding lunged out from under the tree, galloping into the storm.

The children held on tightly as they raced across the storm-swept meadow.

❧ ❧ ❧

*D*avey stepped out of the inn, pulling his coat about him; he approached his coach and team under the porte-cochère. The innkeeper's two boys stood alongside empty feed and water bags, waiting expectantly to be paid for their chores. Davey grunted with satisfaction and tossed the boys a couple of coins. "There ya are, lads, a halfpenny fer each of ya."

With words of thanks, the boys scampered off for the barn.

The driver turned back to the inn and yanked the door open, yelling, "Passengers! Time to go."

Lucy, relieved to be leaving before the constable arrived, rose quickly from her chair and followed Molly out through the door. The innkeeper bustled after them, carrying their bags and, with a hand from the driver, helped them climb into the coach.

Davey untied the reins and stepped up onto his seat. "See you tomorrow, Simon."

The innkeeper waved. "Stay dry!"

Davey smiled and cracked his whip, and the two women were jostled back into their seats as the team of horses sprang to life, pulling the coach out into the deluge.

✿ ✿ ✿

onstable Hardy rode through the inclement weather with stoic determination. His mount trotted at a steady pace, paralleling the muddy track. Somewhere ahead of him was Lucy Sims. He was confident he would catch up to her and make his arrest. His biggest problem at the moment was the cold and damnable rain. What should have been an easy pursuit had turned into a miserably difficult one.

✿ ✿ ✿

ercy led the Squire's matched pair of grey horses and covered buggy out of the barn and into the downpour, noticing that the reins had become entangled with the harness. "A minute, me Lord," he said to the Squire who was keeping dry under the barn's overhanging roof. Percy dropped down onto his hands and knees in the mud and crawled in between the horses to untangle the slippery straps.

"Hurry along there, Percy." The Squire stamped his foot with impatience, spraying his trousers with brown sludge. He cursed and brushed at his pants. *If only he could brush away this whole situation! That damnable little governess could cause him considerable embarrassment; he wished he could remember what had happened between the two of them. Perhaps the tart was intelligent enough to keep her mouth shut, thinking he might drop the charges against her. He fervently hoped so.* He patted a heavy bulge in his coat pocket, his insurance for adding years to Miss Sims' prison sentence if need be. He grunted. *He hoped it wouldn't come to that; he didn't wish to stir up more trouble than he already had. In fact, if the blasted girl got away completely, it would be best for both of them. The little bitch could keep the cursed stolen goods. He would placate Gerty by sending her on a shopping spree to replace her pilfered items. The fool woman loved any excuse to spend money.*

"Ready, yer Lordship," Percy said. He stood up, covered in mud as he gathered the lines together. "I be drivin' you, Sir?"

The Squire stepped away from his shelter and grabbed the reins. "No, Percy. I be driving meself. Ya look like a bog. Get cleaned up."

The Squire climbed up onto the seat and grabbed the buggy whip. With a flick of his wrist he snapped it over the horses and the carriage lurched away.

orothy struggled to control the nervous horse that pulled her borrowed trap along the muddy track. The scrawny roan shied with every stroke of lightning and subsequent thunder roll. She had never considered herself much of a horsewoman and felt ill-at-ease in these conditions, as well as with the unfamiliar animal. Suddenly, the way narrowed, climbed a low hill, and Dorothy could see that the normally calm stream below had become a raging torrent that had eroded its banks and carved slices of earth away.

As she reined the buggy around a curve, her heart jumped into her throat; she barely avoided a collision with the large horse carrying her brother and two children!

"William!" she gasped, passing within inches of them.

"Hold on!" he yelled back.

Pulling on the reins, she searched for an area wide enough to bring the buggy about. She found one and was circling back when William and the children came alongside her. He quickly explained the mystery of the runaway horse. "These two were riding double when they fell off."

"We didn't fall," the boy said. "We was knocked off by a stupid…"

"Lucy's leaving," William interrupted. "There's a chance she's still at the King's Head Inn, waiting for the morning coach. I'm going after her. These two are her charges." He twisted in the saddle to face Emily and Henry. "Slide off. You're to ride in the buggy with my sister." Emily slipped down but Henry grabbed William tightly about the waist. "Not me. I'm going with you."

"Suit yourself." William turned to his sister. "I'll take the lead to make sure the road is passable. Follow me."

Dorothy shook her head as she helped Emily up into the buggy. "No, go on without us," she urged, knowing how anxious he must be.

"It's too dangerous. Just follow me." William prodded the horse and they surged ahead, leading the buggy along the hazardous ribbon of road.

he mail coach jostled Lucy and Molly about like two ragdolls. Lucy did her best to ignore the servant girl while above them the driver was yelling and cursing, urging his team to greater effort. Thunder rumbled overhead, momentarily drowning out sounds of the driver and his team. The coach swayed, and creaked like splintering wood. Lucy, alarmed, thought that at any moment her transport would certainly break apart.

The wheels hit a pothole and they bounced hard. Molly slipped off the seat and landed unceremoniously on the floor. "Bloody hell!" she shrieked to the roof. "Ya tryin' to kill us?"

Lucy helped Molly regain her cushion and picked up the girl's travel bag, which had landed beside her. As they braced their feet against the seats in front of them Molly stared at Lucy's satchel. After a moment her mouth twisted into a smirk.

"What is it, Molly?"

"Ya got more'n yer clothes in that bag of yers, I'm thinkin'."

"I beg your pardon?"

The smirk widened. "Maybe some of the Hawkins' property?"

"No, Molly," Lucy said. "I am more scrupulous than you."

"Tell it ta King George, Dearie," she said with a snicker. "Ya don't have ta worry about me. I know how ta keep me mouth shut. We women got ta stick together. The world is full of pigs like the Squire and that wife of his." Molly's eyes narrowed. "He was ticklin' yer fancy, weren't he?"

Lucy felt the heat of indignation rise to her cheeks and then exhaled slowly, deciding the girl wasn't worth getting upset over—not now, anyway. The servant's crude imaginings and suspicious nature never failed to amaze her. *Was it even worth the effort to explain her reason for fleeing Hawkins House?* She shook her head, choosing to ignore the comment.

"It's alright, ya don't have ta tell me nothin'," Molly said. "I knew the two of ya was doin' it. Otherwise the Squire would've given me a spin. He should've, too. He didn't know a good thing when he saw it right before his very nose."

"Maybe you should have stayed and given him a chance," Lucy said, curious why Molly would leave Hawkins House.

"Nah, I've me own plans. Got meself a lad … and no cabbage-head neither. He's got brains; you can be sure of that. We're ta open our own pub in London. What about yerself?"

Lucy shrugged, not wanting to share her plans. "I'm going to stay with relatives."

The girl snorted. "Ya ain't got no relatives."

The coach lurched wildly as it hit a much deeper pothole and bounced Molly's head against the roof. She screamed and fell back, grabbing her mouth. "Damned driver! I bit me tongue. I think it's bleedin'."

Lucy, who had gripped the coach seat, had avoided injury. She suppressed a smile.

❧❧❧ ❧❧❧ ❧❧❧

Constable Hardy was cold and irritated as his mount plodded on, making less progress than he had anticipated. He'd rather be home in front of a blazing fire than pursuing some fool girl halfway across the county. He hoped he would find Lucy Sims at the King's Head Inn, but he was no longer optimistic. More than likely, he'd have to chase after her in this Godforsaken weather. If he failed to catch her before she got to Bath, he might lose her in the city. Bath, with more than twenty-five thousand souls, was no London, but a person could easily vanish in it.

❧❧❧ ❧❧❧ ❧❧❧

The Squire yelled at his team as the two horses struggled to pull the carriage through the mud, "Git on there! Move on! Go! Go!"

He grimaced from the pain in his gloveless hands, which had blistered on the wet reins. *Damn it all to hell! He should have brought Percy along to drive. But then, the bulge in his coat pocket reminded him why he hadn't. In all probability, Lucy would discard the stolen goods when she saw Constable Hardy approaching, claim she was innocent, and then accuse him of rape. Gerty would throw him out of the manor without a farthing. Well, he promised himself, that wasn't going to happen. He would outsmart the little bitch. He had brought along his cache of pilfered silver, which he planned to plant along the road, close to the area of her arrest: He would then conveniently find the silver and claim Miss Lucy had discarded the stolen goods for fear of being caught with them on her person. She could protest all she wanted, but he was sure no one would believe her. He was rather proud of his plan.* His buggy lurched, bringing him back to the reality of his struggling team. He picked up the whip and laid it on the horses' backsides. They lunged ahead: He had to reach

Constable Hardy in time to offer his buggy as a means of conveying the thief to her cell.

The Squire grinned as he reviewed his plan, one that would solve all his problems. *The Sims girl would never reach her destination. It was a long journey to the big city and somewhere along the road he would find a way to separate the governess from the constable. Then he'd explain her options to her. She could either go to prison or she could accept a few pounds sterling from him and he'd **allow** her to escape.*

The Squire was certain she would take the quid and run. Later, he'd make the excuse to Hardy that she had jumped from his carriage and eluded him. Hopefully, that would be the last he would ever see of Lucy Sims.

ray of light fell upon the page Geoffrey Walsh had been reading. He snapped his head up from William's writing desk to glance out the window. A small patch of blue had momentarily appeared in the stormy sky. His eyelids blinked rapidly like those of a newly-surfaced gopher, adjusting to the daylight. He glanced at his pocket watch and was amazed: He had been reading the journals for an hour and a half, unexpectedly engrossed by Wordsworth's poems. Even the titles he had found fascinating: *The Prelude, Tintern Abby, The Idiot Boy, A Forsaken Indian Woman, The Last Of The Flock, Her Eyes Are Wild,* and on and on, page after page, some complete, others merely works in progress. Not a single line had offered a clue to Wordsworth's seditious activities. To the contrary, he had found the man's writing hauntingly beautiful … the sort of poetry he might have written himself, had he been born wealthy and had the idle time to spend on writing.

At first, he had been mildly amused by the poet's rhythmic simplicity and avoidance of classic structure, but then, an odd thing had occurred. He began to experience the writer's observations. Where Walsh had expected mediocrity, he had found lyrical beauty with emotions and images so easily understood that no scholar was needed for translation: Wordsworth's verse was written so that all men could understand it.

He returned to the last verse he had been staring at … the one that distressed him most:

> *I traveled among unknown men,*
> *In lands beyond the sea;*
> *Nor, England! did I know till then*
> *What love I bore to thee.*
> *'Tis past, that melancholy dream!*
> *Nor will I quit thy shore*
> *A second time; for still I seem*
> *To love thee more and more.*

Walsh closed the book and buried his head in his hands. It appeared that Wordsworth loved England as much as he, himself, did. Anyone who read the poem would see that this poet could never be a French spy, nor a threat to the Crown.

A surge of acid soured Walsh's stomach and he recognized envy, his old nemesis. God was unfair, allowing a man like Wordsworth to spend his life pursing the joys of writing poetry, while he, a devout family man, had to work long hours as a menial assistant investigator. Had he been given the same opportunities, he, too, might have been able to use his creativity.

Walsh stopped himself in the middle of these thoughts. *Was he being honest? Perhaps not entirely,* he admitted. He was much too cautious to risk starving for the sake of art. The love of composition, while his fancy as a young man, wasn't really ingrained in his adult personality. He was a pragmatist more than a poet. The question that confronted him now was:

what was he going to do about Wordsworth? He had already written the Home Office, declaring he had accumulated incriminating evidence that would lead to the poet's demise. If he were to write a retraction, he knew what would happen to his chances for promotion: They would be non-existent and, in fact, he could be dismissed. Sighing, he withdrew his black notebook and stared at it, cognizant that the pages held only hearsay and—at best—circumstantial evidence that would be laughed out of court. Walsh envisioned his superior's wrath. *How could he ever face his colleagues and family if he made such a fool of himself?* His future as an investigator, his pride, his livelihood, his pension—his whole world would evaporate.

Walsh decided he had to save himself. He could cleverly fabricate his notes, naming sources, so that Wordsworth would indeed appear guilty of traitorous acts. He opened his black book and, quelling a disturbed conscience, began to write.

illiam opened the door to the King's Head Inn and ushered Dorothy and the children in, out of the wind and rain. He swept his hat off and quickly scanned the interior as he searched for Lucy, but she was nowhere in sight.

The innkeeper, who had been warming himself by the fireplace, rose to his feet when the burst of cold air hit him. "Close the door!"

William swung it shut and, taking care to duck beneath the low beams, crossed over to him as did the rest of his party. "Simon," he breathed out quickly. "I'm looking for a young lady. Lucy Sims is her name. Have you seen her?"

"Yes, she was here half the night. Left on the mail coach."

"How long ago did it leave?"

The man shrugged. "Half an hour, maybe less."

William's hopes jumped. There was time to intercept the coach.

Henry yanked on his sleeve. "We can catch her!"

"Thank you, Simon!" he exclaimed, already turning for the door.

"Hold on," Simon said, removing an envelope from his pocket.

William turned back, his eyes on the innkeeper.

"I've a letter here with your name on it." He handed it to him. "Ain't that right?"

William read his name printed on the envelope and the return address: Calvert Properties. "Yes, it's addressed to me."

Simon grinned, obviously proud that he had read the Wordsworth name correctly.

As Dorothy hurried to his side, William said, "It's from the Calvert family. It must be news on Raisley's legacy." He broke the wax seal and quickly withdrew a single piece of stationary, recognizing the engraved Calvert family crest on the letterhead. As he read, his hands began to shake.

"It's from Raisley's father. The estate has been settled. I'm to receive a draft for one hundred pounds by the end of the month and a final distribution of eight hundred pounds, minus a few claims, by year's end." He turned to his sister. "After two years in the courts, my inheritance has finally come through!"

She cried, "Oh, I can hardly believe it!"

God bless you, my dear friend Raisley. Now there was no longer any reason for Lucy to leave for Bath! He had the funds for them to get married; if she wanted to wait awhile, so be it. He would lease a cottage for her when they returned from their trip to Germany; it would be close to one he intended to lease in Nether Stowey. He began to hurry toward the door, then turned back to his sister. "I have to get this news to Lucy. I'm going on ahead. "

"Yer not goin' anywhere, Wordsworth," said a voice, heavy with drink.

A chill traveled down William's spine. He turned to see Ben and Walt Sutton stagger through the front door, dipping rain and hostility.

"Shut the damned door," Simon yelled.

The door was kicked shut and the two brothers advanced into the room. William noted the makeshift splint on Ben's right hand and Walt's black and blue nose. Their desire to get revenge had evidently been building since their last encounter. William tightened his jaw in resignation; it appeared he was in for a fight. His hickory stick would have come in handy about now but he had left it at home. Then he spotted a potential weapon and edged closer to the hearth.

"Not this time, Wordsworth," said Ben, slurring his words. Reading William's intention, he lurched unsteadily to the fireplace, scooped up the set of andirons and threw them into the pub's farthest corner.

Dorothy cried out. Emily ran to hug her skirts while Henry pugnaciously stood his ground; a pup in a pit of circling pit bulls.

William's hands brushed the back of a chair and he gripped it. *Maybe with a little luck...* "Dorothy, take the children away!"

"Do as he says, ya stinkin' French spy," Walt said.

Ben came at him from the left, pushing aside tables, while Walt kicked a chair out of his way and came at him from the right.

Ben said, "Heard ya lost yer lease an' are plannin' ta leave us. We couldn't let that happen without settlin' any injustices now, could we?" He withdrew a razor-sharp butcher knife from his belt.

William felt perspiration on the palms of his hands as Walt also pulled out a curved butcher knife. William tightened his grip on the back of the chair. "You're both drunk. I suggest you put those knives away and go home."

"We'll put 'em away... ," Ben raised his blade. "After we cut ya inta little pieces. This is fer all the sons of England that've died because of disloyal turncoats like ya."

"No! Stop this, immediately!" Dorothy yelled, holding Emily to her skirts. "My brother is not a French spy! This is ridiculous! For God's sake, put away those knives."

"Back off, or we might be slicin' ya up as well," Ben threatened.

William's eyes never left the two brothers. He raised the chair and churned the legs before their faces, attempting to keep them at bay. He said, "Dorothy, take the children out of here, now!"

Simon, who had edged his way behind the bar when he first noticed the Suttons enter, had retrieved his club and gripped it out of sight.

William held the brothers' gaze. Now, he thought skeptically, all he had to do was incapacitate the two brutes intent on eviscerating him. He really wasn't ready to die, but living didn't look too promising at the moment. And, damn them, he had to get to Lucy! Sweat trickled down his sides as he waited to see which brother would make the first move. If he could knock one of the brothers off- balance, he would attack the other, and maybe live long enough to shatter both of their heads before he was stabbed. It wasn't much of a plan, but it was all he had. Again, he jabbed the end of the chair at their faces but when he saw how nimbly they were able to sidestep his maneuver, he realized the brothers were *not as drunk as they appeared.* They moved in closer, grinning confidently while slashing the air between them with their sharp blades, enjoying the moment before they went in for the kill. Sweat dripped into William's eyes and burned. *Damn it, why wasn't Dorothy ushering the children outside? And, what in blazes was Henry doing, sneaking up behind Dorothy with a brass spittoon in his hands?* William's heart sank. *This could be a tragic blood bath.* "Dorothy," he said sternly, keeping his eyes on the Suttons. "Henry's behind you. Grab him and take both children away!"

Dorothy stood her ground and said with a tremor in her voice, "They can't hurt you with all of us as witnesses." She shouted at the brothers, "You'll both be sent to Newgate Prison and hung from the gallows!"

Walt grunted out a laugh and said, "Ya dumb wench, can't ya see yer brother's armed hisself with a weapon. We just be defendin' ourselves." He prodded his blade toward William, forcing him to take a step back.

"Ben," Walt said with a wicked laugh, "last one ta draw blood buys a pint."

"Ya'll be the one buyin'," Ben replied, with an air of malice.

William's peripheral vision noted Henry, as the boy swung the spittoon at the large man's head; it bounced off Walt's skull, momentarily distracting the pig farmer. Taking advantage of the diversion, William lunged at Ben, swinging the chair low. The legs splintered against Ben's left knee with a cracking sound—the man bellowed, dropped his knife and then lunged at William, managing to grab onto one of his legs. William was pulled to the floor.

"Hold onta, him!" Walt yelled, hurrying over. William rolled out of Ben's grasp and raised his knees, slamming his boots into Ben's chest, which propelled him into Walt's path; they both toppled over.

"Walt, kill that traitor!" Ben yelled. "He broke me kneecap!"

William and Walt scrambled to their feet and turned to face one another. There it was: Bare hands against a razor-sharp knife.

Walt jabbed at him with the blade. "Yer a dead man now, ya weasel."

William backed up, searching for another chair but none was within reach. Walt sliced the air, coming toward him like the Grim Reaper.

"Son!" Simon yelled.

William glanced for an instant at the innkeeper, who threw his club to him. William caught it out of the air and swung it just in time to deflect Walt's blade—aimed at his throat. Without hesitating, William spun around and swung the club, hitting Walt's shoulder. The big man grunted, hurt but not disabled, as he crashed into William, knocking him to the floor. Walt quickly straddled him so that he could no longer maneuver the club. He saw Walt's wolfish grin a split-second before he raised the knife and plunged it down. Instinctively, William blocked the deadly thrust by grabbing hold of the man's wrist, stopping the blade inches from his chest. William tried to push the knife away but the farmer's strength left him little hope as to the outcome of their struggle. He was helpless as he watched the point descend centimeter by centimeter—he felt it nick his flesh. William strained against the inevitable. *Suddenly, an image of Lucy in a mail coach floated before him.* Utilizing all of his strength, he pushed upward. The point of the knife began to rise, but as his muscles strained, his hopes diminished. Abruptly, a figure in black appeared behind Walt and clubbed him over the head with the blunt end of a pistol! Walt, unconscious, fell to the side, hitting the floor like a sack of grain.

Ben, holding his useless leg, yelled, "You sneaky bastard!"

The man whirled around to Ben, aiming the flintlock at his head. "Call me that again and I'll put a bullet between your eyes."

The newcomer confiscated his knife, and Ben snarled an oath but remained relatively silent, nursing his pain.

William sat up. After noting that the blade had merely pricked his skin, he said, "Sir, I owe you a great debt of... ."

The man raised a hand to curtail his thanks as he eyed the fallen brothers. William studied the stranger in the black suit. His sharp features looked vaguely familiar. Images flashed in his memory—the man's face as he peered out of a coach window—the same fellow again at the fair. *This was the individual who had been following him. Who was he and why had he helped him?*

The man gestured to Henry. "Boy, grab me one of those spittoons."

Henry gulped and quickly did as he was told.

The man in black upended the brass jug over the unconscious brother. Brownish syrup splattered onto his face, awakening Walt who spat and cursed, as angry as a cornered wildcat.

The man stared hard at the Sutton brothers and then spoke without the least bit of emotion. "You two broke your promise to stay away from Wordsworth."

Ben, balancing himself on one leg, said, "We heard he was leavin'. We had ta stop 'im."

Walt, attempting to wipe the filth from his face, saw the pistol in Walsh's hand and his face contorted with rage. "Ya hit me, ya dung-eatin' swine! What kind of writer hits people? I'll kill ya fer this!"

"I'm not a writer," the man said as he calmly raised his pistol and pointed it in Walt's face. "I am an agent from the Home Office. Threatening a representative of the Crown is a prison offence, Mr. Sutton, as I'm sure you and your brother are well aware."

Walt and Ben stopped cursing and froze as the portent of their assailant's words sank into their befuddled skulls.

"Yer the Crown's agent?" Ben asked.

"That I am. Now get back to your pig farm. You are never to interfere with the Wordsworths again or, I assure you, you'll be spending the next ten years of your miserable lives in prison for attempted murder and interfering in a Crown investigation."

The brothers recoiled as if they'd both been slapped across the face. "Bloody Crownsman," Ben muttered. "Walt, gimme a hand."

Walt struggled to his feet and put his arm around his brother's shoulder.

"Curse all of ya," Ben said with diminished hostility, then motioned to Walt. "Get me outta here."

Walt helped his brother limp across the pub to the front entrance. They pulled open the door and slammed their way out into the rainstorm.

William suddenly realized the stranger in black now had the flintlock leveled at his chest. The man waved him over. Stepping forward, William was aware of the floorboards creaking beneath his feet. *What was this all about?* He stopped within an arm's length of the agent and found himself staring into eyes as black as coal.

The man nodded slightly and introduced himself. "My name is Geoffrey Walsh. As you heard, I'm a government agent from the Home Office in Bristol. I was sent by the Duke of Portland to investigate you, Mr. William Wordsworth, for sedition and spying against our government."

William's heart sank. A nightmare was coming true at the worst possible moment. He was certainly going to be arrested and lose his opportunity to overtake the mail coach. "What are your charges against me, Sir?"

311

The Crown's man ignored his question and asked, "Who is Spy Nozy?"

"Spy Nozy?" he said, taken aback. "I don't follow you, Sir."

"I have witnesses who overheard you conversing about a man named Spy Nosy a fortnight ago."

William was puzzled. He tried to decipher the accusation and repeated the name to himself several times. "Spy Nozy... Spanozy... Spinozy... Ah, you must be referring to *Spinoza*."

Walsh's brow furrowed, as if he had heard of the name but couldn't place it.

William added, "Benedict Spinoza, the late Dutch philosopher. I may have spoken about him recently. Spinoza was a Rationalist, a man who spent most of his life in peaceful rebellion against religious traditions and unjust authority... A man I admire."

Now Walsh's mouth twisted tightly, as if he'd just tasted a bitter plum. His shoulders sagged. He lowered the flintlock and finally said, "Mr. Wordsworth, at the moment, there are no criminal charges against you that would hold up in a law court."

"Then I am free to leave?"

"You are ... at least temporarily," he said, pocketing his pistol and turning for the bar.

William felt a great weight had at last been lifted from his shoulders. Dorothy ran to him. She was shaking, crying. "My sweet brother," she managed, as she enveloped him in her arms.

He kissed the top of her head. "God protects fools and poets." He pushed her gently away. "I'm sorry to leave you but I must go after the mail coach." His eyes fell to Henry. "I'll be taking your horse if I may."

"You may not!" Henry said.

"Henry!" Emily admonished. "He needs to bring Lucy back! Let Mr. Wordsworth take Dobbin."

Henry stamped his foot. "No. `Less'n he takes me with him."

"Sorry, Henry, but you'd slow me down," William said, hurrying for the door.

Henry ran after him. "You be stealing me horse! The Crown's agent is here to witness it! You'll be sent to Newgate Prison."

William pulled the door shut behind him, slamming it in Henry's face.

❧ ❧ ❧

*H*enry's bottom lip quivered. He held back tears as he muttered to his sister, "He just wants Miss Lucy all to himself." William's sister came up to him and took his hand. "We can't allow that now, can we? Come along, children. We'll follow after them in the buggy and give Miss Lucy a ride home."

Henry wiped his eyes with the back of his hand and smiled up at her. He followed the woman and Emily out of the inn.

As they rode from the yard, they passed a misty figure on horseback. Looking back through the rain, Henry recognized Constable Hardy.

CHAPTER EIGHTY-THREE

*L*ucy's mind was on William as she gazed out the coach's window at a blurred countryside. The last time she had felt this kind of loneliness was after her parents had died; and it was now actually making her feel physically ill. She flinched when lightning flashed overhead, illuminating the grey sky. Soon thereafter a fusillade of thunder erupted over the coach. The vehicle suddenly lurched forward in a burst of speed. Molly was propelled off her seat, but Lucy caught her with her legs and pushed her back. Lucy noticed that the driver's voice had become strident: His tone had risen several octaves as he yelled, "Whoa! Whoa! Stop, I tell ya!"

Molly thumped her fist on the roof and began to scream at Davey, but she was bouncing too hard to get any words out. The two women held fast to hand straps, bracing themselves against the jarring ride that punished muscle and bone.

As the out-of-control coach tore through the storm, Lucy could hear her heart pounding, its volume rivaling that of the wind, rain and hammering hooves. She squeezed her eyes shut and prayed.

※ ※ ※

*D*avey struggled with the slippery reins atop the coach, trying to pull the team in, but there was no controlling the terrified animals. They galloped on blindly, this way and that, as a torrent lashed the earth. His hat whipped off and, held by a chin strap, danced furiously behind his head. Rivulets of water washed down from the hills. Gullies and hollows flooded, eroding earth from the edges of the road.

A flashflood roared out of a gorge a hundred feet in front of Davey's team. The violent flow washed away everything in its path—mud, rocks and earth, leaving behind a gaping hole. Davey screamed, "Mother of God!"

※ ※ ※

*L*ucy heard the driver's cry a split second before the coach dropped into a deep hole; it hit the side, and bounced into the air, dropping the floor out from beneath her. Then the coach slammed back to the earth, landing on just two wheels—it was now tilting over precariously! Molly howled! Lucy looked out the window and gasped; they hovered over an abyss—the raging river forty feet below! Suddenly, the team broke loose from the hitch-ring; the front wheel splintered, and the vehicle slid off the edge of the road!

Davey leaped free from his seat as the coach plummeted down the hillside; it tipped and rolled over and over.

Lucy and Molly tumbled inside the cab, banging and slamming into each other. Time stood still as images flashed before Lucy's eyes—*her mother's beautiful face—her father painting at his easel—the children playing on the hill—William smiling that first smile.* Reality intervened as the coach crashed into the river with a jarring splash. The vehicle sank heavily, coming to rest on the bottom of the riverbed, with less than a foot of the cabin exposed above the swirling currents.

Lucy gasped for air and fought to an upright position, as icy fingers of water poured in from a broken window. Molly, rigid with fear, huddled in a corner, wailing. The water rose swiftly, first to their waists and then to their chests. Lucy knew she had to keep her wits about her or they would surely drown. She placed a calming hand on the terrified girl's shoulder and said firmly, "Molly, stop it. Stop it!"

Molly stopped yelling, her terrified eyes darting in all directions. "Help me! I can't swim."

"I know how to swim. I'll help you, but you have to calm down. Do you understand?"

"I'll drown!" Molly bawled, throwing her arms around Lucy's waist with a death grip. "God, help me!"

Lucy struggled to pry Molly's hands away. "I'm going to help you, Molly. But you have to let go of me!"

When Molly released her she added, "I'm going to climb through the window and then I'll pull you up after me."

Molly, trembling, on the edge of hysteria, cried, "No! I want to go first. Please. Let me go first."

"All right, but after I help you out you must hold onto the coach railing or you could fall off and be swept away. Do you understand?"

The servant girl's eyes widened with horror. She nodded her head. "Yes, yes, but hurry! Hurry!"

As more water spilled into the cabin, Lucy could feel their dresses becoming dangerously heavy. Swimming would be almost impossible. "Molly, take off your cloak and dress, they're too heavy ... they'll pull us under. Quickly!"

"Help me!" Molly pleaded.

With no time to waste Lucy grabbed onto the back of Molly's dress and pulled, ripping the buttons off, and then reached around to the back of her own dress and did the same. The water had risen to their throats by the time they had stripped down to thin petticoats. Teeth chattering, Lucy commanded, "Molly, in front of me. Hurry!"

Molly's face suddenly transformed into a mask of horror. "Me bag!" She looked around frantically. "I've lost me bag!"

"You can buy a new one," Lucy yelled above the sound of the river.

"Everything I own is in it," Molly cried.

She grabbed onto the girl's arm. "We'll die in here unless you move!" She pushed the girl toward the opening above them. "I'm going to lift you out."

Molly nodded, too distraught to speak. The waters lapped at their chins. Lucy sucked in a breath and slipped beneath the surface where she placed her hands under the girl's buttocks and pushed.

Molly shrieked as she rose up through the window, where she became stuck, half-in and half-out of the cab. Feeling resistance, Lucy shoved hard and felt the girl pass through the opening.

Free of the servant girl, Lucy braced her feet against one of the seats and thrust herself up and out through the window. She climbed atop the cab and fell in an exhausted heap beside a blubbering Molly, catching her breath. She stared up at the roiling sky. A single raven flew overhead, its black form swooping in close above them, screeching loudly. The bird landed in a nearby tree and continued to squawk. Beneath the gnarled sycamore Lucy could see that the bank of the river was less than a stone's throw away. But between them and the shore was a churning, raging flow. Suddenly, the coach groaned like a dying animal, quaking and shifting beneath them. They held fast as the vehicle began to slide downstream.

Icy water surged over the top of the coach, partially engulfing their figures, causing them to shiver violently. Lucy could see outcroppings of rocks ahead; they had to abandon the coach before it broke up beneath them. Lucy felt confident she could make the short swim to shore, but pulling Molly along as dead weight would make the trip far more hazardous. Yet, as much trouble as the servant girl had been, she couldn't abandon her. Lucy was searching for the closest jut of land when suddenly Davey appeared and ran along the bank, keeping pace with them.

"Swim for it!" Davey yelled. He cautiously waded ankle-deep into the swiftly moving waters, gulping with fear as he stretched out his hand. "Jump! I'll pull you out. You have to jump. Hurry!"

Molly shuddered and looked to her. "No! Don't leave me. I'll drown. You said you'd help me!"

"I'm not going to leave you," Lucy replied and then yelled to the driver, "We'll jump together!" Uncertain that Davey had heard her she clutched Molly's hand, just as the coach slammed into a rock and hurled them into the river.

Lucy hit the water first, with Molly landing on top of her, pushing her beneath the murky current that carried them downstream. Lucy pushed the girl aside and kicked her feet, bursting to the surface, gasping for air. She reached out and grabbed the terrified servant about her chest with one arm. "Don't struggle, Molly," she gasped. "I'll swim. You just try to kick your feet and stay afloat."

Molly cried out incoherently and attempted to move her feet. Using one arm, Lucy crawled toward the river bank, fighting to keep her head above the surface. The cold numbed her arms and legs. She spat out a mouthful of water and looked to the shore. Davey was running, still following them, yelling words she couldn't hear.

When Lucy's foot brushed against a sandbar, a surge of hope shot through her. A moment later, her feet touched solid ground. Gulping air, fighting against the torrent, she managed to stand up in the chest-high water. Drained, panting, yet filled with a new sense of optimism, she said, "Hold steady, Molly, we're going to make it."

The girl's feet must have also made contact with the riverbed, for she stood up and struggled like a wet cat to free herself from her rescuer.

"No!" Lucy yelled, glancing over her shoulder at the girl. "Hold still, Molly! Stop! Let me do it."

Davey ran up to the edge of the river. He inched his way into the swirling waters until he was only six feet from them. He stretched out his hand. "Grab onto me!"

Molly, seeing help so close, screamed, "Help me!"

Lucy felt the girl twist and wrench her hand free. The sudden release caused Lucy to stumble and fall into the current.

As Molly edged past her toward Davey's outstretched fingers, her elbow struck Lucy in the side. Gasping from pain, she struggled after Molly.

"Pull! Help me!" Molly yelled as she grabbed onto Davey's hand. "Get me outta here!"

"I've got you!" he said, pulling on her hand. Molly slipped and fell, dunking her head. She came up screaming and kicking. Lucy, following close behind, reached forward to help, and one of the servant girl's feet slammed hard into her face. She reeled back and the world suddenly went dark. Fighting for consciousness, she felt the water sweep her away.

illiam instinctively pulled back on Dobbin's reins as the cavernous hole in the road loomed before them. The gelding skidded in the mud, halting abruptly at the edge of the chasm, where water whirl-pooled in a vicious circle and flowed over the side of the hill to the river below. The big horse snorted, releasing a shrill whinny and pranced nervously at the edge of the swirling vortex. William reined the horse away from the rift and noticed deep gashes in the mud to the side of the road. He surmised their implications: A team of horses pulling a heavy vehicle had skidded off the embankment. His eyes followed the tracks to an area forty feet below where they ended at the swollen river. Squinting through the rain, he peered downstream and could just discern part of the mail coach, lying on its side in the current. He scanned the area for signs of life. There were none. A chill, colder than any of the elements, pierced his soul.

William dug heels into Dobbin's flanks, urging the gelding down the steep incline. Moments later, at the base, they bounded over a narrow stretch of land littered with uprooted trees and shrubs and then splashed along the bank of the river. Coming abreast of the coach he guided Dobbin into the strong current until they came alongside the broken vehicle. He ignored the icy water that slapped above the top of his boots and flooded inside as he stood in the stirrups and gazed into the coach. Except for swirling waters it was empty. William sat back in the saddle and scanned his surroundings, cursing the downpour. He thought he heard the sound of someone calling in the distance. Wiping rain from his eyes, he peered downriver but, if anyone was there, they were lost in the mist.

Then he heard it again. A distant voice. Someone was yelling. He slapped the reins against Dobbin and, guiding the big horse to the bank, lunged out of the current and raced, as fast as he dared, downstream.

❦ ❦ ❦

Lucy, after suffering the kick to her head, had become disoriented and had been carried into the deeper flow where the undertow had grabbed her in its cold embrace and pulled her beneath the surface. She was caught now in the whirling darkness, knowing she was being dragged to a watery grave. She steeled her will to live; and with lungs about to burst, lashed out with her arms, stroking furiously and kicking her feet, using every ounce of her strength in one final effort. Seconds seemed like hours as the current held her down. Air, sweet oxygen, was only inches above her, but it might as well have been a mile. Her limbs tired quickly and soon behaved like lead weights. On the verge of despair, she felt a crosscurrent swell beneath her. It was propelling her upwards! Her head burst above the surface and she gasped in great draughts of air.

Lucy's eyes fell upon Davey running along the shoreline, searching for her. Molly was trailing along behind him in her under garments. She seemed to be searching for her lost bag. Davey, spotting Lucy, waved excitedly and yelled words she couldn't comprehend, motioning to an area downstream, evidently trying to direct her to the nearest outcrop of land. Forcing her deadened limbs to move, she slowly began to swim, inching her way toward Davey on the shoreline. Suddenly, she sighted a large, swiftly moving object out of the corner of her eye. As she turned back to observe it more fully, the gnarled roots of an uprooted tree slammed into the small of her back.

Lucy's cry, as plaintive as a wounded dove, was drowned by the thunderous current. Writhing in agony, struggling to extract herself from the mass of tangled roots, she was swept downstream. She couldn't see the jagged edges of a large rock in her way and, seconds later, she was rammed into the splinter of granite, cutting flesh and bone, causing pain unlike anything she had ever experienced. The roots broke free and were swept away. Lucy reached out blindly, her fingers tightening around the rock. Broken, and in shock, she clung to the momentary sanctuary of cold stone... . A fiery ache stabbing her ribs told her she was seriously injured.

CHAPTER EIGHTY-FIVE

Illiam, riding with cautious haste, threaded Dobbin through the rocky, debris-strewn shore. He could see the man who was yelling now. It was Davey, the coach driver. The young man had his hands cupped to his mouth and was shouting to someone in the river. Reining the gelding to an abrupt halt beside the driver, he now could see Lucy clinging to the thin slice of rock in the middle of the turbulence. "God, *no!*" he breathed.

"She can't hold on much longer," Davey yelled. "I'd go for her, but I can't swim."

William's adrenaline surged, propelling him from the saddle. His mind raced with fearsome details: *Lucy could be swept away and drown before he got to her and, not being a strong swimmer himself, knew if he attempted a rescue, they could both perish. Better that than to live life without her! Dear God, help me!* He whipped off his hat and cloak in a single sweep. His eyes never left Lucy as he tore off his topcoat and boots and hurried forth to splash out into the torrent. He yelled, "Hold on! Lucy, hold on!"

❦❦❦ ❦❦❦ ❦❦❦

*R*ain stung Dorothy's face as she squinted to look past the spooked mare pulling frantically on the buggy's traces, and she tried to focus on the mucky road ahead. The rain was still making visibility poor. She wrestled with the reins, fighting for control, feeling certain the mare was on the edge of rebellion. The children seated beside her stared ahead, petrified, and held on with all their strength to the bouncing seat.

Next to her, Emily stiffened. "Stop!" the girl yelled. "Stop now!"

Dorothy yanked back on the reins. The startled roan skidded to a stop in the mud, whinnying with terror. Dorothy was alarmed to see they had come to a halt only inches from the edge of a treacherous, water-swirling hole. "Sweet Jesus!" she cried.

Henry pointed down the embankment. "Emily, look! The coach is crashed."

Emily stood, her face stricken. "Miss Lucy? Do you see Miss Lucy?"

Dorothy was severely shaken when she saw the wreckage in the middle of the river, with no signs of life. Her eyes came back to the road and followed the tracks of a single horse that had plowed down the incline. That must be William. "Both of you sit back. We're going to turn back and find a way to get down there."

❦❦❦ ❦❦❦ ❦❦❦

*S*wimming hard, William ignored the bone-chilling water as he raced toward Lucy. *Hold on*, he prayed. *Lucy, hold on!* A moment later he reached out and grabbed onto her wrist with one hand, and onto the rock with the other. A monumental sigh escaped him as he drew her close to his chest but, when he felt no response, he realized she was unconscious. Holding precariously to the outcropping, he gently lifted Lucy's face to his and caught his breath: Blood

324

was flowing from a deep gash on her forehead. Her face was ashen. His fingers trembled as he tried to detect a pulse in her neck and, finding none, felt for a heartbeat. He prayed for some sign of life; but he couldn't perceive one. Suddenly, he heard a soft moan. Her chest rose. She was breathing!

William choked back a sob, and kissed her lightly on the lips. A wave of panic rolled over him like a dark cloud. If he didn't act quickly, they would drown. Cradling her close to his chest with one arm, he kicked away from the rock.

The current, like an evil spirit lying in wait, eddied, trapping William and Lucy inside its swirling grasp. William's face tightened with a strained effort, as he fought an ineffectual battle against the raw power of the river. His muscles, cold and weakening, no longer responded with coordination. A feeling of hopelessness overtook him, not so much for himself, but for the young woman he held in his arms. With a strange sense of detachment William observed that the forces of nature he so admired were showing him the fragility of man.

orothy could plainly see there were no passengers in the half-submerged mail coach. She drove the trap carefully past the wreck and continued downriver, with the children clinging to her. As she paralleled the water's edge, her troubled eyes peered through the misting air, searching for any sign of William. The mare balked, bringing the buggy to a halt: A jumbled mass of rocks, tangled driftwood and debris littered the shoreline before them.

Henry stood and pointed. "There's a man down there and he's got Dobbin!"

"Is it William?" Dorothy asked with hope in her voice.

Emily rose to her feet and squinted, trying to identify the figure. "I don't think so. He's yelling to someone in the river, but I can't see to whom."

Henry leaped from the buggy. "I'm going to go see."

"I'm coming, too." Emily jumped to the ground and followed her brother.

Dorothy looked apprehensive as she stepped down and tied the roan to a fallen log. Her breath shortened as she gathered her skirts and ran after the children.

❧❧❧ ❧❧❧ ❧❧❧

*A*s William was nearing the end of his capacity to fight, the furious force of the eddy suddenly abated as quickly as it had arisen. Buoyed with a new wave of hope, William gathered the little strength he had left and began a one-armed stroke to the shore. He swam to within several feet of the bank, where he found a foothold in the shallows. He planted his feet on the river bottom, and stood unsteadily in the current; tightening his hold on Lucy, he lunged forward and fell to his knees in smaller waves that lapped upon the shore. They had made it.

As he lay Lucy down in front of him, he recognized the excited voices of Dorothy, Emily, Henry and the coach driver as they raced up and kneeled beside them. Dorothy reached out and touched William's shoulder, tears welling in her eyes. "Thank God you're all right!"

Emily, plainly worried as she stared at her governess, asked, "Is Miss Lucy going to be all right?"

Henry held back tears as he studied Miss Lucy's grey face, and avowed, "She's goin' to be fine, Emily." He looked to William and asked anxiously, "Ain't that so?"

William didn't know how to answer. He could see Lucy was unconscious, scarcely breathing, with blood flowing more insistently now from the wound on her forehead. Her torso, barely covered by her torn undergarment, reminded him of fine Carrara marble—except for an ugly reddish bruise beneath her left breast, which gave an ominous indication of internal injuries.

"She needs immediate medical attention" he asserted desperately. "Where's the buggy?"

Dorothy pointed. "Back by the turn in the river."

Davey lent a hand as William rose unsteadily with Lucy's limp form again in his arms. William said, "I have to

327

get her to Doctor Deegan. We must hurry." He moved off toward the buggy with Dorothy and the children following. The coach driver stayed behind. "I pray the young lady recovers," Davey called after them. "I'll be finding me team. Good luck to you and God speed."

❧ ❧ ❧

*H*enry ran up to Dobbin, who stood nearby, and gathered the reins. Pulling the big horse behind him, he caught up quickly to his sister; she had stopped by the edge of the river and was retrieving a wet canvas from the water's edge. "It's one of Miss Lucy's paintings!" she said excitedly. She turned the painting over and, after inspecting a broken frame, said, "Not a tear in it. She'll be so pleased."

Henry kicked a rock into the river. "Is Miss Lucy going to die?"

"Of course not. She's going to live."

"How do you know?"

Emily suddenly realized she had never considered the possibility that their beloved governess might die. Now that she did, it was simply unacceptable. "Because we need her, that's how I know." Emily held the canvas to her as if she were grasping Hope itself.

Henry bent and picked another item out of the water. He beamed, "Miss Lucy's paintbrush."

She nodded and smiled. "It's surely a good omen."

Henry tucked the brush into his waistband at the small of his back and they scrambled off to catch up with the others.

CHAPTER EIGHTY-SEVEN

*W*illiam fought the wave of fatigue that swept over him as he rushed along the riverbank, carrying Lucy in his arms. Shifting her weight as tenderly as he could, he pressed her closer to his chest. *She was so cold.* His heart ached as he gazed at her sweet face, this face that meant everything to him. His bare foot hit a rock and he almost tripped, but Dorothy quickly grabbed onto his arm and steadied him.

"Dorothy," he said quietly, "I fear time is running out. She's barely breathing."

"We must think positively," she said.

Hurrying toward the buggy, they came to the spot where William had discarded his clothing by the river's edge. Dorothy quickly retrieved the items.

William knew in his heart that Lucy could die on the long, muddy road to the doctor's residence, which lay five miles east of the King's Head Inn. While he was thinking of an alternate plan, Emily and Henry ran up behind him, pulling

Dobbin by the reins. William had an idea: "The ride to Deegan's is too far. It will be much faster, Dorothy, if you take Lucy in the buggy to the King's Head Inn while I take the horse, ride to the doctor's home and bring him back there."

"Yes, that's best, William," she said, carrying his apparel over to the buggy. The skittish roan whinnied at their approach, trying to pull free from its tether, but the reins held fast.

"Hold these for a moment, Emily," Dorothy said, handing her his garments. "William, I'll climb in first and then you pass Lucy up to me."

"All right," he said, hoping he had the strength left in his arms to lift her up to the seat.

Dorothy untied the horse's reins and scampered up onto the bench. She leaned down with outstretched arms.

"Easy with her now," he said, as he lifted Lucy's limp form up toward his sister.

The nervous roan pulled on the harness and rocked the buggy. "Whoa," Dorothy said with conviction, pulling on the reins. "Whoa." As the horse settled, she wrapped the straps around the whip stand and turned back to William, reaching down again for Lucy. Together they hoisted her up onto the seat, so that Lucy's head was on Dorothy's lap. Taking the reins once more, a worried expression appeared on Dorothy's face. "William, I'm afraid she might fall."

He could see Lucy's precarious position. "Henry," he said, motioning to the boy, "give my sister a hand." He took the gelding's lead from the boy and his clothes from Emily. "We'll be needing you up there, too."

As the children clambered up the side of the buggy, William jammed his arms into his top coat and hurriedly slipped into his boots. Emily sat at the far end of the seat, taking Miss Lucy's feet onto her lap, while Henry stood behind the bench. "I'll hold Miss Lucy, too," he said, reaching between Dorothy and his sister to put his arms around Lucy's waist.

"Dorothy," William said, passing her up his cloak, "put this around her. I'm afraid this arrangement isn't going to work. That horse is a handful. It's not safe."

"I won't let her drop, I won't," Henry said, his arms tightening protectively around Miss Lucy's waist.

"We can hold her," Emily said, cradling her governess's legs.

William shook his head. He couldn't allow the children to assume the burden of Lucy's safety.

Suddenly, a figure approached out of the misting rain. Molly slogged up behind them. "Has anyone seen me bag?" she implored.

William answered swiftly, "Forget any bag. I need your help!"

"What fer?"

"I need you on this buggy to hold onto this young woman so she doesn't fall."

The servant girl seemed to weigh the request. "I'll do it, but only if ya help me look fer me missin' bag."

William was infuriated. "This girl is near death. We need to get her to the doctor immediately. You *must* help."

Henry said sternly, "Molly, she needs yer help, *right now!*"

"Yes!" added Emily.

Molly's face fell. Cursing under her breath, she circled the buggy and climbed up to sit beside Emily, lifting Lucy's feet and stretching them out across her lap.

William turned to the large gelding and placed a foot in the stirrup. Pulling himself up, he said, "I'll bring the doctor as soon as I can. God speed."

"God speed," Dorothy rejoined.

William kicked Dobbin and they galloped off, avoiding rocks and debris, as horse and rider charged up the incline.

Dorothy slapped leather against the roan's hindquarters and the skittish horse pulled the heavy buggy around. They set off at a slower pace as she guided the animal to the gentle path she had found earlier when searching for a way down to the river.

\

❀❀ ❀❀ ❀❀

*D*avey saw the horseman approaching through the meadow and called, "Hey, Hardy ... over here." Constable Hardy turned in the saddle, looking surprised to see the mail coach driver jogging toward him through the rain, rain that had now diminished to a drizzle. He urged his mount across the grass, his lawman's eyes registering the young man's disheveled appearance. "Davey, where the hell's yer coach and passengers?"

Davey stopped breathlessly before him. "Road washed out and we went into the river. One of the passengers got banged up pretty bad."

"What's the passenger's name?"

"Lucy Sims."

Hardy eased back in his saddle and listened to the rest of the driver's explanation. He was in no hurry now. His suspect had been seriously hurt and was in no condition to travel. Lucy Sims wouldn't be hard to find. He would help the young man find his team and then backtrack to arrest the injured thief.

❧ CHAPTER EIGHTY-EIGHT ❦

mily thought her heart would break as she stood, teary-eyed, beside her brother and Dorothy Wordsworth. They were keeping a silent vigil over their beloved Miss Lucy, who lay unconscious on a cot before the King's Head Inn fireplace. The young girl was crushed to see that blood still dripped from the wound on the governess's forehead and from the corner of her pale mouth; her breathing was labored. She was grateful for the presence of Miss Wordsworth, who appeared to be deeply saddened, and was wiping a trickle of frothy red bubbles from Lucy's lips with a cloth. Emily prayed Miss Lucy's eyes would open so everyone could see the beauty and light that shined so brightly within. There was no one, with the possible exception of her brother, and, in theory, her parents, whom she loved more. Miss Lucy was intelligent, understanding, strong, kind, loving and fun, more of a mother to her—in many ways—than her own. She fervently hoped her governess would be able to return home and then never leave, at least not until she and Henry were old enough to attend University. As soon as Miss Lucy recovered from her injuries, Emily planned to have a private talk with her to discover the cause of her sudden departure. She hoped it wasn't because of any transgression she or Henry had inadvertently committed.

Emily sneaked a peek at her brother; she could tell he was doing his best to be brave. Tears glistened in his eyes. As she watched, one tear brimmed over and ran down his pudgy cheek.

Henry brushed the drop away. "Is she going to be all right?"

Emily nodded. "When Doctor Deegan arrives he'll make her better."

The innkeeper carried a tray with mugs and a steaming teapot over to them. "Have some. It'll keep ya warm."

She and her brother shook their heads. The old man grunted and crossed the Squire who, having arrived awhile before the others, sat alone at a table. "A cup, yer Lordship?"

Emily noticed her father didn't respond. He just sat there, staring down at Lucy's canvas, which she had left on the table. When the innkeeper asked a second time, he barely nodded. Simon set a mug before him and bustled over to another table, where Molly sat by herself, looking despondent. Emily had been wondering, *What had the servant girl been doing out by the river?*

❧ ❧ ❧

The Squire, sober for once, sipped tea and reflected upon the last twenty-four hours: *How had things twisted into such a cockle-headed affair?* He had reached the inn hours ago, and discovered that Constable Hardy had missed the governess and had gone off again in pursuit of her. The Squire had decided to stay out of the rain and await Hardy's return; hopefully, he would bring the little thief back with him. After quite some time, Emily and Henry had burst into the inn with news of the accident, and he had been elated; the little filcher had been caught! But upon watching Dorothy Wordsworth and the innkeeper carry the governess inside, and upon observing the extent of her injuries, his vengeance had abated, replaced by a creeping sense of remorse. To make matters worse, the heavy bulge in his pocket had reminded him of his own chicanery: yes, he had taken the Apostle Spoons from the dining room chest and allowed the servants and Miss Lucy to become suspects. And yes, his plan had been to use the silver to bargain with the governess for her favors. But the wench had snubbed him and run off with his wife's earrings! And now, his secondary scheme to plant the spoons along the road, had been thwarted by the damned accident.

*T*he front door flew open and Constable Hardy stepped in. He wore his rain cape and was carrying a satchel.

Molly jumped to her feet, almost knocking the innkeeper over as she rushed to Hardy. "Me bag! Me bag's been found! Thanks be ta God."

Molly tried to grab the satchel away from the constable but he held it in a firm grip.

"That be me lost bag," she said. "Give it ta me."

Hardy's eyes narrowed. "This be yours and not Miss Lucy Sims'?"

"Of course it's mine. I know me own bag when I see it."

The constable knocked Molly's hands aside and opened the satchel, showing her the contents. "Everything inside belongs to you?"

Emily watched the servant with curiosity: Molly looked furtively toward the Squire, who was showing no interest in their conversation. Then her eyes darted back to the officer and she inched closer to him. The maid lowered her voice and Emily could barely hear her. "Yeh, they be me personal things, me property. Give it ta me!" Molly grabbed the bag again and began to wrest it away. Hardy released the satchel and, while Molly studied its contents, he withdrew a pair of iron handcuffs from his coat pocket.

"Henry, look," Emily whispered.

Her brother's mouth fell open when the constable snapped the manacles around the servant girl's wrists.

Molly's face contorted with shock and then fear. "What the bloody 'ell?"

"I'm parish Constable Hardy," he said. "You're under arrest for thieving." He motioned to Emily's father and raised his voice. "Yer Lordship."

The Squire was surprised to see Molly in handcuffs.

"I've recovered her Ladyship's earrings, and apprehended the thief who stole them. By her own admission, it be this woman here. I'm sorry ta say the Apostle Spoons must have been lost in the river."

Emily smiled when she heard her governess had been vindicated and gave her brother an exuberant hug, but when she looked toward her father, she sobered; he looked as if he had suddenly taken ill.

The Squire nodded to the constable with a noticeable lack of emotion. "Her Ladyship will be pleased."

Hardy took ahold of Molly's arm. "Simon, if ya don't mind, I'll put this one in your cellar for awhile and then visit your kitchen."

The innkeeper nodded. "Help yourself. 'Ere's the key."

"Come with me, Miss."

The Squire's tongue tasted of bile. His stomach contracted painfully, the result of deep-seated guilt. *Miss Lucy was not the culprit after all.* He lifted his head to stare at his children. He could see they were struggling to control their emotions as their love and affection for their governess shone through red-rimmed eyes. He exhaled heavily. They would hate him for the rest of his life if they ever discovered it had been his loutish behavior that had forced Miss Lucy's hasty departure and subsequently had brought her to the brink of death.

The Squire made himself a promise. If the governess recovered, he would make amends. He knew she wouldn't consider returning to Hawkins House. Perhaps that was best. But he would send her off in style with a grand letter of recommendation and a gift of twenty-five pounds sterling to help her start a new life.

 illiam rushed into the inn with Doctor Deegan at his side. Seeing that Lucy lay on the cot in front of the fireplace, and that his sister and the children were tending to her, he quickly led the doctor over to them. "Stand aside," Deegan said as he immediately began to examine Lucy. When the children remained crowded around the cot he motioned them away. "Please, go sit with your father."

Emily took Henry's arm and led him over to the Squire's table.

William gazed down at Lucy, his eyes lingering lovingly on her pale face, his heart aching. A fine line of blood trickled from her lips, those he had so lovingly kissed. He took the cloth from his sister's hand and pressed it gently against the flow. He, who seldom prayed, prayed silently now, imploring God to allow Lucy to live: she was more than his love; she was his heart, his spirit, his very being.

Deegan lifted Lucy's arm and felt her pulse. William watched as concern spread across the doctor's features. Deegan then raised her eyelids and examined her pupils. The lines on his face seemed to grow longer. The doctor placed his ear on her chest and listened to her breathing. William's heart skipped a beat when Lucy's eyelids fluttered, but after a moment they were still again. *Had she heard his prayers and tried to respond? Was it possible she could hear his voice if he spoke to her?* He bent to her ear and whispered. "I'm here beside you, my love. Doctor Deegan is here, too. You're going to be fine and you and I are going to have a wondrous life together. I have grand news to tell you ... amazing news. I won't trouble you with it now, but I'll tell you this: When you awake and are feeling better I'm going to take you home with me. We'll be together forever."

She coughed very faintly, startling him, as a fresh trickle of blood appeared. He gently wiped it away. *What if she didn't survive?* He shook his head, forcing that question from his consciousness; he would not consider that option.

William studied the doctor with mounting anxiety. Deegan wore a dire expression as he examined Lucy's discolored ribs. Perhaps, William hoped, it was just fatigue that weighed upon his features. Any man half his age would have been exhausted after having ridden miles through a cold and bitter rainstorm.

"May I help in any way, Doctor?" he asked.

Deegan shook his head in response. After a few moments, he looked up with sad eyes, eyes that revealed the prognosis before the words were uttered. William heard him say, "It's worse than I feared. She has broken ribs. They've punctured her lungs and caused internal hemorrhaging. I'm unable to stop the bleeding. I'm afraid she is passing."

William's breath left him, draining his soul. The children, having heard the doctor's words, cried out and buried their faces in their father's arms. The Squire was ashen; he stared off into space.

Dorothy came to William's side and placed her arms around his shoulders. He managed to hold back a sob as he heard his sister whispering, trying to comfort him.

A low gasp drew his attention to Lucy. She was trying to talk. He gently pried Dorothy's arms away and moved closer, bending to listen as her breathing became more labored. He could see movement beneath her eyelids; and then her eyes opened, startling him; he was once again staring into the loveliest blue eyes he had ever known. He took her hand in his; it was so very cold.

In a barely audible whisper, Lucy said his name. Then she called softly for Emily and Henry.

William motioned to the Squire's table. "Children."

Emily and Henry left their father's side and hurried to Lucy. Her eyes drifted to them as they crowded in as close as they could. Her voice was a low breath. "Emily ... Henry ... ."

"Miss Lucy," Emily said, with tears streaming down her cheeks. Henry whimpered and wiped his eyes.

"I'm so cold. So cold ... ."

William pulled the blanket up to Lucy's throat. Emily helped tuck it under her chin. Henry ran to the hearth and threw large chunks of peat onto the fire.

Struggling to speak, she made a small noise and William and Emily bent lower, trying to catch her words. "It's ... hard to breathe ... I ... I heard the Doctor. I know I'm dying. So many things ... to say ... to do. Sorry ... I'm sorry ... I left ... without saying ... ."

William put a gentle finger to her lips. "You don't have to explain anything. I've read your letter. I understand." He shook his head, dislodging tears that flowed down his cheeks. "Why would a just God allow this to ... ?"

Lucy squeezed his fingers with an almost nonexistent grip. Her eyelids fluttered. "We ... have God ... to thank ... for our love ... my only love ... ."

Henry hurried from the fireplace to stand beside Lucy. "I thank God for you, Miss Lucy. Don't leave us, please."

Emily sniffled and wiped away tears. "I found one of your paintings by the river, Miss Lucy. It has a broken frame but it's not torn or anything. We can fix it."

"Emily ... Henry ... I want you ... keep ... it. Promise me ... to do ... your verbs ... and ... learn ... proper English ... ."

The children, tears streaming, nodded. Henry suddenly pulled out Lucy's favorite paintbrush. He placed it in her hand.

She shook her head. "You ... keep ... ."

Henry sniffled. "No. You'll need it ... so you can paint the angels."

A whisper of a smile flitted across Lucy's features.

Henry, no longer able to control his emotions, turned into his sister's arms and sobbed.

"William," Lucy said, her eyes closing. "I'm so cold ... hold ... me."

"I want to hold you forever, my truest love, my very soul. Would I had Nature's power to keep you with me!"

"You ... have ... God's power ... in your pen ... your mind. Never ... stop ... using ... ."

She caught her breath ... exhaled softly ... and slipped away from the earth.

William laid his head upon Lucy's breast and wept silently.

illiam wound his way through faded, weather-beaten tombstones as he walked toward a lonely corner in the Saint Mary's Church graveyard, where several newer headstones reflected the cool morning's sunlight. It was a pilgrimage he had made daily for the last few weeks, and today would be his last visit for a fortnight or longer. Since Lucy's passing, a depression had enveloped him, causing emotional distress unlike anything he had ever experienced. Dorothy, worried for her brother's health, had persuaded Samuel to make arrangements for their planned trip to Germany and they were to leave today. William, who wore his hat and his heaviest cape for the journey, carried two red roses. He stopped before a new tombstone and glanced at the carving. His heart ached as he read:

Lucy Sims
Born 1781 – Died 1798
"Forever Loved"

William knelt beside the grave that held two wilted flowers in the small container below the stone, and replaced them with the two new blooms. He noticed new shoots of grass had begun to sprout through the soil, weaving together the churned earth. William had always heard that time had the capacity to heal all. *But did broken hearts ever really mend?* He doubted it—there would always be scars on his heart that the passage of time could never erase.

The cry of a gull drew his attention to the sky, where a lone bird circled and then swooped low over Lucy's grave, calling plaintively. William was taken by a sudden musing; he imagined it was Lucy's spirit, attempting to send him a message. The gull circled overhead for some time, and he tracked it, allowing himself to be comforted by his fantasy. The mere thought of her being close to him helped to ease the burden he carried.

The west wind blew in from Bridgeport Bay, sweeping up the bluff to the graveyard, causing leaves to roll and swirl among the tombstones. As it did, William saw that the two roses he had placed before Lucy's headstone were bending, their blossoms moving toward each other ... until the petals were touching. The gull cried out again. The hair on the back of William's neck rose. *Surely Lucy's spirit was here with him now.*

The squeak of the small cemetery's iron-gate shook William from his thoughts. He stood slowly, reluctant to be parted from his reverie, and brushed grass from his trousers. He turned to greet Samuel, who approached. His friend was dressed in traveling clothes, and a rented carriage and driver stood on the road behind him; the rear of the vehicle was packed with bags.

"I went by your house. Dorothy said I might find you here. We'll pick her up on the way."

"And Sara and Hartley, where are they?"

"It's just you, me and Dorothy. Sara has decided to stay at Nether Stowey; she wants nothing to do with Germany, which is fine with me. I'll miss the little one, but not the woman's nagging."

Samuel waved a hand at the marker. "'Tis a shame we never met. From what you've told me, I would have been very fond of Lucy. Dorothy tells me you've dedicated a poem to her."

"Yes, I've mailed a copy to the publisher to be included in *Lyrical Ballads*. I'm working on two additional poems about her. Care to hear what I have so far?"

Samuel shook his head. "No, only the one you've finished. Please. I can think of no better place than this."

William recited from his heart:

> *"She dwelt among the untrodden ways*
> *Beside the springs of Dove,*
> *A Maid whom there were none to praise*
> *And very few to love:*
>
> *A violet by a mossy stone*
> *Half hidden from the eye!*
> *—Fair as a star, when only one*
> *Is shining in the sky.*
>
> *She lived unknown, and few could know*
> *When Lucy ceased to be;*
> *But she is in her grave, and, oh,*
> *The difference to me!"*

Samuel was silent for a moment, then let out a deep, audible breath; "Extraordinary," he said. "Your words will outlive us all."

"As will my love."

William grabbed onto his hat as a fresh breeze blew in from the bay and the lone gull soared and called high above. He looked to Lucy's marker and noticed that the petals of the roses were now intermingled, as if they were lover's limbs.

He smiled. One day he would put the image into a poem. After several moments he took Samuel's arm. They turned and walked silently away.

T H E   E N D

illiam and Dorothy Wordsworth traveled to Germany with Samuel Taylor Coleridge and stayed for almost two years. During this time, *Lyrical Ballads* was published anonymously, with neither poet receiving credit. "Wordsworth's name is nothing," said Coleridge when their publisher, Joseph Cottle, suggested their names should appear, "and mine stinks." The first printing was a financial failure and ruined the poetry-loving publisher.

In January 1801, Cottle's reputation was redeemed when *Lyrical Ballads* was reissued by another publishing house, this time with the poets' names on the cover; it was generally well-received. The book has since been publicly and academically proclaimed to be "the most influential book of poetry in the history of English Literature."

Wordsworth, his sister and Coleridge returned to England in 1800 and, several months later, settled in the Lake Country in the far northeast corner of England, near the border of Scotland. William and Dorothy took up residence in Dove Cottage in Grasmere, an area where Wordsworth would live for the remainder of his life. Coleridge settled in Keswick, a thirteen-mile walk from Dove Cottage, where he continued to be a frequent household guest. Samuel eventually divorced Sara and found another wife.

With the death of Lord Lonsdale in 1802, Wordsworth came into his father's long-disputed inheritance. That same year he married Mary Hutchinson, a childhood friend and schoolmate. They had five children.

Wordsworth and Coleridge had a squabble in 1808. Neither had a clear definition of its cause and were estranged from one another for three years. Finally, older and wiser, they reconciled, but never regained the closeness they once shared.

Over the years, Wordsworth's reputation grew and he became one of England's most celebrated poets. He received several honorary degrees and was appointed Poet Laureate in 1843. Wordsworth died April 13, 1850 at the age of eighty.

Following the poet's death, his fame has continued to grow, and his work has influenced and inspired new generations of readers and poets.

❧ ❧ ❧

Many events in this book are true: Wordsworth's travels to France; the fathering of a child there; his subsequent return to England and inability to find work; the problems in receiving his inheritance; his outspokenness on sociopolitical issues; his suspicious neighbors, and the investigation by the Home Office; his close personal relationship with his sister, Dorothy; his poetic collaboration with the colorful Coleridge; and, of course, the authoring of the Lucy poems.

❧ ❧ ❧

The Lucy poems leave the mysteries of Lucy's identity and Wordsworth's relationship to her open to speculation.

It is possible that William and Lucy met and had an ill-fated affair that has no record in history. If so, the answer to the mystery is one the poet carried to his grave.

ℰ ACKNOWLEDGEMENTS ℰ

First and foremost, my sincere thanks goes to Ron Sharrow, a fellow novelist, a new friend, an attorney and a Renaissance man who generously gave time and effort to help publish this novel. Without his encouragement, suggestions, editing skills and knowledge of self-publishing, this manuscript would still be stored away in a computer file.

I also wish to thank my long-time friends, Richard Jones and fellow-writer, Amy Hawes, who proofed the text and generally helped make William & Lucy a better novel.

My sincere gratitude and love goes to my very patient wife, Holly, who read the first and final drafts and offered her helpful comments—the final touches are always the most significant.

Any remaining errors are mine alone.

ABOUT THE AUTHOR

*M*ichael Brown is a three-time Emmy Award winner for editing movie-of-the-week films as well as mini-series. He has also won the American Cinema Editor's ACE Eddie Award in addition to receiving seven other nominations. In 2011 he was awarded a Lifetime Career Achievement Award for film editing by ACE. He is a member of the Writers Guild of America, having sold television scripts to ABC, NBC & CBS. He is also a member of the Director's Guild of America. He lives in Southern California with his wife, Holly. This is his first novel.

This book is available in KINDLE Editions and online for all other eBook formats from: www.Smashwords.com.

Print editions may be purchased online from most on-line Booksellers or by special order through most bookstores.

TARN
PUBLISHING

www.tarnpublishing.com